The Burns We Carry

MARAE
GOOD

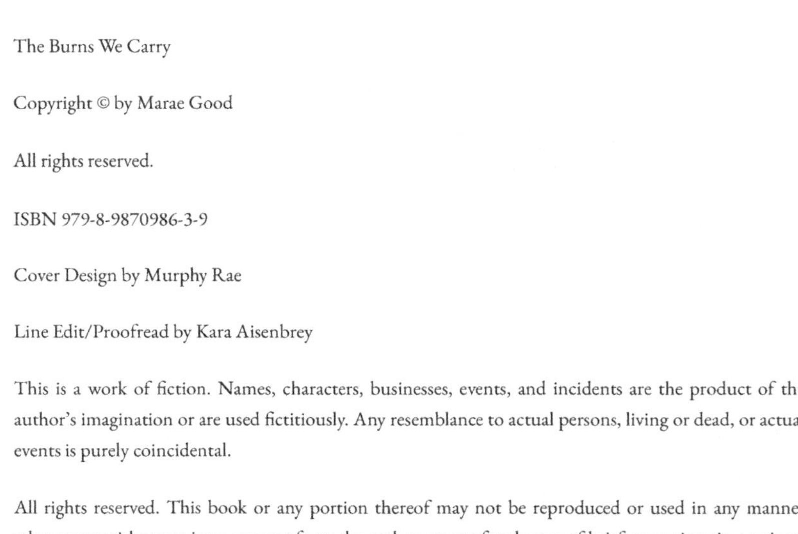
The Burns We Carry

ISBN 979-8-9870986-3-9

Cover Design by Murphy Rae

Line Edit/Proofread by Kara Aisenbrey

To those who listen to "Matilda" by Harry Styles on repeat.

Dear Reader,

Shay is a character who's left an emotionally abusive relationship that was slowly crossing into physical abuse. This story doesn't focus on the abuser, but rather the journey Shay faces after leaving. It's a story of healing, learning to love and trust yourself again, as well as the world around you. However, there are memories of narcissistic abuse weaved throughout, along with a brief memory of physical abuse. There is light, family, humor, goodness, and the fierce love that comes only from a mother balanced through the story, but it's important to me you know the general content so you can respect your boundaries.

Content warning:

Mentions of mental/physical abuse (not by the main characters)
Child abandonment (not by the main characters)
Grief/loss of a parent
Loss of a loved one due to cancer

Playlist

In the Blood—John Mayer
Cardigan—Taylor Swift
Lose You to Love Me—Selena Gomez
She Used to Be Mine—Sara Bareilles
Home—Phillip Phillips
How Do I Say Goodbye—Dean Lewis
Break On Me—Keith Urban
Beneath Your Beautiful—Labrinth
Yellow—Coldplay
Brother—Kodaline
Someone to Stay—Vancouver Sleep Clinic
Yours—Ella Henderson
Paper Rings—Taylor Swift
Dancing in the Sky—Dani and Lizzy
Gone, Gone, Gone—Phillip Phillips
I Don't Dance—Lee Brice
Making Memories Of Us—Keith Urban

Chapter One

It's illegal in all fifty states to interrupt anyone mid-song, right? Especially when I was bellowing—fine, crying—to Taylor Swift's "cardigan," my voice lost in the crisp mountain air and endless pine trees. And it's definitely a crime punishable by death to interrupt Taylor's melancholy heart.

Alas, the forest ranger who pulled me over must not have been well-versed in the laws.

I bit my lip and slowly edged my car onto the shoulder of the road, praying my little Altima didn't roll into the ditch. But really, what was one more dent?

I slipped my hair out of its bun, scrunching my nose at the strong aroma of color clinging to it. Not a blonde strand was in sight, only chestnut waves as I brushed it over my shoulders. I peeked in the rearview mirror as the white truck behind me opened its door, getting a flash of the Law Enforcement sign plastered on the side, along with the brown Forest Service badge.

Wait. Was a forest ranger even allowed to pull me over?

I reached in the back seat and grabbed my denim backpack to retrieve my license, jumping at the abrupt tap on my window. Blowing out a deep breath and slapping on my best smile, I turned and cranked the window down. It screeched with each wind of the handle, resembling a mewling cat being mauled to death. I didn't dare let my smile break.

I was not going to break.

"Hi, Officer—Ranger—sir . . ." *What the heck do I call him?* "How's your day—"

"Are you aware I trailed you for a mile before you finally pulled over?"

I furrowed my brows at the deep voice, positive I hadn't been that oblivious. "I'm sorry, I didn't realize." I smiled brighter, the sun's rays blocking me from seeing if it was getting me out of this. "I'm new in town—I must've been so focused on not missing my turnoff that I didn't see you." I hitched my thumb over my shoulder, where a small cabin sat off the side of the dirt road. "And it actually looks like I missed it—but just barely, thanks to you, Officer."

I squinted and leaned against the door, unable to view the man's face. I waited for a response, maybe a laugh—even a polite question asking where I was traveling from. But all I got were two large tan arms crossed over a sturdy chest. He exhaled, his frame not loosening one bit. "Are you aware you were doing fifty in a twenty?"

I frowned, gripping the peeling steering wheel. *I'm going to light you on fire, Betsy.* "I'm sorry." I sighed, dropping my hands to my lap. "Betsy was reliable in getting me here, but I can't say she's without her faults. I thought I noticed her speedometer being a little wonky, but I thought maybe I was seeing things after driving for twelve hours." I laughed, shaking my head. With only a crinkled map as my guidance, I thought I might've taken a wrong turn after a two-hour stretch of nothing but winding roads and enchanting pine trees. But then the trees thinned and opened up into a valley, welcoming me to the quaint town. A gem, hidden in the middle of nowhere—exactly what I needed. "I mean—I thought I was delusional when I saw that bear statue holding a gun back in town."

I grinned—and enjoyed five seconds of serene silence, nothing but the blissful breeze and crooning birds—waiting for the forest ranger to crack a laugh. But then, with a tone so gruff I swore it made the birds scurry away, he asked, "Betsy?"

I patted the steering wheel, wincing when I hit the horn. "Sorry—this is Betsy. Isn't she cute? She's all mine—"

"I'm going to need you to step out of the vehicle, ma'am."

I swallowed. "Why?"

"Step out of the vehicle, ma'am."

I frowned at the sternness in his tone. *Did he call me ma'am? Am I a ma'am now?* The door creaked as I climbed out, adjusting the hem of my jean shorts. Showing my booty wouldn't win me any points with this hard-ass.

"Look, I'm really sorry." I leaned against Betsy, slowly skimming over the ranger's green pants and gray shirt, up to his face. A face I might've found handsome, were it not hidden behind a tight beard and black sunglasses—not to mention a scowl. "I promise I had no idea I was going that fast, or that there was even a speed limit out here."

He didn't budge, his brows and mouth tight, as though I was lying. But if he'd seen me puttering through the modest town before I'd taken this turnoff, he'd know I'd followed the speed limit exactly. I opened my mouth to reveal that, stopping when he said, "I'm going to need you to walk a straight line for me, ma'am."

"What?" I squeaked, my cheeks burning. "I'm not—I'm not drunk. I don't even drink."

At least, not anymore.

He raised a dark brow. "Or I can take you back to the station."

I clenched my fist, wondering if I'd get jail time if I tackled him. I could say I tripped, right? Plead insanity? But since I couldn't afford bail, I pushed off the car, refusing to let him squash my day. Only I feared he might when I stopped mid-step, frowning at what I believed to be my cabin and the man leaning against a rusty single-cab truck next to it. That had to be my landlord.

Great. Now he's going to think I'm some sort of delinquent.

I waved at him and silently cursed the ranger behind me as I dragged one foot through the center of the dirt road, already scuffing my brand-new hiking boots. "Since it's a dirt road, you know," I called out over my shoulder. "I want to make sure there's no doubt I can walk straight."

"It's crooked."

My nostrils flared, but I brushed it off and walked the line. I walked so straight, if this was the 2008 Beijing Olympics, I was positive Shawn Johnson would request me to sub for her on the US gymnastics team. "See?" I crossed my arms over my chest and glanced at the badge below his left shoulder. "I'm clearly not intoxicated, Officer Graham."

He flexed his jaw. "License and registration."

I swallowed, my throat tight, but nodded and reached through the open window. I unlatched my bag and handed him my documents—both with Elle's address on them. My heart longed for my friend, worsening when Officer Graham said, "These are registered in California, ma'am."

I glared at him. "It's pronounced exactly how it looks." I pointed at the license in his hand. "My name's Shay, in case you weren't sure. And yes, that's where I'm moving from. I'll go to the DMV as soon as I confirm I have a place to stay."

I bit my lip, squirming beneath his scrutinizing stare. "This says you're blonde."

I rolled my eyes. "Is it against the law to color your hair in Arizona? And while we're at it . . . You're a forest ranger—are *you* even allowed to pull me over?" There was a pistol attached to his belt and what looked to be a body cam on his shoulder, but what did I know? Maybe he was playing dress-up.

I froze, wholeheartedly believing the glare behind his sunglasses was on the verge of firing lasers. He grinded his teeth and clenched out, "You're on National Forest land, so yes, I *can* pull you over. Even write you a nice ticket too, *ma'am*."

My eyes burned, my stomach twisting—I shouldn't have been so careless. I couldn't afford a ticket. "I'm so sorry. I promise I had no idea I was speeding. I've never even been pulled over before." Tears welled, my spirits dropping as he remained hard and unreadable. "I promise you'll never deal with me again. And if I had a phone, I'd let you call my friend Elle. She would tell you how anal I am about keeping my promises. Do you like pie? I saw a diner back in town—"

He lifted his hand at the chatter coming through on the radio at his hip, and I stopped. I couldn't make out the muffled words—but I didn't care when my life was on the brink of falling apart. I was supposed to be moving forward, not backtracking.

I needed to prove the haunting voices I'd left behind wrong.

I wasn't going to fail. I couldn't afford to.

But maybe Mother Nature's grace was stronger in these woods, because whatever message came through had him handing my items back. His hand squeezed, crumbling the edges of the registration when I grabbed it. I craned my neck up to look at him—had mountain water made him grow so large? "If I see you inch one mile over the speed limit, I'll give you a ticket. I'm sure you're used to batting your eyelashes to get your way, but that Cali bull won't fly here." He dropped his hand and glanced over my shoulder at the cabin behind me. "I'll let Jake know you won't be staying long. It's only a matter of time before you're running back home."

I gaped at him. The only thing keeping me from shouting—or monkey-rolling him through the dirt—as he walked away was solely that I was broke. I slammed the door shut, not starting Betsy until he drove away. It didn't matter what he thought. I wouldn't run back home.

I was running to a new one.

Solemnly, I placed a hand on my lower stomach, on the life protected from the cruel realities of this world. I'd keep this baby safe, hidden, for as long as I could. For as long as time would let me.

Thanks for the big welcome, Wallowpine, Arizona.

Chapter Two

I was indeed not *walking on sunshine,* despite what the song implied as I flipped a U-turn and drove to the cabin I'd missed, the ecstatic lyrics unable to salvage the day. I hadn't slept longer than an hour straight in days, and my back ached—but I was in the driver's seat and taking control of my life.

I tossed my bag over my shoulder, leaving my suitcase behind in case this place didn't pan out, and climbed out of Betsy, the loose gravel crunching beneath my boots. "Hi, you must be Jake." I stuck out my hand to the elderly man leaning against the rusty red truck. "I'm Shay. I emailed with your daughter Jules about renting your cabin."

He grunted, his wrinkled hand firmly squeezing mine. "So I heard. Doesn't seem to matter where they live or how old I am—my kids seem to believe I need parenting." I bit my grin. Jules had warned me he'd likely say something close to that effect. "Well, come on in. I'll show you around." I followed him around his truck, halting when he paused on the lopsided wooden steps. "I hope you're not picky, because she's really not much to look at."

I nodded, bracing myself as I followed him into the log cabin encased in aspen and pine trees, sidestepping the gaping hole in the center of the porch. I hadn't expected much after the photos, but it was clear those were outdated. By centuries.

Jake stepped aside in the kitchen, allowing me a full view of the single-room cabin, save for the bathroom. One look suggested the wood stove might have bats living in it, that the dusty twin mattress in the corner might be infested with moths. The creaking floor beneath me might even be half a footstep away from caving in.

Those were truths my former life screamed at me.

But I shoved them away. I'd done worse than this—I could do it again.

"It's perfect." I moved to the kitchen, opening and closing the four peeling orange cabinets—all of them bare. I peeked in the yellow fridge, only to slam it shut, trapping whatever had died and rotted inside. "It's exactly what I'm looking for."

Jake's lanky arms loosened, and he ran a tan hand through his scruffy gray beard. "That's good to hear, kid. As much as I don't appreciate Jules meddling in my business, I'm afraid with my wife's treatments, the extra cash wouldn't hurt."

I tucked my thumbs in my back pockets, not wanting to pry. There was plenty I hoped to never share. "I'm sorry to hear about your wife. I hope good health is in her future," I offered, allowing him to decide how much he divulged.

"Ah." He waved a hand at me. "Wren's a fighter—as stubborn as a mule. Even with breast cancer. If she'd caught wind of the trouble Brooks was giving you, she would've dragged him away by his ear." I stared at him, not knowing what—or who—he was speaking of. "That reminds me. You're not in trouble with the law, are you? As good as the money would be, I can't say I'm desperate enough to put this cabin at risk. It's been in the family a long time."

"Oh." I laughed and brushed my hair over my shoulder, realizing who Brooks was. "No, Officer Graham and I had a misunderstanding. He said to let you know I plan on staying a long time."

He grinned, his smile gap-toothed and adorable. "Sound carries pretty well out here, but I'll take your word and just assume I heard him wrong before. Might be fun to see those Graham boys get their britches in a bunch."

Wait—there's more than one of them?

I followed him to the table and sat in one of the two mismatched chairs. "Now, you seem like a nice girl, so I want to make sure you know what you're getting into out here." He paused, waiting until I nodded before he continued. "I'm sure you saw how empty the road was on your way in. The next cabin is about a mile from you. So you'll be out here mostly on your own—except for the bears, of course. Might want to get you some bear spray while you're at it."

I strained a smile, running a soothing hand over my turning stomach as he said, "My wife and I live back in town, and there isn't much service out here, so you'll have to come holler at me if you have any issues. I'm not sure how much I'll be around—Wren has treatments from time to time." He sighed, his shoulders falling with the motion. "We're considering moving to Phoenix temporarily. It's about five hours from here, and after three months of driving back and forth for her treatments, she's tired of riding in my truck. Something about it not being comfortable. But don't you worry, I can always send my nephews to come help you."

Perhaps it would've been wiser to stay somewhere in town, to slowly ease into life in the mountains. But I couldn't resist when I saw the ad for this cabin. It was off the beaten path, a wide-open meadow just a few steps short of being my front yard. The forest was dense, with sturdy pine trees and slender aspens. There seemed to be infinite space to move, to breathe. After living in a world where I was constantly holding my breath, I needed some air.

Jake leaned back in his chair. "Jules mentioned you originally reached out months ago to rent the cabin, but that she hadn't heard from you again until a week or two ago. Did another place fall through?"

I shrugged and glanced around the cabin, ready to make it a home. "Something like that."

His gaze flickered to where my hands rested on the table. "Should I be expecting a significant other or someone to be joining you out here?"

"Nope. It's just me." I dropped my hands to my lap, resisting the burning urge to look at my bare finger. "How do you want rent paid to you?"

He stood, mercifully freeing me of the small talk. "Cash or check is fine. If you have the first and last month's rent now, I'll take it from ya."

I gripped my bag, only having exactly enough for one month. "Oh . . . uh. I wasn't aware you needed more than one month's payment."

He shrugged and glanced out the torn curtains at our vehicles. "That's what Jules told me to do. She mentioned something about a security deposit, but I figured I'd wave that since there's not much for you to damage anyway."

Internally, I yanked out my hair, pleading for it to turn into money. But on the outside—okay, I was doing pretty much the same thing. I sucked in a few quiet breaths, grateful Jake's attention wasn't on me.

You can do this—don't panic.

"So," I started, "I can give you rent for this month, but I don't have enough for two payments. At least not yet—maybe after I've found a job, I could arrange something." My stomach rolled. I was in way over my head. I glanced out the window at Betsy, one of the many poor decisions I'd made recently.

What was one more, really? And I was desperate.

"Um . . . you can have my car if you want. Betsy's a real nice lady."

He looked over his shoulder, raising a brow. "Betsy? I had a cow growing up named Betsy. She was a real pain in the rear."

I blew out a shaky laugh, hoping this was my solution. "You can change her name if you want. I only named her that in spite of my—" I shook my head. *Not important, Shay.* "I know she's not fancy or anything, but she's reliable. Besides the speedometer being iffy, she got me here from California with no real issues. Maybe Wren would feel more comfortable driving to her appointments in it, and then you might not need to move."

He stared down at Betsy, rubbing his jaw. "I don't know . . . What are you gonna drive? You're about two miles from town. And I'm going to assume a young lady like yourself isn't a hermit."

I shrugged. "I'm used to being alone." This sort of solitude was different from before, when I was lonely, invisible, even as I was held. "Maybe I can find a bike or something to get to and from town. If not, I don't mind walking."

He bit his lip and looked me over, likely believing my petite frame would snap under pressure—not knowing the miles of running I'd built on these legs. I opened my mouth to beg, stopping when he said, "I think Jules or one of her sisters has an old bike sitting around back at my place. I can get it for you if you'd like."

"Yes." I nodded, biting my grin. "That would be great."

He frowned, looking back and forth between Betsy and me. "You seem like a nice girl, Shay. So I'll strike a deal with ya. If Wren agrees to use your car, I'll swap with you and let you drive my truck. But"—he stuck up a finger—"if it's not working out for you, we can swap back at any time."

My throat swelled, eyes brimming at his surprising generosity. Needing to keep my head in place, I cleared my throat. "I don't know," I said, fearing his deal meant I'd still have to pay the second month's rent—considering he'd be giving up his truck. "As kind as that offer is, I'll be straight with you, Jake. I'm broke. But I promise, I won't ever be late on a payment and I'll take good care of your home. I just can't afford to pay for two months right now."

"I know," he said slowly, his brows furrowed. "That's why I agreed to trade vehicles with you."

It was my turn to furrow my brows—I'd be lying if I said I wasn't wary, having been burned too many times before. "Are you sure? I'm not trying to be rude—but are you aware you're getting the worst end of the deal? I'm cutting you short on money."

He shrugged. "You'll pay it to me sooner or later. I trust ya." He grinned, his laugh raspy and rough—but nice, genuine. "Besides, it might be fun to watch Brooks chase you out of town if you decide to stiff me."

I snorted, hoping to never see Brooks Graham again. I stood, my arms twitching at my sides, resisting the urge to wrap Jake up in a hug. "So you're saying I can stay here?"

He raised a brow, looking at me like I'd smeared mud all over my face. "I wasn't aware there was a moment you weren't?"

I squealed and threw my arms around his neck, pulling him down to my height. "Thank you. Thank you so much. I promise I'll take such good care of your cabin."

He grunted, his arms stiff at his side, barely letting my words settle before he shifted out of my hold. "I have one rule." He moved for the door, dropping the cabin key on the table. "If I find out you've painted something pink, or whatever ungodly things you do in California, I'll have Brooks escort you out."

I laughed, cherishing how right it felt. "I won't, I promise." I snagged my car keys, dangling them between us. "Do you want to take Betsy for a ride?"

He stared at the keys—and the hot pink fuzzy ball attached to them. He shook his head, closing the door behind him as he said, "I'm gonna leave before my common sense catches up to me. But I'll swing back later with the bike. We can trade then."

I thanked him, waiting until his truck roared to life and drove away before I broke out into a happy dance, unable to control myself. I lifted my middle finger in what I assumed was the direction of California, hoping Declan could sense the big *screw you.*

The universe must've sensed my confidence and decided I needed to be knocked down a notch, because my keys clattered to the floor. I stared, not at them, but at the butterfly hair clip that'd fallen off. It was purple and small, similar to the ones worn in the early 2000s. It was plastic and therefore flightless, and shouldn't be responsible for the tears prickling in my eyes. But it was a harrowing, painful reminder of who I was—and what I'd fled.

"If I have to clip your wings to keep you with me—then I will, butterfly."

I shook my head, determined to beat the haunting voice to the punch, and crunched the clip beneath my boot. But was it enough? I might've outrun him, but he was everywhere in my head.

What if I never escaped him?

Chapter Three

"Well, you're just a big ol' moron, aren't you?" I wheezed down a breath, the mountain air growing thicker each time I pedaled. "Swapping vehicles with an absolute stranger."

I'd believed Jake was getting the poor end of the bargain, but little did I know it was me all along. I initially planned to get to work on the cabin immediately, but I'd barely lasted five minutes before I passed out on the mattress, dust and all. I'd been slumbering so deeply, I missed Jake returning to swap vehicles—but that hadn't stopped him.

I woke up to not only his truck outside and his keys on the kitchen table, but a shiny pink bike on the porch, sparkly streamers and all. I'd found it strange—not only that Jake had come into the cabin while I was asleep—but the bike appeared new. I shrugged it off. Maybe it was normal behavior out here, and who was I to judge if one of Jake's daughters rode a bike that said *Barbie Girl.* Especially since I'd be riding it often, considering one look inside Jake's truck told me I couldn't drive it.

It was a standard. And I didn't know how to drive a stick shift.

I huffed down air and dirt, positive if I fell over and died, I'd be fantastic fertilizer for the trees—or bear food. My legs ached and complained, years of running suddenly worth nothing. I peddled up the last of the dirt road, the edge of town within sight, and grunted as I dropped my foot to the ground.

Wallowpine was a sight for sore eyes, a town set in the central-eastern part of Arizona, near the New Mexico border. After living in San Francisco and enduring its traffic jams, it was strange to see the road open and clear. I could hear the wind in its fullness, bellowing through the mountain range, and there wasn't a single traffic light.

If only I'd come sooner. I shouldn't have backed out when I initially reached out to Jake's daughter, should have just run away then. I'd gone back and forth, giving myself whiplash over it. Insisting I needed to prepare, get some money and myself in order. In the end, waiting only cost me more. But maybe this modest mountain town would be the answer to my soul's needs.

I pushed off the gravel and started toward town, the breeze and slow decline carrying me along. Gripping the handlebars, I stole glances at the open valley alongside the road, unable to help admiring the view.

Lush green grass flowed with the wind, sprinkled with golden and ivory flowers. Scattered homes sat along the perimeter, some with fenced-in horses and cattle. The herd of elk I'd seen on my way in remained there, drinking from the glistening streams, while others pressed closer to the dense forest. I'd heard some describe Arizona as dull. A desert, with nothing but dirt and cactus. But they must've never stepped foot here. Never heard the mountain breeze swish through the forest, carrying tales of endless hopes.

New beginnings.

I steered across the road and past the homes within town, pedaling toward the town square. There looked to be no more than fifteen small buildings staggered about, their frames wooden and rustic. There was a post office, a public library, and a handful of other small businesses, including a bar called Ye Olde Trusty Tavern. Through email, Jules had warned me Wallowpine didn't have much to offer, and I'd have to travel to the next town, Hillshire, if I wanted a Walmart. I smiled to myself, knowing Elle would lose it when I told her there wasn't a coffee shop.

I rode past a country store and the farmers' market set up in front, avoiding the curious gazes of the locals and their offers of fresh fruit, and continued to the diner. I parked my bike beside the adorable, yet concerning, carved wooden bear outside, hoping thieves would be wary of stealing from Smokey the Bear and his shotgun.

I shook my head, hair clinging to my neck as I flapped out the sleeves of my loose tee. It was August, and cooler temperatures couldn't come soon enough. The surge of hormones pumping through my veins had me feeling like an oven. I opened the door to the Struttin'-Ruttin' Diner. Tin signs lined the wall, ranging all the way from *A Love for Huntin' to Suspicions of Bigfoot.* Deer antlers were strung about, and there was a wall of memorabilia for veterans. From the lack of customers, I must have missed the lunchtime rush. I stuck by the door, teetering on my heels, before I finally approached the waitress and ordered a cup of hot chocolate.

"Thank you." I scooted my pile of quarters across the counter as she poured my cup, hoping it was worth the last few dollars to my name. "Do you like working here?"

"It's fine." She snagged the quarters with a light brown hand, dropping them in the register. "You need anything else?"

"Nope," I said, popping my lips. She made her way to a new customer a few stools down, then glanced my way once more before she disappeared through the door behind her. I stared at my steaming mug and my stomach squirmed. What was the best way to approach this? I hadn't seen a hiring sign outside.

"Excuse me," I called out after she delivered a plate to the customer. She rolled her brown eyes, and I paused, the words *never mind* on the tip of my tongue. She looked younger than me—likely in high school—but that didn't help me feel any less intimidated. She wore leather pants, and there were pops of pink and purple in her thick dark braid. She looked like a total badass, and I was . . . well, there was vomit dribble on the collar of my shirt.

I thought I'd done the hardest part—leaving. But now I was wondering if *this* would be the most difficult challenge yet. The rebuilding, the mending. Except I was shoveling sand into a broken bucket, scrambling to form something out of nothing. I was exhausted, but I didn't have time to spare. I needed to be reliable, a steady force in a matter of a few months. I had to become the person I never had.

But I couldn't seem to catch my footing on an already broken foundation.

I shoved it aside, because dang it—I'd driven all this way and I wouldn't give up yet. "Do you have whipped cream?"

She peeked down at my nearly empty cup. "Do you have another quarter?"

I leveled her stare. "I've got two quarters."

Either she thought my broke ass was funny, or she believed I was kidding, but she smiled and reached down behind the counter. She shook the can and filled my mug to the brim, stopping only when it seeped over the edge.

"Perfect." I smiled and quickly asked, "So, are there some sort of requirements to fill mugs with whipped cream, or is the owner handing out jobs to just anyone?"

She grinned, shocking me when she shouted over her shoulder, "You owe me five bucks, Lila. She finally asked." I rubbed my forehead, not quite sure what was happening, but then she brushed her braid over her shoulder and said, "Wait here. The owner will be right out."

"Oh, okay—thank you." I bit back my smile, nearly jumping in my chair. *Relax, Shay—now is not the time for a happy dance.*

It was a mercy I'd chosen not to boogie when a petite woman with cropped red hair walked out from the door behind the counter and said, "Alright. You've got two minutes—let's hear it."

She cocked her head when I said nothing, not understanding in the slightest. "Your spiel," she said with a tired sigh. "Why I should give you a job. And save me the sob story—I don't have a ton of time to spare."

I wiped my damp palms against my thighs. "My sob story?"

She looked up to the ceiling, muttering something under her breath. "Look, I'm sure you're a nice girl. But to be frank, I've been burned by your sort too many times."

I blinked. "My sort?"

She looked me up and down, waving a wrinkled hand. "You know—a Valley Girl who left home with wild hair, determined to experience the world on her own. Only, you and I both know the adventure will only last a few weeks—maybe a month, if you're lucky—before you're racing home to Daddy or whoever it is you're running from." She shrugged. "I've seen it before and I'll see it again, even after you."

I stared her down, carefully chewing on my response. I knew how this looked. I'd watched the movies, read the books. I didn't blame her for being wary, especially if she'd been left empty-handed before.

I dipped my finger in the whipped cream and stole a bite. "I'm broke and hungry—I'm not really in the mood to waste time. Mine or yours. And I know you're comparing me to every out-of-towner who's crossed your path." I followed the blunt trail she'd paved, pretending I knew what I was doing. "But the difference is, no one wants or needs this as bad as I do. I don't want to tell you my story. All you need to know is my name's Shay. I haven't worked in nearly six years, but I promise I'll bust my butt for you, scrubbing dishes, skinning squirrels—I'll do whatever you need for as long as you need me."

She silently held my gaze, the few customers quiet too. Her thin lips quirked up to the right as she said, "I've got a fresh squirrel out back you can skin. I was about to fix up some stew."

I willed my face not to react—or barf. *Who the heck eats squirrels?* I grabbed my bag and stood. "Alright, sounds delicious. Lead the way."

She dipped her chin to the floor, but not before I saw her grin. "Okay, you win." She looked up and rested her arms on the counter, oblivious that she held my whole world in her small hands. "I really wasn't looking for help—so I can't promise you a lot of hours, okay?"

"That's fine," I agreed, taking anything I could get.

"We'll do a trial run. I'll start you on dishes, but you can trail my waitress, Layne, when it's slow on the floor." She raised her hand, stopping me before I could thank her. "We'll start with a week, okay? If it's not working out, I'll have to cut you loose, regardless of how pitiful your life is."

Chapter Four

Dishwasher was not my life calling. I didn't believe there was only one task or career we were destined for. But if Declan could have seen me elbows deep in bubbles and floating grease, I was positive he would've believed he'd prepared me for the task.

I was great at cleaning up messes. Especially his.

The first few days had gone swimmingly—I'd only broken two glasses and one plate. And as far as shining silverware went, I was a pro. I'd done my fair share for Betsy—Declan's mother, not the car—at her gatherings. And I'd gladly scrub sticky barbeque sauce off a fork if I never had to attend one of her functions again.

"How ya hanging, Shay?" Seth—Lila's husband and the cook—asked as he slipped off his apron to take a break.

"Not bad," I called out. I'd quickly learned Seth was hard of hearing from serving in the Gulf War. "Do you need me to prepare any food while you're out?"

A sly grin crossed his wrinkled face as he ran a hand over his bald head, his tanned arms covered in faded tattoos. "There's some potatoes that need washing—but you leave the peeling and cutting to me, alright?" He winked and left.

I smiled as I wiped my hands dry on a towel, ensuring my two band-aids were in place. It was a mercy Lila hadn't fired me when I, not only once, but twice made a bloody mess all over the half-peeled potatoes. Since then, I'd been stuck on dishwashing duty, only trailing Layne once on a near-dead afternoon.

I did my best not to mind. I was grateful to have something to do, to keep my mind from wandering too far—except I had to split hours with Lila's high school staff, meaning I only worked a few hours a day. It was exhausting, a constant effort not to acknowledge the cloud looming over me, growing heavier with each breath. But I knew this was normal—grief didn't simply vanish. Someday, I'd acknowledge it—maybe write something on that blank page I stared at nightly—but not now. Not until I'd rebuilt myself, found something worthy in this mess.

"I got you a special delivery, Valley Girl." Layne ushered in a towering stack of plates, the beginning of a long night. I didn't know much about her, just that she was born and raised in the White Mountains and was a whopping eighteen. Freshly graduated from high school, she was six years younger than me. She leaned against the counter, her deep brown eyes narrowed. "I thought you were prohibited from venturing further than your sink."

I suppressed the urge to roll my eyes. "Seth said I could leave my box."

She snickered down at the red square taped off beneath the sink—placed by Layne herself. "There's a customer out front asking for you."

My heart dropped, a half-peeled potato thumping to the floor with it. Who was looking for me? I'd been here less than a week. Since I didn't have a cell phone, I'd planned to use the diner phone to call Elle—but I hadn't risked calling her yet. I wanted to wait until I was positive I was staying.

Instinctively, I wrapped my arms around my stomach, dropping them when I caught Layne watching me. "You alright, Shay?" She hesitated and glanced over her shoulder. "I promise Jake's harmless—he's a good guy. He even called Lila before you came in, vouched for you and all."

I scrunched my nose—this was the first I'd heard of it. Why would Jake do that? And why would Lila agree? *They don't even know me.* Doing my best to let it go, I blew out a breath, resisting the urge to snap at Layne for not saying it was him in the first place. My issues weren't because of her, and it wouldn't do any good to project them onto those around me.

I exited the kitchen and scanned the full diner, thrumming with chatter and absolutely no music. Lila had a no cell phone, no music policy. Something about her food, and that the people eating it deserved the utmost attention. Finally, I settled on Jake, his lanky legs sprawled out in a booth, stopping when I noticed the two men sitting across from him.

"Shay!" Jake hollered, earning a hard look from Lila and giving me no choice but to head over. "I was just telling these boys a funny tale—thought you might like to hear it."

Boys.

Boys was *not* the appropriate term to describe these men.

I'd seen my fair share of men—California offered quite the variety. But never had I seen any who were equal parts handsome as they were rugged. I met the gaze of the one on the outer edge first, a pair of baby-blue eyes I could lose myself in, his hair as bright as golden silk. Eyes I realized were full of trouble when he winked and extended a tan hand to me. "Hmm . . . so you're the one we're supposed to steer far away from. I'm Nolan."

I nodded, not sure what that meant, but shook his hand anyway. His grip was firm, squeezing when I looked to the man beside him with deep, dark eyes locked on me. His hair was darker than Nolan's, brown and blond weaved together. But by the similar sharp jaws and straight noses, I believed they were brothers—falling on either side of a few years younger or older than me.

He stuck out a hand, both his arms clad in tattoos. "Levi."

I accepted it, wondering what the heck Jake was doing. And why was he grinning? Oh lordy, he probably thought he was doing me a favor and setting me up with one of them.

I'd take the cabin, even the bike—and of course, the job. But I did not want a boyfriend. These men did not want to be strapped down with my particular . . . *baggage.*

"Have a seat, Shay." Jake scooted over, continuing on when I didn't move to join him, "Ah, Lila won't mind. She's all bark—besides, it looks like she's running you ragged."

I frowned, wishing I'd done more than roll out of bed and throw my hair into a bun. I had nothing against looking presentable, but I was in an awkward stage right now, trying to sort through the former pieces of myself to find what *I* liked.

I waited to sit until Lila gave me a nod of approval, unwilling to risk this job. There was too much on the line. Jake rested his arm on the back of the booth, dipping his chin my way. "How's the cabin working for you?"

"Good." It had everything I needed—four log walls and a roof.

"And the truck?"

"Good. I decided I'd use the bike while the weather's nice." I mumbled my lie, too afraid to ask for my car back, not trusting I wouldn't lose my place to live. "Thank you again."

He grunted, shuffling in his seat. "I hope the bike's okay. All my girls' old ones were shredded, so I asked my nephew to pick one up for me. He said you were sleeping when he dropped it off and swapped our vehicles. I won't lie, I hadn't expected him to pick something so . . . bright."

Before I might've contemplated Jake's words, Nolan said, "Ah—so that really was you riding your bike just before dawn the past few days?" He bumped his shoulder against Levi's. "Levi said he saw you, but I thought maybe he was seeing ghosts. Or maybe he was slipping something sharp in his coffee."

"That would be you," Levi said under his breath before he looked up, pinning me with his gaze. But it wasn't intimidating, nor did it make me squirm—there was something soft in his eyes. "You might want to get some reflectors, or maybe a headlamp. It's only going to start getting darker in the morning."

"Ah, she's fine. It's only us on that road." Nolan winked, and my heart didn't race one bit. "And now that I've met her, I know not to hit her."

I swallowed. "You guys live out there?"

"Yup. These are those nephews I told you about. These two and their brother are your neighbors. Thought you should meet 'em in case you ever need a hand."

There's a third one? What was in the water to make men like this?

Jake snapped his fingers. "Ah, I got distracted. Anyway, like I was telling you boys, Wren and I were out on a joyride in Shay's car, enjoying our time before her treatment here in a few days. Well, we *were* driving, at least until Wren got a good look at me or something and decided she couldn't wait to have me until we got home."

I choked on a laugh, and Levi's face flushed along with mine. Nolan only grinned. "Attaboy. I always knew you were hot with the ladies."

Jake laughed, wiggling his brows. "Wren and I were just getting to the good stuff when all of a sudden, there was this blaring siren."

I groaned, mourning the once-innocent life of Betsy, positive she was scarred for life as Jake continued on, "I thought maybe my hearing aid was acting up, so I kept going, only the siren grew louder. I nearly had a stroke when there was a thud on the window. I'm not sure who was more shocked, me or your oldest brother when he caught Wren with her hand down my pants."

Nolan tipped his head back, howling in laughter, and Levi hid his scarlet face in his hands, shaking his head. I laughed quietly beside Jake, feeling sorry for Betsy—and the third brother. Or at least I did, until he said, "But here's the best part—Brooks only got one look at us before he scurried back to his truck and sped away." His bony shoulder nudged mine. "You really must've ruffled his feathers, Shay. I reckon he thought it was you and was ready to chase you outta town."

His words had barely settled before a new, deep voice said, "You're in my spot."

I looked up at who I now knew to be the eldest of the Graham brothers—Brooks. The buttmunch who pulled me over, then apparently tried to again. He wore the same forest ranger uniform, only this time his sunglasses were pushed up in his black hair, letting me see every bit of that daunting gaze.

I didn't know why I did it, but I looked right into those green eyes. "Are you going to write me a ticket for it?"

The men at the table snickered, but Brooks stared me down, a force to be reckoned with. Across from me, Nolan taunted, "Jake was telling us how you might be some sort of Peeping Tom." Brooks clenched his jaw, snapping his head toward his brothers. Nolan lifted his hands in defense. "Well, at least now we know what's had you in a piss-poor attitude the last few days. Can't say I understand why pretty little Shay is responsible for that."

"Let's go," Brooks bit out. "I'll make us something to eat at home."

I stared at the table, hiding my burning eyes, clueless why he so clearly disliked me. I'd been disliked before, of course, but they'd at least known me. But Brooks . . . he had no problem letting me know he couldn't stand me.

And he didn't know me at all.

"You're lucky I can look past what others can't. They don't see you like I do. They can't forgive you like I can—"

I shook my head, not liking how familiar Brooks's disdain tasted. "I should get back to work anyway. But thanks for introducing me to your nephews. And for everything else." I patted Jake's hand on the table. "Give Wren my best, will you?"

"Why don't you come over soon? Wren's been asking to meet you."

I smiled. At least someone wanted to know me. "I'd like that. Maybe when you guys get back from her treatment, I can swing by on one of my days off."

He winked and leaned in to whisper, "Maybe we'll work on driving the truck too, huh?"

I nodded, not sure how he'd figured it out. I crawled out of the booth, careful to avoid the brooding statue. "It was nice to meet you both. Maybe I'll see you around."

Nolan smiled and raised his brows, as though he intended to ensure that happened, but it was Levi who said in a low voice, "Don't forget to get those things for your bike. You can find them at the game shop. It's just down the road."

My heart warmed at his genuine care. Maybe the people in this town were truly good—besides one sour forest ranger. It was why I looked at Brooks, pretending I wasn't wearing a crusty apron and yesterday's underwear, and said, "Do you think you can find a hot pink helmet and basket to go with my bike?"

He met my gaze, not admitting that he'd dropped off my bike—and come into my cabin unannounced. His neck flexed, and I didn't fail to notice the tightly corded muscles as he crossed his arms over his chest. Too bad he was an asshole. He proved that notion true when he mumbled, "Ma'am."

I clenched my hands and stepped around him, not looking back once. Only when I made it back to the kitchen did I unfurl my fists, solely so I could peel potatoes beside Seth. He said nothing, not stopping me as I sliced away, oblivious that I was imagining Brooks's stupidly handsome face as the spud.

Chapter Five

I ached.

Figuratively and literally.

In the figurative sense because I didn't know how to let go of the past. How could I when I could barely think of it? In the literal sense because the mattress was lumpy, aggravating my already sore back and feet, despite only working a few hours a day. But I'd survived a week at the diner, and I assumed Lila hollering she'd see me in a few days meant I wasn't fired.

Today was my first designated day off since high school, when I'd worked part-time bagging groceries. And what does one do on their day off? Well—if you're me—you stare up at the light fixture, wondering why they call it a boob light.

Please tell me my boobs won't grow that big in a few months.

I snorted and rolled over, blaming the bizarre thought on the lack of sleep and the surge of new hormones. I didn't know if it was nerves, or perhaps living alone in the mountains—well, mostly alone—but I hadn't slept well since arriving in Wallowpine.

No, that wasn't true. I hadn't slept well since I started sleeping alone. But that was to be expected after sharing a bed with the man I believed I'd love forever. That's the part they don't warn you about when you dedicate your life to someone. You assume it'll never change, you get comfortable sharing a life with another soul. Accepting and loving their strange quirks.

I hadn't known I'd have to live without those quirks again.

But some of them I didn't miss. It was why I didn't make the bed when I rolled out of it, why the pants I'd worn yesterday were discarded on the floor. Why the toothpaste lid was off, the dishes piled up. One might've looked in the cabin and seen a mess, a slob. But the little messes, the clutter—it was an act of defiance. I was taking back my life.

I slipped on a pair of denim jeans and a baggy T-shirt before pulling on my boots. I hadn't had the chance to hike yet. Well, given I wasn't working more than twenty hours a week at the diner, I'd had the time to hike—to do more than that. To write. To fully acknowledge the life growing inside me. But despite what I believed, that I'd taken the hardest step by moving here, fear wasn't releasing its claws.

There were moments when its grasp seemed to loosen. Not enough to actually do something about it, but to at least dream. To imagine what it might be like to climb a mountain, to smell a tree—the ones I heard kids in the diner talking about, that smelled like chocolate or strawberry. To feel my legs burn. I hadn't experienced that sort of exhilarating pain in too long. I wanted to prove to myself I was capable of doing new things . . . and old things.

I stepped into the bathroom, for once not jumping at the sight of the brunette in the mirror, finally accustomed to no longer being a blonde. I'd never colored my hair before—I'd always worn it with pride. My mom had talked herself hoarse with the tidbit that men preferred blondes, saying how envious she was that I'd gotten my father's hair. Not that I knew him, so I'd have to take her word for it.

I stared at the girl in the mirror, and I didn't know her. Blue eyes that I swore were once bright were dull. I frowned at the puffy dark circles beneath my eyes, the freckles scattered across my cheeks. My fingers itched to grab the makeup on the counter, to hide my exhaustion and flaws. But my confidence was shattered in a way that was much deeper than beauty, and I didn't know how to fix it.

Broken.

Unworthy.

Damaged.

How was I supposed to fix *that*?

I sighed, frustrated, and hit the bathroom light switch, before heading out the door instead. I paused with a foot on my bike, considering staying home. I was tired. My body was sore, adjusting, and the bloat pushing against my jeans had me wanting to do nothing but sleep. But I pushed off the ground and wheeled down the road. Any sort of physical exhaustion was better than what I might experience if I let myself sit still.

Sweat dripped down my brows and my eyes stung, the sun's punishments for glaring up at the creaking wooden sign for so long. A sign that read *Graham—Bait and Game.* It couldn't mean the Graham brothers. Graham was a common last name, right? But life kicked me swiftly in the rear when I walked inside and saw Levi behind a counter, his nose stuffed in a book.

I paused in the doorway, planning to sneak out before the spiteful brother emerged, but I'd barely managed one step when a smooth voice said, "I was wondering when you'd be coming around, darlin'." I turned and found Nolan—whom Layne had revealed was the middle brother, clocking in at twenty-five. He grinned, a dimple in his cheek, and crossed his arms, not possessing a single ounce of the intimidation his older brother radiated. "Could you not find what you needed, or did you lose your nerve in asking me out?"

I gripped the door handle, unsure if I should leave or not. "I didn't know you worked here."

He shrugged and looked around the store, full of items I assumed were for hunting and fishing. I'd never actually stepped foot in a place like this. Declan had no interest in such activities. "Yup. I can probably find you some pictures of me waddling through the aisles in nothing but a diaper."

I dropped my hand and stepped closer, grateful for easy conversation. Too often, all I had was my thoughts. And that was too much. "That's okay. I'm sure one of these days when I stroll in here, I'll find you doing just that—only you'll be nursing a beer."

He grinned, waving a tan finger at me. "You'll have to earn that, darlin'. I save that for my special ladies."

I trailed Nolan's gaze as he winked at a woman leaving the store, remembering how Layne had called him the town flirt. But I wasn't annoyed, and my stomach didn't sink in his presence. He was harmless. As I turned back to Nolan, Levi waved, catching my eye.

He smiled faintly when I raised my hand in greeting, and I could've sworn red washed over his cheeks before I faced Nolan and asked, "Um . . . Is it okay that I'm here?"

He furrowed his brows, running a hand through his light hair. "Yeah? I mean—Jake did say you showed up with nothing to your name but a bag, but I assumed you wouldn't just straight-out rob me." He winked and my heart didn't falter, didn't jolt into a race. Would it ever again? "But I imagine it'd be hard for you to pack much on your princess bike."

"Barbie," I corrected him, deciding Jake was the town gossip. But I didn't care. No one here knew me, and they likely never would. "I meant because your brother seems to think I'm a walking plague." I might've been overreacting, but all I could think of was how Nolan had said he and Levi were supposed to stay away from me. Had Brooks told them that?

"Oh, Brooks?" He waved a hand, his muscles bunching beneath his white tee. "Don't take to heart anything that cranky ass does. He has a thing against all beautiful women, regardless of who they are."

I opened my mouth to protest, sure it had to be much more than that, when Levi called from across the store, "I grabbed those items I was telling you about, Shay. I can check you out when you're ready."

"Oh." I glanced between him and Nolan—the latter now conversing with a customer, something about fishing lines. "Let me walk around a bit and I'll be right up." I waved goodbye to Nolan and started down the aisles. I nabbed a loaf of bread, stashed beside a case of bullets. Strange that a game shop carried food. But what did I know? Maybe with the combination of the shop and the country store down the street, I'd never need to worry about finding a way to the next town over. Hillshire was an hour and a half away—a home to a Walmart and just about anything you couldn't find here. I rubbed at my chest, relieving the aching pressure there. I desperately needed to learn how to drive Jake's truck—or ask for Betsy back. But he and Wren were already in the city for her appointment, and I couldn't risk losing the cabin.

Was I doing the right thing?

I shoved the doubt aside and grabbed what I needed—bread, peanut butter, and a dusty bottle of prenatals I found hidden on a back shelf. I hadn't been to a doctor, and could only guess how far along I was, but I knew Elle had said it was important I took these. Guilt swept through me—I should think about my pregnancy more, about the baby inside me. Maybe once I had a chance to catch my breath, to slow down, I would be brave enough to fully acknowledge it. But for now, I'd start by taking these vitamins. I stared at the fliers behind Levi, avoiding his gaze as he silently bagged my items, along with what looked to be a reflector and a bike light.

I frowned at the total, not because I couldn't afford it—Lila paid weekly, and in cash per my request, since I'd yet to set up a bank account—but because of the price. "Did you scan everything?" It had to be more than twelve dollars.

"Yes," he mumbled, his hair covering his eyes, not letting me see what lay there.

I narrowed my eyes and grabbed the light. It cost more than the entire total. "You forgot this."

He looked up, his cheeks flushed. "The items for the bike are on the house—don't worry about it."

My eyes burned, my throat constricting to the point of pain. "No. I want to pay."

He shook his head, his voice milder, younger, than his brothers. "It's fine. Doesn't seem fair to charge you for something I suggested you get anyway—especially with Brooks being a jerk to you." He ran a hand through his hair, which fell just short of his chin. "If you want, we can order you a better bike through the shop."

I bit my lip, chewing over my words. There was a quiet, timid piece of myself that wanted to trust him. To believe he didn't have a condition hidden beneath his kindness. But that piece was quickly smothered out by the truth. Levi had no reason, absolutely no reason to help me—he wanted something. And I had nothing to give. I wouldn't stumble down this familiar path again, unknowingly giving up who I was. Giving up my voice.

Never again.

I swung my bag off my back and grabbed my wallet, pulling out more than enough in cash. My stomach twisted, sick as I pushed the money across the counter and grabbed my items. "Leave me alone. I don't want your charity."

"Shay—"

I shoved open the door and fled outside, cursing when I realized my error—I had nowhere to put the paper bags. Carefully, I dangled one on each handle and pushed off the porch to peddle away. But in my haste, I'd failed to notice a truck pulling in. I skidded to a stop and reached for the bike light before it fell, only to lose my balance in return.

I hissed as I landed, my hands and knees burning, grateful I hadn't flopped face-first in the dirt lot. As I rose I heard the store door open, and Nolan called out, "I saw the whole thing, Shay. We can go right to the police station and report that Brooks tried to run you over."

Of course. Why wouldn't the devil pay me a visit?

I stared at the ground as I stood and saw only black boots as the devil slammed his truck door. "Don't give her any ideas. I'm sure she'd jump at the first chance she'd get to take a man for everything he's worth."

My lungs burned—I wanted to shout, to reason that he knew nothing about me. That his assumption of me was way off. But I couldn't find it in me to care. He'd formed his opinion of me with one look.

I brushed the gravel from my hands and clung to the last bit of my pride, having done so for weeks. I straddled the ridiculous bike and became the stone-cold woman he assumed I was. "Pretty sure that requires you to be worth something."

I didn't stay for his rebuttal, knowing my heart couldn't survive it. My eyes swelled with moisture, but somehow no tears broke through until my wheels hit the dirt road, though I wasn't quite sure where it was leading. To the cabin, of course, but it didn't feel like home. What if I never found home again? I'd moved hundreds of miles to escape a life others had molded for me, but what if I just allowed the same thing to happen again?

Chapter Six

What was home?

It wasn't walls, whether they were sturdy or shaky. It wasn't the floors that supported you, no matter how crumbly or sure they might be. It was supposed to be the ones who dwelled with you, who shared the same air. But was it home, really, if it could be destroyed in one thoughtless moment?

I'd thought I had a home once—only once. But it was gone, and now . . . now I was questioning everything. Had it even been a home at all? I wasn't sure, but at least I'd had stability and comfort. And while I knew, believed with my entire heart, that what I was chasing—freedom—was worth more than anything my former life could offer, I missed it.

Being loved. Cared for.

Privileges with a price I was no longer willing to pay.

There was nothing I could do to ease my aching heart as I leaned against the diner counter, watching a father eat dinner with his daughter, even treating her to dessert. I'd been enamored with them their entire visit, stealing peeks in between batches of dishes. His daughter was young, with small pigtails and chubby ankles and the largest chocolate eyes. Eyes that glowed for her daddy. She giggled as he tickled her beneath the table, both wrapped up in one another.

Something unfixable in my chest squeezed, then plummeted to my feet when a young woman walked in and joined them. The little girl glanced up, grinning with delight in her booster seat and squealing for her mama to pick her up.

How was it possible to grieve something I'd never had? Would never have?

The man kissed the woman's cheek just as there was a pinch on my shoulder. I turned, finding Layne beside me. "How much longer are you going to check out my brother? It's weird."

"I'm not," I scoffed, lowering my hand from my stomach. That was the last thing on my mind. "I just thought they were sweet, that's all." I nudged my elbow into her ribs, hoping she wouldn't deck me for it. "But at least now I know why you were checking on their table so much. I thought maybe you had a thing for dads."

She stuck out her tongue and gagged. "Gross." Reaching into her apron, she pulled out a wad of cash. "As annoying as my brother is, he's a fantastic tipper. So I'll serve him as long as I have to if it gets me out of this town."

I nodded, grateful Layne was opening up to me—I hadn't anticipated starting over to be this lonely. "Why are you wanting to leave Wallowpine?"

She waved goodbye to her brother and his family, waiting until they were gone before she said, "Believe me, Valley Girl—after you spend any real amount of time here, you'll be running for the hills."

I shrugged. "I don't know . . . I don't hate it here."

"That's because you think you're on some grand adventure. You think you're going to find yourself in these mountains, don't you?" She sighed, shaking her head. "Your story will end exactly how it did for the rest of the Valley Girls before you. You'll grow bored and wonder if what you're searching for doesn't exist—or maybe if you already had it all along. But soon enough, you'll head home and be grateful for how good you had it."

I looked at her, seeing so much potential and life in her young brown eyes. It was why I didn't hesitate to disagree, needing to not believe her. I wouldn't go back. "You know, Layne, I could say those exact words to you. I could say: you're going to leave here and head off into the big world, determined to make something of yourself. But guess what? The real world sucks. It's messy and painful, and I can assure you—there aren't many Lilas or Jakes in the world who will help out a complete stranger like they did me." Even now my heart burned, swelling as I thought more of it. How Jake had rented me the cabin, helped me out with the rent, and gave me a bike. Even put in a good word for me with Lila, who'd offered me a job despite not needing the help. "I could tell you you're going to get swallowed whole and come crawling home, remembering how good you had it." I smiled then, softening my tone. "But I won't tell you any of that—because I don't believe it. I think anyone, even you and I, are capable of surviving anywhere. And yes, I know I could've stayed where I was, but I was tired of surviving, Layne. I wanted to *thrive*. And if you think you'd thrive somewhere other than Wallowpine—then I want that for you."

She tightened her lips and said nothing as a group of customers arrived. I shifted and returned to my dishwashing post. I was arms deep in muggy water when Layne strolled in with a tower of plates. I expected her to drop them off without a word, but she stayed, lingering in the doorway. "Did you go to college?"

"A few years ago," I murmured, feeling like the knife I was scrubbing was wedged in my chest. "I never finished."

She narrowed her eyes, looking me over. "What were you doing before you came here then?"

A whole lot of nothing.

That wasn't true. But in the hindsight of things, it felt like a whole lot of nothing now. "I fell in love. Got engaged." I swallowed, my hands shaking beneath the water. "And I lost myself somewhere in between that."

She shook her head, not bothering to hide her smug grin. "See, I told you. You're a walking cliché. So what happened—did he cheat on you?"

"No." I scrubbed the dishes harder. I wish Declan had cheated on me. Maybe then I wouldn't feel guilty for running. I knew I was right to leave, but guilt strangled me regardless. And I didn't know what thoughts were mine, what was manipulation. "If you're wanting to go to college, let me know if you need any help with the applications or anything."

There was a long pause before she asked, "You'd do that?"

I looked up and flicked dish bubbles at her. "If it gets you off my butt, I'll do anything. Besides, with you gone, maybe Lila will let me have more hours."

As though summoned, Lila and Seth walked through the back door, both returning from a break. She looked at me and then Layne. "Do I pay you to stand around and gush on one another? I could hear both of you blabbering on from outside."

Layne raised a hand to her chest. "Shay practically cornered me, saying all sorts of things to convince me to stay. She warned me I was going to leave here and fall in love—only to be deserted by my fiancé, abandoned with his child."

I let out a shocked laugh, my cheeks burning. "I did not, you bratty hillbilly," I fumbled out in a rush.

Seth chuckled under his breath and adjusted the stove, kissing Lila's head goodbye before she walked by and said, "Don't be scaring her, Shay." She wrapped her arm around Layne's shoulder and not so quietly whispered, "You don't know how long I've been trying to get rid of her. At least now I'll have you to replace her."

I laughed as they left, the ache in my chest easing, washing away the emotions Layne's conversation had brought up. It felt like a lifetime ago when I was young like her, the world at my feet, ready and willing.

I'd once thought I was independent, strong. I'd taken care of myself as well as my mom since I was old enough to understand electricity. And if you didn't pay, the power was shut off. My mother wasn't lazy—she always worked some sort of job to keep us afloat. But she was easily distracted, namely with men. And I guess after three days of not being able to watch *Scooby Doo*, I'd had enough. I didn't know if it was my raggy pajamas or if I'd pitched myself well enough, but I convinced a handful of neighbors in our apartment complex to let me do some odds and ends for them in exchange for cash. I remembered the smug grin I wore late that night when my mom hobbled in, reeking of smoke and beer from the club she bartended at. She tossed her bag on the table and stared at the glowing lights—and then me. She asked if I'd paid the bill, and when I admitted I had, I grinned. I waited for her to dote on me, to tell me how proud she was, how grown-up I was at the age of seven. But she only nodded and disappeared into her room. I was on the cusp of sleep, hands aching from pulling weeds, when I was stirred awake by a fit of giggles and the front door opening. I opened my eyes just enough to see my mother glance back at me, her arm looped with a man I'd never seen before. And when she slipped out, I couldn't help but wonder if I'd done the wrong thing. If now my mother didn't think she needed to take care of me.

And maybe I didn't need her. I'd convinced myself I didn't need anyone—that is, until I met a stranger. A handsome, likable man who wanted to know me. And then I really wasn't that independent after all. I'd thought it might be nice to be cared for, loved. And for a time it was. It was refreshing to know someone was watching out for me, freeing me of unnecessary stress. Yes, it had been nice.

Until it wasn't.

I'd made mistakes in the last few years. Grown dependent, reliant on someone other than myself. Moving here had been the second largest pivotal moment in my life—the first happened just a short time before. And I had to believe, had to hope I hadn't made those decisions in vain.

Maybe I wouldn't ever have the world at my feet again. But maybe . . . maybe I could make something of myself in this quiet town. Where I was safe, hidden.

Maybe pain couldn't reach me here.

Chapter Seven

Maybe it was the hormones, or the lingering effects of watching Layne's brother and niece the other night. Maybe it was the crackers I'd thrown up earlier. But my stomach was twisting with regrets.

I'd been here less than two weeks, and I'd yet to go to the doctor or conquer a single hike. Summer was barely hanging on, fall drawing nearer each breath. And soon enough, I wouldn't be able to hike—at least not comfortably. But my biggest regret was how rocky my relationship with my neighbors was. The loneliness I'd felt in California had followed me here, and I was tired of wearing it as an extra layer. I needed something more. I didn't know quite what it was, but I was determined to find it.

I'd watched my mother for eighteen years—and not a day more—and I'd learned plenty. It was why I'd clutched on to my virginity for all of high school, after seeing her sob in the bathtub over too many scummy men. But I'd also watched her bake. It was never for me, and it wasn't often—but anytime a new neighbor moved in, she baked a treat for them. I imagined it was more out of nosiness than kindness, but she'd always done it.

It was why I'd gotten down on all fours and scrubbed the iron stove in my kitchen last night after Lila handed me a bundle of ripe bananas, claiming they'd be too far gone in the morning. I didn't have a recipe, nor a phone to search for one, but I'd gone to the country store and grabbed what ingredients seemed best, deciding I could wing it.

So that was how I found myself walking down the dirt lane, venturing deeper into the forest with a loaf of bread. Jake hadn't taught me to drive stick yet, and I was too chicken to risk smashing the bread on the bike. After the hell I'd endured cleaning the oven, this loaf was my child, and I'd treat it with all the tender love and care in the world.

I cradled it to my chest, silently praying like I never had before. *Please don't let a bear maul me.* It was probably unwise to live in the mountains among wild animals and strangers and not have a phone, but I wasn't ready to give in just yet. There was a different sort of freedom that came with being unreachable. Besides, the closer I drew to the two-story cabin on the right, my palms sweaty, the more I wondered if being eaten alive might be a kinder fate than willingly facing the Graham boys.

One in particular.

I didn't know his schedule—why would I? I wasn't the devil's keeper. But I'd hoped the bunnies and birds needed tending, or whatever forest rangers did. I scrunched my nose, frowning at his white truck in the driveway, parked next to a navy pickup and a red Jeep I'd seen outside their shop.

I paused in the driveway and took a step back. Were they married? There wasn't an extra vehicle parked out front, but I knew that meant little. Until Betsy, I'd never owned a vehicle. Before, I'd relied on the car service Declan paid for, or him to drive me around. I hadn't heard of or seen a significant other in their lives, but what if they were having a sleepover and I was crashing it?

I shook my head and started forward again. It didn't matter if they were married, taken, or *it's complicated*. I wasn't interested in any of them like that. I only wanted to start off on the right foot. I climbed the steps of the sturdy porch and let out a steadying breath before I tapped my knuckles against the faded maroon door, the house silent behind it. It was too late to back out now.

But then there was a ruckus, shouting and what sounded like a barking dog. I dropped the loaf—*sorry, my sweet child*—and turned and ran, claiming the title of ding-dong ditcher. I only stopped when a voice bellowed, "You know, trespassing is illegal."

I halted in the gravel lane, and maybe the mountain air had poisoned my brain, but I considered—seriously considered—grabbing the largest rock I could find and chucking it straight at the ranger's truck. But because I wasn't insane, I turned and faced him.

Brooks stood in the doorway, his glare framed nicely by his disheveled dark hair, looking like he'd rolled straight out of bed. I realized he had, my eyes widening, when I spotted his bare feet and boxers, his white T-shirt folded up on his waist, like he'd thrown it on in a hurry.

Did he have a half-naked girlfriend behind him?

"Um—" I forced myself to hold his glare, not daring to linger down south. "I made banana bread. I thought maybe you guys would want some."

He glanced down at the bread wrapped tightly in foil on his porch and nudged it with his toe. "It poisoned?"

"Maybe."

He looked up, this time the glare gone, replaced with something I couldn't place. It was questioning, searching—like maybe he was trying to figure me out. *Nope, don't like that.* I turned when he shifted his attention back through the partially open door and mumbled words beyond my hearing, using that as my chance to leave.

"Shay!"

I turned, this time finding not Brooks but Nolan running down the steps in only boxers, a wolf chasing after him. Nolan must've noticed my half-hearted attempt to brace myself in case the animal tackled me because he whistled and firmly said, "Stand down, Cash."

The wolf—or rather, dog—halted, its large pointed ears perked up and ready, eager for another command. "Sorry." Nolan smirked. "He gets as excited as the rest of us when a lady comes around."

I stared at the German shepherd, deeming that better than ogling Nolan. I'd never seen muscles like that. His skin was golden, tight and firm. Were his brothers in such good shape? I shook my head—bad Shay. "I—" I cleared my throat. "Did you need something?"

Nolan tilted his head, blond strands falling over his forehead. "Did you?"

I pointed at the empty porch, seeing red when I realized Brooks had abandoned my bread at the doorstep. I blew out a steadying breath. "I had bananas that were about to go bad, and I thought you guys might like some banana bread," I explained like I was the Pioneer Woman and this wasn't my first time baking it.

He grinned and stepped back toward his log-cabin home. "Well, come on in."

"What?" I glanced at the trees surrounding us, like one of them could offer me a way out. Maybe if one fell on me. "That's okay. I'm sure you just woke up and would like to relax, not entertain me."

He clicked his tongue and Cash moved, following him up the steps. "Nah. We've been up for hours. Come on in, darlin'."

I hesitated. I didn't know these men, and being murdered wasn't high on my to-do list—it was at least number forty-five. But when Cash jumped up and stretched his front legs onto Nolan's chest, I started forward again. Animals were a good judge of character, right? They didn't lick serial killers.

I wrapped my arms around my stomach, grateful I'd actually brushed my hair and thrown on cut-off jean shorts and a white tank top, a brown flannel thrown over it. Nolan grinned in the doorway, not at all bashful at being nearly naked.

But I guess if I had a six-pack, I wouldn't be shy either.

"Thanks," I mumbled when he closed the door, lingering in the entryway as he moved to the kitchen and unwrapped the foil.

I scanned what I could see of the house, Brooks and Levi nowhere to be seen. The staircase was empty, clean of dirty socks or underwear. The walls were warm, mounted with antlers, artwork, and what looked to be family pictures, not bare, as I would've imagined a bachelor pad to be. Adjacent to the kitchen was the living room, with a large sectional and matching recliner in front of a television. I stared at the stone fireplace in the far corner. There was a guitar beside it and a vase on the mantel above it—perfect for hanging Christmas stockings. Had they done that? Was this home a happy one?

"Do only you three live here?" I asked, deciding they must've had someone who'd made this house a home, who'd cleaned it. "Or four, I guess," I added, correcting myself when something wet nudged my leg and I looked down to see Cash beside me, his tongue hanging out.

"That's right." Nolan reached into the beautiful oak cabinets lining the kitchen wall, a window above the sink offering a perfect view of the forest. "Which means we don't have the opportunity nearly enough to share breakfast with a lovely lady such as yourself. So thank you for that."

I snorted and stuffed my hands in my back pockets as Cash stirred at my feet, his claws clattering against the wood flooring as he moved to the hallway where Levi stepped out, his eyes wide. Mine were even wider, though, at learning he was not only in *fantastic* shape, but his tattoos didn't end on his arms, the ink carrying onto his chest.

"Shay?" he asked, rubbing his eyes. "What are you doing here?"

Brooks stepped out of a door behind him—the only brother who bothered to be clothed, his jeans worn with holes. "What part of *she's here to deliver us death* did you not understand?"

Levi glared at him, as I did. "I thought you were kidding. I didn't think she was actually here."

Nolan waved a knife—perfect for gutting stupid girls like myself. "Well, wake up, little brother. Because the Lord has delivered us an angel bearing bread."

Levi turned, muttering something under his breath, and slammed the door behind him as Nolan mused, "Do you think that's the first time a woman's seen him almost naked?"

"Don't be a prick," Brooks said and opened a sliding glass door, letting Cash out back into a fenced yard. "And don't think I missed how you stripped off your clothes when you heard her voice."

I laughed, only to stifle it when Brooks glared at me, no hint of a smile on his tight lips. "I'm gonna head out," I said, refusing, absolutely refusing, to stay anywhere I wasn't wanted. I'd done so for too long. "Thank you for inviting me in, Nolan."

"You're leaving already?" Levi's voice stopped me before I'd managed a step. He was fully dressed in jeans and a flannel, only his face and neck visible, and I smiled, unable to help myself. "You just got here."

"She's not leaving." Nolan sliced into the bread, giving Brooks a hard look. "I haven't had breakfast with a woman in too long, and I'll be damned if you take this from me."

Brooks laughed, and I stared, unaware he was capable of such a thing. He poked his brother in the forehead, standing hardly an inch taller. "That's your own fault. Commit to something more than just sleeping around."

"Nah. It makes this all the more special." Nolan winked at me and opened the fridge, pulling out a jug of milk. "Do you want milk or coffee, darlin'?"

"Neither." I glanced at Brooks, sweating beneath his glare. I doubted he was the sharing type. "I'm good, really. I ate before I came."

Nolan shrugged, dishing himself a plate. "More for me."

Levi came up, distracting me from seeing if Nolan was enjoying the bread or not. "Hey, you," I started, uncertain how to greet him after our last encounter—when I'd told him I didn't want his charity. "You guys don't work today?"

"No." His tone was faint, and he glanced over his shoulder to where Brooks was watching us, his brother's eyes narrowed. "It would probably be better for business to open up on Sundays . . . but we're still figuring it out. Dad wanted us to make time for church."

Nolan had said only he and his brothers lived here. But then where was their dad? Or mom? I leaned back on my heel, straining to see if someone was upstairs, when Nolan said, "You should come with us."

"Um—" I bit my lip and stepped back, edging closer to the entryway. "I'm not really the church-going type."

"That explains it," Brooks murmured and leaned against the counter, making no move to try my bread.

I rolled my eyes. "I just meant I've never been." Though I didn't have an interest in going. Elle was religious and had invited me, but I'd never gone—and now it seemed sort of pointless. "Sorry."

Levi shrugged, not seeming nearly as put off as Brooks. "Don't apologize. Regardless of Dad's wishes, this is our first time going in over a year. Nolan must be feeling guilty over something, considering it was his idea last night that we go," he said with a grin, and I might've smiled with him if I hadn't seen the way Brooks's shoulders dropped, his frown deepening.

Was he ever happy?

Nolan turned from the window and chugged a glass of milk, his jaw dusted with morning shadow. "That's because I knew an absolute angel would come visit us." He reached for the bread, folding the foil together. "I might have to break one of my rules and marry you, darlin'. This was too good."

I bit my smile, my heart warming. "You liked it?"

"Liked it?" Nolan put a hand over his bare chest. "I loved it."

Brooks raised a dark brow. "Why don't you have another slice then?"

Nolan shot a look at him, but before I might've examined it more, he said, "Fine—but I demand my brothers have a slice right now. It's too damn good not to share."

I smiled wide, my cheeks aching. I wished Declan was here—so I could shove the bread down his throat. He'd hated everything I'd ever made, so I believed I was a lousy cook, but maybe he was just a lousy fiancé. "That's great. If I get bored, maybe I'll make you another one sometime." I glared at Brooks, whose cheeks were red, his hand over his mouth—blocking out the slice Nolan was waving. "Can't promise there won't be poison, of course."

Levi left my side and cut himself a slice at the counter. I stood on the edge of my toes as he took a bite, giving little attention to Brooks and Nolan in the corner, the latter still attempting to cram his piece into Brooks's mouth.

Red bloomed on Levi's cheeks as he swallowed and beat his chest, choking. "I'm fine," he croaked and grabbed the milk, guzzling straight from the jug.

"Shut up," Nolan hissed at Brooks, both of them heaved over and laughing. "Eat my damn bread."

"Are you okay?" I stepped forward, brows furrowing, as Levi cleared his throat, his face and neck flushed. "You don't have to eat it," I said, my voice straining. "I know I'm not very good—"

"I like it," he insisted, wolfing down another bite. "I just got excited and swallowed too fast."

I rolled my eyes. But when he took another bite and smiled, I relaxed—maybe he wasn't lying. After all, Declan had always spoken his mind, so why would the Graham boys be any different? I shifted on my heels, tilting my head toward the string guitar. "Does one of you play?"

All three stilled and looked at one another, like I'd dropped a bomb. But it was Levi who said, "No. That's Dad's."

Before I'd fully registered the strain in his voice, felt the heaviness in the room, Brooks stalked by me. He grabbed the guitar and placed it in one of the rooms down the hall . . . like I was going to steal it.

What an ass.

"Alright." Nolan dropped the bread he'd failed to give Brooks back in the foil, wrapping it up. "As repayment for this delicious treat, we'll be taking you to church now."

"Okay," I said, before I might've thought better of it, agreeing more out of habit than anything. But I made no effort to take it back. I had no interest in church, or in spending time with Brooks, who I was doing my best not to look at. But I wasn't ready to go back to the cabin, remembering the reason I came here bearing bread in the first place.

I was lonely.

Lonely and running.

And I didn't mind their company—at least Nolan and Levi's. It was fun, something different to watch how they interacted with one another. I'd never had a sibling of my own.

"But wait—" I bit my lip before I teased, "You're going to put on clothes, right? Unless you're involved in some sort of nudist religion."

Levi choked on his last bite of bread, and Brooks, to no surprise, rolled his eyes. But Nolan grinned. "No. But dammit, now I really wish I was."

Chapter Eight

Even though I wasn't a virgin—and was pregnant, at that—fiery flames didn't engulf me when I snuck into the church with the Graham brothers and stole a bench in the far back. I planned to sit on the end—a clean getaway—but somehow I was sandwiched between Levi and Nolan, with the devil on the corner. I spotted Jake across the room, his mouth wide open as he snored. I gave a small smile to the elderly woman beside him, assuming it was Wren, her brown eyes on us since we'd crept in.

"What is wrong with you?" I mumbled when Nolan widened his legs like a starfish, cramming mine against Levi's. "Stop moving."

He adjusted in his seat, pulling at his jeans—different from any kind I'd seen in California. "I didn't put on underwear. Everything's sitting funny."

I feigned an apologetic smile as the preacher speaking at the front of the room glanced our way, likely silently warning Nolan to be quiet. I scooted to the edge of the bench when Levi leaned behind me and whispered, "What happened to the underwear you were wearing before?"

Cheeks burning, I dipped behind the bench in front of us as Nolan not so quietly explained, "Those are my house boxers. My out-on-the-town ones are dirty."

I hid my face in my hands—I was never going to church again. "Please tell me you have more than two pairs of underwear."

"Wouldn't you like to know, darlin'?"

I rolled my eyes and glanced to the right, catching Brooks's eye. To my surprise, he didn't look away, watching me like he had outside his house. His emerald eyes weren't shy, but soft and focused solely on me. Like he was trying to figure me out, like maybe he *wanted* to figure me out. Regardless, my blood was pumping, afraid he could see through me, separate the truth and the lies.

I didn't have to know Brooks to see he didn't trust me.

His gaze stayed on me as a piano began to play—the signal it was time to go, if the children sprinting out the back door were any indication. The Graham brothers stood just as fast, and I couldn't help but wonder why we'd come. Not one of us had listened to a word of the service.

I didn't dig into it and followed Nolan and Brooks out. Levi leaned down and said beside my ear, "Nolan probably thinks he's a shoo-in for heaven now."

I grinned and whispered over my shoulder, "Not if he doesn't wash his underwear."

Levi looked down at me again, his grin boyish and young, innocent. And it was because of that I didn't regret tagging along. Maybe I might find a friend in Levi Graham.

I walked beside him back toward Brooks's truck, stopping when we heard a loud holler. "Levi Graham—you best not be walking away before you introduce me to your girlfriend."

I bit my lip and turned to face the woman who'd sat beside Jake, who was nowhere in sight. "She's not my girlfriend, Wren," Levi murmured. "This is—"

"I know who she is," Wren finished for him, clearing the last of the church steps. "She's the girl who named her car after a cow." I swallowed, my throat dry. Her hair was short and dark, peeking out from beneath her sage scarf. She looked to be in her seventies, her skin bronze and warm, aged with wrinkles. But she didn't look the least bit sick. Especially when she said, "Now I know why you haven't come by to see me. You're too busy running around with these hooligans for little ol' me."

"Um—" I fumbled for a response and looked to Levi, only to realize I stood alone. The coward had retreated to his brothers. I swallowed, her chestnut eyes hard on me, feeling like I'd done something wrong. "I don't run around with them. They don't even like me that much." I wrung my hands behind my back when she said nothing and looked me over, all too aware of the amount of leg I was showing.

"I can visit with you now if you're not busy. Or I can go home and bake you something," I offered. *Because I'm the Pioneer Woman, remember.* "I can come over after. I'm really sorry for not making time—"

She lifted her hand, stopping me mid-ramble. "It's alright, Shay. I was only teasing." She glanced up at Jake when he sidled up beside her, his arm over her shoulder. "You weren't kidding. She scares quicker than a deer in headlights."

What?

"Nah." Jake smiled, kissing the top of her head. My heart did a little drop and roll at the way he looked at her—I'd never seen such love and amusement in anyone's eyes before. "You're just an intimidating, beautiful woman."

Wren scoffed, proving Jake's observation to be true when she shouted, "I'm going to pretend you three boys haven't been back there cowering this whole time."

"We were letting you have a clear shot at the city slicker," Brooks said, the first of his brothers to step forward and wrap Wren in his arms, surprisingly capable of being a good human. "It's good to see you out and about."

She smacked his arm, her frame frail next to his. "I'm not dead yet, asshole."

I choked on a nervous laugh as she hugged Levi and Nolan, both of whom tightly embraced her back. Levi scooted away, scuffing his boots against the ground as Nolan teased, "Ah, even when that happens, I'm sure you'll still be out and about, Wren, busy haunting this mountain."

"Someone has to keep you in check." Wren raised a brow at me. "Although—I guess if Shay can drag the three of you to church, I may not need to haunt you after all. Question is: which of you will snatch her up first?"

My cheeks heated, worsening as Brooks said something in Nolan's ear, both of them stifling a laugh. If they replied, I didn't hear it, looking back to the truck instead, considering walking home. Something was off. Not with Wren, or anyone else, but me. A haunting whisper, reminding me I didn't quite fit in here. They had each other. They were a family; Wren and Jake were their aunt and uncle. And I wasn't a part of that family—of any.

Where was my place? My family?

I looked up, eyes burning, when Levi's boot nudged mine. His lips didn't move, but his furrowed brows and dark eyes said it all as he searched my face, not bothering to jump in the conversation around us. Against my will, a tear slid down my face and my chest squeezed. I didn't know what to do with how he was looking at me. I didn't believe there was romance or longing in his eyes, but rather concern. And I didn't know what to do with that either.

Brooks cleared his throat, and I looked away from Levi, staring at my feet as the former said, "It was good to see you, Wren. But we should head out."

"Alright, alright." She looped her arm through Jake's and faced me. "Hopefully you'll come see me before I'm dead. Maybe you can convince these boys to come have dinner with me too."

I nodded, praying she couldn't see the moisture in my eyes. "It was nice to meet you."

I turned and was trailing Levi to the truck when I heard Jake faintly say, "I hope you'll consider what I asked, Brooks."

I climbed in the back seat and shut the door before I could hear what Brooks replied. I stared out the window, doing my best to not look at Brooks when he climbed in, but I could tell his jaw was tight. I wondered if Jake had said something to upset him or if my presence was the culprit.

"Levi," I said as Brooks started down the road, remembering one of my other tasks for the day. "Are there any good hikes nearby?"

Brooks scoffed, and my chest clenched, not hearing what he muttered under his breath. I glared at the back of his head, contemplating smashing it when Levi said, "Turkey Ridge is pretty good this time of year."

"You know," Nolan piped in from the passenger seat, not letting me ask more about the hike, "something Wren said got me thinking—do you have a boyfriend, Shay?"

I fidgeted in my seat, the silence pressing in on me. I pulled at the loose strands on my shorts. "No, I don't."

He turned to face me, raising a light brow. "Is it true you had a fiancé?"

"You're such an ass," Levi muttered, shooting me an apologetic look.

I swallowed through the lump wedged in my throat. I should've gone to a larger town. "Yes. I was engaged."

I tucked my hands beneath my thighs, as if hiding my bare ring finger made it any less real, when Nolan asked, "Did he cheat on you?"

"That is none of your business," Brooks snapped, surprising me.

And while I agreed with Brooks, I wasn't angry with Nolan. He was only being nosy, not cruel. I blew out a shaky laugh and shook my head. "No, he didn't cheat on me." Why was that always the first question? Was that the only reasonable explanation for why a relationship or promises might end? Sometimes it was simple—as simple as no longer wanting the same things. "He just didn't want to be a family anymore."

Simple or not, it hurt.

"Thank you for spending time with me," I murmured, like today was my idea, and climbed out of the truck, not waiting for Brooks to fully stop in my driveway. "I'll see you around."

"Shay," Levi said, stopping me before I could shut the car door. "Come by the shop tomorrow. I'll draw you a map of some hikes."

My eyes burned—and I blamed it on Nolan's nosiness, not Levi's kind gesture. I nodded and closed the door, reaching into my bag for my keys. Exhaustion hit me straight on as I walked inside. I stared at my bed, longing to sleep, and had started to shuck off my boots when there was a thump against my door. I halted, one leg in the air.

I shuffled over, my feet now uneven, and peeked through the kitchen window to see Brooks's truck idling outside. I opened the door, expecting Levi, or even Nolan, but I stepped back—it was the devil himself, brooding in my doorway. "Do you need something?" I asked when he said nothing and stared over my head, searching my cabin. "Brooks?"

His gaze flicked down to mine, his deep voice pinning me to the spot. "I need to talk to you."

I waited, looking up at him expectantly—but he only stared, his jaw not loosening even an inch. I blew out a heavy breath and stepped aside, letting him in. I paused with a hand on the door, my stomach twisting, unsure how I felt being alone with him.

I glanced out the door, to where both Levi and Nolan were eagerly watching, and deemed it fine. But my mind and my heart were racing. I looked at Brooks and did my best to slow my breathing, telling myself I was safe. His shoulders were loose, his hands lax at his sides, and while he might not like me, he didn't look angry.

But I couldn't trust myself, not after failing the last time.

I grabbed a chair and wedged the door open, relieving the feeling of being trapped. Something in his face seemed to soften, the crease between his brows easing. "Shay—"

"What do you want?" I asked, my tone gruffer than I intended.

Before I could apologize, maybe explain that I was tired, Brooks dryly said, "I need you to leave my brothers alone."

I blinked, not understanding why it felt like my heart had splattered to the floor. "Excuse me?"

He didn't look at me, but at my unmade bed, and I internally winced, wishing I'd done better at cleaning the cabin up. Why did I ever think the mess would prove anything to Declan? What if he told Jake and I got kicked out? But before I could curse myself for being so foolish, Brooks said, "Look, I get it. You're sad and trying to move on. But you need to leave Levi and Nolan out of it. Levi is young and naive, and Nolan—" He snapped his mouth shut and breathed through his nose. "I don't need you screwing with their minds."

I blinked, expecting him to vanish into thin air. This conversation was ridiculous, surely a nightmare. But he only confirmed his presence further. "I'm going to give you the benefit of the doubt and assume you're lonely and mean well. I wanted to say something this morning, but I didn't want to embarrass you in front of them." He hooked his hands on his pockets. "But leave us alone, okay? We don't have time for you."

"Okay . . ." I rubbed the back of my neck. "I know you're their oldest brother and this might be your way of looking out for them—but they're grown adults. They can decide for themselves what they do," I reasoned, not sure if I cared if I saw them again or not, more put off by Brooks demanding I stay away.

"Levi is only twenty. He's—"

"He is an adult," I snapped back, an all-too-familiar bitterness filling my mouth. I stepped closer to the partially open door, hoping that could calm the pressure in my chest. But I felt as hopeless as I had in the situation I'd barely left.

He shook his head, his lips curling. "I saw how you were looking at him. He's too young for you—"

"Are you kidding me?" I cut him off again. "I'm not interested in him like that. Don't forget, Brooks—you were also looking at me, and I watched you right back. And I absolutely can't stand you." My breaths were raspy as I held onto the last of my courage. "I want to believe you're doing this because I'm a stranger and you don't know my intentions. But the problem is—you think you do know me. You think I'm a spoiled, selfish brat, looking to use someone until I feel better about myself. That I want to hurt someone like I've been hurt. Or like you said, that I want to take a man for all he's worth." I shook my head and swallowed hard. Was that how I portrayed myself? Did everyone think I was here to take something and leave?

I lowered my voice, my courage falling with it. "I didn't come around today, or any other time, with an ulterior motive. All I wanted to do was thank your brothers for being kind to me. I'm sorry for not realizing sooner that I wasn't allowed to return that kindness."

The truck honked its horn, and I flinched. Brooks shook his head, his tone hard and focused, intent on breaking me. "We don't want your kindness. All we want is for you to figure out your life. Alone. The sooner you do that, the sooner you can go back home."

"I am home," I insisted, the words for me and not him, my heart needing reassurance.

"Fine." He stepped past me and pulled the chair out of the doorway. But he didn't leave, turning to face me one last time. "But understand that me and my brothers—we want no part in your life."

My chest caved in, a sob at the edge of my throat. But I wouldn't let myself break, refusing to give Brooks the satisfaction. To let him—a complete stranger—know he held that much power over me. Even though it was likely obvious when I cleared my throat and nodded. "I'm sorry." He seemed to falter at that, the corners of his eyes dropping, like he'd expected me to fight back. And I wanted to. I wanted to scream and throw him out. But no matter how much I tried to rally the fight, I couldn't bring myself to argue any further. I knew all too well I couldn't force my way into anyone's life. "I didn't mean to cause any problems. I'll keep my distance, I'm sorry."

He stepped forward, as though he might try to stay, maybe regretting his words, but before he could say anything, I grabbed the door, stopping him from coming any further. My hands shook—needing him gone—and he didn't protest, letting me close the door gently in his face.

I locked it, a frail attempt to stop his words from slithering into my heart. But his words . . . they weren't new. It was the same message, only with a different voice, a different story. My mom. Declan. The ones who were supposed to love me, to be there—except they weren't.

I'd thought I was brave in leaving, for believing I deserved more. But when I sat down in my crumbling cabin, alone within those four walls, I wondered if I was wrong. If the problem was indeed within me, if I wasn't worthy of being happy or cherished.

Maybe I was a fool for leaving it all, leaving the only family I'd ever known.

But I couldn't change anything about it now.

I couldn't make anyone want me.

Chapter Nine

"You doing okay?" Layne asked as I knotted my apron, switching out the soggy one I wore for dishes for a fresh one. Lila needed extra hands on the floor with the influx of hunters in town.

"Yeah. Why?"

She shrugged, rolling up the cuff of her flannel sleeve. "Because you've been moping for the last three days. I thought I'd do you a favor and ask about it so you could move on."

I turned to face the mirror in the corner of the kitchen, pulling half of my hair up into a clip, leaving the rest to fall to the middle of my back. "I've had a lot on my mind—that's all."

"Your ex?"

I huffed a laugh. I wished it was that simple. Declan did often squirm his way into my thoughts, along with the life I'd left behind. But I was stuck on Brooks. Not him, but what he'd said, how I should stay away. I'd gone to bed that night determined to ignore him. He didn't know me, and if his brothers wanted to be my friends, that was fine by me.

But when I woke up Monday, I didn't get out of bed.

It was a blessing I was entirely reliant on myself—meaning I couldn't miss work. So for the last three days, I'd dragged myself in and steered clear of the Graham house and their shop. I wanted to prove Brooks wrong, but I didn't have the energy or heart to spare. I needed to focus on why I came here, and that wasn't to make friends.

I needed to get myself back on my feet. Make a life for myself. Silence those voices haunting my every thought.

Unwanted.

Mistake.

Useless.

"He's been on my mind, yes, but I'm moving on," I admitted, because I was. It was easy to move on, to walk away, when your choices no longer solely affected you. And my feelings toward Declan had wavered long before I left—it just took longer for me to see it, to accept it. "Do you have a phone I could use? I've been meaning to call a friend."

She reached into her back pocket and handed it over. "You know how to use it?"

I laughed, rolling my eyes. "I'm only a few years older than you."

She raised her hands in defense, wiggling her brows. "Well, you're the one who doesn't have one. You should go to the country store—they have those prepaid ones you can buy for pretty cheap."

"Thanks," I mumbled, telling myself it was probably time I got one—if I could afford it. Rent was cheap, but with my lack of hours, it stole a hefty amount of my wage. And I was doing my best to ensure any left over went to essentials and savings. Savings I'd hidden in my freezer, as I'd yet to go to the bank and create an account.

I really needed to get my life together.

"I'll be right back," I called over my shoulder and stepped out the back kitchen door into the alley. I stared out at the valley across the road and dialed the number I'd memorized long ago. I focused on a distant family of elk as it rang, expecting to get her voicemail.

But then the rings halted, and a voice said, "Hello?"

"Elle?" My throat swelled, eyes brimming with tears. "It's me."

She said something inaudible over shouting kids on the other end, and then there was a slamming of a door, followed by, "Are you kidding me, Shay? You promised you would call as soon as you got there—and that was weeks ago."

"I know, I'm sorry." I paced up and down the alley, a rush of relief and longing filling my soul. "I need to get back to work—"

"Shut the front door, world. Shay's a working girl!"

Tears slipped down my cheeks, and I choked on a laugh. "It's nothing much—I'm just a dishwasher."

"Don't you do that," Elle said, gentle, loving firmness lining her words. Oh, how I missed her. "Don't degrade anything you've done. I'd be proud of you if you were slapping food on lunch trays."

"Well, then you'll be mighty proud because sometimes my boss lets me waitress. Which I'm doing tonight." I glanced around the alley, the parking lot full, with more piling in. "I should head back in. I just wanted to let you know I'm okay."

There was a brief pause before Elle, my sincerest friend, asked, "Are you doing okay?" My lip wobbled, and I opened my mouth to say I was—but the words wouldn't come out. But even with miles and mountains between us, words weren't necessary with Elle. "Shay . . . I know you might not feel okay right now. But I promise you will be, alright?"

"I know," I rasped, not quite sure I believed it.

"Have you . . . have you been to the doctor?"

I bit my lip, wiping my cheeks with my spare hand. I hated what I was about to say, revealing how much of a coward I was. I could barely let myself think about it. "Not yet."

"Alright." There wasn't judgment or disappointment in her voice—only understanding. "I know you're scared, but you need to take care of yourself, okay? It's important that you get seen, though. I know you have a lot going on, so why don't I look up a list of doctors near you? I can text what I find to this number."

"Okay. Thank you." I sucked in a breath and then let it out, composing myself. I could ask Layne to keep it to herself—she didn't know why I would go see a doctor anyway. I couldn't hide this forever, but for just a little while longer I'd keep it quiet. It wouldn't hurt anyone if they didn't know right off the bat I was pregnant. I didn't even know how far along I was, so it wasn't like I could answer anyone's questions. And I couldn't bear any more disappointment. "I do really need to go back inside. But I miss you."

"Me too, Shay." Her voice broke, followed by her clearing her throat. "I went into the firm to check on a few things while I'm on maternity leave . . . and I saw Declan."

My eyes widened, my heart racing. "You didn't tell him where I was, right?"

I knew the answer before she said, "He didn't ask."

"Oh." It was all I could manage.

"Have you considered coming home? Maybe trying your mom again?"

Despite her difficult questions, I smiled. It was why I loved Elle. She was honest and real—I could count on her. Two years ago, Declan had brought me along to a gathering at the law firm he worked at, and I met her there. She was one of his coworkers—apparently one of the best criminal defense attorneys in the state. I didn't know if that was true, but if Elle was as fiercely loyal to her clients as she was to me, I believed it. She was nearly fifteen years my senior, more successful than I could even dream, and she was everything to me. I doubted Elle knew how much she'd truly saved me. She'd come to my aid when no one else had.

"Sometimes," I admitted quickly, not wanting to give the thought power. "But Declan's not an option, and my mom made it pretty clear I wasn't welcome . . ." I drifted off, unable to voice it. "And as much as I loved staying in your casita and eating waffles with your kids, I'm good here. Besides—" I paused, pulling the phone away from my ear at the abrupt beeping on the other end. "What the heck is that noise?"

"Hold on—" Elle's voice weaved in with the beeping, and a laugh bubbled in my chest at her choice of colorful curses. At last, it fell silent, and she said, "Sorry—I was in the middle of recording voice memos for myself when you called. I was trying to turn my recorder off, but I hit the wrong button."

"Oh lovely, you and your dang recorder," I teased, knowing her habit of using one whether she was at work or not. "When you're bored later, you can listen to my wailing."

She laughed over the line, the sound soothing my wavering heart. "That's fine—it'll go perfect with the meltdown I was having earlier."

I straightened at that, wishing I'd thought to check in with her. "Are you doing okay?"

"I'm fine," she assured me, exhaustion heavy in her voice. "I'll be better once I get back to work, and I'm able to have a little bit of time to myself again." I pursed my lips and considered pushing her on it. Elle had a supportive husband, but I didn't imagine having a newborn and two toddlers under four was easy. But before I could say a word, she said, "I'll let you get back in. But call me more often, alright? I was about to throw the kids in the car and come looking for you."

"I will. I promise."

"Love you, Shay."

I closed my eyes, one last tear falling. I didn't know the last time I'd heard that, felt that from anyone. Likely the last time I saw Elle—the day I left for Arizona. "Love you too."

The line fell silent, and I crouched down to my knees. I sucked in a deep breath, willing the ache to go away. If only I could change my heart, forget how I longed to go home and be cared for. But I couldn't trust my heart. It was raw and broken.

But homes can be rebuilt, and hearts can mend.

—ele—

"I've got just the thing to turn your mood around," Layne declared after I came back, giving me space until my blotchy cheeks had eased. "We've got orange-vesters in town."

I raised a brow. "What?"

She rolled her eyes, and I eyed the new, edgy bangs across her forehead and the fresh red weaved in her braid, wondering if she'd done it herself. "They're out-of-state hunters. Elk season is just around the corner, so they're coming in to scope out the area. They pay big bucks for the best guides and tags. So," she drawled, "that means tips could be really good tonight. And like the kind coworker I am, I'll split their tables with you."

"I don't know, Layne . . ." I peeked my head out of the kitchen and into the full diner, assuming the men and women clad head to toe in camo were them. "Why don't you take their tables? I'll stick to the usuals."

"Don't you need the money?"

"Well, yeah." But I also needed this job, and I could trust the usuals not to complain when I messed up their orders—sometimes twice. "But you're wanting to leave, so you need it too."

She shrugged. "I don't see why it has to be one or the other. Why can't we both work toward our dreams?"

I paused, at a loss for words. She wasn't wrong, not at all. But I'd once said very similar words to someone, and I'd gotten a much different response. How had I been so blind? And what was worse, I didn't know if that moment—when I gave up on my dreams—was the first time I'd sacrificed a piece of myself for Declan.

But it wasn't the last. No, it certainly wasn't the last time.

But Layne didn't want that. She was okay if I slowed her down. She was supporting her dreams *and* my dreams.

"Fine," I agreed, not letting on how much it meant to me. "But if Lila fires me and I can't pay rent, I'm moving in with you."

She lifted her brows, backstepping into the diner. "Slow your roll, Valley Girl. At least buy me dinner first."

To my—and likely Lila's—surprise, I didn't screw up any orders. I mistakenly delivered a Coke that should've been a Pepsi—high treason, punishable by death—but we weren't counting that.

Most of my success was due to Layne, surprising me when she helped usher out my tables' plates and drinks, not sweating under the extra flow of customers. I didn't know if she'd overheard my conversation with Elle, but she said nothing of it when she handed me a list of doctors, having already written them down for me. I hid the way my eyes burned as I stuffed it in my back pocket and thanked her, promising to get my own phone. And thanks to tonight's tips, I'd be able to.

"The next table is yours," she said in passing as I went to the kitchen, delivering dirty plates to the high schooler washing dishes tonight.

I inhaled a breath and blew it out my nose as a wave of nausea hit me. I munched on a cracker from my bag, hoping that would do the trick, and quietly groaned when the door rang again, signaling another customer. "You can have it."

"Fine by me."

I sat for only a moment before the door rang again. For once I wished I was on dish duty. I slapped on a smile as I walked out of the kitchen, praying I didn't vomit. Except I'd taken a wrong turn and gone straight to hell—as Brooks and his two brothers were right there.

I dipped back to the kitchen, banging my shoulder on the way and earning a concerned look from Seth at the stove. "Layne," I hissed when she came back in, hanging up another order. "Switch me tables. Now."

She furrowed her brows. "Why?"

I groaned, resting my forehead against the wall. "Because the Graham brothers just came in and they can't stand me."

"Can't stand you?" Seth cut in, stirring a pan. "Didn't look that way when I saw you canoodling with them in the back of the chapel."

"Ohhhh, you were canoodling?" Layne wiggled her brows, like either she or I knew what that meant.

"Please," I moaned, on the verge of begging—or throwing up. "Brooks really has something against me, and if I do their table, I'm positive he'll set my cabin on fire. Please switch me."

"Are you sure you're talking about Brooks Graham?" Seth asked, his brow raised. "Last spring, my truck got stuck in a mudslide, thought Lila and I were gonna have to hike back to town—but Brooks came and pulled us out in the middle of the night. Even washed my truck."

"I didn't say he would light you on fire," I muttered, my twisting stomach making me grouchier than normal. *What the heck, isn't morning sickness supposed to be in the morning?* "But I have no doubt he would delight in listening to my screams as I burned to death." I snatched Layne's wrist, stopping her escape. "Please, pleeeease."

She pouted, sticking out her bottom lip. "But my table has some really cute guys—"

"The Grahams are cute," I reasoned—because they were. It was absolutely ridiculous. A total gene pool. Who did they think they were, the Hemsworth brothers?

"Not when you've known them your entire life."

"Please." I'd drop dead if Brooks demanded I get lost in front of everyone. "I'll do anything you want. I'll cover your shifts—I'll even give you the money from the table."

She laughed, shaking her head. "How about you just help me with my college application?"

I nodded like I was a life-sized bobblehead. "I was going to anyway, but deal."

"And you need to come out with me and my friends sometime. Your life can't only be work and wallowing alone in your cabin."

"Okay," I agreed, despite knowing I'd regret it later. But I was desperate to avoid Brooks. "Thank you, thank you—"

She walked away, cutting me off, her long braid swishing the entire way to the Graham table in the far corner. I kept my head down and walked to her previous one, wishing more than two tables separated us. But it wasn't my fault—Brooks knew I worked here.

He'd have to deal with sharing the same air as me. And if he suffocated, so be it.

"Hi," I greeted the two men dressed in camo, refilling their water glasses. "Layne was requested at another table, so I'll be serving you both tonight. My name's Shay."

The one on my right looked me over, like my black apron and hiking boots deserved such attention. "Hi, Shay."

I returned his smile. "I know you already ordered, but is there anything else I can get for you?"

He looked to his friend, whose face was buried in his phone, ignoring the diner's no-phone policy. He adjusted his cap, flicking his friendly blue eyes back to me. "I'll let you know if something comes to mind?"

I nodded and walked away to tend to my remaining customers, counting down until the night was over, not sure if my feet or back ached worse. I'd murder for a bathtub—or at least, I'd break into someone's house and kindly ask to use their bathtub. That's how desperate I was.

Shoving breaking-and-bathing aside, I grabbed two plates and ushered them off, careful to keep my gaze away from the Grahams. "Thank you," the blue-eyed man said as I set the plates at his table. "You working all night, Shay?"

"I'm almost done."

He smiled again, running a light brown hand through his curls. "Listen, I'm supposed to guide some hunters around here in a few weeks. You know of any secret spots I might impress them with?"

I snorted. I didn't know what they were hunting. Bunnies? Turkey? "No, I'm afraid I can't help you. But I can ask Layne—"

"That's alright," he said, making no move to touch his plate. "Are you not familiar with the area?"

"Nope." I slid my hands into my back pockets. "I moved here not too long ago."

"Ah." His smile grew, revealing it was kind of crooked—kind of handsome. "Well, maybe I ought to show you around then? Maybe we can discover something together."

I waited for my heart to beat uncontrollably, for butterflies to fly through my stomach. He was clearly asking me out. At one point, this would've been exciting. He was handsome and looked near my age, but something about his confidence was too familiar, too similar to the men I typically dated.

The man I once was engaged to.

"I'm not sure I'd be great company. I tend to get a little carsick." I stepped back, swallowing a rush of nausea. "Give me one second," I sighed, catching a glimpse of Nolan waving his arms like he was on an airstrip.

"Shay!" Nolan shouted, somehow believing he hadn't caught my attention. I stared at him and only him—not the protective asshole beside him. "Shay, come here."

"What?" I hissed, grateful Levi was across the booth so it wouldn't be obvious I was ignoring him. "I'm working."

"Clearly." Nolan smirked, shaking the ice in his glass. "I need a refill."

I clenched my hands into fists. "Where's Layne? She's your waitress."

"She's busy." He lowered his glass back to the table and cocked his head. "I gotta say I'm hurt—and a little surprised. I thought we were on our way to a beautiful friendship. But then Layne says you're too nervous to come wait on us. What's that about?"

I wiped the back of my neck, my skin flushed with nerves. I spared a glance at Brooks. His brows were pinched together, eyes intent on me, likely daring me to rat him out. "I didn't want you to heckle me in front of everyone. That's all."

"Is that why you never dropped by the shop?" Nolan asked, this time without a trace of humor. "I told Levi he ought to tear that map up."

I stepped back, at last seeing what was going on. I didn't have siblings. Declan did, but never once had I seen this sort of loyalty. It was like the Graham brothers were more than siblings. Friends. Choosing one another always.

There was something admirable about that—about them. Even if it was proving to be a real pain.

"I'm sorry," I said to Levi, who was glaring at Nolan, his tattooed arms strained. "Thank you for doing that. I've been pretty busy, and I haven't felt great recently." It wasn't a lie—even now, it was an effort not to heave over.

"It's fine, Shay," Levi murmured, his posture loosening. "I didn't care."

"Like hell you didn't care," Nolan snapped, red creeping up his neck. "I haven't seen you put that much effort into your drawing in months."

"Stop it," Levi hissed, kicking him beneath the table. "She did nothing wrong."

I wavered back and forth between their responses, feeling like I was in a movie, only I hadn't received my lines. I blinked, struggling to keep coherent thoughts—feeling absolutely sick.

"I'm not saying she did anything wrong." Nolan leaned back. Brooks was silent beside him, staring at his hands, likely enjoying the movie he was secretly directing. "But Shay needs to know: around here, we stick to our word and do it. That's all."

My stomach cramped, and a ripple of chills swept through me. "Okay," I rasped, needing to get out of here. "I'm sorry, Levi—that was wrong of me. I'm sure it's a beautiful map."

"Shay," one of them murmured quietly—but I didn't know who. I was already gone. I kept walking, ignoring the blue-eyed guide.

"Seth, I'm sorry, but I'm not feeling well," I said, fumbling with the strings of my apron. "I need to go home."

"Everything okay?" Seth dipped his head to meet my gaze, concern in his amber eyes. "What's going on? You're looking flushed."

My hands trembled against my cheeks as I wiped my tears. I felt ridiculous for crying, especially for leaving work, but I didn't know what the heck I was doing. "I just need to lie down."

"Okay . . ." He frowned, looking me over. "Why don't you wait a few minutes—I'll get Lila to give you a ride home."

"That's okay, thank you." I grabbed my bag and slipped into the dim alley, walking around front to where I'd parked my bike.

I'd experienced moments of true loneliness before. I was ten, and we'd moved to a different apartment. Again. Mom had gone out of town last minute for some sort of concert—I couldn't remember—but she hadn't made arrangements for me. I'd gotten off the bus, planning on binging *Hannah Montana* until she got home from work, only to find a note and realize she'd be gone the entire weekend. She'd left ten bucks on the table and told me to go next door if I needed anything. But I didn't know our neighbor—I wasn't sure *she* knew him. Even to a ten-year-old it had seemed strange that a bunch of people always knocked on his door, but never went in.

I'd spent the entire weekend coiled up inside, alone. I was alone a lot, but there was something different that weekend. I felt . . . abandoned. And once the sun set, all I could focus on was my fear. I wanted my mom, but I would've settled for anyone to come over and sit with me. To hold me, to stay with me and ease my fears. Remind me I wasn't on my own.

But I'd never felt more lonely, more hopeless than I did as I stared at my bike. And no matter how justified I'd been in leaving, *I wanted my mom*.

But I didn't have a phone. And even if I did, she wouldn't pick up.

In an attempt to suck it up, I straddled the bike. The handlebars were cool as I rested my forehead against them, breathing through my nose. I was about to climb off and ask Lila for a ride home after all, feeling like I might pass out, when a voice asked, "Ma'am, are you alright?"

Ma'am.

"Get away from me," I hissed as I sat up, ready to rip Brooks a new one. Except it wasn't him—but the man from inside, his blue eyes alert and on me. "I'm sorry. I thought you were someone else."

"That's okay. I snuck up on you," he said with a shrug, scanning the parking lot. "My name's Jacob. Sorry to see you're heading out. I'll leave your tip inside."

"Oh. Thank you." I wiped my hand across my forehead, my skin slick, before putting both on the handles, ready to get home. "It was nice to meet you, Jacob."

I pushed on the pedals, and my heart jolted when Jacob stepped forward and stopped me, his hands covering mine. "Could I get your number? I'd like to get to know you . . . maybe see you next time I'm in town."

There was a time I appreciated a straightforward man. Someone who wasn't afraid to go after what he wanted. I'd liked that about Declan. But I was young and didn't see his entitlement for what it was, unable to predict the times he'd barrel over my needs and desires.

"I really need to go," I pressed, praying he didn't hear the fear rattling my voice. "Have a good night."

He didn't budge, not even when I put both feet on the pedals and pushed, holding me in place. "Maybe I should drive you back to your place. You're not looking too hot right now."

"Shay," a deep voice shouted, stopping me from ramming my bike into Jacob's groin. I blinked in the dim light as Brooks walked toward me—was I imagining things? "Everything okay out here?"

"I've got her," Jacob answered for me. "I'm gonna take her home."

"Yeah, I don't think so," he shot back, something strangely fierce in his tone.

I shook my head, unable to find the words. I focused on my breathing. I was not going to throw up. Faintly, I could hear muffled words being exchanged, but I missed them. Was it normal to feel this sick? Had I done something wrong?

Why did I think I could do this?

I hadn't realized I'd sat down and curled myself up into a ball until there was a crunch of gravel in front of me. Warm, firm hands peeled my arms away from my face, and I looked up, finding Brooks kneeling before me. His dark brows were furrowed, his lips tightly pressed together. "Are you alright?"

I stared at him, distracted by the freckles dusted across his cheeks, the surprising concern he wore, before I said, "I'm fine." I sniffled, wiping snot off my nose. "Thanks for ruining my fun. I was about to break his wiener with my bike."

He laughed, the sound abrupt and full, but that wasn't what caught me off guard. *He's smiling.* I'd never seen him smile, at least not for me. And though I was sure it was his attempt to relax me, fearing I was on the brink of hysterics, it was a smile nonetheless.

I opened my mouth—to smile, or maybe say something—but I never had the chance before my stomach knotted and hot liquid filled my mouth, splattering onto both Brooks and me.

"Shit," he muttered and shot to his feet as I heaved again. I scrambled to roll to my knees, refusing to sit in a pool of vomit. I whimpered, a piece of my soul dying from embarrassment as I emptied the last of my stomach's contents. Warm fingers grazed my neck, and I jerked, the movement dragging me back to a haunting memory. "I'm sorry—" Brooks's hands were up, his eyes wide as I spun toward him. If I hadn't already been on the receiving end of his hate, I would've thought he was the most considerate man I'd ever met. "Your hair . . . I wanted to get your hair out of your face."

My lip wobbled, my eyes unable to meet his and confirm how pathetic he must think I was. *I am pathetic.* Crying and puking in the diner's parking lot. I wiped at my mouth, ignoring the vomit plastering my shirt to my skin, and stood, straightening my bike.

"Shay," Brooks said, stopping me from pedaling away. "You're sick. Let me give you a ride home."

I stared at him, at the vomit on his jeans, his boots. And then I looked at his hands. Hands that appeared to be considerate and careful. Understanding. Different from the last man who touched me. My breaths were shaky as I blinked the memory away, the sudden jolt of pain, the vise grip on my neck. I couldn't breathe—

No, no—I will not give it power. I will not give him power anymore.

"You didn't finish your dinner," I said weakly, not sure I had it in me to refuse Brooks. I didn't trust him, didn't particularly like him—but I wasn't sure I'd make it home on my bike with how woozy I was feeling.

"My brothers are still eating. I'll finish when I get back," he said, already fishing his keys out of his pocket. He glanced at his pants and shook his head. "Can't say I'm honestly that hungry anymore."

I gave him a subtle nod, feeling a twinge of guilt as I followed him to his truck, pushing my bike alongside me. I let him load it on the tailgate, nerves fluttering through me at the thought of being alone with him. I just needed to get home, and then I'd never talk to him or his brothers again.

But why was he helping me?

That question consumed me throughout the short drive, as I struggled to grasp why Brooks had involved himself in the first place. He couldn't stand me, had told me to stay away, yet he was here. I didn't believe Jacob had meant any harm, was more so overly pushy, but thanks to Brooks, I wouldn't have to find out. He'd come to my aid, made sure I was okay . . . and tried to hold my hair.

I shook my head and chalked it up to Brooks being a decent human. He didn't care about me. "Here's some gas money. Thank you," I murmured, reaching into my bag, grateful for the extra money I'd made tonight. I rolled my eyes when he just stared at the bill in my hand, likely believing it was diseased. I knew I hadn't put him out much by driving me home, but I wasn't about to owe him anything. I tossed it on the dash and hopped out of the truck as soon as he pulled in front of the cabin. Assuming he'd stay inside, I pulled down the tailgate, but before I could retrieve my bike, he was beside me. His large arm brushed mine, and without a word, he grabbed it, towing it over to the cabin.

I hovered on the shaky porch steps as Brooks leaned against my door like he owned it. Why wasn't he leaving? Sighing, I slid the key into the doorknob. He grabbed the handle before I could and let himself in, invitation be damned.

Yeah. I'm glad I threw up on him.

I swallowed and flicked on the light, careful to avoid the hole beneath the rug as I walked in, Brooks holding the door open. Rather than closing it—or leaving—he grabbed a kitchen chair and propped the door open.

What was happening?

Realizing he had no intention of leaving just yet, I sat on the bed and shucked off my boots, careful of the vomit splashed on them. I felt the heat of his gaze, watching my every move as I knelt and searched through the pile of clean clothes on my suitcase and then slipped into the bathroom to change.

After brushing my teeth twice and changing into sweats and a baggy T-shirt, I stepped out, catching him snooping through my fridge. My cheeks flushed as he scanned the almost bare shelves, even more so when he asked, "What are you doing here, Shay?"

I hooked an arm behind my back, not knowing what to say. I knew why I was here, but could I tell him that? Before I could decide, he pulled out a chair and sat, stretching his long legs out. "I'm not trying to be a jerk. I get that you're wanting to start over—but look at this place." He waved a hand around the single-room cabin, as though I'd been blind to its emptiness and age. "Is this really the life you want? Working part-time at the diner to make ends meet and coming home to this? There's barely any food, you have a pile of money in the freezer, you're living out of a suitcase, and it's going to get cold soon. There has got to be somewhere else you can go. Someone you can stay with while you figure yourself out."

I huffed a dry laugh—so this was why Brooks had helped me. I was sick, vulnerable. Why wouldn't he use it as a chance to convince me to leave? I didn't bother to respond, to explain I had nowhere to go. Maybe it was stubbornness, or maybe Brooks had pushed me too far. But I wanted to be here. I didn't care if I didn't have a dresser, or that I had to watch my steps, afraid the floor would cave in.

Because it was *mine.*

I'd used every penny I had to buy Betsy and move. It was my hard work, my own money paying the rent. I was providing for myself.

Did I miss the comfort I'd once taken for granted? Of course.

But I'd get there eventually. I'd be ready when it mattered.

But Brooks didn't bother to see that. He saw what I wasn't, not what I could be. Exactly like the last man I left.

"Look," he started, running a hand down his tired face. "I'm sorry . . . I'm not always the best with words and that came out wrong. But I'm gathering the sense that you have a lot going on, and it might be easier on you if you stayed with someone you can rely on." He reached into his pocket, pulling out his wallet. "Let me help you. I can give you some cash to at least get you on your way."

I stared at him, at the stack of money in his hand. He didn't want my money, but he expected me to take his. I wasn't sure if he was offering his aid out of genuine concern, or if this was an attempt to get me out of this town. But I knew one thing.

I couldn't trust anyone.

"I don't need or want your money." I thought I might've seen surprise cross his face, like he fully believed I'd take the cash and run. "Just please leave me alone." I moved for the bed and slid beneath the covers, facing the wall. I wouldn't be telling him the truth, wouldn't tell him I was pregnant. He didn't deserve to know, and he'd likely use it against me. "After you've finished coming up with the narrative you'll spin for your brothers, please lock the door on your way out."

I braced myself for the door to slam, maybe even for him to yell at me. But I only felt the blaze of his gaze on my back for a moment before there were three hushed footsteps, the sound of the chair sliding across the floor, and then the door clipping shut. I shut my eyes, grateful he'd left the light on. The darkness was too heavy tonight. I was already drifting off when the truck started, and I reminded myself this wasn't for nothing.

I'd do it again and again, endlessly—if it led me right here.

Chapter Ten

"I'm not sure this is such a good idea, Valley Girl."

"You already started, Layne," I cried, my voice pitchy and high. "If you stop now, I'll look like freaking Cynthia from *Rugrats*." Layne laughed, and I winced, wary of the scissors skimming along my neck. "Are you almost done—"

"Stop talking," she hissed, pushing the top of my head down until my gaze rested on the inches of cut hair beside my feet. "You wrangled me into this *fantastic* idea, so be quiet and let me finish."

I bit my lip, resisting the urge to jerk away. I'd hardly slept last night, and clearly it was making me delirious. I'd woken up to Layne pounding on my door, taken one look at the colorful strands weaved into her braid, and asked her to cut mine. Either she hated me, or she was confident in her ability, because she didn't put up a fight at all. The only reason she was here to begin with was to inform me Lila had given me the day off. I'd initially protested, but after a rush of wooziness had me running toward the toilet, I thought I could use a day.

It hadn't hurt that Layne delivered the tip Jacob left behind, an amount that was atrociously high for diner food. He'd even left a note, apologizing if he'd scared me. I had half a thought to deny it—the gesture reminded me too much of Brooks offering me money last night.

I'd pondered last night a lot, what Brooks had said, and I decided to make a change. The first was my hair, but neither Layne or I had scissors on us, so we made a quick trip to town. We'd stopped at the thrift store, too, scouring it for over an hour and walking away with several bargains. And after that, I yanked up my imaginary big-girl pants and went to the bank, where my thawing money now dwelled.

Suck it, Brooks.

Somehow sensing my thoughts, Layne teased, "Well, at least your panties aren't sitting on the ground anymore. I'd be surprised if Brooks didn't snag a pair of them last night."

I rolled my eyes, huffing a laugh. "I think the last thing Brooks wants is my panties."

She hummed, running a comb through my hair. "Does he remind you of your ex?"

I blinked, pausing to think it over. Brooks had hurt me, but it was different than Declan. Declan knew what he was doing. He *wanted* to hurt me. But Brooks just didn't seem to know what to do with me. "No."

"Then why don't you like him?"

"He doesn't like me."

"Look up," she instructed, and I did, straightening my spine. I held my breath, aware the ends of my hair now grazed the middle of my neck and not my back. I stared at the heaping pile of hair on the porch. "All done."

Don't cry. Don't cry. Don't cry.

"Thank you," I said, resisting the urge to run to the bathroom and look. I wasn't necessarily attached to my hair, but it felt like I was cutting off much more than that.

"You look cute," Layne said, admiring her work as I swept the hair off the porch. "Back to what I was saying . . . Brooks doesn't know you. And maybe he is misunderstanding you, but I think you're doing the same to him. You heard Seth—the Grahams are good people."

I tossed the hair in the trash bin and straightened the new-to-me woven tablecloth on my kitchen table. I did think the Grahams were good, or at least enough for Brooks to help me out last night. Maybe I was misunderstanding him. He'd basically told me to get lost, but even then, I thought I might've seen honest concern in his eyes. I didn't know what to believe.

"My ex . . . Declan was straight to the point. He knew what he wanted, and once he decided it, nothing could stop him. I'm pretty sure he was born knowing he wanted to be a lawyer."

My chest throbbed as I remembered what I'd given up to make sure Declan could reach his dreams. I was in my second year of my English degree, and he was about to take his bar exam, again. He'd failed it twice before, and we were fighting. I thought we were going to break up.

I was a distraction, yet I somehow wasn't giving him my full support. Support he deserved as my fiancé. All I knew was that I wasn't making him happy, and I was *devastated*. At the time, I hadn't talked to my mom in a year, I'd moved out of my dorm and into Declan's place, and I'd quit my job. I was entirely dependent on him, didn't know how I could live without him. How I'd ever lived without him.

Declan seemed hopeless too. At least, until he suggested I drop out. It made sense, he reasoned. My school was almost two hours away, my schedule was full—and it was taking up too much time. Time I could be giving to him. Time I *should* be devoting to him.

"I won't have to worry about you this way, butterfly. I'll know where you are, and we'll have extra time together. I'll take you to the beach, on those hikes you're always bugging me about. You can build a garden. Imagine the home we can have, the life I can give you. You're wasting time in school—and it's not like there's any sort of money in your degree. Let me give you the life you could never make on your own."

I was so flattered. Grateful to be loved so much, that he wanted me around. And I believed every word he'd said. I'd dropped out of school, promising myself I could create stories in my free time.

But I never did.

I had better things to do. Like wash the sheets—and make sure the edges were perfectly folded. Iron his suits and shine his shoes—heaven forbid there be a scuff. Answer his calls and lick his letters. Clean the house and cook his meals. Maybe a quick lay in the sack to clear his head.

Ready and willing, always.

It made my stomach churn. How blind and naive I'd been, not wanting to see how my wings were clipped. I knew better now. Letting someone take care of you was a weakness, a way to give up your freedom.

I blinked away the burning in my eyes and grabbed a drink of water. "My point is, Declan always spoke his mind. When he was upset, he'd tell me what I'd done wrong so we could work through it. So I could be better—"

"So *you* could be better?" Layne scoffed, her lips curled as though I'd said something foul. "Sounds like he was more your trainer than your fiancé."

I blinked, not anticipating the blow to my heart. Was there truth in her words? Was that how it was? Had I let Declan train the life, the will, out of me?

"Like I was saying," I started again, refusing to focus on that right now, "Declan was blunt. He was that way with everyone. So when Brooks keeps telling me to leave town, it's hard to see it as anything else." How else was I supposed to take that?

"I hear you, Shay, but I also think you're forgetting everyone has a story. And just like me, and everyone else here, Brooks doesn't know your story. And you don't know his either." She eased her words with a smile, offering no clue as to Brooks's *story*. "I need to get going, but call me if you need anything." She pointed at the flip phone I'd bought, sitting on the kitchen counter. I'd already used it to schedule an appointment with an ob-gyn. The practice was in Hillshire, and since I wasn't about to ask anyone to drive me, I'd have to ask Jake if I could borrow Betsy for the day. "Are you coming to the festival tonight?"

I shrugged, only now remembering what Lila had mentioned weeks ago. Apparently it was a big enough deal the entire town shut down for the evening. "I'll think about it. Thanks for today." I smiled at her as she left, letting it drop as soon as I closed the door. I stared at the purple throw blanket tossed atop the bed, the wicker dresser in the corner. The vase of fake flowers, the pine candle beside it. It was such a weak attempt at sprucing up the cabin, at fixing me.

There was no quick fix for anything.

I should've stayed home, said every introvert ever.

I stared at the lively festival across the street, fumbling to catch my breath after riding up the last of the dirt path. I longed to crawl back to the cabin and into bed, maybe read *Pride and Prejudice* and fall in love with Mr. Darcy.

But my conversation with Layne played on repeat. No one knew me or my story. I wasn't about to air out my dirty laundry—but I couldn't stay cooped up in it either. If I was insisting this was my home, I needed to plant roots.

I swallowed and pushed my bike across the main road, the sun almost having fallen behind the tree line. I'd never seen the town so full. Rows of canopies and tables lined the street, waves of individuals walking up and down the road. There were games of bean bag toss and bobbing for apples. Children screamed and squealed, laughing as someone fell victim to the dunk tank. A live band was set up in the middle of the square on the grass field, filled with swaying bodies and chatter.

I stepped back, ready to retreat, just as a pair of pointed ears ran straight toward me. Cash's tongue dangled out of his mouth as he greeted me, like we were best friends and his owners didn't despise me. Hot on my heels, he trailed me to the diner, where I parked my bike. He whined at my feet, and I scanned around, failing to find the Grahams. I knelt and rubbed his head. "At least I'll have you as a friend."

He brushed up against me, leaving a patch of hair on my jeans. His wet snout pushed my hand, nudging me forward, but I couldn't get past the nerves fluttering through me. I'd attended plenty of events—Declan's mother loved to throw them—but I'd only attended them as his guest, happily existing in his shadow.

I didn't mind the shadows. Maybe it was the lack of attention during my childhood, but I'd found comfort in not being the center of attention. Maybe that's why Declan and I worked for a time. He liked having someone who didn't push for more, who was grateful to stand behind him, to have anyone to stand with. I hadn't realized until now how much I'd used him as a crutch. I couldn't hide behind him any longer.

Cash whined and shoved his head against my thigh. "Okay, fine. You win," I huffed when he pushed me again. Apparently I was fluent in dog. "Are you hungry?" I stared into his large brown eyes and waited—only to shake my head. I was losing my mind. I drifted through the crowd and stopped at the first mouthwatering booth I saw. Cash leaned against me, his ears shifting with the laughing children in front of us. I watched silently, smiling as sticky fingers exchanged coins for ice cream cones, already melting down their arms. I half expected Cash to run off, maybe steal a cone from an unsuspecting kid, but he stayed with me, moving only when I did.

I ordered two cones—why wouldn't I treat my friend?—and wandered away, in search of a quiet corner, when a smooth voice asked, "You gonna eat both of those, Betsy?"

I turned and found Wren, wearing a large sun hat and even larger sunglasses despite it being nearly nighttime, her red-lipped mouth turned up in a grin. "I just might. Unless you'd like one?"

She didn't shrug or feign hesitation, just grabbed it and gave it a big lick. "Thanks—guess I'll forgive you for not visiting me and call you Shay now." I looked at Cash, who I swore grumbled, and silently promised he could have mine as she asked, "How are you feeling? Heard you blew grits all over Brooks."

"I'm fine," I murmured, choosing to sidestep the *blew grits* comment, whatever that meant.

I followed after her as she led the way to the sidewalk and sat, waiting until she'd gotten down safely. "Ginger helps with nausea." She hummed under her breath and pulled off her sunglasses, eyeing me like she could see beneath my skin. But rather than confirming it, she said, "I chopped my hair when I was around your age, too. Can't say it fixed anything, but it felt good to get rid of that extra weight."

"I do like it." I'd be lying if I said I hadn't hoped it would magically improve everything. I might regret cutting it above my shoulders at the end of my pregnancy, when I was a swollen puff ball—but I'd worry about that later. "How are you feeling?"

She took a bite of her cone, traces of lipstick staying behind in the vanilla. "Annoyed. I'm heading up to Phoenix tomorrow for two weeks of treatment. I hate it up there. It's too stuffy." She pinched her nose, like the muggy air reached her here.

"How long ago were you diagnosed?" I asked, fortunate enough to not know much about breast cancer.

"Almost three months. They caught it at stage three," she said, a distant look in her eye. "They did a double mastectomy, and now I'm doing chemo—it's aggressive, but the doctors are hopeful." Her laugh was bitter, and I couldn't help but wonder if the Wren I'd met outside the church was a front, especially when she said, "I can't wait for it to be over. I'm sick of everyone hovering over me. Do you have any idea how many people I've had apologize to me? Or to Jake for his loss?"

I licked my cone and then tilted it to Cash, my stomach twisting at the taste of it. I wanted to tell Wren how sorry I was, how unfair this was—but stopped. She didn't want my apology. She wanted someone to listen. "You could always mess with them by pretending you don't know what the heck they're talking about," I said, hoping she'd appreciate my attempt to lighten the moment.

"Oh, you just might be trouble after all." She winked, her brown skin warm in the fading light. "My daughter Jules says you're from California?"

"All my life."

"Give that to the furball," she said, handing me her cone. I hesitated, wondering if he should have this much dairy, but I caved when Cash pawed me, assuring me he'd be fine. "I've got three kids. Jules is in Michigan, and my other two girls are in New Mexico. There isn't a day that goes by when I'm not missing them, worried about how they're doing." My mouth turned bitter when she paused, anticipating her next words. "What do your folks think about you moving here all alone?"

I pressed my lips together. "They don't know I'm here."

"So they're oblivious and think you're still in Cali?"

I ran a hand through my hair—I should've stayed home. "I don't know where they think I am. I don't have much of a relationship with them."

"And why's that?"

I furrowed my brows, about to say it was none of her business. I'd offered her privacy, and she should give me the same. But I paused and thought it over . . . How it might feel nice to hear it outside my own head. "You love your kids, don't you?" I asked, waiting until she nodded. "I don't want to steer you wrong and pretend my life was full of pain and misery. I know plenty have it worse—"

"Pain is pain, Shay. Whether you die from a car accident or cancer—it still kills you. And I imagine both hurt like hell."

My eyes burned, my smile strained. I'd never thought of it that way. "I don't know who my dad is. Well, I have a name, but nothing beyond that." Noah Lewis. He was forty-five, a mechanic, married with two kids in Oakland, California. My parents' relationship never went farther than a one-night stand—he didn't know I existed. Or at least that's what my mom claimed. She told me who he was when I was fifteen, after I'd pestered her enough. Despite my curiosity, I'd never broached meeting him. At least, not until we got into a fight, and in a bout of anger, I told her I wanted to live with Noah. It was laughable, really, living with a man who was oblivious to being my sperm donor. But I'd never forget the anger, the fear I saw cross her face—the possibility of losing me. My mom was a lot of things. She was loud, irresponsible, and a bit of a drunk. But it wasn't until then that I understood she was a human, one who'd had me alone at the age of eighteen. She wasn't a great parent, mostly just tolerated me. And while I suspected she kept me around solely because I paid a portion of the bills, she'd stuck with me. I never mentioned Noah Lewis again.

"My mom raised me. I'm grateful she did, but I'm not sure she truly cared about me. At least, not beyond what a parent might feel biologically for their child. As a kid, I remember thinking how exhausted I was trying to earn her attention. She worked a lot and always had some sort of boyfriend. I just sort of felt like a burden." I'd done all I could to ease that, to slip into the cracks and stay out of her way. I wasn't dumb—I knew when she wanted to be anywhere but with me. So I'd assured her she could leave, made my own meals, stayed on top of my grades. When I was old enough, I joined clubs and sports at school. I got a job. I showed her I could pull my own weight. I wanted her to think *she needed me.*

"I thought it would be better when I started college. I'd be out of her way, and we could almost be friends. But she was hard to get ahold of, moved apartments a lot. One time when I was out with Declan, my ex, we ran into her. She'd dodged my calls for months, but when she saw us, she started talking to me like we'd braided each other's hair the night before. I don't know . . . maybe I was wrong. But it seemed like she was interested in Declan and his money, and it just felt gross. So I stopped calling." I'd been filled with regret for weeks, worried about her. But Declan had comforted me, saying he thought she would try and use me, too. Besides, *he* was my family. "Um—" I blinked hard, wringing my fingers together. "After I left Declan, I went to my mom, but she made it pretty clear she didn't want anything to do with me."

Before I could stop myself, I was swept back into those moments of desperation.

"Mom?" I whispered, my hands shaking against my lips, huddled in the tub. I was so afraid the music on the other side of the line would wake Declan up. "I need you. Can—can you come get me?"

"Who is this?" a man slurred. I didn't know his voice.

I gritted my teeth, tears falling down my cheeks. "I need to talk to Dina."

The exchange went on for several minutes. I couldn't make him understand. But before I lost all hope, there was a shout, followed by a curt, "Who is this?"

My heart surged. I didn't even know the last time I'd heard her voice. "Mom—it's Shay. I need you."

The relief quickly vanished, and reality set in. "Oh, you need me, huh? Now, that can't be true. You're too good for me, with that fancy house, that fancy boyfriend. Oh, don't tell me . . ." She laughed lowly, and my soul withered at the sound, begging, pleading with me to hang up—to run and protect myself. But I couldn't bring myself to do it. I was helpless and alone, hiding in the shower. "You've gone and done it, huh? I warned you, Shay. I told you: no man will want you—"

Wren patted my knee, pulling me out of the memories that haunted my every breath. She slipped her fingers through mine, and in her silence, I thought she might know, might be acquainted with fighting silent demons. We sat there, Cash licking his cone beside us, and despite what I'd shared, I felt relieved. Grateful to have someone listen, while understanding there was nothing they could do to ease the burns I carried. Only time could do that.

I rasped a wet laugh when Cash rested his head on my lap, the cones discarded beside me. Apparently he was a picky eater. I slipped my hand out of Wren's and was scratching his ears when a gruff voice sliced through our moment of vulnerability. "Did you give my dog ice cream?"

Shock stole my voice as I looked up at Brooks, gaping beside us. He wore a pair of blue jeans, and I couldn't help but wonder if they framed his behind as well as they did his long, sturdy legs. Before I made a fool of myself, Wren came to my rescue. "Your scoundrel tackled me and stole my cone. When Shay tried to save me, he stole hers, too."

My cheeks flushed as I strained to hold back my laugh. His gaze was hard and full of disbelief, worsening when Cash nuzzled against my stomach. "What did you do to my dog?"

"Nothing." I shrugged. "What can I say? He's got good taste."

He crossed his arms, and heaven help me, but I didn't miss how his chest flexed beneath his white tee. "Let's go." His jaw clenched, looking on the verge of snapping as Cash whined. "Now, Cash."

"You better go," I whispered to my not-so-little furry friend. "Otherwise your daddy will hang me by my toes." I bit my lip, pleading that Brooks hadn't heard me calling him *daddy* over Cash's whining.

He must've missed it, because when Cash finally climbed off my lap, Brooks only shook his head, smirking at his dog. He looked at Wren, not wasting another breath on me. "I'll see ya around, Wren."

"Why don't you and your brothers come over for Sunday dinner soon?" She nudged her shoulder against mine. "Maybe you can bring Shay along." Before Brooks and I could protest, both of us red-faced and uninterested, she said, "I am a dying woman, after all."

"You're not dying, Wren." Brooks shook his head and walked away.

She laughed under her breath and held out her hand. "Help me up, will ya? My ass isn't what it used to be." I grabbed her hand, slowly easing her onto her feet. "So you'll come then?"

"What?"

"To Sunday dinner sometime?"

"Oh, I . . ." I found the Graham brothers in the crowd—Brooks's jeans did indeed frame a certain asset nicely. "I don't know if that's such a great idea."

I must've stared too long, or drooled, because when I glanced back at Wren, she was grinning. "Wrangler butts drive me nuts."

"Uh—" I blinked. "Excuse me?"

She smiled wide and laughed, looping her arm through mine. "I'm guessing since you can't stop looking, you didn't see them much in your parts of Cali. But, dear," she said, dipping her chin toward Brooks and his brothers—her nephews—"those are Wrangler butts."

My cheeks heated as I remembered Wranglers was a brand of jeans. "I don't know what you're talking about," I muttered, palms sweating, pretending Wren hadn't caught me checking out Brooks.

She sighed, letting me off the hook. "I've known those boys their entire lives. They were as annoying and inseparable as kids as they are now. They're probably worse now. But you'd think, after all they've endured, they'd leave this place—and each other with it. But I don't think there will ever come a day where they don't stand together."

I brushed a loose strand of hair behind my ear, wanting to ask more, if only so I could better understand them. Understand Brooks. "Did something happen to their family?"

"Their father died almost a year ago," she told me, her eyes deep and distant, carrying something that looked like longing. "But their mama left them when they were just kids. Levi was still in diapers at the time."

My heart throbbed for Wren, for her nephews. "Their mom passed away too?"

Her tone shifted, no longer gentle, but bitter. “No, she walked away and never looked back.” She placed her hand on my shoulder, giving it a squeeze. “We all bear pain differently, Shay. Some of us better than others. You ran from yours. But I think those boys—they’re haunted by theirs.”

Chapter Eleven

Wren's words lingered with me the remainder of the night, a pesky thorn. Each time I caught a glimpse of one of the Graham brothers beneath the gleaming moon, I couldn't see them as anything but little children, confused and longing for their mama, wondering why she'd left them.

Our situations were different, but I knew something about heartache.

It was why I pushed aside the hurt Brooks had given me and walked to where he stood in the grassy field. He wasn't in the middle of it dancing like the other adults, but rather tossing a football to scrambling children. I didn't let myself falter, determined to show him and his brothers someone would fight to be in their lives—no matter how that might be.

I tapped on his shoulder, willing the butterflies in my stomach to slow. *He's playing with kids. He can't be that bad, right?* He turned with a raised brow and glanced around, probably wondering what the hell I was doing. "Do you need something?"

I smiled. *I will not pee my pants.* "Would you dance with me?"

He didn't blink, probably didn't take a full breath. "No."

Despite everything, I couldn't say I'd anticipated that—nor had I expected it to feel like I'd been punched in the gut. I supposed his rejection was fair. I'd pushed him away last night, and now he was doing the same. But I must've worn my hurt on my face, and something in Brooks must've cared, because he said, his voice softer than before, "I'm sorry . . . I'm just not so sure it's a good idea."

I dipped my chin in acknowledgment and walked away. He was probably right; it wasn't a good idea. After all, I'd told him to leave me alone. I was on my way to bury myself deep in the forest when a hand latched onto my wrist. I peeked over my shoulder, and it wasn't Brooks there—it was Nolan. "I'll dance with you, darlin'." I didn't know where he'd come from, but he didn't give me a chance to decline, wrapping our hands together and leading me onto the field in front of the live country band. He winked, his eyes glistening in the moonlight. "Follow my lead."

He led me in what I learned was a swing dance, our hands palm to palm as we pushed and pulled each other, our bodies brushing. His steps were smooth, his arms fluid as he spun me out left and right, and his grin was wide as he watched me stumble my way through, lacking his grace. But he didn't seem to care, laughing as he twisted me around his back, our arms in a pretzel, before he spun me back to his front.

"I'm sorry about Brooks, darlin'. I hate to admit it, but he's as stubborn as they come," he said as I marveled at a couple beside us, the man swinging his partner between his legs.

"Did I do something to offend him?" I asked, sighing in relief when the music shifted to a slower pace, not having expected Nolan to be so enthusiastic.

He lifted my hands to rest on his shoulders. "No, don't take it personal. He's closed himself off. It's nothing new, he's been doing that since Bonnie."

"Bonnie?"

He shrugged, and I did my best to focus on him and not Brooks, aware he'd been watching us the entire dance. "His high school sweetheart. Ever since then, he's been downhill." He smirked, like the idea of his brother getting his heart broken was funny. But I realized he might've been grinning over something else when he said, "Though, it probably doesn't help that you're absolutely gorgeous."

I rolled my eyes and pinched his neck, not sensing any sort of romance between us. "I bet you say that to all the ladies."

"Maybe." He leaned down, his voice low. "I bet we could get him all sorts of red if you let me kiss you."

I reared back, a shocked laugh bubbling past my lips. "Absolutely not."

He grinned, his hands playful. "We don't even have to use our tongues. Unless you want to, then I'm all game—"

"Oh my gosh." I tilted my head back and laughed. "I refuse—Brooks will murder me, and you'll feel guilty when you have to help him bury my body."

Both of us were red with laughter, sloppily moving to the music. "Figured it was worth a shot," he said with a shrug. "But listen . . . I owe you an apology for the other night at the diner. I said some things I shouldn't have, and I'm sorry."

"Oh." Nolan had been a jerk, but in his defense, he thought I'd straight-up ditched Levi after he'd drawn for me. He probably had no idea Brooks had demanded I leave them alone. Having no desire to further rock the boat, I said, "It's okay. I'd say we're even with you dancing with me."

"Deal." He released my hand and slowly stepped back. "Can I grab you a beer?"

"I don't drink," I said at the same time Levi appeared beside me and said, "She doesn't drink."

I raised my brow at Levi as Nolan walked away. Had I told him I no longer drank? "How are you?" I asked instead. Levi had watched me buy the prenatals, so I suppose there was a possibility he knew I was pregnant. But I doubted it. If he knew, he would've told his brothers and kept his distance, right? I wasn't necessarily trying to hide it, but process it myself. When I'd first gotten the positive test, I'd barely had a second to breathe before the air was stolen from my lungs.

"Good," he murmured, scuffing his boot against the ground.

I tucked my hands in my pockets and searched the crowd, Brooks's warning hot in my mind. I didn't know if I should push my luck, especially after dancing with Nolan. But then I thought of what Wren had revealed. How Levi might've felt when I didn't show up at his shop after he'd generously drawn for me.

"Do you want to sit?" I asked. To hell with Brooks.

Even if his mom abandoning him sucked.

He nodded and followed me to where I sat on the grass, folding my legs in front of me. We said nothing for a long while as couples danced in front of us, some moving like they were on fire. "What did you say?" I asked, missing what Levi had mumbled. I was too busy watching Nolan and Brooks across the square, worried by the rigidness in Brooks's frame that their conversation was heated.

He plucked out a weed, his tattoos stark against his skin. "I asked why you hadn't put the light on your bike yet."

"Oh." I paused, not realizing he'd noticed. "Um—I dropped it when I was trying to put it on and broke it. But I put the reflector on," I added like it made me any less ridiculous.

"I would have helped you."

"I know." I pulled my knees to my chest and rested my chin on them, not understanding why he wanted to help me. "I didn't want to be a burden."

His voice was low, no more than a whisper. "It's not a burden to need help, Shay."

I sucked on my bottom lip, chewing over my words. "I had a bad habit of relying too heavily on someone before. I don't want to ever be that way again."

He didn't respond, but he stayed firmly planted beside me. I waited for the awkwardness to drift in, for one of us to attempt to break the silence, but we just sat there.

And it was nice.

I didn't know Levi well, but I thought he might like the quiet, the stillness. He was different from his brothers—and not just in looks. Yes, he had tattoos and wore his hair longer, but he was softer. Reserved. I didn't know if that was entirely from shyness, or if Levi's silence allowed him to see things others often missed.

I couldn't help but worry that he might know more about me than he let on.

The crowd slowly thinned as the band packed up, and I was on the verge of panicking just as Levi stood. "I'm giving you a ride home. Where's your bike?" Before I could decline, he said, "I'm giving you a ride home, Shay. It's too late and not safe. You'd be riding home in the complete dark."

I groaned and followed him when he walked away, not surprised stubbornness was a shared trait in his family. "And don't worry about Brooks. Nolan and I both gave him hell for what he did. He had no right to ever say that to you." He shook his head, huffing a laugh. "Despite what he thinks, I'm a grown man, and if I want to be your friend, then dammit—I'm going to be."

I smiled, kind of liking Levi all riled up. Had Brooks come clean, or had they figured it out? "Who says I want to be your friend?"

He side-eyed me as I walked beside him, a smile playing on his lips. "Do you have any other options?"

I feigned hurt, lifting my hand to my chest. "Layne's my friend."

"Doesn't count. You work with her."

"Fine. Then Jake and Wren."

He laughed and rounded the diner, grabbing my bike before I could. "They're your landlords—and like seventy years old. That's just sad if they're your only friends."

I followed him through the parking lot and let him load my bike onto the back of the red Jeep I'd seen outside their cabin. "I planned on dipping out earlier tonight, so I drove alone. Brooks doesn't drink, so he'll drive Nolan home." He opened the passenger door before I could, motioning for me to climb in.

"Thank you." The Jeep whirred to life, and I buckled myself in. "I want to be your friend, Levi. I really do . . ." I paused, debating if it was worth saying anything at all. But I'd caused enough problems in my life by not speaking my mind. "But I can only be your friend. Nothing more."

He raised a brow, his words slow. "I know."

"Not because I don't think you're a catch," I blurted, fearing I'd hurt his feelings. *Great, I suck.* "Believe me, I think you're so handsome and even kinder—"

He laughed, his wavy hair skimming his jaw, and lifted his hand to stop me. "And I think you're beautiful, Shay. We all do. But I can think that without wanting more from you. And I have other things I'm focusing on right now than who I'm wanting to date. I mean—maybe if Layne wasn't leaving . . ." He shook his head, but not even the dim light could hide his flushed cheeks. "That's beside the point. I'm cool being your friend, Shay. I wanted to be the moment Brooks came home ranting about our new neighbor."

"Okay," I agreed, my chest lighter than before. "I'll be the greatest friend you've ever had—but first, I need to ask you a favor."

"Anything," Levi said without pause as he pulled into my driveway, his lights bright on Jake's idle truck. I hadn't driven it once. But despite his assurance, I couldn't bring myself to ask. "You know," Levi started, shifting the Jeep into park. "My brothers baby me. A lot. They'll deny it until they're dead, but they do. It's why Nolan overreacted about the map and why Brooks thought he needed to protect us from you. And I hate it. It drives me crazy, and someday I'll probably lose it on them. But no matter how annoying they can be, I don't think they're doing it because they think I can't take care of myself—they just wanna help me out. And that's all we want to do for you, Shay. Even Brooks does. He's just an idiot," he said with a laugh, looking up at me. And in that look, I couldn't help but think again that Levi Graham might someday be the greatest friend I ever had. "So if you need help, then I'm here. As your friend."

I stared at my hands, resting in my lap, telling myself I could trust Levi. There was nothing wrong with needing help. "I have a doctor's appointment this coming week. I was going to ask Jake if I could use my car, but Wren told me they'll be gone for two weeks, and I know she's more comfortable in it—"

"I'll take off work and give you a ride," he said, not asking why I didn't use Jake's truck, nor why I was seeing a doctor. "I've got you."

"I know," I breathed. Maybe it wasn't such a bad thing to let someone in. To welcome their support, trusting they desired the best for me.

And for the first time, when I lay awake that night and silently promised myself *I've got this*, I believed it.

Chapter Twelve

Empty.

The words that had once flowed easy and strong, nearly brimming over, were gone. My ability to write, a piece of my soul that had offered refuge and peace, had withered away. It had been a gift, a tender mercy.

And now it was gone.

I cursed, the lead of my pencil snapping against the empty page—the first mark I'd yet to make in my notebook. I couldn't even pinpoint the last time I'd written. Perhaps sometime within the first year after I'd dropped out of school?

Lila had called to tell me she didn't need me to work today. I knew I had no reason to worry just yet—after all, before Declan, I was accustomed to being frugal—but it weighed differently on me than it did when I was eighteen. Needing comfort and longing for inspiration, I'd gone on a short run and then wandered out to the meadow.

The sun had been high when I first sat down, but now it was nearly set, shedding shadows on the wildflowers beside me. I stared at the daunting blank page, those empty blue lines making a mockery of me. As though they were telling me: *Ha! You have no story to tell. Your story is over.* Maybe it served me right. I didn't deserve to weave words together, to form stories and voice pain in a way I never could aloud. I didn't know how to bring that piece of myself back to life.

"Screw this," I hissed and tore the journal limb from limb. I carelessly ripped the pages, pieces scattering about my feet, the trees forced to watch as I mutilated one of their ancestors.

Before I might've reaped further carnage, I froze, not only at the abrupt barking, but the smooth, mocking voice that said, "Can't say I'm surprised to see you're a litterer."

This is not happening.

I snatched the remnants of the journal and stared out at the tree line, unable to face the devil. Regretting my actions—not only because I'd been caught, but because I was indeed not a *litterer*—I crouched down and slowly picked up the shreds.

I stayed silent, even when Cash nudged my side and slipped his head under my arm. He licked my cheek, his tail slashing the tall grass, distracting me enough I failed to notice Brooks until he was right beside me, kneeling. I froze, taken aback when his hand wrapped around my wrist.

"Sorry," he said, releasing me immediately. "I was just trying to hand you this."

I stared at the paper in his hands, waiting for him to tear it into a thousand pieces and leave me to clean it up. "Thank you." I grabbed it from him, ensuring I hadn't abandoned a single piece before I stood. I brushed off my knees, yet to look his way. "I'll leave you and Cash to it."

I turned and started back toward my cabin, veering wide in case Brooks threw a hissy fit for breathing too close to him. Stalks of grass crunched behind me, and it was the effort of my life to keep my attention directed on the last of the setting sun, licks of orange and red kissing the trees. I quickened my pace, on the verge of jogging as Cash nudged my hand.

"You're going to get me in trouble," I murmured out of the side of my mouth. "Go with Brooks."

"You know I can hear you, right?"

I frowned, catching a glimpse of him now, several feet between us, his long legs keeping up with ease. I didn't reply, not in the mood for one of his lectures. I could only imagine he was raging—not only had I danced with Nolan, but Levi had given me a ride home.

I slowed my breathing, not wanting to give him further ammunition as I walked down through the ditch and up onto the dirt road. I rubbed Cash's neck once, a suitable goodbye, and continued on my way, steering clear of Brooks's truck parked alongside the road. I listened, waiting for him to climb in and slam his truck door, maybe run me over—but he didn't, his boots crunching on the gravel with Cash's paws.

"I'm going to bed," I said, my voice dry, unwelcoming.

"The sun's still out."

Thank you, Lucifer.

"I'm still tired." I reached into my pocket and fished out my keys. "Good night."

I imagined wedging them in his lovely green eyes when he asked, "Are you still not feeling good?"

"I'm fine." I turned and put my back to the door, facing him at last. My gaze slowly trailed up his legs and sturdy chest, still wearing his forest ranger uniform. His pistol was gone, so I assumed he was off duty. His beard was cut and clean, his eyes pleasant and inviting—even his lips weren't pressed in a hard line. And not for the first time, I couldn't help but think how handsome he was.

And now my heart was pounding for an entirely different reason.

"If you're here to lecture me about the other night, there's no need," I bit out, not liking the sense of vulnerability I felt looking at him. "Believe me, I had no idea what possessed me to ask you to dance."

He raised his brows, likely revolted at the reminder. Not wanting to experience his rejection again, I gripped my keys and dryly said, "What do you want? If I did something wrong, just tell me. That way I can dream of all the ways I managed to piss you off, yet again."

He clenched his jaw, his tongue pressed against his cheek. "You can't drive standard."

I can't—what?

I forced my gaze to remain on him and not Jake's truck. "That's not true—" I stopped, not caring how incapable the truth made me. I was sick of feeling small. "Fine. I'm not sure why that matters—but yeah. I can't drive standard. Big deal."

"My dad taught me when I was fourteen."

What was this? An attempt to stroke his ego?

Congrats. Your dad taught you to drive. I learned how to appear invisible when my mom's boyfriends had too much to drink.

I rolled my eyes and turned, jabbing the key into the doorknob. "Good for you." I cracked the door open just enough to slip through and turned, prepared to lock it.

Brooks wedged his boot in the doorway, stopping me. "I can teach you."

"Ha! Fat chance." Arms straining, I pushed against the door, letting up when Cash's nose nudged through. "Traitor." Back pressed to the door, I fought to not lose an inch.

"Come on. It's not that hard." He blew out a deep breath, muttering something I failed to hear. "Wouldn't it be nice not to ride Jake's bike everywhere?"

I ground my teeth—of course he'd point out the bike wasn't mine. Nothing was. "I love my Barbie bike," I lied, pretending my legs didn't cramp up every night in bed. "Now go away."

"It's going to get cold soon. You won't want to ride it in the snow."

"Maybe I'll freeze to death. Bet you'd like that."

There was a long pause, and I imagined Brooks tearing at his hair, regretting not running me out of town the first day we met. "I'd really like to teach you so I can move on with my life."

I scrunched my nose at his exasperated tone. "Why do *you* want to help *me*?" When he didn't respond, I spun and yanked open the door. My nose tapped his chest, and I stumbled back, not expecting him to be so close. "Did Jake put you up to this?"

He didn't bother to deny it. "So what if he did?"

I crossed my arms over my chest, narrowing my eyes. Of course Brooks wouldn't help me on his own. "Just tell him no. Or ask one of your brothers to do it."

His eyes flared, and I bit my lip as he said, "No. I gave my word to Jake and you're gonna let me keep it."

I gaped at him, my hands shaking, itching with the need to give him a friendly shove off the porch. "And I gave you my word that I'd leave you guys alone—so bye." I grabbed the door, planting my feet when his hand halted the movement.

But he didn't struggle, holding the door open with ease. "Yeah, sure seemed that way when you rode home with Levi the other night. Which you wouldn't have had to do if you knew how to drive."

I grunted, cheeks flushed. "I know how to drive."

He groaned, not from exhaustion, but aggravation. "Stop being a pain and let me teach you."

"No."

"Why?"

"Because I have absolutely nothing I can give you in return," I breathed. Brooks's face shifted, but before I could read what lay there, his hand lowered and I stumbled forward. The door clipped shut and I fell on my knees, hitting my chin.

My lip trembled and I bit back a cry. Not from pain—at least, not the visible sort—but because I refused to let Brooks witness me crumble. There was a soft rap against the door. "Did you fall in that hole beneath your rug? If so, I'm coming in so I can take a picture of you in all your glory."

I forced a dry, hollow laugh and rolled to my feet, careful to avoid the broken floorboard. He must have seen it when he snooped through my cabin on his last visit. The door opened and I shifted out of the way, unable to face him, to see the smugness that was surely there.

I rubbed Cash's neck, fingers deep in his fur when Brooks asked, "You alright?"

I nodded and, despite myself, looked up, shocked with what I found. He didn't look like a man who'd won, who'd successfully knocked me down. No . . . I thought it might be pity in his eyes. And that was somehow worse.

"Let me teach you," he said, his voice mellow, gentle. "Trust me, if you don't let me, Jake's gonna do it when he gets back. And I promise that's something you don't want to experience."

I smiled to myself, thinking it might be fun to have Jake teach me, an experience for sure. But he had enough to worry about, Wren being the most important. I wrapped my arm around my stomach, my voice timid. "And what will I have to give you in return?"

He rubbed the back of his neck and glanced over his shoulder, the sun almost fully set behind him. "I—I don't want anything from you, Shay."

I resisted the urge to snap that he'd made that more than clear, but I paused—I was too exhausted to fight. "Fine," I agreed. I couldn't ride this bike forever. "But I don't want you doing me any favors. So I'll pay you."

I didn't have the cash to spare, but I couldn't afford to let anyone have control over me again.

He pressed his lips together, and his eyes roamed over the cabin, likely judging my lame attempt to spruce it up. Miraculously, he held back his snide remark and said with what I believed was a hint of a smile, "Maybe you can make me a loaf of that banana bread."

I nodded and put my back to him, hiding the way I grinned—refusing to expose my excitement.

Look out, Pioneer Woman.

Chapter Thirteen

Scratch that.

Run me over, Pioneer Woman.

If Ree Drummond were here, her cheeks would burn as scarlet as her fiery hair, and she'd roll with laughter as she watched me suck at stick shift. After which she'd yank me out of the driver's seat and show me how it was done.

Surely, she'd be more helpful than Brooks—who only grunted when I stalled the engine.

"Try again." He glanced in the rearview mirror, likely ensuring Cash hadn't fallen out of the bed of the truck. "Press the gas a bit slower." I nodded and bit my lip, pressing the clutch down as I turned the key in the ignition. "Make sure it's in first gear," he mumbled, the truck shaking to life.

I pressed the brake, double-checking it was in first, then released the brake again. Palms sweaty, I clutched the wheel, and the truck inched forward, the headlights illuminating the dirt road between our houses. I held in my breath, eased my foot off the clutch, and pushed on the gas—

The truck lunged and puttered out, stalling again. "I'm sorry."

"Again."

I blinked through burning eyes and reached for the keys, stopping when my arm brushed his. The truck's space was limited, with only the driver and passenger seats, a gear shift between us. I stared at the ever-shrinking cab, somehow only now realizing the lack of room. I'd bought the Altima—Betsy—because it was cheap, but it also had space.

Where am I supposed to put a car seat in here?

"Can we get going already?" Brooks said, his tone growing more impatient as the night passed. "I'd like to be in bed before sunrise." I shook my head and tried again, pausing at the gear shift where I wished a middle seat was. I was such an idiot. "Let's go, Shay," he pressed, and there was something hard in his tone that made my heart rate jump. Panicking, I floored the gas, the truck jerking in return. "If you would focus, you could do this."

With blurring vision, I stared out my window, unable to see the meadow this late. "I'm done."

The door groaned as I pushed it open, not bothering to slam it shut. Brooks could drive it back. Cash whined, his paws hitting the side of the truck as I walked away into the void of the night, the cabin hidden from me at this distance.

"Where are you going?" Brooks called after me.

I wrapped my arms around myself, holding the pieces of my spirit together. I sucked in short, rapid breaths of the fresh night. It was fine. Everything was fine.

But it wasn't.

"Can't you do anything right?"

"How many times do I have to explain such a simple task?"

"Don't you see? Don't you see how you need me?"

"Really? That's it?" Brooks's voice carried, loud enough to free me of those memories. "You know what—fine. I'm not surprised you're giving up."

My nails dug into my palms, and I spun on my heel. "You don't know me."

"Oh, I know you." His long strides absorbed the distance between us, closing in on me. "I think you're used to getting your way. You've been so coddled and pampered, you don't know what to do when life pushes back. So you give up."

I flinched under the weight of his words—or perhaps I feared the anger in his eyes might come out in his hands. He stopped half a step short of me, likely seeing my lapse. I looked up through my lashes at him, his breath warm against my skin. He was silent, and so was I, but what was being passed between us . . . that was loud. He could see me, see how broken I was.

If I shifted an inch, I'd be pressed up against his heaving chest, feel the confirmation of his hatred with each beat of his heart. I didn't try to reason with him, to prove how wrong his image of me was. He wouldn't believe me, and it was better that way. Safer than letting him know me, see me for who I was. He couldn't hurt me then, couldn't inflict the same pain I was running from.

But I was so tired.

I rubbed my neck, the red glow from the truck's brake lights tinting the air. "It's too small," I cried and gave in, resting my head against his chest. He stiffened, but made no move to shove me off. "The truck's too small—and I'm so stupid. I don't know what I'm doing. Betsy was so good to me, and I gave her away."

"What . . ." There was a long pause before Brooks asked, "Jake's cow? Sunshine, Betsy was slaughtered a long time ago—"

"No," I choked out and wrapped my arms around him, needing to hold something. "My car. The one I gave to Jake."

His arms hung lifelessly at his side, but his voice was lighter, almost edged with a laugh. "Poor Betsy. I'm sure she's heartbroken that you abandoned her, but at least she doesn't have to fear for her life anymore. At least not until Jake takes her to the junkyard."

"What?" I cried, dropping my arms to step away. But then his arms were up and around me, holding me against him.

"I'm sorry," he murmured. "I was only teasing you about Betsy." His hands rubbed up and down my back. I sniffled and leaned into him, savoring his warmth. Savoring being held, even if it was by him. I closed my eyes when his fingers brushed my neck, his touch as careful as his voice. "None of us knows what we're doing, Shay. We're all trying to figure it out." I stepped back and he made no protest, his hold loosening. "I'm sorry. I know you were trying, and I was being an ass."

I wiped my cheeks and huffed a tired laugh. I didn't know what to do with his apology; sometimes words meant nothing. "I suck."

He smirked. "Kind of. But you won't always." He tucked his hands in his pockets, jerking his head back to the truck. "Come on. I want to try something else."

He walked away, but I couldn't bring myself to follow. "I'm tired." My voice was frail, my soul aching.

He leaned against the truck and rubbed Cash's head. He made no move to coerce me forward and only whispered back, "I know." His voice was gentle, so considerate, I wouldn't have believed it was Brooks if he wasn't standing right there. I didn't know if he could tell the exhaustion I spoke of wasn't solely physical, but by the way he patiently watched me, I thought he might understand. Might know what it was like to be nearly spent, to know that there might come a day when you woke up and realized you had nothing more to give.

I'd have to dig deeper, then.

"No more yelling," I breathed, loud enough to reach him.

"No more yelling," he repeated back, his voice as smooth as air.

I rubbed my eyes, clearing my mind before I walked back to the truck. It was ultimately up to me if I succeeded or not. I'd been on my own before. I could do it again.

But when I reached the truck, my nerves faltered as Brooks climbed in the driver's seat, leaving the door open. He adjusted the seat, pushing it all the way back, and patted his thigh, as though in invitation. "Let's go." I realized it was, eyes widening, when he asked, "Are you going to climb in or not?"

I glanced at Cash in the truck bed, wondering if Brooks was calling for him instead. "You want *me* . . . to sit on *your* lap?"

He shrugged like it was no biggie—and it might have not been for him. I didn't know him, maybe he did this often. Yes, that was it. He'd lure unassuming girls into vehicles, under the pretense of teaching them to drive—and then squeeze the light out of them with those deliciously sturdy thighs. But I was unaccustomed to sitting on the laps of men I hardly knew, especially ones who didn't like me.

My hesitation must've been notable, because Brooks said with a sigh, "Don't make it into something it's not. I want to try it with you experiencing the movements instead. I think I can show you better than I can tell you."

"Okay," I agreed, grateful his eyes were ahead of him and not on me as I calculated how to best crawl atop him. "You'll let me know if I'm too heavy?"

He pinned me with a look. "Don't be annoying."

I rolled my eyes and—to hell with it—climbed on his lap, my back against his chest. Nothing but our soft breaths filled the cab as he widened his legs, his hands adjusting me where he needed. And I let him, pretending my bum wasn't on top of his crotch.

"Okay." His voice was breathless. "Put your hands and feet under mine."

His jeans scraped against my thighs as I placed my feet under his, followed by my hands. His hands were rough, large. I'd known Brooks was taller than me, assuming he fell somewhere in the six-foot range, and while I wasn't particularly short at five-five, his body practically absorbed me. His forearms were strained, tight and corded with muscles I knew weren't built in the gym, but the sort you obtained through hard work. I'd seen Nolan and Levi in nothing but boxers, and while I'd only seen him dressed, I knew—I just knew from how his body felt against mine—Brooks Graham was no less a masterpiece.

I swallowed and adjusted myself on his hard thighs, tilting to the side so he could see, our position making me slightly taller. "Move with me, okay?" I nodded, unable to find my voice. What was happening? As I was on the brink of diving out of the truck and making a run for it, Brooks rasped, "Sorry. I've never done this before. This was how my dad would let us drive with him when we were kids." He wrapped our fingers together and gave me a gentle squeeze before guiding our hands to the ignition. I stayed silent, resisting the urge to remind him I was more than capable of at least *starting* the truck.

Instead, I asked, "Are you sure this is safe?" As far as I knew, it was only us who lived on this path, but what we were doing was also far from legal, and I wasn't about to risk the safety of others. "I know you did this as a kid, but I am clearly not a child—"

His coarse, calloused hands tightened. "It's just you and me right now, Shay."

I nodded and spun the key, the truck shaking to life. Rather than repeating aloud his instructions, Brooks silently guided me through it, his feet carefully pressing down on mine, indicating the right pressure, until we had slowly drifted into first gear.

I gripped the steering wheel, his hands holding mine just as tightly—and I couldn't help but wonder if he was as nervous as I was. He lifted our right arms and brought them to the stick shift. "We're going to release the gas and press the clutch while we shift to second."

Our bodies flowed as one, the truck smooth as we shifted and pressed the gas. We didn't speak again as we worked our way through the gears, successfully each time. We flipped a U-turn after reaching his house, his porch light winking through the trees. Releasing my hands and lifting his boots off mine, he said, "Okay. Drive back to your place."

I paused, expecting him to reach for the door handle, maybe to shift beneath me and indicate I should get up. But he turned off the truck and dropped his hands to hold the side of the cloth seat, gripping it like he was in pain.

Okay.

I swallowed and my hands shook, my nerves worse than before. The truck rumbled to life, and I worked the pedals, his legs abrasive against mine. Keeping one hand on the wheel, I reached for the stick and attempted to shift to second.

I silently cursed, cheeks heating when the truck lunged, my chest hitting the wheel when it sputtered to a stop. I'd never hated being a woman more until I'd experienced just how freaking tender boobs could be. Pregnancy was for the birds. Blowing out a breath, I started again, grateful Brooks chose not to scold me. But this time, when I went to shift, I froze as his hands gravitated to my knees. He squeezed in encouragement, and I realized his intentions when his pressure shifted, pushing and guiding me along.

I smiled, nearly stalling—but not—when I successfully shifted to second, a faint trail of dirt behind us. His hold didn't falter and neither did I, slowly working through the gears, not giving up even when the truck was on the edge of puttering out.

"I did it, Brooks!" I squealed as I pulled into the driveway, the headlights shining on the cabin. "I did it!" Before I could think better of it, I let go of the wheel and clapped my hands. Brooks, being wiser than I, grabbed it, his boot coming down hard atop mine on the brake. I covered my mouth in horror, realizing what I'd done. "I'm so sorry. I was so excited—"

His free hand lightly clutched my waist, and he laughed under his breath—he laughed!—instead of screaming at me for nearly driving through his uncle's cabin. "You did it." He turned off the truck, and darkness swallowed our surroundings. "I . . ." He hesitated, clearing his throat. "I knew you had it in you, Shay. I'm proud of you."

My heart drummed with excitement, and I didn't care, didn't think as I spun on his lap and wrapped myself around him, burying my face against his neck. "Thank you, Brooks."

I didn't care how ridiculous I must've looked when I brought my legs up and around him, kicking the stick shift somewhere in between. Or that he didn't embrace me back—I knew he'd only done it before out of obligation. But I was so grateful for his help, that he kept trying even when I struggled. That rather than give up on me, he'd simply adjusted and found another way.

"Thank you." I leaned back. His head rested against the seat and his hands hung loosely, not touching me, even where my knees dug into the seat as I straddled him. But his eyes . . . they were so charming and inviting, openly roaming over my features. Inviting enough, I found myself shifting closer, my hands looping further around his neck. "I really appreciate you helping me."

Before I could've made a further fool out of myself, Brooks's jaw tightened, and he closed his eyes. "It was nothing. I did it for Jake."

I flinched at the reminder. Brooks didn't like me, didn't want to share my company. The fact I was on his lap likely intensified his hatred. And I was pregnant—I had no business even touching him. I crawled off him and into the passenger seat, not missing a beat, and got out, closing the door swiftly behind me. "Okay," I said, when he climbed out and unlatched the tailgate for Cash. "Then you can tell Jake you fulfilled your promise and you're off the hook."

I walked up the porch and unlocked my door. I was already inside, the door halfway closed, when Brooks said, "Shay."

He leaned against Jake's truck, his eyes watching me more intently than I'd ever been watched. "I hope you're prepared to bake at least a dozen loaves of banana bread, because we're not nearly done." He patted the side of the truck and clicked his tongue, Cash following after him. It wasn't until I could barely make them out that he called out, "I'll see you tomorrow night."

Chapter Fourteen

Unexpectedly, Brooks and I fell into an easy routine. I hadn't anticipated our lessons to be nightly, but he and Cash always showed, even on the nights when I didn't get off until the moon was high and the cricket chirps were loud.

But what I had expected was the silence. I didn't speak and neither did he, other than to offer gentle reminders. There was absolutely no invitation to sit on his lap again, both of us firmly separated and planted in our seats. Which was for the best, because I was stalling less and less each night. It was only a matter of time before our lessons were done and Brooks was rid of me.

"Your dad taught you how to do this?" I asked as the engine grew louder and I shifted to second.

His attention was on the dark forest outside the window, his voice gruff. "Why are you asking questions you already know the answer to?"

I pursed my lips and focused on the road. This was why we didn't talk. He gave me whiplash. I drove past his cabin, where both his brother's vehicles sat in the driveway, and edged deeper into the forest. I cleared my throat, pushing the last of my luck. "Um, I'm busy tomorrow . . . and I think I'm good enough to practice alone. So you have officially fulfilled your word to Jake."

"What are you doing tomorrow?"

"Um—" I fumbled for a response, not having expected him to ask. And why was I driving deeper into the woods? I was practically inviting him to murder me.

"Someone finally ask you out on a date?" he asked when I failed to come up with a response.

"No," I answered immediately, choosing to ignore how rude he was solely because I knew he was about to unleash all the mighty wrath of the underworld. "I have a doctor's appointment, and I'm not confident enough to drive the truck long distances . . . so Levi is taking me."

His jaw clicked and I panicked, seeing only one clear route of safety. I went to shift gears but released the clutch too early, grinning wickedly as the truck lunged. Brooks slid forward and braced his forearm on the dash. He slowly turned his head in a way that was purely terrifying, his nostrils flaring. "You did that on purpose."

"Nope." I popped my tongue against the roof of my mouth. "You're just not that great of a teacher."

He smirked. "Good thing your lessons are done."

I gave him a tight-lipped smile and restarted the truck. Flipping a U-turn, I got us back on the road, cutting the night short. I clutched the wheel, bracing for Brooks to reprimand me about Levi, but he was quiet, his hands tense against the door.

He's going to murder me.

"Okay, well, this was fun. Thanks," I started when I pulled up beside the cabin, smoothly switching the truck off. "Have a good night." I was out of the truck before I'd closed my mouth, slamming the door shut. I skipped rubbing Cash goodbye, almost tripping over my boots as I ran up the porch steps. Not because I was afraid of Brooks, but because I really couldn't survive him—or anyone—telling me to get lost again.

The doorknob was in my hand when Brooks called out, "Where's my payment?"

I turned, my brow raised. "Your what?"

He leaned against the truck like he owned it—which was *fine*, since I didn't either. "My bread. I was thinking we do a loaf for each lesson as payment. And seeing as you've had five lessons and only delivered one loaf, you owe me four."

"Okay?" I scoffed. "I haven't had a chance to make any again."

He crossed his arms over his chest and shrugged. "I've got time now."

"I don't have the ingredients," I explained, positive the banana bread hadn't been that great, though I hadn't tried it. "I'll get them to you in a few days. All I want right now is a peanut butter sandwich and to crawl into bed."

He pushed off the truck. "I like peanut butter."

I gaped at him, stuck on the half smile he wore as he put his hand over mine and finished opening the door, welcoming himself in.

What was actually happening?

Did I look like a sandwich-making housewife?

No.

Yet here I was, meandering through the kitchen as Brooks sat at my table, silently scrutinizing the way I smeared peanut butter on bread. I stared at the counter, my back to him, when I muttered, "Do you want it cut in triangles or rectangles?"

Being the smart-ass he was, he answered, "Rectangles. And don't forget to cut off the crust."

Nasty words foamed in my mouth, and I had half a mind to spit them into his sandwich. I swallowed and sought revenge by cutting it in triangles instead, leaving the crust. "Here you go." I slid his plate across the table and pulled out the chair across from him. "You're welcome."

He stared at it, his fingers tapping on the table, seeming to hesitate. "Do you have any butter?" I took a bite and pointed at the fridge, done playing housewife. He stood, his chair scuffing against the floor, and returned with a butter container and knife.

I stopped mid-bite, shocked, not because he smeared butter on his sandwich, but when he revealed, "My dad would do this. I can't eat them any other way." I nodded, unsure what I could possibly say. I never knew what to expect from him. But I definitely hadn't anticipated him putting two fingers on my wrist, halting my next bite. "You should try it."

I shrugged and took the knife from him—how could butter possibly make anything worse?—and smeared it over the peanut butter before slabbing the two pieces of bread back together. "If it's gross, I'm docking you a loaf."

He smiled, and I'd be lying if I said my heart didn't squirm, that I wished he'd smile again. "Thank you for making me a sandwich."

I stared at the plate as we ate in silence, Cash sound asleep at the foot of the door. Not wanting to wake him—nor give Brooks the satisfaction—I swallowed back a moan. Maybe it was the pregnancy talking, but holy moly, this was the best sandwich I'd ever had.

Silently promising to make another when I was alone, I grabbed Brooks's plate once he finished, placing both of ours in the sink to clean. I leaned against the counter, hoping he would take the hint and leave, but he stretched his legs out and asked, "Who taught you how to drive?"

I blew out a tired breath. *Someone's chatty tonight.* "Um—" I paused, unable to stop the way my stomach twisted. "A few of the girls in my dorm taught me my first semester of college."

It was strange how I couldn't recall their names, but I could remember the embarrassment I'd felt when they asked me to be their designated driver, only to realize I couldn't drive. My mom hadn't taught me—it wasn't like we could afford an extra car. It hadn't bothered me; I knew money was tight. But I did wish she'd given me the chance to at least learn.

It wasn't until I was eighteen, and in my first month of college, that I fully understood my success was up to me. I couldn't rely on anyone's support.

He cocked his head, his dark hair slipping down onto his forehead. "How old are you?"

"Twenty-four," I said, not surprised he didn't remember from when he'd looked at my license. "How old are you?"

"Twenty-eight."

I raised my brows in acknowledgment and glanced at the door. He'd had his sandwich—it was time to leave. I was on the verge of voicing that when he said, peering around the room, "I like what you've done with the place." Though the few things I'd added were nothing worthwhile, I was grateful I'd cleaned, deciding I preferred it that way. It wasn't just something Declan had engraved in my head. "Are you planning on visitors soon?"

"No."

"Your parents . . . they aren't gonna come visit you?"

I clutched the side of the counter. My voice was empty. "No, Brooks. No one is coming to see me."

It was silent for a long while, only the sound of Cash's quiet snores accompanying our breaths, until he asked, "Are . . . are your parents not alive?"

My heart ached, plummeted to my boots. "Sometimes it feels that way."

I wasn't sure if I wanted to ever see my mom again, not after what she'd done. Our relationship was severed, family bonds broken, but still I ached for her. Well, maybe not her—but a mother. Someone to love me, to tell me everything would be okay. That I was strong enough to get through this. I didn't grieve for my mom, or even Noah—I grieved for what could have been. I longed for a family I'd never have.

I cleared my throat and blinked through tear-filled eyes. I was so tired of crying in front of Brooks. Tired of crying in general. "They're alive—but before you suggest it, I can't live with them. Sorry to disappoint you."

I looked up to find him watching me. His eyes weren't hard and untrusting, seeking secrets. He wore pity, even kindness, likely because he too knew something about being unwanted. It might've been nice to open up, to sit with someone who knew the sort of burn that left. But all I could think of was the wound he'd inflicted upon me, telling me time and time again to leave. Deep inside, I believed that stemmed from something I knew nothing about, but regardless, I didn't feel like I could trust him yet.

"I should get ready for bed." I faced the sink and started the water for the dishes, hoping he'd catch the hint.

I scrubbed a spotless plate as the floor creaked under his boots and Cash's collar rattled as he shook awake. A balmy draft swept in as the door opened, and Brooks said, "You did good today, Shay." Bubbles dripped off my arms into murky sink water as I stared at the dish, my throat tight from his words. "Good luck tomorrow."

"Thank you." I turned and gave him a frail smile before he closed the door, knowing I'd need all the luck I could get. I didn't know why the reminder made my heart race, why my stomach dropped. Tomorrow's appointment wouldn't truly change anything.

Everything had already changed.

Chapter Fifteen

"Give me one freaking minute," I muttered, hurriedly filling my cup at the sink. Through the kitchen window, I caught a glimpse of Levi's Jeep, where he was likely readying himself to honk his horn again. I slipped on my sandals and grabbed my bag off the table, internally wincing at the catastrophe of clothes I was leaving behind. I'd woken up this morning in a panic—a Grinchy *and what will I wear* sort of panic.

In a sensible part of my brain I knew it didn't matter; it was only a doctor's appointment, after all. But I'd settled for the nicest pair of jeans and the flowy baby-blue top I'd found at the thrift store and deemed it good enough. Levi honked his horn again, and I jumped, water splashing out of my cup and onto the floor. I hadn't known he was such an impatient ass—something I planned to tell him as I locked up the cabin and jogged down the steps to his Jeep. I grabbed the handle and yanked the door open. "What is all the fuss about? It's not even ten—" I halted with one leg in the truck when I wasn't greeted with friendly, youthful eyes and instead met a set of brooding, heart-pounding ones. Brooks.

Welp. That explained the honking.

"What are you doing here?" I peeked over the passenger seat into the back, but no one else was to be found. "Where's Levi?"

"He's sick."

I didn't hesitate, didn't think before I spat, eyes narrowed, "You're lying."

His arms flexed beneath his flannel, and I expected him to snap some snide comment, maybe drive away or run me over. But his breaths were steady, his hands loosening. "Please get inside, Shay. I assume you don't want to miss your appointment."

I scowled, searching for any other option. Of course I didn't want to miss my appointment, but the last person I wanted to tag along was Brooks. What if he tried to come inside? I was more than aware I couldn't keep this a secret much longer—but I wasn't about to admit something so vulnerable to a man who gave me whiplash on the daily. I didn't know him. Who was to say he wouldn't react the same way Declan had?

I lowered my leg and shut the door a fraction of an inch. I'd reschedule the appointment. Except I stopped as Brooks reached into the glove box and pulled out something folded in a paper towel. He placed it on the middle console, and I sniffed—because apparently heightened smell was my choice of superpower. "What is that?"

Brooks ran his hand over his mouth, covering what I believed to be a grin. "A peanut butter sandwich."

I bit the smile itching to break free on my lips, certain I'd drool if I did. I'd never admit it, but last night after he'd left, I'd scarfed down one and a half sandwiches, unable to think of anything else. I'd thrown up after, but it was worth it. My hand twitched, aching to grab it, but not before I asked, "Does it have butter?"

"Get in and find out."

I didn't let my hopes rise as I climbed in and sat, anticipating his large fist to smash it, only for him to hand it over. "Thank you." I laid it on my lap, buckling myself in. "Is it poisoned?"

"Definitely. Figured you were used to that by now."

My smile faltered, and I picked at the edge of the paper towel. "You promise that Levi's actually sick?" I asked, not sure if I'd believe him regardless. "If this is an attempt to protect him from me—"

"He's sick, Shay." He didn't snap it or roll his eyes, but just sighed. "He's caught some sort of stomach bug, probably whatever you had. But he's fine. The only reason I'm here is because he didn't want to get you sick."

I nodded, not bothering to tell him what I *had* wasn't contagious. "Could I have Levi's number?" I asked as he pulled out of my driveway and started us down the road. "Please."

He raised his brow. "You have a phone now?"

I shifted and grabbed it out of my back pocket, showing it off like I was in fifth grade and had the new Razr everyone wanted. "Look at me moving up in the world."

A soft smile stretched his lips, one that seemed to carry into his eyes, the corners crinkling. "Look at you." He turned, directing his attention back to the road as he rambled off Levi's number off the top of his head without a fight, then shockingly gave me Nolan's as well.

I saved the numbers and texted Levi before I tucked the phone away. "Thank you."

Mouth watering, I unveiled my sandwich, only to be interrupted when Brooks asked, "You don't want mine?"

I brushed my hair behind my ear. "Want what?"

"My number."

Isn't the devil's number 666?

I resisted the urge to tell Brooks how clever I was, solely because he was being nice-ish. He was under no obligation to take me to my appointment, nor did he have to teach me how to drive.

Plus he'd made me a moan-worthy sandwich.

"Oh." I sipped from my cup, searching for a response. "That's okay. I don't need it." I internally winced. "I don't mean that meanly," I rushed to say, twisting in my seat to face him. "I just think if I needed something from you, I could text Levi or Nolan to ask you for me."

He raised a brow, a glimmer of sunshine skimming over his cheeks and highlighting his freckles. "But what if I need or *want* to get ahold of you?"

I shrugged, unable to think of any day, or any lifetime, in which Brooks Graham would wake up and want to talk to me. I'd been wary of getting a phone again in the first place—I kind of liked being unavailable. Especially after years of enduring Declan's blitz texts, usually in the form of anger and annoyance. I doubted Brooks would text to tell me what a useless woman I was, but I wasn't going to risk anything. "Then you can ask Levi or Nolan to call me."

He sputtered a laugh, shaking his head. "Okay, that's alright. Don't give it to me. But when aliens invade the planet and I'm the first to know, don't blame me when you get abducted because I couldn't get ahold of you."

I stared at him. Who was this? This loose, at-ease man teasing me was not Brooks. "If aliens were to invade the planet, I highly doubt you'd try to warn me."

"That's a lie. I'd need someone to act as bait so Cash and I could get away."

I shook my head and finished unwrapping my sandwich. It was sliced in rectangles with the crust cut off—exactly how he'd asked for it last night. I grabbed one side, smiling, and held it out to him. "Payment for the ride?"

He rolled his eyes but accepted it, wolfing it down in one bite. I peeled mine off in pieces, slowly nibbling as we drove in silence and I stared out the window at the forest beyond. It was easy to forget a different world existed outside of it. It was why I'd come here, chasing the idea of getting lost.

And while it was a relief to be lost, to escape from it all, I was starting to wonder if it might be even nicer to be found.

"Do you have something to do while I'm inside?" I asked when Brooks pulled into the parking lot of the clinic. The hour-and-a-half drive had gone quicker than I expected.

He shrugged, unbuckling his seatbelt. "I'll just hang in here. Maybe take a nap." I nodded and bit my lip, grateful he'd give me privacy to go in alone. But that didn't stop him from asking, "Is everything okay, Shay?"

I rubbed my hands over my thighs. "I'm fine." I grabbed my bag from the floor, double-checking I had all my things. "I don't know how long it'll take, I'm sorry. I know I'll have to do bloodwork and then—"

"It's fine," he reassured me. "I'll wait as long as you need."

I wanted to demand to know why. To accuse him of being nosy, or that he had forced Levi to stay behind, because I hadn't heard back from him. But I only offered up a frail smile and climbed out, pretending this was real. Pretending I lived in a world where others' actions were sincere. One where I didn't have to question my every thought and decision. One where handsome men offered to teach me how to drive and made me peanut butter sandwiches.

But most of all, one where I was confident that I hadn't thrown my life away for nothing.

Okay, it wasn't for nothing.

No . . . it was for *everything*.

I handed over the forms I'd received from my doctor to the front receptionist, thrumming my fingers over the desk. I ran a hand over my smile to ensure it was real. I hadn't expected to feel this way. I'd walked in so unsure and lost. I still felt that way, yes, but I also felt confident in my ability to withstand the challenges coming my way.

I'm having a baby. A real-life baby.

My lungs burned with the desire to laugh, to cry out in relief. I hadn't felt this courageous, this empowered, since . . . since . . . well, I didn't know. But I loved it. I said goodbye to the receptionist and grabbed my belongings, promising myself I'd chase this feeling more often.

The radio gods must've sensed my high, because just as I was leaving, the hit sensation "Get Back Up Again" from *Trolls,* sung by none other than the troll Poppy, played on the overhead speakers. I laughed, sucked back into the memory of when Elle demanded I watch this with her and her kids after I'd left Declan.

She'd played this song on repeat for a whole week, probably hoping it would take root in my heart.

At the time, I'd hated Poppy. Loathed her entirely.

She was relentlessly optimistic, and every time she broke out into song, I wanted to strangle her with her fluffy hair. But now, you could paint me pink and name me Queen of the Trolls. I spun on my heel and kicked open the front door, singing, "There's nothing getting in my way—"

"Son of a—"

The door slammed shut, blocking out the rest of my unsuspecting victim's curse after I whacked—literally whacked—them with the door. I bolted outside, my worst fear coming true when I found the devil on his knees.

"Brooks?"

He looked up, blood dripping down his hand from where he cupped his nose. But rather than cussing me out, he asked, "Are you okay?"

I ignored him and reached into my bag, pulling out a wad of napkins. I swatted his hands when he reached for them. "Let me." I knelt, holding his gaze as I replaced where his hand had been, gently holding the tissues to his nose. "Does it hurt?"

His lips moved against my palm as he ignored my question. "You were crying."

"I'm fine," I whispered, wishing I'd brought makeup to cover my blotchy cheeks. "I'm so sorry, Brooks. I wasn't paying attention—"

He stopped me, grabbing my free hand with his clean one, giving it a squeeze. "Don't. It was my fault for trying to go inside."

I stared at where our hands touched, my stomach clenching. "Why were you coming inside?"

Maybe Brooks was suffering from blood loss—or a concussion—but his thumb skimmed over the top of my hand. "I was worried about you."

I swallowed, a flush of heat filling me, and dropped his hand. Guilt for not telling him what my appointment was for consumed me, and I retrieved another napkin, ignoring the authentic concern in his eyes. "I hope I didn't break it," I said when I released his nose, letting him take over applying pressure. "I'll check inside to see if they have wipes. You go back to the Jeep."

I waited until he walked away to dart into the clinic, grabbing a handful of wipes from the bathroom. I ran back outside, this time song free—I'd never sing again—and made my way back to the Jeep. "Hi," I huffed, closing the door behind me. I paused and looked him over. His skin was flushed and irritated, and blood smeared down his lips, but his nose looked straight.

I swatted his hand again when he reached for the wipes. This was the least I could do. "Please let me." Without waiting, I placed my hand on his jaw, his short beard bristly against my palm. He winced as I tried to clean him, and I lightened my touch. "I'm so sorry."

"It's okay." His words were a puff of air against my skin. He adjusted himself to fully face me as I leaned over the center console. His throat bobbed, his freckles so near and enticing, reminding me we hadn't been this close since the night he'd invited me onto his lap. "How was your appointment?"

I smiled. Not even busting Brooks's nose could dim that bliss just yet. I was estimated to be thirteen weeks along, and the ultrasound in my bag revealed a baby that looked like a bean with legs, but I was happy. Terrified, overwhelmed—but happy. "It was good. Really good."

His fingers brushed the side of my arm, so teasingly gentle. "So . . . everything's okay?"

I looked at him, and for the first time, I thought I saw a flicker of myself in those earthy green eyes. Here he was with blood seeping out of his throbbing nose, pain I'd inflicted—yet Brooks was concerned about me. *About me.* He'd set aside his needs for me, somehow caring about my well-being more than his own. And all I could think was that I kind of might like him to experience what I was feeling. That I wanted to ease some of his pain, like he was trying to do for me.

Bravely, boldly, I brushed my thumb over his cheek. "Everything's perfect, Brooks."

Chapter Sixteen

"Where are all the babies?" I leaned against the window, the valley along the highway barely visible in the evening light, the last of the warm hues washing over the elk. I'd expected Brooks to speed back to Wallowpine immediately—I did smash his nose, after all—but he'd insisted on getting food. Something about a mom-and-pop joint with fried chicken capable of healing wounded egos. But I must have only jolted him further when I scrunched my nose at it and munched on the fries instead. If he was offended, he didn't let it show, not even protesting when I asked if we could stop by Walmart, needing to stock up on essentials I hadn't found in Wallowpine.

Brooks raised a dark brow. One arm stretched toward me, his hand resting on the back of my seat, the other on the steering wheel. "The what?"

"The baby elk." I dipped my head toward the valley. "I haven't seen any in the herds."

"They're called gangs, not herds," he explained with a smug smile. "The females tend to drop them in early June, so they've had a few months to grow. But they're in there."

"Hmm." I tapped my fingers against my knee. "You're a forest ranger, right?"

"I am."

I fiddled with a loose thread on my jeans, biting my lip. "And what do you do exactly? Besides pulling over innocent drivers?"

He raised a brow, and amusement gleamed in his eyes. "Innocent isn't the term I'd use. Maybe annoying." He nudged my shoulder with his hand, and I did my best to hide my smile, noting his touches were becoming more frequent. It wasn't like he'd avoided it before—*hello, I sat on his lap*—but he'd never touched me casually. And I liked it. Maybe I was growing on him. Maybe he wasn't as bad as I thought. "You were the first, by the way. I'd never pulled anyone over before."

I snorted. Yeah, right. I'd bet anything that Brooks handed out speeding tickets like Oprah gave away cars. It was why I said, "Did you like it so much that you couldn't resist pulling over Jake and Wren a few days later?" I grinned at the sight of his blooming red cheeks, unable to stop myself from teasing him further. "And while we're at it—what were you planning on doing if it had been me getting hot and heavy with someone?"

His jaw line tightened, and my smile faltered under his dark, intense gaze. But his finger was soft as it teased my hair, skimming my neck. I was now truly curious to know what he'd have done, but rather than answer my question, he said, "My job is basically how it sounds. I'm law enforcement for the Forest Service. I tend to the forests, make sure campgrounds are being taken care of. Check permits. Stop morons who think they're Leatherface from illegally chopping down trees."

I laughed, seizing the change of conversation. "Do you like it?"

"I do. I like living here, and I'm not one for being indoors much, so it made sense. I hated those years of school though, especially living in the city," he said, surprising me when he continued on, "but if I'd known my dad would pass away last year, I wouldn't have done it. My schedule is decently flexible, but I can only help Nolan and Levi so much at the shop—and they're drowning as it is."

I stared at my hands in my lap, questioning what I should do. I had no experience with deer, but I imagined Brooks was similar—they both spooked easily. Maybe it would've been wise to be satisfied with what he'd already given me, to admire him from afar. But I wanted more. "How long has the business been in your family?"

He furrowed his brows, pausing to think it over. "Somewhere around seventy years—my grandfather started it when my dad was a kid. He was an only child, so the business was passed down to him." He grew silent, and I fought the urge to look up from my lap, letting him have his privacy as he made himself vulnerable. "When my dad died, we didn't know what to do. We'd never discussed who would take over the shop. Nolan's the only one who really worked side by side with him—and he'd gripe about it every day. But with everything up in the air, we all went in on the shop. Nolan and Levi own most of it, but I have a small share, too. I wanted to keep a piece of my dad." He let out a quivering breath, and I looked up. His gaze was hard and intent on the road, but his voice was frail. "I'm not sure any of us imagined owning the shop, but we definitely never imagined running it without our dad."

I blinked the moisture in my eyes away, not wanting to taint one moment of what he'd shared with me. What he'd *trusted* me with. I reached up and grabbed his hand where it rested on the top of my seat. I squeezed it as I teased, "Something tells me your dad was a real handful if he ended up with the three of you as sons."

He glanced at our joined hands. "Something tells me he pulled some strings in heaven and brought you here to raise a little hell for us."

I laughed, a single tear streaming free. "I'm innocent."

"You're something," he murmured, the corner of his mouth hitched up in a smile. He dropped my hand, placing both of his back on the wheel. "Are you ever going to tell me what led you here? You said your fiancé didn't want to be a family anymore . . . Did he leave you?"

I stiffened, feeling the words clog in my throat. But I willed myself not to shut down, especially after Brooks had opened himself up. I needed to talk, to put down roots. "No, I left him." It was the truth—a slight edge of it. The wholeness of it was Declan had left me even when I was right beside him. "We wanted different things."

He nodded but asked nothing more. Giving me space, I realized. Space I would've usually accepted—but I wanted to share more. Maybe today had given me closure, the ability to accept that Declan and I were truly over. "I met him when I was eighteen. I was in my freshman year at a community college, one that offered me enough in scholarships and financial aid," I explained, though the details didn't matter. "Declan was twenty-six at the time. He attended Stanford and was almost done with law school. We had no reason to cross paths, but a girl from my creative writing class asked me to tag along with her to one of their parties."

I paused, remembering how it felt to be eighteen and unconfident, struggling to find my place. But that hadn't deterred Declan from approaching me that night. I could still feel how my heart had fluttered. He was so handsome, driven, and successful—and he was talking to me. He sought me out like I was the only person in the room.

I'd never experienced that before.

It was warm and muggy, August heat in full effect when I stepped into the house party, where I was swarmed with sweaty bodies and billowing puffs of smoke. I glanced around in search of Claire—was that her name?—but I'd lost her shortly after we arrived. I wanted nothing more than to go home, but with the rapidly growing pile of empty red Solo cups and glossy, dazed eyes of the strangers around me, it felt wrong to ditch her.

Needing a moment, I stepped out into the hall, the pungent fumes of smoke reminding me too much of home. How was it that my mom never smoked, but she'd always found a boyfriend who did? I leaned against the wall and closed my eyes, just as a crisp voice said, "You lost, butterfly?"

Warily, I opened my eyes and stared at the handsome man with cropped honey hair and warm eyes. His smile was even brighter, and I knew he wasn't talking to me. "Butterfly?" He smiled wider and reached for me, his finger skimming the clip in my hair. "Oh," I said, realizing he meant the butterfly clip in my hair. I'd borrowed it from Claire on the drive over, liking how it resembled the ones I'd worn as a little girl. "No, I'm not lost. My friend will be here any second."

"Oh?" He raised a brow and leaned his shoulder against the wall, his frame tall and athletic, on the leaner side. I wondered if he could hear how fast my heart was beating. That I was nervous and fibbing about Claire joining me. "Do you mind if I disagree with you on that? I think you'll be inclined to hear my case."

I sputtered a laugh. "Your case?"

"My case." He leaned in, his voice real low. "I'd be happy to share the evidence I've gathered since I watched you walk through the door twenty minutes ago."

I bit my lip, my stomach swirling with nerves. Doing my best to hide my excitement, I crossed my arms over my chest. "Let's hear it."

He pushed off the wall. "I'll need your name, butterfly." I laughed, shaking my head while he paced in front of me, making a show of himself despite the people around us. "Oh, you're going to make me work for it, aren't you?"

It was a constant effort not to squirm beneath his gaze, the confidence there. Forcing myself to mirror it, I raised my brow. "I'll tell you if you win your case."

His eyes sparkled as he grinned, seeming to enjoy this game. "Right—well," he started, pacing before me. "You see, I was right and ready to leave. I'd done my due diligence and made an appearance at my friend Tyler's party. I sat on that crusty couch over there and didn't complain when, not one, but two drinks splattered onto me. But"—he paused mid-step—"you walked in. And though I was forced to sit there while a couple was getting handsy with one another beside me, I hardly noticed them. I mean, how could I look anywhere but at this small, timid butterfly? Your eyes fluttered to every part of the room, yet you . . . you stayed in the corner. Watching. Alone. At first, I felt sorry for you. I assumed you were longing to join in with the others, searching for your place. But . . ."

My stomach dropped, splatting to my feet. Where was this going? I craned my neck up, holding his gaze as he said, "The longer I watched, the more I realized you weren't watching them out of longing . . . you were just watching. Absorbing. I could see the magic dancing in your eyes, the thoughts weaving behind your pretty little face. And I thought . . . that's a girl who's lost." He leaned closer, and I swallowed as we shared quiet rasps of air. "But not in a hopeless, help-me sort of way. Like someone who just hasn't found their place yet. But they keep searching, wandering, believing that it's out there. And they won't settle until they've found it."

I willed my breaths to slow, for my trembling lip to still. I'd never stood this close to a man—boys, yes, but this was a man—never had one speak to me in such a demanding way, absorbing my attention. My voice was low, timid. "You make a compelling case. And I can't help but wonder if you're speaking from experience?"

He blew out a low laugh and stepped forward, his arms caging me in. "I might know a thing or two about being lost . . . but that was before I saw you, butterfly."

I smiled, and he did, too. He had to know how cheesy this was—but wow, I loved it. I held still, frozen as he leaned in and murmured, "Name, please."

My hands hung at my side. I wanted to touch him, but I was afraid he'd disappear if I did. Or that I'd vanish and never be noticed again. "I never said if you won your case."

"Hmm . . ." With one arm braced against the wall, the other lowered, brushing my hip. "Two things you should know. First: my name's Declan Hallsy." His fingers toyed with the edge of my shirt, and a thrill brewed within me. "I'm confident you'll be acquainted with it soon enough. Second: I always win." His nose skimmed mine, his breath hot and sinful. "You remember how I said you wouldn't settle until you found your place? I'm the same in that way, butterfly. And if I have to clip your wings to keep you with me, then so be it. So please, put me out of my misery and tell me the name of the woman who's captivated me without so much as lifting a finger."

I rasped a breath, my head feeling funny and light—not from a drink but from his words. I'd never felt this way. Pursued. Wanted. Important. Without moving, letting him string me along, I said, "My name's Shay."

"Shay." His smile was so near I could almost taste his satisfaction. "Last name?"

I swallowed, unable to think with him so close. When was the last time I'd taken a full breath? "It doesn't matter. I don't use it." It was Davis—my mother's last name. But the more she drifted out of my life, the less I used it. It didn't feel like I was a part of her anyway.

He hummed, his hands cupping my jaw. His lips taunted me, on the edge of brushing mine. "Maybe someday you can have mine."

I blinked rapidly, shaking the moment away. My stomach twisted as I thought of Shay from a lifetime ago. If only I'd known then what I knew now. Before I might've spiraled, Brooks's finger skimmed the back of my neck. I hadn't realized he'd put his arm behind me again.

Fearing I'd wander down another memory, I cleared my throat and continued on, "It was just my mom and me, growing up. She wasn't the most . . . involved. I thought I didn't mind it, but when I look back, I think I was desperate for any sort of attention. So I fell hard for Declan. Fast too." I blew out a shaky laugh, rubbing my fingers across my palms. "I was used to taking care of things, even taking care of my mom—but all of a sudden, I had this man wanting to take care of me. And it felt so nice to be wanted that I didn't hesitate to drop out of school and move in with him."

I wanted to throttle the Shay from all those years ago. Not for loving Declan, but for giving up her dreams to support his. At the time, it made sense. I didn't need to work; he would provide plenty for our family with his career, his success and his dreams. But my dreams—they were taking me away from him. And he wanted to marry me.

He wanted me.

I swallowed, the truth bitter. Part of me knew now all that was crap. Declan had been failing, struggling to pass his exams. I'd never been a natural student, but I'd worked hard and applied myself. And when he saw me doing well—succeeding without him—he wanted to squash it.

And I let him.

"He proposed before I'd even known him a year. It was quick—but I thought I was in love. And I loved the idea of love. I wanted so badly to have a family, a real one. And it was good for a while." I rolled my hands into fists, wondering how much of my time with Declan hadn't really been that good at all. He might have proposed to me, but we hadn't taken any steps to get married. Anytime I'd broached the subject, he'd brushed it off, and that was that. As it always was with him. "Declan's . . . expectations for our life together were high. I was trying my best to make him happy, until one day I noticed how different the life I had was from what I'd pictured for myself. I was living entirely for him. And maybe that would've been okay if he'd been living for me. Don't get me wrong, Declan's a hard worker, and he always made sure I had what I needed . . . but I was lonely. At some point, I realized I'd traded my old life for exactly the same one. It was just painted in a different hue."

Brooks's hand cradled the back of my neck, not to hold, but to soothe, reminding me I wasn't in that world anymore. I was making a new one. I peeked up at him through my lashes. His gaze was on the road, yet I felt every bit of his attention. "I don't know if Jake told you this, but a few months before I moved here, I reached out to his daughter to rent the cabin. I was going to leave him."

Eyes still on the road, he softly asked, "Did your ex ask you to stay?"

"I'm not sure Declan's ever *asked* for one thing in his life—he *takes* and *demands*, and that's that. So no, he didn't *ask* me to stay." I froze, wanting to curl up and hide. I hadn't meant to reveal so much. Brooks's jaw was unbearably tight, but his hand . . . his hand was so gentle. I stared, focusing on him, on a man I wondered if I'd misjudged. "In the end, I made the choice to stay. I was scared—I'd let Declan take care of me for so long. I had nothing, and I didn't know if I could survive on my own again. But one day . . . everything shattered. It was like I'd lived behind one-sided glass, but then I could finally see. I knew I was existing to make him happy, and I wasn't living at all. And when I realized Declan had no intention of ever changing, of living for me, for our family—I left."

I'd never forget that moment. The fear and heartbreak I felt. The anger and sorrow.

In an attempt to lessen what I'd shared, afraid I'd made it appear worse than it truly was, I shrugged. "We never made sense anyway. Maybe when I was eighteen, we did—but not anymore."

I hadn't intended on sharing so much. But there was something about Brooks, something safe and solid. Part of me wondered if I should've shared more with him, the true catalyst behind me leaving. Maybe even about my childhood, and how I was afraid I wouldn't be any different than my mom. I could've confided in him about a lot of things, but even sharing what I did had drained me. You didn't fill wells of trust in a day. You did it gradually, over time.

I had plenty of time to build a friendship—I couldn't possibly do more—with Brooks.

Something he seemed to understand. He didn't mention Declan or my mom, or even the lack of a father in my life, but just soothed the tips of his fingers over my neck in delicate circles before returning his hand to the wheel. "How did you end up finding Wallowpine anyway? No offense, but it's hard to imagine you dreaming of a life where you live alone in the middle of the mountains."

I smiled and pinched his thigh. "For all you know, I could be very accustomed to living in cabins where I have to pound on the shower wall three times for the hot water to work."

He pinned me with a skeptical look. "I know it's different now, but you said your ex was wealthy and a lawyer, so I kind of imagined you'd be accustomed to that lifestyle. It's easy to spot a city slicker when they come here—they stand out like a sore thumb. But had I not seen your California license plate, I would've thought you belonged here."

I shrugged, pretending Brooks admitting I belonged in Wallowpine didn't have my heart dancing. "It was his money, not mine. I knew it could always be taken away, so I never let myself get comfortable." I smiled to myself. "And I like living here. Though I won't lie—there are some comforts I miss, like a heater and a floor I don't have to worry about collapsing. And I get scared sometimes being by myself, but I lived in some less-than-ideal places as a kid, so this is nothing. But while we're at it—" I raised my brow at him. "You should open your mind a little. California is more than just Los Angeles or Hollywood, and there are plenty of people there who aren't city slickers, as you call them. My mom and I lived in Northern Cali for a few months, and I loved it."

"You're really something, aren't you?" He gave me a small, amused smile. "You mentioned you'd taken creative writing—does that mean you write?"

"Oh, no." I tucked a piece of my hair behind my ear. "I don't write anymore."

"But you did?" I nodded, hoping he'd take my silence as a sign to let it go, but he asked, "Why did you write before, then?"

I didn't have to think it over. I knew the answer as sure as I knew the sky was blue. It was the same reason why I'd always loved movies and books.

"Because I could be someone else for a while."

I stared out the window, focusing on the sun slowly disappearing behind a grove of trees and not the heat of his gaze. I couldn't help but wonder if he could read me like an open book, if my secrets weren't that hidden. But that didn't stop him from pushing for more. "What made you choose Wallowpine?"

"My friend Elle. Before I first reached out to Jake's daughter, I told Elle about my situation, how I felt stuck. She told me about this place she went with her cousin as a kid—some camp or something. She said: 'Shay, I'd never seen anything like it. There was this giant world, completely unscathed, untouchable.' She thought it was overwhelming, that it would be easy to get lost in." I smiled, my voice no more than a whisper. "And all I could think was how I might like to get lost . . . see if I found something along the way."

Maybe what Declan said to me the night we met was true. Maybe I was lost. Not hopelessly, but confidently. I was wandering, searching for more. For home.

Brooks veered off to the right, and I looked up to find his lights shining on the cabin, surprised at how quickly time had passed. But I was more surprised when Brooks didn't drop me off and leave, but switched off the engine instead. He stared at the wheel, his voice soft and intimate. "I'm sorry for trying to ruin that for you, Shay. For trying to steal your chance at getting lost."

I watched him, waiting for words to leave my mouth. But I had no way of properly conveying my thoughts, not when I didn't understand what I was feeling. "Does this mean you're alright if I stick around?" I teased, even though I knew it would hurt if he admitted he wasn't.

He rested his head on the wheel, looking at me as he smirked. "You're gonna do whatever you want anyway, so I may as well be okay with it."

I rolled my eyes, but reached into my pocket for my phone. "I'll take your number then."

He raised a brow, his eyes gleaming with mischief. "What if I don't want you to have it? For all I know, you'll use it to prank call me at one a.m."

"But what if the aliens come?"

He huffed a laugh and reached for the door handle. "Tough luck, sunshine."

I scowled at his grin. *Did he call me sunshine?* "But we're friends."

Brooks climbed out, and the look he wore was so intense, even wrapped in night's shadows, I couldn't find the will to move. His severe green eyes looked me over, his voice smooth. "You and I both know we aren't friends."

He walked around the back of the Jeep, giving me barely a moment to catch my breath. I didn't know if I was offended or afraid. Had he meant our relationship would at most be cordial, or had he meant . . . something I didn't let myself think about. I couldn't go there with Brooks. Either way, when he opened my door, it felt like my heart was going to pound straight out of my chest.

Chapter Seventeen

Brooks and I didn't continue our driving lessons. I knew we'd agreed I didn't need him around for them, but to say my stomach didn't flip a little that first night I puttered down our dirt lane alone would be an outright lie. And I hadn't heard from him in almost a week. Maybe he really did have no interest in being friends.

But I didn't let that keep me from Nolan or Levi. There was something about them I craved to be around. It was why I'd suggested to Layne we meet at their store to work on her college applications.

"Remind me again why, in order for a college to consider me, I have to write an essay on a setback I faced and how it affected my life," Layne whined from where we sat in the back of the store, at the counter for game and fish licenses and tags.

I shrugged, not remembering a thing I'd written for my own essay. "It can't be that hard to think of something."

"I know one: how about last weekend when you dropped that pot on my foot?"

I rolled my eyes and closed my notebook, not sure why I'd bothered. The page was bare. "And how did that affect your life?"

"My big toe aches. I'll probably walk with a limp the rest of my life." She snagged a carrot out of the bag I was munching from. "With a story like that, no waiting list will ever know my name. Or maybe I'll write about how traumatized I was from that time you almost barfed all over me."

"Be sure to send them a picture of your mangled toe," Nolan called, carrying a set of boxes to the back. "I hear folks pay big bucks for photos of feet."

"Gross," Layne and I said at the same time. She followed that up by asking, "Hey, what did you write your college essay on? Or did you not have to write one with that fancy baseball scholarship of yours?"

"You played college baseball?" I asked, unable to help myself from wondering if Brooks had too—namely if he'd worn *baseball pants*. Move over, Wranglers.

"Yes." Nolan set the boxes down, rattling the counter. "And I don't know what I wrote it on. That was a long time ago." Before either of us could ask more, he said, "You should go talk to Levi up front. He's enrolled in some online classes right now. Maybe he can help."

I waited until Layne had walked away to ask, "Levi's in school?"

"Yup." His tone was gruff as he opened a box full of painting supplies. "He dropped out of his graphic design school after Dad passed away, but Brooks and I kind of made him take some generals online to keep him busy. Pretty sure he's half-assing his work, so he'll probably flunk out."

I raised my brow. I was still learning about Levi—all of them, really—but even I thought it seemed out of character for him. But then I remembered how he'd confided in me that his brothers sort of babied him. Maybe his heart wasn't in school.

Nolan pointed to the paint can at my feet. "Can you grab that? I'm setting this stuff out back."

"He dropped out of art school?" I asked, following him out with the can.

"Yeah." He kicked the back door open and set the boxes on the ground beside what looked to be wood flooring. "I keep hoping he'll pick his art up again—but I haven't seen him put too much effort into it."

I internally winced, knowing Levi *had* put effort into his art. For me, for a map I'd yet to see. Silently promising to do better, I looked at Nolan, noting the tension in his shoulders. "Is everything okay?"

He sighed, and for a moment he looked like he'd answer honestly, but he didn't have the chance before the back door opened and a woman I didn't recognize popped her head out. She glanced at me and then Nolan before she said, "Did you not order me those kale chips? I couldn't find them on the shelf, and I need them for that diet I'm starting—"

"I'll be right in," he said, and without a second glance, the woman left, not even pausing when Nolan seemed to deflate.

"Kale chips?" I asked when he made no move to follow her inside, finding it strange that a game store carried those to begin with. I knew nothing about running a business, but I hadn't missed the random items mixed in with the hunting and camping gear.

"Yeah." He rubbed at his shoulder, only to drop his hand when he caught me watching him. He opened the door, motioning for me to go inside. "Gotta keep everyone happy," he muttered, but before I could ask more, he said, "I was supposed to call you last night, but I got home late. Wren's home. Brooks told me to tell you she invited us all over for Sunday breakfast."

I smiled, certain Wren had *insisted* rather than invited. "Do you think your aunt's really up for that?"

"Nothing stops Wren." He shrugged, walking toward the woman waiting for her kale chips before calling over his shoulder, "Oh, and Brooks said to tell you the aliens are coming. Whatever the hell that means."

I laughed, forgetting any worry and unease I had before. I was still smiling when I made it to the front, where Layne was chatting with Levi. "How are you feeling?" I asked. He'd texted me back eventually, confirming Brooks hadn't tied him up to a tree, and he looked completely fine, though that was typical for the Graham brothers. Since I'd met them, not a day had passed when I hadn't thought they were the handsomest men I'd ever seen—even when Brooks was brooding and grumpy. Especially then, but that was beside the point.

"Better," he said, thrumming his fingers on the counter. "Sorry I bailed on you. Kind of figured I'd be a useless driver if I kept pulling over to vomit."

Layne chimed in, "Shay's been throwing up a lot too—almost every day this week. I wonder if there's something going around."

I swallowed, my throat constricting. Levi's eyes were on me, his gaze dark and heavy, and I did my best not to squirm, feeling as though he could see beneath my skin. But if he knew, if he'd put the pieces together, he said nothing of it.

I couldn't keep this to myself much longer.

Chapter Eighteen

"I promise you don't want to taste me," I whined as I crept through the meadow, swatting another bug off my sundress, not realizing until now that the white seemed to attract all sorts of crawling and flying demons. "I am full of peanut butter and carrots, and I can't imagine that'll be very appetizing to you."

I swatted a spider on my knee, wishing I'd stayed in my running gear from earlier. I knelt and yanked up a handful of white wildflowers. I couldn't find any place in town that sold flowers, so this was the next best thing I could give Wren at breakfast this morning. I groaned at a swarm of gnats and bolted back to the cabin just as I heard a rev of an engine. Brooks's truck came into view, coming from the direction of town. I would've stopped and salvaged the last of my dignity, but the sound of a rattle had me running faster.

I stopped at the road, huffing as I adjusted the dress straps that had slipped down my arms, my skin flushed when Brooks pulled up beside me and rolled down his window. "You that excited to see me?" he asked with a smirk.

I blamed my absence of words on the fact I was wheezing down air and not because he'd stunned me stupid. He was so unfairly good-looking—even more so now that I'd gotten a glimpse into who Brooks Graham was. His beard was freshly trimmed, cut close to his face, dark like the smooth, full hair on his head. And those eyes . . . those eyes were fresher, brighter than any grass I'd ever seen.

I shook my head. It had been a few days since I'd seen him. That was all.

"I was getting these for Wren before I left." I raised the sad bouquet of tangled flowers. "Where are you going?" I asked, hating the desperation in my tone, realizing he might be bailing.

"Home. Wren's not feeling up to it."

"Is she okay?" I asked, immediately regretting not doing a better job of checking in on her.

"She's alright. Just tired." He patted the side of his door. "Get in. I'll make you breakfast at home."

He'll make me breakfast?

"You don't need to do that. I have food inside."

"Best to just get in, Shay. Unless you'd like me to toss you in?"

I blinked, blaming the spike in my pulse on the fact I'd just run. "Okay, grump," I murmured and climbed into his truck. I pulled at the hem of my dress, wishing I'd worn pants when I noticed he was wearing a simple gray tee and blue jeans.

"You curled your hair," he said, staring at the soft waves I'd managed to put in, the edge of my hair falling just above my shoulders. "And you're wearing makeup."

I shrugged, crossing and then uncrossing my legs, wishing he'd focus on the road and not me. I'd gotten ready for *me*. Since leaving Declan, it was one of the first times I'd dressed up because I wanted to, not because my fiancé told me I looked like garbage otherwise. But that didn't stop me from muttering, "Next time I'll show up in sweats and a messy bun. I won't even brush my teeth."

He looked at me with a hint of a smile on his lips. "Makes sense to go with your best look."

I scrunched my nose—was he insulting me or not? Deciding on the former, I stared out the window until he pulled up to his cabin and then hopped out, slamming the door behind me before he'd even switched the engine off.

I lingered on his porch steps, feeling weird about entering on my own. In my haste, I hadn't realized I'd left behind the wildflowers until Brooks walked up the pathway with them in one hand, along with a different set of flowers in the other.

He extended the new bouquet to me, keeping the weeds I'd yanked out of the ground. The sun hit the flowers just right, bringing to life the already cheerful yellow petals. "These are for you."

"Oh." My hand crinkled the plastic wrapped around the daffodils. My heart clenched, not solely because I'd never been given such a simple flower—Declan had always done roses—but because no place in town sold flowers.

Had he gone out of town to get these?

Great, now I was an overreacting buttmunch. But I was a pregnant buttmunch—I was allowed to blame hormones. *Sorry, the baby made me do it.* How many times had I heard Elle use that same excuse? As soon as I told the Grahams, I'd go crazy with it.

"They're Wren's favorite," Brooks blurted before I could thank him. He glanced at our feet, hiding his red cheeks. "When she canceled, she told me to go ahead and give them to you."

"Oh, okay." My heart stumbled to a stop. That made more sense. Brooks had no reason to buy me flowers. "Well, I guess you can have the wildflowers then."

He gave me a tight-lipped smile and walked past me. I followed him up the stairs, any and all unease staying outside when I was greeted with a wet snout and pointy ears. "Hi, handsome." I knelt and rubbed his head. I laughed as Cash pushed against me, coating me in slobber and hair as he whined, complaining I wasn't loving him fast enough. "I missed you too. Tell your daddies to let you come play more often."

"Daddies?"

Nolan stood in the kitchen, pouring himself a cup of coffee—this time fully clothed. He grinned, toasting his mug to me. "I kind of like the sound of daddy. Say it again."

"Freak." I whacked him in the chest with my bouquet, only to claim the biggest jerk award when I realized Brooks was placing the wildflowers I'd picked in a mason jar. I gently set mine on the counter, regretting hiding how much the gesture had meant to me. "I'm glad you chose to put on clothes."

"I can take them off if you'd like." He winked, looking me over with nothing but playfulness. "But don't you just look extra beautiful, darlin'. First you bring me flowers—" He snagged the jar of wildflowers, limp petals falling loose. "And now you dress up. I think you're trying to impress me."

I slid onto one of the stools at the counter and shrugged. "You caught me."

"Hey," Levi greeted me, hopping up on the stool beside me. "You look nice."

"Thank you." I smiled—at least two of the Graham brothers thought so. The third, however, leaned against the counter beside the stove, his arms crossed over his chest, silently watching us. Watching me. I fidgeted with my hands in my lap, suddenly worried he regretted inviting me in.

"Can we eat now?" Levi asked, stealing a sip from Nolan's coffee. "Nolan's been guarding the rolls like his life depended on it."

"It did," Nolan insisted, yanking his mug back. "Brooks said he'd sneak Nair into my shampoo if anything happened to his precious cinnamon rolls while he was gone. Why he felt the need to threaten my beautiful hair at four in the morning is beyond me."

I looked at Brooks and raised a brow as Nolan and Levi bickered, the sound already having become a familiar melody. "You made cinnamon rolls?"

"He tried," Nolan scoffed before Brooks even opened his mouth. "None of us are great bakers, but that didn't stop him from stumbling his way through the kitchen last night after Wren canceled."

She'd canceled last night?

Rather than questioning it, I smiled, savoring how scarlet Brooks's cheeks were. I liked it. "I don't know." I put my hands beneath my chin and wiggled my brows. "Brooks makes the best peanut butter sandwiches I've ever had."

"That's because you haven't had mine," Nolan said, reaching for the foiled plate on the counter. "If you're done, I'd really like to eat before Brooks's ego busts the house."

"Like yours already hasn't," Levi muttered, getting up from his seat.

"Hi," I whispered when Brooks sat in the stool beside mine. I waited until his brothers' attention was fully on the cinnamon rolls before I leaned over and placed a fleeting kiss on his cheek. "Thank you for breakfast, and for the beautiful flowers. I'm sorry Wren didn't get them, but I love them. "

He rolled his lips together and nodded, ignoring the gesture. But I didn't mind—he could've wiped it off his cheek, or yelled at me for defiling him. I smiled when he slid me a plate, already topped with a roll. My eyes suddenly burned, threatening to overflow and mimic the creamy icing spilling over the roll's golden edges.

I ate quietly as they conversed, half-heartedly listening to them debate what teams would play in the World Series later this fall. I froze mid-bite, nearly choking as Brooks's thumb brushed my palm beneath the counter. Once. Twice. I swallowed, my throat bobbing as I peeked a glance in his direction. His attention was on his brothers, but his hand was on me. His calloused thumb swept over my hand once more, and my heart raced. I didn't know such intimacy could exist in just an innocent touch.

His hand left mine, but his soothing presence was a constant beside me. My lip trembled, something large and overwhelming filling my chest, my soul. Something I wasn't yet brave enough to acknowledge. And as I finished every bit of deliciousness off my plate, resisting the urge to lick it clean, I couldn't stop myself from wondering if this was what I'd been searching for.

If *they* were what I'd been looking for.

I grabbed their empty plates and carried them to the sink; the least I could do after their kindness was clean the dishes. I was elbows deep in bubbly water when Levi asked, "What do you say, Shay?"

I looked over my shoulder to find each of them watching me expectantly, but I hadn't caught a word of what was said. "About what?"

"We're going camping. You want to come?"

I furrowed my brows, wiping my hands off on a towel. "I've never camped before. I don't have anything."

Levi shrugged. "We have plenty. You can use our stuff."

I glanced between them. There was something suspicious about their smiles. Too broad, eager. "You're all going?"

Nolan grunted when Levi wedged an elbow into his ribs, holding it there as he said, "Yup. We're all going."

"Now?" I asked.

Nolan pushed his brother's arm out of his ribs, shooting him a glare. "Levi and I need to check on a few things at the shop. I messed up on a shipment. But I was just telling Brooks how you both should go early and get things set up."

Brooks muttered something under his breath, and Nolan grinned wider. I opened my mouth to turn them down—sleeping on the ground in tents didn't sound all that appealing. But when I looked at the leftover cinnamon rolls and the flowers, I couldn't bring myself to do it. Not to the men who'd drawn me maps, danced with me, and taught me how to drive. I doubted they had any idea they were teaching me how to *live* again.

I set aside the last plate and leaned against the sink. "You guys aren't going to murder me, right?"

All three answered with a sly grin, but I only felt the heat of one.

Chapter Nineteen

"I thought someone should know where I'm going in case I go missing," I said, holding the phone to my ear as I folded a pair of leggings and crammed them into my bag.

There was the clattering of dishes on the line before Elle asked, "Haven't you already done that?"

"I guess." I switched the phone to speaker so I could slip on my boots. "You've camped here before. What should I expect?"

She laughed under her breath, the sound clawing at my chest. I ached to hear it in person. "I was twelve, and we stayed in cabins." I smiled at the distant sound of squealing laughter. No doubt Elle's two toddlers were up to something. "And it was an all-girls camp. There definitely weren't any hot brothers lingering around."

I made my way to the bathroom, stealing a glance in the smudged mirror to check my appearance. Brooks needed to do a few things before we could leave, so I'd had time to ditch the dress for a pair of jeans. But I almost wished we'd left immediately, if only so I'd stop trying to talk myself out of going. "I don't know," I huffed, adjusting my waistband. I wasn't showing, was more so at that awkward bloating stage, but I'd need to get new clothes soon. "It sounded fun before . . . but now I think it's a bad idea."

"Shay," Elle soothed over the phone, her voice a comforting balm. "You deserve to have fun. Have you gone out at all?"

"No."

"Shay—"

"It would be a waste of time. It can't go anywhere." I'd played it over in my head endlessly. "You know that."

"No, I don't know that," she snapped, and I smiled, easily imagining her eye roll. "What about the grumpy one? Brooks? I thought he was coming around to you."

He was. We were both warming up to one other. And as relieving as it was to not have Brooks against me, I feared the inevitable as we grew closer. I'd have to tell him I was pregnant, why I was truly starting over. I didn't know how he'd react, if he'd be happy for me or full of pity, but my nerves were in knots over it.

I bit my lip and glanced at the daffodils, unwrapped and resting in a vase of water. "We're becoming friends . . . but I don't know. It's hard to trust myself, you know? I get so mad at myself when I think of how blind I was to Declan's shit. Sometimes I can't help but think that if everything hadn't gone down the way it did that I might have never left."

"But you did leave," Elle said, her voice soft, assuring. "You left, and you're better for it. You're free of him, and you can finally live again—hold on. Get that out of your mouth, Lai!" Her voice drifted further from the phone, and there was a series of squeals before she mumbled, "Sorry, it's a madhouse here. I'm running around with my head cut off." I frowned at the exhaustion heavy in her voice, wishing I'd been a better friend and let her vent about her troubles. "Shay, as much as I love Howard and my children and would never give them up, there are days where I'd love to be in your position. Not the crappy stuff—that sucks, obviously." I laughed as she did, doing my best to put myself in her position. An exhausted mom trying to juggle two toddlers, a newborn, a husband, and a home, all while longing to be back at work. "But you're in the middle of nowhere, living in the mountains. Right now, you can live entirely for you. You don't have to worry about a kid peeing behind the sofa or shoving Cheetos in their baby sister's mouth because they 'wanted to share.' Right now, you're free. You have an entire new world at your disposal. Make something of it."

My eyes brimmed with tears, my chest burning with love. "You know I think you're amazing, right, Elle?"

"Say that one more time. Nice and loud—I need to make sure I got that on tape."

"Oh my gosh! Stop recording me, you stalker."

"Oh, don't flatter yourself. Trust me, when you become a mom, you're going to have a million different things running through your mind. This helps me. I can't tell you how many cases I've had where recording conversations has helped push me over the edge."

I raised a brow. "Isn't that illegal?"

"I don't use them in court," she scoffed. "But not everyone is truthful with their words, whether they're innocent or not. This just allows me to dig a little deeper into what they're telling me. It helps me hear the things I might've missed." I peeked out the window at the sound of a door shutting, finding Brooks walking up the driveway. "As I was saying, I know you're afraid. Believe me, I get it. But you can't know joy without pain, Shay. We both know you're accustomed to pain, but it might be time to let yourself chase joy too." The porch steps creaked, and I switched the phone off speaker, grateful I had when the door opened as she continued, "And if that happens to be with a mountain man—then so be it. I bet he's fantastic in bed."

Cheeks burning, I muttered goodbye and flipped the phone shut on her cackling. "Hi," I blurted as I faced Brooks. "All ready?"

"Yeah," he said from the doorway, eyeing the flowers I'd set on my table. "Are you ready?"

"Yup." I waved a hand at myself, apparently believing Brooks to be blind. "I changed, too."

"I noticed." His lips tilted to the side, and I swore there was a flicker of amusement in his eyes. "You look nice. You did before too . . . in case I didn't make that clear."

Nothing was really clear when it came to Brooks.

But I didn't say that and instead scrunched my nose. "Not my best look though, right?"

I fought the urge to squirm as he raked his eyes over me. "I kind of liked how you looked this morning, hollering and running to me."

I rolled my eyes. "There were bugs. Thousands of them."

"I thought you said it was a snake?" he teased with a smile. *He. Is. Smiling.* Oblivious to my awe, he said, "So, there's been a slight change in plans."

"If you need to cancel, it's fine." I made a mental note to stitch up the tear in my heart, surprised by the disappointment seeping through. "I promise."

"No, it's not that," he assured me. "Nolan and Levi aren't coming. Apparently something came up at the shop." He lifted up his ball cap, running his hand through his hair. "But you and I . . . we can still go if you want."

I swallowed. Nolan and Levi weren't coming. But Brooks was here. And we'd be camping alone?

"Do you want to?" I blurted, resisting the urge to fan myself with my hand. I didn't know if it was hormones or if there was a heat wave, but something was going on. "You don't have to—"

"I want to." His gaze darted to the floor, and he bit his lip, a half-hearted attempt to hide his growing smile. "My brothers tend to hog you when we're all together, so it might be nice. I thought we could go on a hike too?"

A small sense of what I'd experienced this morning at breakfast washed over me. An inkling of warmth, comfort—of home. Brooks wanted to spend time with me, and he wasn't trying to hide it, wasn't playing games. And I thought of what Elle had said, how it was time I became acquainted with joy.

Maybe I could experience that with a mountain man.

Chapter Twenty

Living on a mountain and camping in the mountains were two entirely different things. One: there was no bathroom readily available. Meaning all four times I needed to pee on our drive, Brooks had to pull over so I could squat behind a tree.

I'd never been sexier.

Two: if I wanted a roof over my head, I'd have to build it. And trying to shove poles through a tarp and make a home of it was no walk in the park. Or forest. Whatever.

"You are the dumbest creation known to mankind," I scolded and crawled over the flat tent, the pole snagging on the material again. "When I get home, I'm going to invent a tent that builds itself."

"Those already exist," Brooks chimed in from where he sat on a log, firmly planted there ever since I told him I could build it on my own. He'd only brought one tent—for me, since he and his brothers didn't use them, preferring to *rough it.* As if camping wasn't already roughing it. "It's not too late to sleep out under the stars. There's the bed of the truck too."

I considered it for a second, one fleeting second of insanity. But then I remembered I'd be exposed to bears and rabid skunks if I slept in the open. Not to mention, the thin tent acted as an extra layer of protection from Brooks.

I trusted him. But I wasn't so sure I trusted myself.

Hormones. It was ridiculous hormones.

"That's okay," I murmured, silently cursing Elle for her mountain man talk.

Brooks stood and stripped off his red flannel, leaving on his white tee beneath. Despite the clouds brewing in the sky, the sun was warm, beating through the trees encasing our campground, wrapping us in the refreshing smell of pine. "You've really never camped before?"

"When one of my mom's boyfriends kicked us out, we had to sleep in our car for a week. Does that count?" I asked, most of my attention on snapping the pole into place. I froze and looked up, realizing what I'd said.

Brooks must've thought I was kidding, or sensed I didn't want to talk about it, as he cleared his throat and looked up at the sky. "Fishing?"

"Nope."

"Hunting?"

I sat back onto my feet and wiped pine needles off my sleeves. "Do I look like I've hunted before?"

He smirked and crossed his arms over his chest, his forearms flexing. "I don't know. You've definitely got a few looks that could kill."

I stuck out my tongue and directed my attention back to the tent, frowning at the crisscrossed poles. "Are you going to help me or not?"

He laughed, the sound refreshing and full. "You told me not to."

"Help me, Brooks," I whined. I was already on my knees and ready to beg. "I won't survive if I have to fend off mountain lions all night."

He shook his head and knelt down. I smiled and scooted back, ready to watch a master at work, before he stopped me with a hand on my wrist, pulling me close. "Get back over here. I don't want to have to build your tent every time we come out here."

"Okay," I grumbled, even if the thought of him wanting to do this again sent jitters through my body. "How many loaves of bread in exchange for this?"

He laughed and dipped his head like he had a secret to hide. "Just one. I haven't finished the last five you gave me."

I frowned, my heart following suit. "Are they that bad?"

"I love them." His hand slid over mine atop the tent. But before I could feel his warmth, he moved it to his knee. "Now pay attention. You break it, and I'll invite those mountain lions you're so worried about to come sleep in your tent tonight."

Thirty minutes and a few snarky remarks later, my tent was up and standing. All three feet of glorious wonder, suitable for one—two if you snuggled close. I tossed the sleeping bag Brooks had brought me inside and zipped it up. "Thank you."

He dipped his chin and sat on the chopped log he'd dragged into our campsite, large enough to satisfy his *extraordinary* rear end, an asset I verified each time I saw him. I sat across from him in the camping chair he'd brought, an empty rock fireplace separating us, and fiddled with my thumbs.

"So." I clicked my tongue. "Do you and your brothers go camping a lot?"

He nodded. "As much as we can. Less now that we're busier, but we try to make time for it."

I bit my lip, toying with my words. "Did . . . did you do it with your dad?"

"We did. Growing up, we were out here just about every weekend." He paused, clearing his throat. "Sometimes it feels like we lost a lot more than just him, you know? Like he's gone, and we're left trying to figure out what pieces of the life we shared with him we want to keep." I straightened where I sat, surprised by how his words affected me. Our losses were different, our grief not the same, but there was a sort of connection between us. We were both rebuilding, trying to form stone from rubble. My eyes were still on Brooks, my heart warm as he said, "But I'm happy camping's stuck around—I love sharing it with my brothers."

I smiled and shoved the sleeves of my sweater up, wishing I'd worn something less hot. "I like how close you guys are," I admitted. "Even when I first met you and you hated me, I admired that about you."

Brooks straightened like a rod, his brows pinched together. "I didn't hate you."

I shrugged. "It's okay if you did. I wasn't that crazy about you either."

"I didn't hate you," he repeated in a whisper, his voice somehow firmer than before. "You scared the hell out of me, Shay. If I'm being honest—you still kind of do."

"What?" I scoffed, pointing a finger his way. "I was on the verge of peeing my pants when you pulled me over."

He laughed, and I wished the firepit wasn't between us. I wanted to feel his laugh, share his heat. "Imagine how I felt. I thought I was pulling over some city slicker, and instead I found the most stunning woman I'd ever seen."

I licked my lips, my cheeks roasting. "You made me walk to see if I was drunk."

"You named your car Betsy!"

"You interrupted Jake and Wren making out because you thought it was me!"

It was his turn for his cheeks to burn, a deep shade of red. But rather than hiding it, he faced me fully. "I was jealous. It's as simple as that."

I swallowed and ran a hand across my neck. My skin was hot, feeling his eyes everywhere. Rather than starting down that trail, I backtracked to another. "Why are you scared of me, Brooks?"

He shifted on his log, rubbing a hand over his jaw. "You brought up a lot."

"Oh." I cleared my throat and glanced up, frowning at the unruly dark clouds forming more and more. "I'm sorry."

"No, I'm sorry." He stood and closed the small distance between us, surprising me when he knelt, putting us almost at eye level. "I never apologized for how I treated you before, and I need to. I'm sorry, Shay."

I picked at a loose thread on my jeans. "It's fine."

"Please look at me." His voice was a gentle caress. "Please, sunshine."

I blinked a few times, hiding the emotions threatening to engulf me before I looked up, meeting his gaze. He watched me, his thumb brushing my knee. "*Nothing* about how I treated you is okay. What I did to you was wrong. I hate that you'd even try to excuse my behavior. You don't deserve that. Not from me or anyone else."

"Why?" I asked, focusing on his hand palming my knee. "Why did you want me to stay away so bad? What did I do?"

"You did nothing." His voice was low and rough, lined with regret. "What I do, how I react—that's on me. But I was being honest. You scare me, Shay," he repeated, his throat bobbing. "I don't know if you know this, but my mom left us when I was ten."

He stopped and broke our gaze, looking at the hand I'd placed over his. I wanted him to understand I was truly present. I cherished him opening up and apologizing. Especially apologizing. "She'd left a few times before that—just for a few days. But she always came back. Except that time she didn't.

"I waited for her. Each day, I'd come home from school, expecting her to be there. My dad was the same way, but deep down, we both knew she wouldn't come home. Nolan and Levi were younger—hell, Levi doesn't actually remember her—so I know it's different for them. But I remember. I remember when she'd get drunk and reveal how trapped she felt. How she'd scream at my dad that she regretted marrying him. Or that we were holding her back." He stared at our joined hands, his other one clutching my calf, as though he was afraid those memories would drag him away. "I was awake the night she left. I heard my dad begging her to stay, offering to move—anything to keep the family together." He choked on a laugh, his blinks quick. "He even told her they could get divorced, but he begged . . . begged her not to leave her boys."

Hot tears streamed down my cheeks, but I gripped his hand tighter, refusing to leave him in this. I knew all too well the ache abandonment leaves, the questions that haunt you. *Why am I not enough?* "I ran outside when I heard her car start. I thought I could make a difference. But when I asked her to stay, to choose us—she didn't."

He let out a tight breath, and we sat in silence, leaning into one another, his story seeming to take a lot out of both of us. My soul throbbed for him, aching to comfort that small child within. To remind him he was loved. That he wasn't holding anyone back. That he himself was helping me build my own wings, empowering me more than he knew.

"I've spent a lot of time hating my mom. It wasn't until I was older that my dad shared with me that she battled some inner demons, that the reason she lasted as long as she did was because she loved us. But deep down, she didn't know how. Didn't think she was worthy of our family," Brooks admitted. "I don't know if I believe that, but I thought I'd come to terms with it. But then my dad died, and you showed up, and I thought you were like her. That you were only here looking for your fill. You'd take and leave nothing in return. Because that's exactly what my mom did, whether it was intentional or not. She stole a lot of years and moments that should've been happy. And when I saw you with my brothers—" His breaths were shaky as he lowered his head, his hair brushing my forehead. "I love my brothers, but we have our problems. It's a bit better now, but when my dad died, there were days when I couldn't get Levi to leave his room. When I wasn't doing that, I was trying to stop Nolan from drowning himself every waking moment in beer. And me . . ." He shook his head and cleared his throat. "But we've always dealt with our problems together, as a family. And when I saw you with them, when I felt even a fraction of that beautiful light you carry—I felt like I was ten years old again. I was terrified you were going to come into the home I've fought to keep together and destroy it."

"Brooks," I whispered, my throat aching. "I'm not going to take anything from you." I inched closer to him and ran my fingers up his arms until I was cupping his jaw, his beard bristly against my palm. "You're safe with me. I promise."

His fingers wrapped around the back of my knees, and he pulled me closer, into his heat. I closed my eyes and rested my forehead against his. I wasn't sure how we'd gotten here, hadn't expected him to share so much. Yet I wasn't surprised at all. When you spend so long alone, carrying the weight of those around you, eventually you collapse. But I wouldn't let Brooks break. No, I'd support him, be his friend—let him know it wasn't his responsibility to take care of everyone. And I would never take anything from him.

But I needed to be honest with him. I knew that more than ever as I felt his breath on my lips. He was my friend—he deserved the truth.

His fingers tightened on my legs, and I shuddered, but before I could open my mouth, he asked, "How do you feel about going on a little hike? You've been wanting to, right?"

I nodded, at a loss for what to do. Deciding I'd tell him later, I let my hands linger on his jaw, waiting until he stood. He shifted to his truck, and I straightened as he pulled out a backpack. He grabbed my water, tucking it inside. "If you want to put this on, you can," he said, offering his red flannel. "It'll feel cooler than your sweater."

"Thank you," I said, accepting it. I moved to the front of the truck and changed, the slight breeze tickling my skin. When I buttoned the flannel together, the hem fell past my thighs. I walked back around the truck, folding the sleeves so they wouldn't hang over my hands.

I finished and looked up, catching Brooks watching me, his mouth slightly open. It grew into a smile, his eyes crinkling at the side. "That's it. That's your best look."

I tucked my hair behind my ear, staring at my tightly laced boots. I was finally going to hike in them. "I like it, too."

His eyes beamed like he might say more, but he only tilted his head toward the trail. "The hike's not very long, but we should get going—I'm not sure if that storm is going to hit or not."

I nodded and followed him, the clouds drifting in closer, swarming in on the sun. I walked beside him, the trail a mixture of weathered grass and dirt. We weaved through the forest trees, the trunks both slim and broad, and in the far distance there was the trickling of a creek. Despite what we'd just shared, how we'd held one another, we didn't touch, didn't speak. But I didn't mind the silence. I never had—at least, not when I knew I wasn't alone in it.

Brooks and I were carved from the same tree, yet different branches. I couldn't imagine how he must've felt, not only as a young boy, but as an adult. He believed his mother didn't choose him or even love him. I had no relationship with my mom, and I didn't believe I ever would. But if I sorted through the tangles of her neglect, I could see a mother who *stayed*.

Sometime after that weekend when she'd gone to that concert and left me alone, I mistakenly mentioned it to a classmate. I bragged about how cool it had been—hiding the fact I'd spent most of the weekend curled up, crying. I sold my story well enough, though, because she went to her parents and asked when she'd be old enough to stay home alone, complained it wasn't fair that I had. It turned into a whole ordeal.

One where my mom was reported to Child Protective Services.

I'd never seen her so angry, so embarrassed at what I'd done. And shockingly, despite the lack of attention and care I received, I was terrified of being taken from her. Something she swore—threatened—would happen if I ever told anyone another detail of what occurred in my life again.

So I didn't.

The times when I woke up to an empty apartment I kept to myself. When I relied entirely on school meals for a while because my mom couldn't manage our money, I told no one. And through every pang of discomfort I felt from the lingering gazes of my mom's more trashy boyfriends, I stayed silent.

Now, I could see the manipulation. How she scared me into silence so she wouldn't have to change. But maybe . . . maybe she'd done it out of desperation, too. Maybe she hadn't wanted to lose me.

I shook my head and did my best to clear my thoughts. It would take more than a day—probably more than my entire life—to unravel what my mother had done, why she'd never told Noah he had a daughter. To understand why Brooks's mother didn't choose him or his brothers. I had no experience in raising children, but I believed with everything I was that I would never run from my child.

I would be better than what had happened to me.

I looked up when Brooks's fingers brushed mine. I hadn't realized he'd slowed down or heard how ragged my breaths were. But nothing could stop my smile. It wasn't bold or grand. It was soft and gentle, much like what lay between us. Whatever that might be.

I didn't know what I believed in, if there was an afterlife. Some sort of home where our souls rested. But I couldn't help but wonder if Brooks's father really had guided me here. Brought me to his boys—to Brooks.

And maybe what I thought was too complicated really wasn't that complicated at all.

I grazed the back of his hand, and he threaded our fingers together. It was the only acceptance he needed. He held me close, his arm brushing mine as we descended the hill into a meadow.

The ground was flat, with willowy grass and glistening ponds of water, the mountain range beyond us. It was wide and open, with bursts of wildflowers, and if I listened hard enough, I thought I heard the echo of an elk's bugle in the distance. I shook my head, remembering how red Layne's cheeks were when I'd told her I hid under the blankets the first time I heard the high-pitched shriek, afraid of what crept outside. It had taken her five minutes to calm down before she'd explained it was a bull elk's mating call that had woken me up, not bigfoot.

I gripped Brooks's hand tighter as we walked, the ground softening into mud the closer we drew to the water. I thought he might lead us to the water's edge, but he stopped halfway through the meadow. "This is far enough," he said, adjusting his hat to look up at the sky. "We can do a longer hike another day—I just don't want us to get caught in the storm."

"Okay," I agreed quietly, my lips curling up. "I'd like that."

"Yeah?" Brooks asked, his own lips fighting off a smile. I nodded, and only then did he unveil how happy that seemed to make him.

His smile was full and bright, distracting enough I could've stared at him for hours. Choosing not to make a fool of myself, I pivoted and scanned the meadow, my gaze landing on the tree line surrounding us. It wasn't all flourishing, I realized, finding a burned patch right in the middle of it. The bare, ash-ridden trees were stark among the evergreens.

"That's a controlled burn zone," Brooks said, following my line of sight. "We don't do them often, but they have their benefits. Especially when it comes to preventing wildfires."

I stared at the bleak, dark ground, stricken. "You burned it on purpose?"

"Well, I didn't specifically. There was a group of fire experts who came in."

I couldn't find the words to respond, didn't understand the tears brimming in my eyes. All I could do was stare at the charred trees and imagine what they used to be. Strong, beautiful—powerful. And that had all been stolen from them by a single match.

How could they be so careless?

"Shay," Brooks murmured, filling my line of sight. He dipped his head, the concern in his eyes carrying into his words. "What's going on in your head right now?"

I looked up into his eyes. They were so green and inviting, and for the first time I noticed the golden flecks within them. "Sorry." I wiped at the edge of my eyes with my sleeve. "I think I'm just tired." He nodded, but rather than suggesting we go back to camp or head home, he stood there.

Waiting.

I forced a smile, but it wobbled when I said, "Why'd you have to hurt them? They were probably so happy and beautiful. But you burned them, and now they're ugly and ruined."

Brooks grinned as my voice cracked, but before I could call him a jerk, he said, "You're so damn adorable. You know that?" He pulled me close without hesitation, wrapping me up tight in his arms. "They were beautiful," he said, his chin resting atop my head. "But they weren't growing." I shuddered a breath against his chest, not understanding where this was going. "Not all fires are bad, sunshine. They can prevent wildfires, help clean up debris and invasive species that are hurting the forest. They rejuvenate the land and encourage growth that might have never happened. There are even seeds that are dependent on fire."

He pulled back, just enough to sneak his fingers beneath my chin and bring my gaze to his. "It might be hard to understand, looking at it straight on, hard to see it as anything but burned to hell. But I promise," he whispered, tucking a loose strand of hair behind my ear, "in a few years, that spot is going to be stronger and more beautiful than it was before."

A tear slid past my lashes, warm and full on my cheek. I felt silly, crying over something that didn't affect me at all. And I believed Brooks when he promised those trees would be full of life again. But it was more than that. It was about my own pain, my own burns.

I used to be full of life. And Declan saw me and ruined me. I was nothing more than a hollow shell of who I used to be. *Empty. Forgotten. Done.* But maybe . . . maybe I wouldn't always be this way. Maybe I too could grow from fire and ash. Maybe I could take this pain and mold it into something more.

Maybe it was a fool's hope, but I needed something to believe in.

"Do you think it works that way with people, too?" I asked, praying my voice didn't sound as weak as I felt.

If Brooks saw me as weak, he didn't voice it. Instead, he cradled the back of my neck with his hand, easing more pain than he knew. "I didn't believe it until I met you."

There wasn't a piece of me that considered delving deeper into what he said. Declan had a way with words, had always known what to say. But Brooks . . . I didn't believe words were easy for him. I could see how terrified he was of sharing his thoughts, his soul. He feared he wouldn't be enough.

But he'd brought me out here today because he knew I wanted to come. And then when I needed to be built up, he put himself on the line to do so.

He deserved to know he was more than enough.

I pushed up on my toes and wrapped my arms around his neck. Before I could make another move, Brooks's mouth was on mine.

The kiss was slow at first, our breaths mingling as we acquainted ourselves, learned how we fit together. His fingers glided into my hair, and my arms tightened around his neck, leaving nothing between us. Yes, there was pain and fear of the unknown, mountains left to climb. But in the midst of that, two beautifully broken people were whole.

"Shay," he whispered, and thunder rumbled, cool raindrops pelting our skin.

I smiled and slipped my tongue out to taste the drops on his lips. He groaned and coaxed my mouth open further, asking for more, and I let him have it. I wanted him to have me. My hair was damp, plastered against my neck, but I clung to him. To his warmth, his courage—I needed all of him.

And as he kissed me, as he held me so intimately, tenderly close, I thought I could breathe again.

I whined as he pulled back, his breath hot against my skin. Only when I opened my eyes did I see how badly it was pouring, both of us drenched to the bone. He smoothed my hair out of my face and placed his ball cap on top of my head, raindrops falling down his lashes. "Let's get back to camp and get you warm."

I grabbed his hand and held on as we jogged up the hill, even though an impatient, needy part of me wanted to stay. By the time we'd returned to camp, the forest was soaked and slick, rain beating through the trees. I started for the tent, but he snatched my waist and tugged me to the truck. He opened the back door and let me in first, slamming it shut behind him. I shivered, my clothes sopping and cold, clutching to my skin. But I was feverish when I looked at Brooks and saw the desire in his eyes.

I straddled his lap and did what I wasn't brave enough to do the first night he'd taught me to drive. His tongue teased my lips and I opened them, letting him take all of me. I ran my fingers up his neck and into his sleek hair, the contrast of hot and cold sending my nerves into a frenzy. He lifted his hat off my head and dug his fingers into the back of my thighs, hitching me up tighter against him.

"We can stop," he rasped, his breaths heavy. "We've got time. I'm in no rush, sunshine. I brought peanut butter, I can make—"

I laughed against his lips, fingers gripping his hair. "As much as I love your sandwiches, there are other things I want more right now." I leaned in and nipped at his ear, the knowledge of being *wanted* and *needed* making me brave. "I want you."

That was all the confirmation Brooks needed. He cupped my jaw and kissed me fiercely, like a man who'd toed the line of self-control too long. We broke away, and I shivered, gasping as he peppered featherlight kisses down my neck. I slipped my fingers beneath his damp shirt, and he pulled back, letting me lift it over his head. Hot, heavy fog coated the windows as I sat back on his thighs and ran my fingers up his chest, dark hair dusted over his tightly corded frame. "Are you real?" I traveled his core, marveling. I'd never seen such strength and tenderness in a body. "This feels too good to be true—I'm afraid it's not real."

There was no hesitation, no pause on his part. "We're real, Shay." His hand was careful on the back of my neck as he watched me, waiting for me to lead, I realized. I smiled and nodded, welcoming his lips easily, then gasped at the feel of his hard chest against mine, edging on the side of pain. My breasts were more sensitive and swollen than they'd ever been, and it was enough to jolt me back to reality.

"Brooks." I pressed a kiss to his collarbone as clarity overwhelmed my desire. I couldn't go any further—not until he knew. "I need to tell you something."

He smiled and skimmed his fingers over my lips. "Tell me."

I opened my mouth to say it, to give power to what I'd hidden. But fear stole my voice, and the truth wouldn't come out. Everything was going to change. The shaky foundation Brooks and I had barely built was going to fall into ruins, exactly as my life had before.

"Hey." His voice was as light as his hands as they grabbed mine from where they shook between us. "You can trust me. I won't run from you." He pressed a kiss to my palm. "I want to take care of you. And I know that scares you, and there's a lot I don't know about you and what you've endured. But I do know you weren't seen, were pushed aside and forgotten. You weren't cherished and taken care of in the way that matters. But I want to take care of you *right*—"

"Brooks," I cried, shaking my head. I couldn't let myself believe him. I'd ruined everything, I just knew it. "I'm sorry . . ."

"Shay," he tried again, misunderstanding my loss for words. "I'm not going to take anything from you. I trust you—and you can trust me. We can be something better together—"

"I'm pregnant," I admitted weakly, unable to let him believe we were a possibility any longer.

He blinked. And in that one single blink, my world shifted. His brows furrowed, and there was a hint of a smile on his lips as he scanned my face, like he was waiting for me to say I was kidding. "That's not funny, Shay."

I'd never hated myself more. He blinked fast and hard, shaking his head. "But you and I . . . we haven't."

My heart was breaking.

His hands on my waist loosened, though they stayed. Somehow he was still with me. "Is—is there someone else here?"

"No," I rasped, my chest tightening. "Declan's the father."

He glanced at my stomach, his eyes wide, perhaps searching for the proof hidden beneath my shirt—his shirt. "Did you?" His throat bobbed and his hands left me, and it took every bit of my strength not to fall apart right there. "Did you know when you left him?"

At that moment, I knew. I knew everything was over before it had truly begun. Even if I could explain, it wouldn't matter. So I straightened my spine and owned it, welcoming the pain that would surely follow. "Yes."

Tears streamed down my cheeks, washing away the taste of him on my lips as he said, "I need you to get off me."

Chapter Twenty-One

"Brooks," I tried, my voice hoarse. "I didn't—"

"Please." His eyes were closed, his hands lay open at his sides, like he couldn't stand the thought of touching me. "Get off of me."

Vision blurry, heart pounding, I crawled off him. I was barely on the seat before he was out the door. Flecks of rain fell inside before he gently closed it, not slamming it like I deserved. Not even a heartbreaking second later, he sat shirtless in the driver's seat, starting the truck.

"Brooks." My voice was firm as the truck pulled away, the windshield wipers beating furiously. "Would you please stop and hear me out?" He ignored me, his truck revving faster and farther from camp. "You're leaving all of our stuff—"

"I'll come back for it later," he snapped, his tone harder than I'd ever heard. "I can't—" He stopped himself and shook his head, his arm shaking on the wheel. "We're done. I don't want anything to do with you."

I must not have learned my lesson before—from Declan and my mom—because I managed a hopeful, quiet whisper. "You don't mean that."

He said nothing, and that was somehow worse.

I closed my eyes, refusing to let his words take root. They couldn't be true—they weren't. But they were relentless. It didn't matter if I'd never intended to ask anything of Brooks, for him to be involved with this baby in any way. His words slithered in and claimed my heart, confirming the truth I already knew.

I'm not wanted.

I placed a trembling hand on my stomach, one that was changing and re-forming, a home for a slowly growing life—my baby.

But you're wanted.

I promise.

Chapter Twenty-Two

I don't want anything to do with you.

I hadn't expected those words to hurt so much, especially from a man I was only beginning to know. But it was nothing compared to the agony I felt when Brooks parked alongside the road and I saw Nolan's and Levi's vehicles outside my cabin.

I was going to lose all three of them.

"Brooks," I shouted, almost slipping on the slick running board as I climbed out of the truck. His hands were fisted, his bare back strained as he marched away like I didn't exist. "Please listen to me. It's not what you're thinking."

"What the hell?" Nolan called unknowingly from the door, shirtless and with what looked to be a utility belt on his hips. "We're not even close to being done. You ruined the surprise, moron."

Brooks moved with purpose, stomping through the mud. The rain had stopped somewhere along our unbearable drive home. "Let's go. We're done."

Nolan stepped outside, watching Brooks for only a moment before he looked to me. "Is everything alright, darlin'?"

"What's going on?" Levi followed Nolan out onto the porch, a hammer in one hand. "You said you weren't coming back until tomorrow night. We're still in the middle of everything."

So this is pain.

My ears rung and my hands trembled. This was too much. "I'm pregnant," I said, realizing Brooks had no intention of filling his brothers in, too busy throwing wooden planks into the back of Nolan's truck. "It's Declan's—my ex's—baby."

"Get your stuff and let's go," Brooks ordered, grabbing anything in the driveway that wasn't mine. He pointed a firm finger at his brothers. "Now."

"I don't understand why we're leaving," Levi said, his voice light, making no move to leave.

But Nolan walked down the steps, coming straight for me. I braced myself, prepared for my heart to shatter again. But the hand that touched mine was calm, his eyes full of nothing but concern. "Are you okay?"

I nodded, even as tears crawled down my cheeks, worsening when Brooks said, "Nolan, I swear if you don't get in your truck right now—"

"No." Nolan turned, putting himself between Brooks and me. "Not until you tell us what's going on. Because I can't find one reason why Shay being pregnant is any reason for you to be angry."

"How do you not see what's happening?" Brooks's voice was loud, shaking with anger. "She played us all along. She used us!"

"How?" Nolan asked, his voice rising too. "She hasn't asked us for a single thing! It was your idea that we fix her place up. It was you—"

"She lied!" Brooks pointed his finger at me, and it was an effort not to crouch behind Nolan, to hide from his disdain. "What were you going to do? Try and trap one of us? Is that why you wanted Levi to drive you to your appointment—"

"Do you hear how stupid you are?" Levi yelled, his hammer thudding on the porch. "Don't you dare accuse Shay of shit like that. You don't know her at all."

"You're right. I don't." Brooks's voice was suddenly eerily calm, making the weight on my chest worse, forcing me to endure this pain inside and out. "All I know is that she's a liar. She abandoned her family just like Mom—"

"She is not Mom!" Nolan snapped, his hands shaking at his side. "Dammit, this is—"

Nolan fell silent when I set my hand on his shoulder. His frame was tense, his eyes intent on his brother as I said, "It's okay." Except it wasn't. It was anything but okay, as I understood why Brooks was so deep in a rage, to the point that he was unreachable and paranoid. He'd let me in, only to believe his worst fears to be true.

Before, his reaction had made me sad. Heartbroken.

Now I was angry.

"I am not a liar." I left Nolan and marched up to Brooks, so close I could feel his seething breaths, taste his anger. But I wasn't afraid of him. I trusted him—and I hated him for it. "I don't owe you an explanation for my choices. You're going to believe I'm like your mom no matter what I say." I jabbed his chest with my finger, not knowing how I'd let him touch me, know me. "But do you think your dad told your mom how worthless she was? When he found out she was pregnant, did he try to force her hand and demand she either go to a clinic to take care of *it* or get the hell out of his house? Do you think he broke her?" Tears sprawled down my cheeks, not of sorrow—but rage and shame.

"No?" I scoffed at his stunned silence, his wide eyes. "Well, I'm glad you had a good man in your life, Brooks. Because I never have. Declan hurt me—" I choked on the words and swallowed them down. I didn't want his pity, and I didn't want him to know me any more than he already did. I took in a quiet breath, strengthening myself. "I'm not proud of my choices, but I'm not going to let you make me feel less than for what I had to do. And nothing you ever say or believe will change the fact I gave up everything for someone I've never even met. So don't you ever accuse me of abandoning my family."

The air was thick with tension, sorrow and loss. But there was also acceptance. I hadn't come here for him. I hadn't come here for anyone but myself and the life growing inside of me. "I know I should've told you sooner—believe me, I get it. But in case you forgot, you were telling me left and right to get lost. You were pushing me away, and I didn't think it mattered. You didn't even think I was worth something until today."

"That's not true—"

I shook my head, cutting him off. I didn't want his excuses. We were done, and I'd been right to stay away. "I wasn't trying to trap you." My voice was soft, but not weak—never again would I allow anyone to make me feel small. "I would never expect you or anyone else to raise my baby, to take on the responsibility I chose. I told you because I trusted you, because you were my friend. I thought that you, more than anyone, would understand me. But I think you were right—we're not meant to be friends. Because the only thing we share is that we're both unwanted, Brooks. The difference is, I'm choosing not to live in it, choosing to grow into something better. But I think you're okay existing in it. You want to hurt people exactly how you've been burned."

I turned and walked away. I firmly planned on closing that door, forgetting what Brooks and I could've had. But I only managed one step onto the porch, faintly registering that it was filled with building supplies and my belongings—even my cabinets were crammed in the corner—when Nolan said, "Shay, you can't stay here."

I stiffened. I hadn't expected this, not after Nolan came to my aid. But Brooks was his brother, and his loyalty should lie there. "Please," I cried, my gaze on the sanded-down wooden planks. "It's my home. I have nowhere else to go."

It was Levi who said, "No, Shay. You can't stay here because it's a mess." He ran a hand through his slick hair and looked over his shoulder into the cabin. "There's all sorts of chemicals in here. I don't know if you should be breathing it . . . if it's okay for the baby."

"Oh." I stared at the torn-up floor, refusing to turn around and face Brooks, see his anger. "Um, I'll call my doctor and ask. I'm sure it's fine."

"You can call them at our house," Nolan said, coming up beside me on the porch. "You can't stay here anyway—we made a real shit show inside." He grabbed my wrist, putting his keys in my hand. "Go wait in my truck. I'll grab a few of your things for you."

"No." I pushed his key back into his palm. "I'm not doing that to you guys. I'll go stay with Layne—"

"Please," Nolan insisted, the blue in his eyes fierce. "You're my friend, Shay. And I want you to stay."

I licked my lips and, against my will, glanced at Brooks. His shoulders were relaxed, almost sagging. Even his eyes had lost their hardness, as though my words had eased his rage. He looked defeated. But when he only gave us a sloppy wave and walked away, I didn't buy it. Brooks slammed his door and I flinched, squeezing Nolan's hand, and then his tires were skidding through the mud as he sped off in the direction of town.

My hand fell to my side when Nolan dropped it and followed Levi into the cabin, leaving me alone on the porch as night pressed in more and more. It was then, and only then, after the storm had parted, that I was able to see the disturbance it had left.

Brooks had touched me, held me, whispered soothing words of affection. He'd taken me camping so Levi and Nolan could make repairs to the cabin. Help me make it a home. And for a moment, a pure, fleeting moment, I'd thought I'd found my place—my family.

Brooks was afraid I'd destroy his home.

But he'd never stopped to ensure he wouldn't destroy mine.

Chapter Twenty-Three

Our bodies can adapt to pain.

Not always, and not immediately, but over time, our bodies can become so accustomed to it, the pain begins to feel natural, acceptable.

But hearts are a different matter. When the pain is not solely physical, but mental, it's that much harder to endure. It doesn't matter if the pain is second nature; it's agonizing, draining.

I was numb. But everything hurt.

I hadn't spoken when Nolan led me to his truck, suitcase in tow. I didn't know if he tried to talk to me on the short drive to his house. All I knew was silence. A hollow echo, reminding me of what was gone. I didn't really know what happened next—I'd been too busy trying to keep myself afloat as I drifted back and forth between the present and the past, the feeling of loneliness and abandonment intertwining.

I should've told Brooks sooner. I knew that. I should've revealed why I was here straight from the get-go. But at the time, I hadn't wanted to be that person. I didn't want to claim the title of sad, pathetic girl whose fiancé had kicked her aside, whose absentee mom dodged her calls.

I didn't want to be me.

I sank deeper into the couch cushions, curling my legs tighter around Cash, who hadn't left my side since I'd arrived at the Graham house. Initially, Nolan and Levi had insisted I take a room upstairs, but I held firm on my no—I wasn't staying long. Silence swallowed their house. They all stayed in their rooms, giving me privacy. I hated it. Hated how the dark suffocated me. I had nothing but space to think, to drown, to see how far off I was from who I wanted to be.

I wanted to be the mom who knew she deserved better. Who chased the life she believed was best for her child. Who believed she was capable of starting over, of forging a new world. One where she and her baby would never know loneliness, would always have each other.

But I wasn't her.

"I don't think you should be here."

I stirred awake, a low, golden hue from a light in the kitchen slipping past my lashes with each blink. I closed my eyes again, sleep and stress weighing heavily. I'd nearly succumbed to it, drifting away from this world, when a deep voice pulled me back. "I just want to talk to her."

I lay with my eyes open, listening. Cash stirred and, with a low grumble, nuzzled deeper against my legs, making no move to greet the voices behind us. I waited, staring at the stone fireplace across the living room, but when the silence lingered, I thought maybe I'd imagined the voices. It was still dark outside, maybe Levi or Nolan had come into the kitchen and forgotten to turn off a light.

"She's asleep, Brooks." Nolan's voice was a sharp whisper. "And if you wake her up and I have to listen to her cry for two hours again, I'll kill you."

I swallowed, my throat dry and sore, unaware I'd cried for so long—or that Nolan had heard me. And when had Brooks come home? I lay still on the couch, trapped, waiting for him to further break my heart. But he only asked, "Is she okay?"

"You're an idiot," Nolan muttered. "She's been crying for hours. We inadvertently made her homeless. You accused her of trying to trap us with her baby. Not to mention, you did it shirtless—so I can only imagine what you guys were up to before you decided she was trash and tossed her aside, exactly like her worthless fiancé did. Do you really think she's okay?"

"Fine," Brooks said, giving me no time to absorb Nolan's words. "That was a stupid question. I know she's not okay, but I'm struggling to understand what happened. One minute I thought she was mine, and the next I find out she's pregnant with another man's child. And with a waste of a man at that. What he did to her . . . that he even had the nerve to try and force her hand. It makes me sick." He let out a tired breath, his words sounding as helpless as I felt. "So much happened at once . . . I don't know what to do." Nolan was silent, as though he too was confused and overwhelmed. *Welcome to the club.* "Did you know she was pregnant?"

"No." I expected that to be the end of it, but then Nolan said, "You're not going to like this, but I talked to Levi, and he said he suspected she was when she first moved here and bought prenatals from the shop."

It fell silent again, as though Brooks was as stunned as I was that Levi had known, or at least suspected. Maybe I shouldn't have been surprised, not when I remembered how he had told Nolan I didn't drink, hadn't protested when Layne thought I'd given him a stomach bug.

But if Levi knew this whole time, he never let on to it—never told his brothers.

And he'd still been my friend. Hadn't pushed me away.

I stored that sacred treasure deep in my heart, hoping it might lessen the misery within.

"I don't know what to do." A stool slid against the floor, followed by Brooks whispering, "Trying to keep Shay an arm's length away has been so damn hard, and it felt so right to let her in. When I told her about Mom, it was the easiest thing I've ever done. You should've seen her light up, like me being vulnerable meant everything to her." It had meant everything to me, and if I could go back, I would've told Brooks the truth before today. But there was no going back now.

"I thought I was making promises to her, but really all I did was make a fool of myself. I told her things I've never told anyone, but she kept this from me. She waited until I was completely gone for her before she told me about the baby. And now she's in our home, a part of our lives. I don't want to believe it, deep down I know it's not true—but I'm afraid she's using us."

"She's not using us," Nolan assured him, something like exhaustion in his tone. "You wouldn't have let her in."

"We've been fooled before."

I furrowed my brows, waiting for any further explanation, but Nolan only said, "This isn't like that." He cleared his throat, his voice drawing nearer. "In a perfect world, Shay would've told you before you had feelings for her. But to be fair, Brooks, you liked the girl the second you saw her. Hell, I hadn't seen you so fired up in years. So I'm really sorry it didn't work out the way you planned. But that doesn't mean you have any right to be angry at the choices she's had to make alone. The only thing you get to decide is what you're going to do about it now. And just like you get a choice, so do I." Tears welled in my eyes, not from pain, but gratitude. "I don't care if Shay's having one baby or four—she is my friend. I'll be damned if I let you push her out of our lives. And I'll tell you this—our little brother is furious at you right now. So I'd choose your choices carefully."

I never wanted this. No matter how angry I was toward Brooks, I didn't want to hurt him, to disturb his home. I found no joy in Levi being angry at him. And while it warmed my heart to witness how fiercely Nolan had come to my defense, I almost wished he hadn't. I couldn't help but feel like I'd meddled my way into their life and blown it up.

"I'm really trying with you, Brooks. I've tried to stay calm, but Shay trusted you—she trusted all of us—and you screwed up." I closed my eyes, wishing I'd never woken up when Nolan's voice grew louder, closing in on the couch. "I've always looked up to you, even when you're being a controlling bastard, because I know you've always had our best interests at heart. But it's time you stop worrying about my and Levi's issues and fix your own, otherwise you're going to end up exactly like the person we hate most."

"I know I messed up. I never should've said what I did to her outside the cabin . . . but I can't be with her, Nolan." Even though I already knew that, there was nothing I could do to stop my heart from constricting, the sob from building in my chest. "Not because of the—" Brooks paused, leaving me broken and hanging. "I can't."

Nolan let out a short laugh, but there was nothing affectionate or humorous about it. "I think you're right, Brooks. You can't be with her, and it's your own fault."

I clenched my eyes tighter when a door shut, leaving their conversation to settle in. The consequences, the truth of tonight, had fully taken root. Anything Brooks and I had planted, anything we'd grown together, would no longer flourish.

Let me take care of you.

Despite how empty I felt, I was on the verge of tears again, mourning for what could've been. I'd been honest when I told Brooks I expected nothing from him. It had never crossed my mind to have him fill in as the father for my baby. It wasn't why I'd let him in. But it never occurred to me he'd obliterate my heart. A heart I hadn't realized I'd offered him in the first place.

The kitchen light flicked off, and I was engulfed in darkness again. I foolishly hoped Brooks hadn't meant what he said. So I waited, assuming Nolan had gone to his room and it was Brooks shuffling in the kitchen. But when the front door opened and closed, and an engine started, and his truck drove away, I knew he'd meant every word.

Before, in the truck, and even outside my cabin, I could excuse his actions. I could say his reaction was because I'd caught him off guard, that he'd panicked when he told me he didn't want anything to do with me. He'd even voiced his regret. But he'd had hours to calm down when he confided in his brother—someone he trusted, loved—that he didn't want to be with me.

For too long, I'd wasted time excusing the actions of others. I'd done it growing up with my mom and I'd done it with Declan, always giving them the benefit of the doubt. But it was time I stopped looking for what I wanted to see and focused on what they were telling me. Like Elle, who used a recorder to hear what people weren't telling her.

But I didn't need one.

Brooks had been loud and clear—he didn't want me.

Chapter Twenty-Four

"Here's your sugar," I mumbled as I set two sugar packets on the diner counter for the customer drinking his coffee. I stifled a yawn, my heavy eyes reminding me how little I slept last night. "Let me know if you need anything else."

I wasn't supposed to work today. Lila was scraping to give me hours as it was, even with the influx of hunters. But when I'd showed up this morning, my face must've said what I couldn't, because she'd patted my shoulder and handed me my apron. I'd work for free if it kept me out of that house, kept me from slipping too deep into my head.

I'm drowning.

But I'd been offered a small amount of relief when I heard back from my OB this morning. I'd called last night, worried I'd potentially harmed the baby by breathing in chemicals. She assured me it was fine, especially since I hadn't stepped foot inside. Despite that, she'd gone out of her way and offered me an appointment for later today if I needed further reassurance. But I'd declined—I wasn't confident enough to drive Jake's truck that far. And I wasn't about to ask one of the Grahams for a ride.

I really needed to get it together. I'd be doing the next twenty-five weeks on my own. I was due in March, and I hadn't begun to fathom what came after that, how I'd bring and raise a baby into the world alone.

"Alright," Layne drawled as she trailed me back to the kitchen and set a stack of cups beside the sink. "Are you going to tell me why you're moping, or do I have to work for it?"

I plopped the cups down into the water, disturbing the resting bubbles. I stared at it, as though the frothy water could give me any clue what to say. I didn't know how to answer, how to piece my mind together.

I swatted at a patch of bubbles and ran my hands back through my hair. I was feeling too much. Too much, yet nothing at all. "I'm pregnant."

"Shay." She paused and scanned the empty kitchen. Both Lila and Seth were outside. "I'm sorry."

I turned on my heel and faced her, wearing a smile that didn't quite reach my eyes. "I'm not." My voice was steady and sure. I wasn't haunted over the fact I was having a baby. No, I'd panicked over that tidbit much earlier. With fifteen weeks under my belt, I'd made my peace. It was all the stuff that came after that was tangling me in different directions. "I'm almost four months along, so I've had a while to accept it. I wasn't trying to hide it from you or anything . . ." I rubbed my face, feeling like I hadn't slept in days. "I haven't exactly had the best reactions when I shared the news, so I think I was trying to protect it. Keep this one thing safe with me for as long as I could."

I didn't just mean Brooks's reaction. His words had gutted me, torn apart my repairing heart, but I knew they had been said out of fear. I'd blindsided him, had been in the middle of tearing his clothes off when I told him, feeding his paranoia.

But he hadn't promised to love me. To raise a family with me.

Declan had.

"Your ex . . . He's the father?" Layne asked, and I nodded. "He didn't want it?"

"No." My voice was low, on the edge of nonexistent. I might as well have mouthed the words. "He didn't want us."

"But you do? You want to be a mom?"

Months ago, when I peed on the stick and was greeted with a big fat positive, I hadn't been able to confidently answer that. I was excited, scared, nervous, and sick in one breath. It didn't help that only a few short months before, I'd tried to leave Declan.

If I'd been smarter, I would've packed faster, had all my things ready. If I'd planned better, steeled my heart and mind, I might've been strong enough to leave then. To resist Declan when he came home and realized I was done. Maybe his promises wouldn't have broken through my resolve. Promises to work less, to be home more—and not just home, but present. That he'd make time to do things I wanted, that he'd take me to the sea or even the mountains. We'd go running, go on dates. He'd do better to show more patience, to not snap or speak over me.

When he said I owed him the chance to try, after all he'd done for me, I thought he was right. When he made love to me and admitted how much he needed me, craved me every breath, told me we'd be lost without each other, that no one could ever love me as much as he did—I believed him. It was my fault for not seeing the lies carefully placed between his words. I should've seen the little web he weaved, slowly, carefully, easing me back to where he wanted me.

And it worked. Because when the weeks passed, and the love bombing faded, and the flowers wilted, I was back where I began. Afraid to leave, to live and breathe without him. I might've stayed had I not gotten that positive test. If what came after I told Declan I was pregnant hadn't happened. I might've stayed. But I didn't.

It's easier to change your life when your choices no longer affect solely you.

It's easier to love someone more than yourself—to believe they deserve more.

"Yeah." I stuffed my hands in my pockets. "I want this baby. I want to be a mom."

Layne smiled, and I wished I'd told her sooner, if only so I wouldn't have carried this alone for so long. "Then I'm excited for you." She nudged her elbow against mine. "Except I might have to request different shifts from you when you start showing. My tips are going to plummet when the customers see you waddling around all cute."

I forced a laugh, one that only drained me further, did nothing to lift my spirits. But I was grateful, so very grateful, for Layne's easygoing nature. It felt good to announce my pregnancy and have it celebrated.

I cleared my mind and burrowed into work, losing myself until the sun was near dropping and it was time to hang up my apron for the day. I had one foot out the back door when Lila said, "Hey, Shay—wait around for a second. I'll be right with you."

I sat on a stool in the kitchen as she slipped to the front, tended to a customer, then returned. "Thanks," she said, running her fingers through her copper bangs. "I'm glad you came in today. I've been needing to talk to you."

"Thank you for letting me work an extra shift. I needed it."

She gave a tight-lipped smile. "Look, I'm going to cut straight to the point. You're a great kid and I really like you . . ." Time seemed to slow, and there was a warning ringing in my ears. "But I've gotta let you go. I was scrambling to get you hours as it is, but I can't afford it any longer. I'm really sorry."

"Oh," I breathed, running my hands over my thighs. "That's okay."

"You were a great worker. Best Valley Girl I've ever had," Lila offered, wrapping an arm around my shoulder when I stood. "And hey, if you're still around when Layne heads off to school after the New Year, come see me. The job will be yours."

I steeled my spine and smiled, not wanting to take my disappointment out on Lila. She didn't have to give me a chance in the first place. "Sounds great." I grabbed the door and stepped out. "I really appreciate you taking a chance on me. I'll see you around."

She smiled and tucked her hands in her pockets. "Swing back by in a few days and I'll have your pay for you."

My smile lasted the amount of time it took for the door to close.

You're fine.

I silently manifested those words with all the might I could muster as I pedaled my bike through town. My breathing grew more ragged with each turn of the wheels, and I wished I hadn't had the grand idea to forgo driving Jake's truck for as long as I could in an attempt to save money. Make it home, and I could lose it. I could panic for a moment and then regroup, form a new plan.

Just make it home.

Wait.

The realization had me gripping the handle brakes. My tires grinded against the dirt road as I screeched to a stop. My foot hit the ground, stopping me from falling as I swiveled to the side and panted down great breaths. What was I doing? Where was I going?

My home was gone. The floor half ripped up and the kitchen demolished. And spending the night at the Grahams' had been a one-time thing. I wouldn't stay there again. Brooks had spent the night elsewhere, but eventually he'd come home.

And I didn't have a job.

Even if I managed to make Jake's cabin livable, I had no way of paying for it. I'd managed to build up a savings, but it wouldn't last long. And I'd yet to buy a single thing for this baby.

I sucked down a few gasps of rich mountain air and steeled myself to take off on the bike. But when I pushed down on the pedal, the bike resisted. The tire was twisted to the side. "You've got to be freaking kidding me," I groaned at the flat front tire, air still seeping out. Refusing to cry again, I stepped over the bike, dropped it on its side, and kicked the useless wheel.

It was laughable, really. I'd lost everything in a matter of twenty-four hours. And this time, I didn't have a slimy ex to blame.

This was *my* fault.

I wanted to cry. I wanted to sob, to moan and whine about how freaking hard this was. But instead, I kicked the bike again and again, furious at myself and the situation. I scrubbed at my eyes, uttering flying curses and kicking dirt, unraveling along with my life.

I'd given up everything—only to lose more in the end.

How had I failed my baby before it was even born?

Foot throbbing, I kicked my bike one last time before I tugged it off the road—I'd tell Jake later. I started toward my cabin to fetch his truck, hoping he'd understand and trade Betsy back. I'd read somewhere that doing the same thing repetitively and expecting a different result was the definition of insanity. I'd done that with Declan, stayed when I should've left, and everything had just gotten worse.

And now, living here—it wasn't working.

So I'd leave.

Chapter Twenty-Five

I was going to set the Graham brothers on fire.

Two in particular.

After my meltdown, I'd gone on a run. I needed to clear my head, make sure I was doing the right thing. Deciding I was, I'd returned to Jake's cabin for my belongings. I was all set for the perfect getaway, especially since I hadn't left anything behind at the Grahams. I could avoid an awkward goodbye. Only, when I went to Jake's cabin, not only was the flooring still missing, but so were my things. It wasn't like I had much, given they'd managed to stuff all of it in the bathroom and the corner of the porch when they'd made repairs to the main room, but it was all gone. And assuming Brooks had no reason to think of me again, it would be Nolan and Levi I would douse with gasoline.

If they thought they were stopping me from running, they were wrong. In the end, they were only deterring me—and pissing me off.

I'd parked down the road, hoping the night would conceal me. If Brooks was home, I was leaving, stuff be damned. I slammed Jake's truck door shut, and only after I'd confirmed Brooks's truck was gone did I stomp up their driveway.

I rolled my hand into a fist, ready to pound down their door. But before I'd even lifted my hand, the door swung open. "Are you done hiding?" Levi said in greeting. His eyes were hard, and there was something tense in his tone. "We tried calling you—even tried the diner. But Lila said you left hours ago, after she let you go."

The annoyance I'd felt was gone, replaced with gratitude as I stared at a man who might really care about me. "My phone's dead," I admitted truthfully, considering I didn't have a home to charge it in. "And I wasn't hiding . . . I needed some space."

"It's about time," Nolan said, coming up from behind Levi. "Thought we'd have to send out a search squad. Get in here, darlin'."

"Um—" I stepped back, strengthening my resolve. "No, I'm here for my things. I'm leaving."

Levi pursed his lips, and I prepared myself to say to hell with it and leave, but it was Nolan who said, "Well, c'mon in and gather your stuff. I don't want to be left with more shit."

I forced a half smile, pretending his quick dismissal didn't gut me. I hesitated in the doorway when Levi let me past and scanned the room for Brooks just in case.

He wasn't here.

So why did my heart ache?

Tums. I needed Tums. It was heartburn—not heartache.

I stuffed my hands in my pockets as Levi locked the door, including the chain lock, apparently believing I was a major flight risk. And I was, considering how I backpedaled into the wall when a shadow moved in the dim hallway where the bedrooms were. I held my breath, willing myself to vanish when Brooks stepped out.

His hair was freshly washed, wet strands falling to his brow. But his face was heavy, with deep circles beneath his eyes. He stared at me, and I him, and the world seemed to stretch thin. It overwhelmed me, the power we had. The potential to forge something astonishing, or decimate everything and everyone around us.

Whatever worked.

"I'm sorry," I stammered, clutching my hands behind my back. "I didn't know you were here—your truck wasn't out front." He furrowed his brows in question, but I ignored it—I needed to get out of here before I did something I'd regret. "I'm here to get my things and leave. That's all."

I planned to say more. Maybe beg for forgiveness or get struck by lightning, but before I could, Brooks moved. I stepped toward the door, only to bump into Cash lying behind me—*traitor*—as Brooks pulled me to him.

I stiffened, hating how well I molded against him. My head rested against his chest, my hands dangling at my sides. The hug was brief, over before it started. He stepped back, staring at the floor, but nothing could hide the pained, distant look he wore. Perhaps because I hadn't embraced him back.

How could I with all that lay between us?

I cleared my throat and moved to the couch, pausing when I noticed the guitar against the fireplace. I hadn't seen it since Brooks hid it from me, and I'd have bet anything he put it back thinking I'd already left. "Where ya headed?" Nolan asked as he sat on the kitchen counter, his legs swinging.

"Um—I'm going back to California." Brooks's head snapped in my direction, and I rolled my eyes before I clarified, "I'm crashing with my friend Elle until I figure out where I want to go."

Nolan nodded, giving me no clue as to where my stuff was. "Her couch better than ours?"

"What?"

He hopped down and landed on his feet beside Levi, and I couldn't help but notice the obvious line drawn between them and Brooks, the latter now looming at the edge of the hallway. "Well, it's gotta be pretty damn comfy if you're willing to drive hundreds of miles to it, rather than sleep on the one right here."

I bit my lip and looked down at Cash leaning against my leg, not bothering to correct Nolan that I'd be sleeping on a bed in Elle's casita. "I lost my job." My voice was miraculously even. "Even if I could afford to live here now, I can't. No offense, but you guys kind of made my home unlivable."

Nolan brushed it off, waving a hand at me. "We'll finish it. Have you back inside in no time."

I glared, my nails digging into my palms. "I don't have a job, Nolan."

He shrugged, and Levi stepped closer to the doorway, likely sensing I was on the verge of tackling his brother. "There aren't any other jobs here?"

"No."

"Really?" Nolan raised a brow. "You went to every spot in town and got turned away? That's pretty impressive."

"No."

"Then why?" he asked, his throat bobbing. "Why are you leaving?"

My resolve faltered, and I thought of what Nolan had done for me, how he'd stood by me. I shook my head, releasing an exhausted breath. "There is nothing for me here."

"That's not true and you know it."

"Nolan," Brooks said in warning. "That's enough."

I rolled my eyes. Of course—of course it wasn't Brooks trying to get me to stay. He might've expressed regret to Nolan last night, but nothing had really changed. "It is true and you know it," I continued on. I needed to say my piece and get out. "I am grateful. I'm so grateful for each of you and what you've done for me. But it is not working out here—"

"You can work at our shop," Levi interrupted me, tossing his hands up. "We already talked it over."

"No—no." I shook my head, refusing to hear him. "I won't. I promise I didn't come here so you'd pity me. I don't want anything from you guys."

"We don't pity you, darlin'." Nolan crossed his arms over his chest. "In order to pity you, I'd have to believe there's something sad about your life, and I just don't see it that way. You've got three friends here asking you to stay. You've got a job offer. There's a couch waiting for you, possibly a bed, if you play your cards right. And I imagine there's a really cute tater tot cooking in your belly."

I choked out a laugh at the last part and ran my hand over the small bump. I stopped, cheeks flushing, when I caught Brooks's eyes zeroed in on the movement. I stretched down the hem of my shirt. "No. I'm not taking anything from you guys."

"Shay—"

"No, you don't get it, Nolan." I pinched the bridge of my nose, hating that I had to explain this. "I spent the last few years entirely dependent on someone, and I can't . . . I won't do it again." Never would I allow anyone to have control over me again, the ability to change my life on a whim.

"Well shit, Shay—" Nolan ran a hand through his messy blond hair, his eyes a bit wild. "We're not giving you this for free. Trust me, Levi's a hard-ass. He'll fire you if you slack off at work. He won't care if you're puking up your guts or not."

I smiled, unable to leash the desire I had to stay. I didn't want to start over, especially when I didn't believe there were many places I could call home. I hadn't even realized that was what Wallowpine was for me until I was leaving it. "I—I don't know."

"You can pay to live here," Levi pressed. "And Nolan's an ass. You don't have to sleep on the couch. We have spare rooms."

"I thought the couch would further entice her to stay since Shay's made it clear she'd rather go without to prove a point," Nolan added, as though that would persuade me further. "But we already put some of your stuff upstairs. The rest is in a shed out back."

I couldn't lie—it was endearing to see the fuss they were putting on for me to stay. But even if I trusted them, there was one key factor keeping me from agreeing to their demands and putting an end to their pleas.

Brooks. Who'd been nearly silent the entire time, not once asking me to stay.

And maybe I shouldn't have needed it, shouldn't have cared what he wanted. But it would've been nice.

"I appreciate the offer," I started, interrupting Nolan and Levi, who'd shifted to bickering. "But I can't. There are too many unknowns, and I can't waste time. I'd like to get settled . . ." My cheeks heated as I waved a hand at my belly. "You know. Before."

I bit my lip, resisting the urge to bend over and curl up as all three men stared at my stomach, likely searching for the proof that hadn't quite *popped*. "I'm not due until March, and I'm only fifteen weeks," I murmured. "That's not very far along, so that's why you can't really see anything yet." I mean, when I was naked, you couldn't miss the cute round pooch I rubbed every night, but I wasn't about to strip down. "I guess most women, especially with their first, don't show until much later. So if you still don't believe me, you'll have to wait at least a few more weeks. Although, at the rate I'm eating peanut butter sandwiches . . ." I trailed off, aware I was rambling and now worried Brooks had silently forbidden himself from ever enjoying peanut butter again, if the empty look on his face indicated anything.

I would have avoided them for the rest of my life, too—but the baby goblin inside me had other plans.

Nolan moved to the recliner and kicked his feet back. "Why do you need to leave now? In the middle of the night?"

I crossed my arms over my chest, my nipples wincing at the abrupt motion. "Because I don't have anywhere to sleep, genius."

Okay, that was meaner than I intended, but I plead the fifth—aka, sore nipples.

Nolan grinned, raising his brows. "See why I can't have you leave, darlin'? I'll be too bored."

Levi leaned against the front door, blocking my way out. I rolled my eyes and bit back my smile when he smirked. I was about to remind him I could crawl through the window, but then there was a low, steady voice. "Stay."

I swallowed and looked at where Brooks stood at the edge of the hallway. His hands were tucked in his pockets, and every bit of those enticing green eyes was on me. But then he looked down, and my heart slowed, the power of his words lessening. "I mean, not forever. But at least for a few days. You can see if you like working at the shop. And the house is big—you can have the entire upstairs to yourself if you want it. At least until Jake's cabin is livable again."

I wanted to throw Brooks through the wall. *That* was straightforward. I had no idea what to do with his plan. What did he want? For the first time—and only the first time—since I'd left Declan, I wished for his bluntness.

He'd tell me to stay or get lost.

But even if Brooks was angry at me, wanted nothing to do with me, I knew he wasn't cruel.

He pitied me.

And I hated pity.

But I liked living here.

"Can I talk to you?" I asked. I cleared my throat when all three brothers moved, each up and taking a step toward me. "With Brooks, I mean."

Out of the corner of my eye, Nolan and Levi exchanged a look, but I was too busy watching Brooks give me the subtlest of nods. Rather than waiting for privacy, I walked to the front door. Levi immediately moved out of my way, and I smirked. I'd known he'd never keep me against my will.

But to my surprise, he put a tatted arm up and blocked Brooks from following me. I didn't know what was said, but something Levi muttered had Brooks's entire posture tightening. A pang of guilt rippled through my conscience as I walked away from the porch and onto the road, offering them space. I hated the anger between them. Maybe it would be better if I left.

Brooks stepped out onto the porch and groaned. "Where is my truck?"

"I moved it out back," Nolan called from inside. I didn't have to see him to imagine the grin he wore. "Even with us taking her stuff, we doubted Shay would show up if she knew your grumpy ass was here."

I shook my head. The last thing I needed was them interfering between Brooks and me. I wrapped my arms around myself, the nights growing colder as fall settled in, resisting the urge to run as Brooks approached me. He lingered on the edge where the dirt road met his driveway—like he couldn't decide where he stood.

"Do you want me here or not?" I blurted. I'd make him decide. I refused to stand on shaky ground any longer.

His brows pinched together. "What?"

I rolled my eyes. "Do you want me here?"

"Does it matter?"

Just stab me, Brooks. Surely you'd find more pleasure that way.

"Fine," I said. "It doesn't matter. I just need to know if me being here—even if it's only for a few more days—is going to be an issue for you. I'd rather leave now if it's only going to make matters worse for all of us."

He looked at me.

And I hated it.

Hated that there was no smile in that look, none of the tenderness and care from before. Now it was hard, empty and searching—exactly as he'd first watched me, back when he didn't trust me.

"Brooks." My voice cracked, the all-consuming anger I once felt leaving. I closed my eyes and put a hand to my chest, sucking in a whiff of soothing air, composing myself. "Forget it." I wouldn't do this again, live in a world where I fought to prove my place. "I'm going to spend the night at Layne's, then I'll be out of here. Tell your brothers I said thank you."

I'd barely managed two steps down the road before Brooks asked, "Do you ever stop running?"

I froze and forced a breath. "Do I stop running?" I turned to find him with both feet in the driveway. At least he'd chosen a side. "I don't know. Do you ever stop pushing everyone away?"

He ignored it, because really, how would he respond? *No, because I'm a stubborn man who pushes everyone away?* Instead he said, "You didn't care whether or not I wanted you here before. Even when I made it clear that I didn't."

I ran a hand down my face, my voice tired. "I'm aware how clear you made it, Brooks."

"Then why does it matter now?"

"I'm not doing this." I started back toward the truck. My heart raced and my steps hastened, as though I could outrun the stomping feet of doom behind me. "Let go of me," I hissed when his hand wrapped around my wrist and pulled me to a stop. "Let me go."

"No," he said, his voice gruff, but his touch was careful, always careful, breaking my heart that much more. "Not until you tell me why it matters to you—"

"Because before you didn't know me." My hand fell limp in his. I refused to enjoy his touch. "I was fine with you hating me when you didn't know me. I thought it was more your issue than mine. But now—" I paused, staring at the dark forest encasing us, anywhere but him. "You know me, Brooks. *You know me* and now . . ."

You still don't want me.

"No." His hand held on to mine, giving me nowhere to run. "You can't put that on me. You can't stay or leave because of me. You have to be here because you want to be. Not because I, or even my brothers, told you that you could."

"I don't want to make you uncomfortable—"

"Forget how I feel." He stepped back, letting my arm fall to my side. "Forget about my brothers, Wren, Jake, and whoever else—even Declan. Forget about them and what they want. What do *you* want?"

My lip wobbled as I stared at him. I wanted to hold him, cry with him, and maybe even *love* him. Because not once had I ever considered what *I* wanted. All these years, I'd been drifting, searching for anywhere I might fit, taking anyone who accepted me—and I never wondered if I wanted to be there in the first place. My voice was meek, small, as though I feared he might smash my admission. "I want to stay here."

"Then stay."

My eyes burned, and I fought the urge to throw my arms around him, to seek comfort and friendship. In the end, it didn't matter if he was empowering me to make my own choices—there was no going back after last night. "I'm sorry," I whispered. "Not for being pregnant and the choices that led me here. But I'm sorry for not telling you sooner."

His eyes softened, looking so damn tired. "I'm sorry for what I said—"

"It's okay."

"No, it's not." His hands wrapped around my arms, his touch light and airy. "What I said to you, how I reacted—that came from a place of anger, and I was wrong. And I hope you know you deserve more than that, Shay." His throat bobbed on my name. "I was scared—and I'll admit, you caught me off guard. Nothing about how last night went was okay. But this was supposed to be your chance to get lost, and no matter what, I won't run you out of your home, okay?"

I was lost. But not in the way I wanted.

I swallowed and peeked up at him through my lashes. The last time we'd been this close, I'd tasted his breaths. Experienced what it might be like living with his air. And now I couldn't remember how to breathe. "I can get lost somewhere else."

He dipped his head, his forehead against mine, and I breathed him in, savoring the certain sort of comfort and warmth that was all Brooks. "I don't want you to. Not if you want to be here."

Again with the evasiveness. I wanted to shake him, demand he decide what *he* wanted. Yes, I appreciated him for advocating that I do what was best for me. But it still was nice to be wanted. To be needed.

But then I opened my eyes and remembered. Remembered the conversation he'd shared with Nolan in the privacy of his own home.

I can't be with her.

I stepped back and reinforced my barriers, resisting the urge to gravitate back to his heat. Reminding myself of the times I'd let Declan string me along, fool me with his words. I didn't believe Brooks was similar to Declan, but I couldn't take chances. "If I stay, I don't want to go back to how it was before, when we first met—"

"Shay—"

I ignored him, aware of my fading bravado. "And I know we can't be together . . . how we were. And believe me, I don't fault you for that. But I don't want to stay if we're going to go back to you wishing I'd leave or not trusting me. I know how sketchy last night looked, but I promise, I wasn't trying to trap you. I wanted you to know before we . . . I just didn't want you to think it was a mistake afterward."

He thought it was a mistake regardless, but at least I hadn't announced it after we'd done the deed.

Gold medal for Shay. Yay.

He rolled his tongue against his cheek, his gaze hard on the meadow beside us. "I never should've accused you of that, Shay. I regret every single thing I said to you." He paused, as though he'd heard my heart break. I didn't miss it—he regretted *every single thing*. Even the good.

Let me take care of you.

I shoved it away, watching the hardness in his gaze melt away when he met mine again. "I trust you wouldn't do that. And honestly, it's my fault for not noticing you were before then."

I furrowed my brows. "I'm not sure how you could've known. You probably thought I always walked around looking like I'd eaten twelve Dorito Locos Tacos."

He huffed a laugh, and the sound lightened some of the tension, even when he glanced down to my stomach. "It really doesn't look like there's a baby in there."

I shrugged. "It's little—imagine a tiny baby avocado."

"You would have a green alien baby."

A laugh bubbled up my lungs, and I snorted. "If you want to see, I'll show you."

"What?"

"My baby bump."

"Oh." He stepped away, and the invisible barrier was between us once more. We were never going to be okay again. "No, it's fine. I believe you."

Hey, universe? It would be really great if a meteor blasted out of the sky and wiped me off the planet. Thanks.

"Sorry," I murmured, stretching down the hem of my shirt.

He clenched his jaw and looked over my head. "So you're going to stay, then? You'll work at the shop and live at our place while we finish up Jake's?"

"Um—" I paused, the thought appealing, but also not. When I looked at Brooks, I saw everything I'd lost. Not just him—though he was a big loss—but a home. The feeling I'd experienced with his family. I'd felt like I was a part of them. Nolan and Levi had made it clear they wanted me to stay, but I knew it wouldn't be the same.

I was having a baby.

And no one—three bachelors especially—wanted a baby hanging around.

But I didn't want to start over. Not again. And I did believe I had the Grahams in my corner in some way, as well as Layne and the other relationships I'd established here.

"If I stay," I started, my voice low but firm. "I have a few requirements." Brooks watched me, probably resisting the urge to snap that I wasn't in a position to make demands, but he nodded anyway. "First: I pay rent. I don't want to be freeloading off you guys in any way. And the moment Jake's cabin is finished, I'm moving out." I lifted my finger, backtracking. "Unless I have the baby beforehand. Then I'll find somewhere else to live. You guys don't need a baby in your house."

He scrubbed his jaw with his hand, and despite the moonlight, I thought I saw red creeping up his neck. But if he was disgruntled with my conditions, he held it in. "Okay."

"That reminds me—I'm sorry if I gave you the impression that I wanted you to fix up my home. I'll pay you back for everything you guys did."

"No."

I rolled my eyes. Us being cordial with one another was going to be a task in itself. Maybe I'd been right, that what we shared wasn't *real* at all. "I'm not about to owe you more than I do."

His eyes flared, but his voice didn't convey his frustration. "You don't. It's Jake's cabin, and he asked us to do it. He paid for the material and everything."

"Oh," I said, pleading he didn't hear the disappointment lining the word. I should've suspected that. After all, Brooks had only taught me how to drive standard because Jake asked him to. It made sense they'd help him out with the cabin. "Okay, then second—"

"Darlin', you doing alright out here?" Nolan shouted from the house, the door closing behind him. "I hope you're alive and well, and that it's Brooks who's six feet under right now."

Brooks rolled his eyes and muttered something under his breath when not only Nolan but Levi joined us on the road. "Shay was telling me her conditions for staying."

I didn't miss the way Levi grinned, and my heart fluttered—I was so grateful for his friendship. "Yes, and as I was saying: you can only give me the regular hours and pay you would any other employee. I don't want special treatment,"

I said to Levi and Nolan, assuming I'd be working with them and not Brooks. At least I had that going for me.

Nolan shrugged. "Suit yourself. Anything else?"

I nodded, following the strange pulse crawling through me, powering me to speak my mind. "Yeah." I waved a hand, motioning to the four of us. "If this isn't working for any of you, I need to know. I don't want to wake up with my bike tires slashed because I stole the last piece of toast or accidentally walked in on you with a girl." I grimaced, not only because the thought of Brooks touching anyone else made me want to declare WWIII—hormones, I blamed hormones—but because my bike tire was already busted, tossed aside on the side of the road. "I mean, just let me know if you need me to get lost for a bit because you want the house to yourself."

Nolan smirked. "Darlin', you're acting like we haven't lived together our whole lives. Believe me, I'm real good at pretending these two don't exist—even with them down the hall. So don't worry about messing up somebody's groove or stepping on our toes."

I swallowed, my lungs pressing in, remembering how well it went the last time I'd lived with someone. Declan had been the first and only man I'd lived with, so I'd expected an adjustment period. I'd basically raised myself, so I had my own rules, my own quirks. To me, it wasn't a big deal to leave my toothbrush on the counter, a dirty plate in the sink. But Declan thought differently, and I was fine changing. I thought I needed to embrace the life he wanted.

But his patience didn't extend far.

Despite how I was brought up, I'd never cared to cook. Not when ramen and Easy Mac were readily available. But it was important to Declan, so it was important to me. The first time I overcooked chicken, it was cute. When I broke the yolk of an egg, I was unfocused. When I didn't have dinner ready and waiting by the time he was home, I was lazy. The first time I made Declan's favorite risotto and it was too clumpy, I was ungrateful. It was his birthday, and while I was hesitant, I served it anyway. I thought it would be something we'd laugh about when we were older.

Do you remember that time I made your favorite meal because I loved you, and you ate every charred, chunky bite because you loved me just as much?

Declan threw his dish instead. I'd never seen him like that, so I jolted, accidentally shattering a bottle of wine. But the most broken of all was my spirit as I sat there and silently endured a verbal lashing, a tirade of what I'd done wrong.

I was wasteful, careless. Declan worked so hard, and I'd repaid him with a half-assed meal. Plenty of women would beg to be in my position—taken care of by him. I didn't know how long I sat there, listening to those words, but eventually he left, leaving me to clean up the mess.

As I picked up the broken glass and rubbed at the red-wine stain until my knees ached and my fingertips were near raw, all I could think was how *lucky* I was. The red stain could've been my blood, and the broken glass my bones. I was so lucky my loving fiancé had chosen to hurt me with his words rather than his hands.

He'd come home with roses. He'd made love to me, assured me all was forgiven. He would help me be better, would love me regardless of my downfalls. And I'd told myself it was enough.

I had a home, and it was fine.

I closed my eyes and forced slow breaths through my nose. That wasn't my life anymore. I wasn't that girl. And the Grahams weren't Declan. "You don't need to feel obligated to do this."

"Darlin'." Nolan's tone was light and teasing, but his blue eyes were sharp. "You've gotta stop believing we're that great of people. We don't do anything unless we want to." He bumped Brooks's shoulder with his fist. "Except him. You'll do anything for her banana bread, right?"

My stomach flipped—and I couldn't even blame the baby—when Brooks just stared at where Nolan had touched him, not acknowledging his words. "Anyway," I started, resisting the urge to rub my eyes. I was so tired. "Are we agreed?"

To no surprise, Nolan and Levi both eagerly agreed, the latter pulling me in for a brief hug. And despite having told me it was my choice, Brooks was silent, his attention forward, searching past the meadow. In what I assumed was an attempt to distract me from him, Nolan joked, "Ah—don't worry about it. He's in. He's just trying to decide if he can handle you bringing home other men."

I glared at him. "I would never."

Nolan shrugged and glanced at Brooks. "Well, you're welcome to. You're allowed to make your own decisions. Don't be fooled into thinking your baby bump will steer anyone away. Moms are hot."

I frowned, not missing—or appreciating—Nolan trying to get a rise out of Brooks. And by the way Nolan returned the glare Brooks gave him, I knew they stood on unstable ground. "Well, I'm not going to. And that's not because I'll be living with you guys. I just don't want to," I said, needing that to be clear. I'd only ever slept with Declan, so it wasn't like I'd be changing my lifestyle. "Even if someone was okay with me being pregnant, they'd be wasting their time. I couldn't trust just anyone to be around the baby."

"Are we done here?" Brooks asked, his gaze still hard on Nolan.

It was Levi who said, "We're waiting on you, Brooks. We know you like to give your approval and all."

Nolan and I exchanged a glance, and he stepped closer, like he thought he might need to intervene. But Brooks only smirked and shook his head. He stepped back, his attention wholly on me. "Welcome home, Shay."

Chapter Twenty-Six

The Graham household was sort of home.

That is, if the home had been crafted from the bleak pits of hell itself.

I'd anticipated it would be awkward—why wouldn't it be? I was intruding on three grown men in their bachelor pad, none of whom were my baby daddy. I'd happily tangled tongues with one of them, and they weren't exactly getting along.

Within that first week, I did my best to brush off the less-than-ideal circumstances. Like when I accidentally walked in on Nolan stepping out of the upstairs shower—yowza—I taught him how to use the little lock on the handle. Or when, out of the goodness of my heart, I cleaned the skillet Brooks had left out on the stove for the third day in a row, I learned you're not supposed to wash cast iron with soap and water. Oops. And when Levi intentionally drank the remaining milk in the jug after Brooks had called dibs, I realized siblings fought in the most ridiculous ways.

But we were adjusting. Everything was *fine*.

I'd be back in Jake's cabin in no time.

I didn't understand how a project that Nolan and Levi had initially planned on finishing in a weekend could turn into a whole ordeal, but what did I know?

So when Jake strolled into the shop clad head to toe in camo, I assumed he was a bearer of great news. Good news. Even mediocre news.

"So," he started, setting the unappetizing freeze-dried food on the counter for me to ring up. "I'm about to head out—a buddy of mine is elk hunting, and I'm tagging along. But I wanted to let you know I swung by the cabin and talked with Brooks."

I was glad Brooks was talking to somebody. We'd barely spoken since the night I decided to stay and officially moved in. I hardly saw him—but it probably didn't help that I burrowed in my room the moment he got home.

"And?" I asked, not trusting myself to say more. As much as I appreciated the gesture, the whole thing kind of peeved me. As my landlord, shouldn't Jake have given me some sort of notice that he was fixing up the cabin in the first place? Elle had pushed me to ask more about it, but I'd decided against it. He had a lot going on with Wren, and I was walking a fine line as it was.

"Turns out there's quite a bit of termite damage."

I blinked. "Okay . . . so what does that mean?"

"Well," Jake started, handing me cash for his items, "my daughter advised against you living there until it's fixed. Something about you possibly suing if it caved in on ya."

"I wouldn't do that," I offered. "I mean, I probably wouldn't be alive to sue you if that happened."

"That's what I told her." He snorted and I smiled, remembering why I liked living here. The people were good. "But I can't in good conscience send you in there. And that's not just because, you know, you're having a baby. I care about you."

I hadn't told Jake I was pregnant, but I wasn't surprised he knew with how quickly word traveled in this town. Plus, I'd stopped wearing baggy shirts and said to hell with it—give the town gossips something to feast on.

Is she pregnant? Or did she eat twenty-four chili cheese dogs?

The world may never know.

"I appreciate your concern, Jake. I really do." I braced my hands on the counter. "But I need somewhere to live."

"I thought you were staying with my nephews?"

"I am," I said, forcing my voice to remain steady. "But it's not permanent. How much longer do you think it'll be?"

He pursed his lips. "I don't know. I'm fixing to head out of town for a bit—Wren's got more treatments."

My heart lurched. I should've asked about her first. "How is she doing?"

He shrugged, but the way he avoided my eyes told me a different story. "She's Wren. Still hollering at the chickens when they wake her up too early."

I laughed. "Sounds about right."

He patted the counter and grabbed his items. "I gotta hit the road, but I promise I'll get you back in the cabin as soon as I can. Those boys of yours are on it." He was out the door before I could protest—or suggest he bring in professionals to do the job.

I blew out a heavy sigh and scrubbed my eyes. I was going to be homeless by the time this baby came.

"Hey darlin'," Nolan murmured. His eyes drifted from the television to watch as I walked down the stairs, my hair still wet from the shower.

"You want a sandwich?" I offered as I went to the kitchen and pulled out a slice of bread from the cupboard I'd claimed as my own.

"Sure, thanks."

"Levi?" I said loud enough to reach him in his room, where he'd been since we got home from work.

"No, thanks!" he called back.

I glanced at the clock—I still had half an hour until it was six. I smeared a bit—fine, a lot—of peanut butter and butter on sliced bread and grabbed a glass of milk for me and a beer for Nolan, joining him in the living room.

"You're too good to me." Nolan grabbed the beer and sandwich from me.

"Thank you." I smiled and did my best not to frown at the laundry piled up on the sofa, which had sat there for the last two days. I plopped down, the towering pile of boxers and socks between us. "How's Tater doing tonight?" he asked, just like he had every day since he'd found out.

I shrugged. "Good, I think. I haven't felt any movement yet, but maybe soon." I thrummed my fingers against my belly, summoning the baby to move. I was barely seventeen weeks, but I was getting impatient.

"You're feeling alright, though?" Nolan asked when the game on the TV shifted to commercials. I nodded, my mouth too sticky and full to respond. "Good. I hadn't seen you throwing up much at the shop, and I didn't know if that was normal or if something was wrong."

"Oh." My heart squeezed at his concern. His reaction to the news was the most surprising. I'd expected him to be sort of indifferent, but Nolan seemed genuinely interested. "No, I'm fine. Morning sickness tends to ease up in the second trimester." At least, that's what I'd learned from the pregnancy book I was reading, where I also learned babies drink their own pee while in the uterus. *Freaky.* "I have an anatomy scan in a few weeks. That's where they check the gender, organs, and all that. But I feel good. Probably helps that I'm not on my feet as much as I was at the diner, so thanks for that."

Nolan nodded, and with that, texted something on his phone. I glanced at the clock, double-checking I was okay on time. "So." I set my plate on the end table. "Jake told me that the cabin won't be done for a while—something about termites. I might be here a bit longer . . . if that's still okay?"

"I heard. Brooks and Anika called me back at the shop." Before I could process that—*who the heck is Anika*—he continued on, "You're welcome here as long as you want. I'll hide you under my bed, toss you and Tater snacks every now and then."

I nodded, and despite his reassurance, reached for the laundry. I folded a flannel, setting it on the cushion beside me. "When are you going to stop calling my baby Tater?"

"Well, you got another name I can use?" I shrugged; I hadn't gotten that far. But I wished I'd made one up when Nolan smirked. "Then Tater it is."

I rolled my eyes and bit my grin so as to not encourage him as I folded their laundry. "Are you going out later?"

"No," he said absentmindedly, focused on the game. "Unless you wanna join me?"

I scrunched my nose and folded together the last pair of socks. I hadn't been to the bar in town, and I had no interest in going now. "I don't think I'd make the best wingman—besides, I'm pretty beat."

He hummed and glanced at me out of the side of his eye. "I would've thought you'd be plenty rested with how much you're sleeping. When was the last time you weren't in bed before sundown?"

I stared at him, not missing the accusatory tone. "I am tired," I said with a sigh, grabbing both his and my empty plates. "I'm growing a baby. It's a lot of work."

I set the plates in the sink, my back to him as he said, "I'm not saying it's not. Guess I'm just saying I thought it would be more fun with you living here."

I tightened my grip on the dishes. "Sorry to disappoint you. Guess I broke the *fun* part of me." I scrubbed at the plate, hard enough it was sure to shine. Glancing over my shoulder as I set the plates in the drying rack, I found Nolan watching me. He looked liable to say something, his gaze darting between me and the folded laundry, but before he could, there was a pair of headlights in the driveway. I wiped my hands and the counter real quick, ensuring it was crumb free before I started up the stairs. "Good night, Nolan."

I didn't look back, feeling his gaze hot on my trail, likely believing me a coward. But I already knew that. Truth was, I was riding on stolen time. Eventually one of them—probably Brooks—would grow tired of the situation and ask me to leave. So was I really a coward if, in the end, I was only doing what was necessary to survive?

Chapter Twenty-Seven

"Shay! If you don't waddle your little tush down here in five seconds, you're walking."

I scowled from my room, Nolan's voice carrying through the door. I knew I was pushing my limit and we needed to get to the shop. I glanced out the window again, confirming Brooks's truck hadn't left. Why was he still here?

"Don't think I'm kidding," Nolan shouted. "I'll pop both your bike tires and steal your keys so you'll have no choice but to walk."

Rolling my eyes, I grabbed my bag off my bed. One positive about my living arrangements was that I'd upgraded in space. The bed was large—leaving plenty of room for Cash, who accompanied me nightly—and I even had a closet and desk. It was funny how the little things could grow to mean so much once you lost them.

"I'm not sure why we're friends," I muttered, stomping my boots down the stairs. I'd plastered on my best glare when I stumbled, catching myself on the rail. It wasn't just Nolan and Brooks, but a woman too. A woman who was sidled up tight to Brooks's side, both too immersed in each other and the eggs in his pan to notice me nearly falling.

Someone kill me.

And I was definitely smashing that stupid pan later.

"Sorry." My voice was breathless and light—I blamed the stairs—and I cleared my throat. "I lost track of time getting ready." Nolan gave me a look, like my leggings and wrinkly T-shirt said otherwise, but I ignored it and reached in my cabinet for a granola bar, forgoing the sandwich today.

Sorry, Tater.

"You must be Shay," a mild voice said. I turned, putting a face to the stranger in the room. Her eyes were blue and bright, as warm as her hazelnut hair, and she looked to be in her twenties. Great. She was banging, and I was a cave troll. She offered me her hand. "It's nice to meet you, I'm Anika."

"Hi." I shook her hand and did my best not to frown—or stomp my foot—when I noticed the peanut butter sandwich on the counter behind her. It was crustless and cut in rectangles—exactly how Brooks used to make them for me. "Are you a friend of Brooks?" I asked, even though I knew she was the one who'd helped deliver the news to Nolan about me staying longer. And was eating *my* sandwiches.

My sandwich! You ate my sandwich!

Okay, calm down, Shay. You're not Ross Geller.

"You could say that." She shrugged and smiled as she peeked a glance at Brooks, whose back was still to me. "I have to say, I think it's so great what he's doing for you. So generous—"

"We should really go," Nolan interrupted, jabbing his thumb toward the front door.

I gripped my granola bar. I wasn't that hungry—I'd survive if I tossed it at Brooks's head. What was he doing that was so generous? Beyond letting me stay here, of course. But I was paying rent. A tidbit I was sure he'd left out, making himself all that more honorable.

I deserved a medal for not rolling my eyes. "Yes. I'm so glad Brooks found it in his heart to take on a stray such as myself." I turned on my heel and walked to where Nolan waited in the doorway, his eyes wide.

"What?" I hissed when he closed the door and headed for the Jeep, where Levi was ready and waiting. Another one of the perks of living here—I could hitch rides with them to work.

"Nothing." Nolan shrugged, a hint of a grin on his lips. "Remind me to never get on your bad side."

I tucked a loose strand of hair behind my ear, grateful there wasn't any tension between us after last night. Nolan was easy like that. "I'll apologize the next time I see her."

He raised his brow, opening the passenger door. "Can't imagine why she'd come around again."

I climbed in the back seat, left to stew in regret. Not solely because of Anika; I didn't think I'd been directly rude to her. After all, my words were intended for Brooks. But if anything, I'd given him a reason to toss me out. I needed to be better—needed to lie low.

"Can we listen to Taylor Swift?" I asked and reached forward to grab Levi's phone from the center cup holders.

"That's it—you're walking," Nolan hollered as Taylor Swift's "You're on Your Own, Kid" started to play.

"What do you mean you don't have any Halloween candy?"

I flashed a fake smile at the local Karen—*Is that her name? I don't know, but it is today*—and repeated for the third time, "Like I said, our shipment hasn't come in yet. It's only the end of September. But I'm sure if you check back in a week or two—"

"How am I supposed to prepare?" Karen scoffed, her black hair sharply cut at her chin. "Some of us like to have a plan, you know? We don't fly by the seat of our pants."

I sighed, and for a brief second, I missed the diner and the regulars I'd grown accustomed to. But then I felt the stool beneath my bum, reminding me I was off my feet, and moved on. I didn't have to ride my bike or pay for gas, because I lived with my bosses.

How scandalous.

I smiled. That was the first thing Elle had said when she learned I'd moved in with them. Along with—

"What's so funny?" Karen snapped, making me wish I was tied up in a pit of snakes right now. Anywhere but here.

"Nothing." I shuffled to my feet, scrambling to check out the rest of her items. "If you're looking to prepare, there is some candy down aisle six."

She lifted her brows, her mouth and eyes wide like I'd slapped her with a bag of jerky. "But it's not Halloween candy."

I blinked. "It's candy."

"Don't they just change the wrappers anyway?" Layne chimed in from behind me, her feet propped up on the counter. "Seems like a scam to me."

"She's got a point," I added, bagging her final item. "But why don't I mention something to Nolan, see if he can get something in sooner?"

She pursed her red lips. "You know, I might just have to start taking my business elsewhere. Is this place incapable of making a simple order? If they're not out of cereal, it's toilet paper—"

"Well, it's a bait shop, so . . . And there's the country store down the street. Where they sell actual groceries," Layne muttered under her breath.

Karen's gaze flicked to her, and I willed on my best smile—this was not in my job description. But rather than snapping at Layne, she set a hand on the counter, tapping her nails. "I'm sorry, but this place has gone downhill since those boys took over."

"*Those boys* are doing the best they can," I corrected, the bite evident in my words. I probably wasn't supposed to snap at customers, but I didn't particularly care for her attitude. "But I understand, and like I said, I will see if Nolan can get the shipment in sooner."

She closed her eyes and sighed heavily. "Fine. If that's all you can do. Tell him it's for Karen, that might help." I bit back my laugh as she handed me cash—she really was a Karen! "That baby is just sucking everything out of you, isn't it? You should have him order you some vitamins. Your skin is looking a bit dull."

"I'll do that." I smiled, pretending I wasn't mentally wringing her little neck. "Oh my heck," I muttered as Karen left, waiting until she'd climbed into her car before I turned and faced Layne, finding her grinning. "Tell me if I act like that when I'm a mom."

"You'll probably be ten times worse, but . . ." she drawled as she reached into her bag and pulled out a large envelope. "I won't be around to see it."

"You got in!" I squealed, not needing any further explanation. "Where at?"

She handed me the acceptance letter, beaming. "It's nothing major. Just some community college in Boston."

"Don't do that," I warned, waving her paper. "Don't you dare lessen your achievements. Oh, Layne, I'm so proud of you."

She rolled her eyes, but the apples of her cheeks darkened, blooming with red. "You're such a mom."

"And you're such a brat," I teased, plopping down on the stool next to her. "When do you leave?"

"I'll leave at the end of December, right before New Year's. So I still have a few months."

I nodded. I hadn't anticipated the ache filling my heart. "That's so great."

She bumped her knee against mine. "You gonna miss me?"

"Hardly," I lied. I was thrilled for Layne, but I was dreading her leaving. I didn't want to lose another friend. "But I'm bummed you won't be around when the baby's born."

"I'll be back this summer." She stood, slinging her bag on her arm. "Besides—who else will teach Tater all the best curse words?"

I groaned. "Nolan got to you too?"

"It's a cute nickname." She shrugged, rounding the counter to leave. "Hey, you should come by the diner tonight. With the hunts going on, there's been a bunch of cute customers coming in."

I scrunched my nose. "No, thanks."

She laughed, brushing her hair over her shoulder. "See ya, baby mama."

I checked out another customer, then double-checked no one was lingering in the aisles as I walked to the back room, where Levi and Nolan were. Before working here, I hadn't realized they were the sole workers, beside the occasional employee they had fill in from time to time. At least with me helping out, maybe Levi could focus on school more and I could ease Nolan's plate too.

"Hey, darlin'," Nolan said from where he sat in front of the computer, mounds of papers scattered over his desk. "You need something?"

I opened a cabinet, drooling at the sight of the single-serve peanut butter tubs I'd stumbled upon my second day. Levi or Nolan must've brought them in for me. "How long until the Halloween candy comes in?"

He hummed, rifling through a folder on his lap. "There's candy up front, Shay. Grab whatever you want."

I licked my spoon. "Not for me. A woman named Karen came in looking for some. She was hoping you'd push the order up."

He looked up from his lap, his brows furrowed. "Who is Karen, and why would I order Halloween candy? There's candy out front."

"That's exactly what I told her."

"Did you not order any?" Levi asked from behind his laptop, his pencil pressed to a notebook.

"No," Nolan scoffed, pointing to the front of the store. "Because there's candy out front! I can barely keep up with everyone else's demands—I don't need hers. Give the kid some fish bait."

I laughed, only to choke on it when Levi shook his head, his voice tense. "Dad always ordered it."

"Well, I didn't know."

"Well, you should've," Levi muttered under his breath. "Maybe if you weren't so busy making special orders for everyone, you'd remember."

Nolan's jaw tightened, a warning that had me stepping closer to the door. "Well, I didn't," he spat back. "How would I know Dad wasted his money on Halloween? In case you missed it, I'm a little busy trying to run this place on my own."

"I could help more if I wasn't wasting time in school!"

"You're not wasting time," Nolan said, red sneaking up his ears. "Dad wouldn't want you to just give up—"

"Dad would've wanted you to order Halloween candy," Levi hissed, his eyes pooling.

"I'm gonna go out front," I said, wishing I'd never brought it up. "I'm sorry—" I turned to the doorway, stopping when I almost walked face-first into a solid surface wrapped in grey and forest green.

Brooks cleared his throat, and I stepped back. His brows were raised, his gaze wary—and not on me, but Levi. "Is everything okay?"

Levi muttered something inaudible, and I shifted to sidestep around Brooks, stopping when I was greeted with a wave of hazelnut hair. "Oh . . . Hi, Anika."

She smiled wide, not at all put off by our last encounter. Great, now I really was a cave troll. "Hi, Shay. I was hoping I'd see you again. I just heard the best story about you from Jake—"

"You should probably check on the front, Shay," Brooks butted in, one of the few things he'd said to me in well over a week. "I need a moment alone with my family."

"Yeah, sorry." No longer hungry, I tossed my half-eaten container of peanut butter in the trash and moved around them. I pivoted outside the doorway, expecting Anika to follow me out, but she'd already stepped inside. I caught a glimpse of her pulling out a chair before Brooks closed the door.

I swallowed and started toward the front of the store, my chest and throat unbearably tight, not at all comfortable with this feeling. It was too familiar. I was at someone else's whim here. And it was clear whose whim that was. Brooks might not outright kick me out the door, but he'd never let me in again. And in return, I'd never fully have Levi or Nolan—Brooks would always be between us.

Chapter Twenty-Eight

"You sure you don't want me to tag along?" Levi asked, pulling the Jeep alongside the diner.

"Nah, you have homework," I said, grabbing my bag and pushing open the door. "Plus, someone has to go back to the shop and nag Nolan to order that candy."

I bit my lip, wishing I'd kept my mouth shut when his smile faltered. I hadn't heard any more about the candy fiasco. Brooks and Anika had slipped out the back door, and I'd interpreted the silence as a sure sign to stick to the front of the store and mind my own business. "Alright, I'll be back at the shop if you need anything. You want me to swing by when I'm done?"

"That's okay, thanks." I hopped out and stole at peek at the front button of my jeans, making sure the hair tie I'd looped around it in an effort to make them fit on my growing hips was still in place. "I'll ask Layne for a ride, but I'll text you if something changes."

I waved goodbye and slipped into the diner, busier than I'd ever seen it. Every booth and table was full, much different than the slow flow Lila tried to keep. I stole the last stool at the counter and ordered a side of fries from one of the high school waiters Lila kept on. I glanced around and waved at Layne, grinning from across the room, before grabbing the book my OB had given me from my bag.

Immersed in reading about what to expect for week eighteen—*Tater's the size of a sweet potato! Ha!*—and nibbling on a fry, I fumbled the book when a voice snuck up behind me. "Did you really think you could hide here and I'd miss ya?"

I looked back and smiled at Wren. "I'd never hide from you."

She rolled her eyes, but her sass didn't warm my heart—not when I noticed the deep, hollow pits beneath her eyes. "Well, let me have a look at you."

I stood and let her make a fuss, doing my best not to watch her too closely. "I hope you're not mad you found out from Jake."

"Jake?" she scoffed, pausing to pat the gentleman on the stool beside mine on the shoulder. The man didn't put up a fight at all in moving, and I laughed as she slid up on the seat. "Honey, I told Jake weeks ago. Old man didn't believe me either. Said I was seeing things."

I furrowed my brows and lifted my hand in greeting at Jake, who was across the diner, sitting with men and women dressed in hunting gear. "What? How?"

She snatched one of my fries, dunking it in ketchup. "I've had three kids. Trust me—no one touches their stomach as much as I saw you doing unless there's a baby in there. Or I suppose they have some sort of intestinal problem."

I snorted, shaking my head. "I'm surprised you didn't call me out on it."

"I was letting you go at your own pace, honey. It's important to let people do that." She pulled my plate between us, grabbing another handful of fries. "I was sad to hear about the cabin—but I knew it was time. At least now you've got a handsome landlord. How's that going with Brooks?"

I groaned. That's what Brooks was, wasn't he? My landlord. "It's fine."

She grinned, and there was a look in her eye that I once believed meant trouble. "Never thought I'd see the day when not only one but three Graham boys were at the mercy of a woman."

"Ha!" I pointed a fry at her. "That's where you're wrong. I'm one-hundred-percent at their mercy."

"Are you telling a dying woman she's wrong?"

"No," I started, my voice high, only to shake my head when I caught her grinning. "That's not funny, Wren."

She shrugged, her feet swinging beneath the stool. "It's the truth. Might as well have some fun with it."

"How are you feeling?" I asked when she grabbed my soda, claiming it hers when her lipstick stained the straw red.

"Perky as a turkey. I leave for another round in the morning."

I eyed her, pressing my lips together before I said, "Are you sure you're alright? You weren't feeling well when we were supposed to have breakfast—"

"That was weeks ago, Shay," Wren said, something edged in her tone. "Those first few days after treatment are always hard. But I feel good now." She grabbed another fry, but froze, peeking at me from the corner of her eye. "You don't mind, right? My doctor's a real stick-in-the-mud and doesn't like me to eat this during treatment."

I laughed and slid the plate over to her, feeling guilty for pushing her to talk about it. "Would you stop if I did mind? You're stealing food from my child."

She chuckled, glancing down at my belly. "Nolan said you named your baby Noodle or something. Sort of a strange name if you ask me. Though I guess it works for you, Betsy."

I tilted my head up and laughed—and not just any laugh. It was real, genuine, sort of like Wren. "It's Tater, and Nolan picked it!"

Wren smiled, letting me have my moment of joy—before she gutted me, going straight for the kill shot. "So, how long are you gonna make me sit here until you tell me what's going on with you and Brooks?"

I closed my mouth, only to open it and close it again. "Um, nothing. He's my landlord."

She stared me, deadpan. "Rumor is he found out in the middle of ripping your top off."

"What?" I choked, heat crawling up my chest. "Who is saying—"

"Relax," she said with a laugh, patting my wrist. "I'm only teasing you. No one's saying anything, and believe me, they'd hear an earful and catch a foot in their mouth if I caught them speaking a word about what's brewing between you and Brooks."

Gratitude swelled in my chest, thankful to have her in my corner. "Wren . . . there's nothing going on with us."

"Well, why not?"

"Why?" I scoffed, resting my head between my hands. "Well, I'm having a baby. Another man's baby at that. No one willingly takes on damaged goods unless they have to." I stared at the counter and breathed through my nose, wishing I could suck the words back in. "Sorry," I muttered. "I'm not trying to have a pity party, I promise. I'm fine being a single mom—I've accepted it. I'm not naive enough to believe any man could fix me."

"Well, at least you have that. Because you're right—no man can fix you." Tears brimmed in my eyes, but I willed myself to meet her gaze, to face the sternness in her words. Her lips were pursed; even her hold on my hand was tight. "Only you can fix you, Shay. Only you. But I'm willing to bet, and don't you dare argue with me, that there are a lot of good men—good people in general—who are willing to sit with you as you sort through the pieces." She dropped my hand, the tightness in her shoulders easing, and grabbed another fry. "Did you know I'm not really related to the Grahams?"

I shrugged. I saw little to no resemblance between Jake or Wren and the Graham brothers, so I'd assumed the relation was distant. "Is Jake their biological uncle then?"

"Nope," Wren said, making a popping sound with her lips. "We're not related in the least bit—heck, I might share more blood with you than I do them." I sat up and wiped at my nose with my sleeve. "Even before their daddy died, I considered those boys part of the family. Even when I wanted to wring their necks as teenagers for letting a skunk into my house." She laughed softly, and so did I, hanging on to her every word. "And the fact you didn't know until this moment that those boys weren't truly my nephews tells me they claim me as much as I do them. So I guess what I'm trying to say is family has everything to do with heart and nothing with to do with blood. And I think someday, wherever you are, you'll find it. You and Tater."

I nodded, unable to do more. I didn't know if I believed her, if I thought anyone would take Tater and me in. And not just in a romantic sense, but the sort of safety you find only in a family—blood or not. The kind where you can look around a room and be confident in those around you, in yourself, knowing that no matter what, you have a safety net to catch you.

I wasn't sure I could *trust* anyone to catch me to begin with.

Wren must've sensed my doubt, felt my lack of faith, because then her hand was on my wrist and she was yanking me to my feet. "Come on, let's go break something."

Wren had lost her mind.

Or marbles, as she'd probably say.

"Is this legal?" I asked, warily glancing at the stack of glass plates in my arms, ones Wren had us grab from her house before she'd driven us out to the middle of nowhere.

"Oh my hell, Shay," Wren said with a groan, slamming the car door shut. "Are you planning on squabbling the whole time? If so, you can stay in the car with Jake."

I bit back my grin. Jake hadn't even batted an eye when Wren told him what she was doing, as though it was completely normal to create chaos in the middle of the night. I followed her as she led the way down a dirt path, sticking close enough to the car that its headlights still reached us.

I stood beside her, arms straining from the weight of the plates, as I waited for her instruction. I realized there were none when she yanked a plate off the top and chucked it right at the ground, shattering it. "Woo!" she said, winding her arm like she was a major-league baseball player. "That felt good." She grabbed another, smashing it into smithereens. "Come on, it's past my bedtime, and I've got an early morning. Get throwing."

I warily set the stack on the ground between us. I'd never been to a panic room, though I'd seen videos of people destroying things for the fun of it. When Wren suggested we go smash plates, I'd imagined this would have the same effect, but now I just felt silly. Sensing my hesitation, she said, "It can only break you if you let it, Shay. So let it go."

Let it go.

I didn't believe she was telling me to get over it. Or that my pain or grief weren't valid. I didn't think she was telling me I was weak. As I watched her throw another plate, her eyes full of fire and determination, instead it seemed like she was telling me to keep pushing, fighting.

Fingers shaking, I snatched a plate and tossed it at the ground, frowning when it only broke in two. With better resolve, I grabbed the two pieces and chucked them, smiling as they shattered. Using even more force, I tossed plate after plate, aware Wren had sat down. But I didn't think of her—I didn't think of anyone but me.

I thought of the girl who I believed to be a burden. The one who was a disappointment, a waste. One who was small, insignificant, a failure. I stared at the broken plates, feeling a lot like that. Like someone had taken me and carelessly tossed me around, not second-guessing their actions. But the more plates I shattered, I thought of what Wren had said at the diner. How the right people would sit with me as I sorted through the pieces.

These plates were broken—but they weren't unfixable.

They were *resilient.*

And maybe I was too.

I waved goodbye to Wren and Jake as they dropped me off in front of the Grahams', stifling a yawn. It had taken us an hour to pick up the broken plates, not wanting to leave any glass behind. My back was aching, but my heart was rejuvenated. I was reminded why I wanted to stay in Wallowpine. Because of Wren—and people like her.

I smiled, remembering how she'd asked me to keep her updated on the *babe*, but my confidence wavered when I stepped inside and found all three brothers waiting for me in the living room.

"Hi," I mumbled and tucked my hands behind my back, feeling like a teenager who was caught out after curfew.

"Late night." Nolan wiggled his brows like it wasn't only nine p.m. "I was starting to think you skipped town."

I knelt and greeted Cash, his tail thumping from side to side, and gave his head a good rub. "Unfortunately, you won't be able to get rid of me that easily."

"What were you doing?" Brooks surprised me by asking, his attention not on the television, but me.

"I was at the diner," I replied stiffly as I stood and walked to the kitchen for a glass of water. "And then I hung out with Wren for a little bit."

"Did she drive you home?" he asked, apparently now my keeper.

I frowned, not only at him asking, but because of the sandwich sitting on the counter. Had Brooks made this for Anika and she forgot to eat her dinner? I rolled my eyes and tossed it in the trash, deeming myself their maid. But at least she wasn't here. "Nope."

Okay, that was a lie. But Jake had been the one driving—so technically Wren hadn't given me a ride home.

He stared at me, clearly waiting for an explanation. I knew it was a little bratty to not give him one, but it wasn't like he was divulging anything to me. He was the one who'd closed the door on me so they could have a *family* meeting. I guzzled from my glass, holding his gaze the entire time. Only when it was drained did I say, "Levi, are you still willing to drive me to my next appointment? It's still a few weeks away, but I need to call and schedule it in the morning. And I'd like to try and schedule it around you—"

"Schedule it whenever and I'll make it work," Levi said, his attention on the empty sketch pad on his lap. "But only if you promise not to torture me with Taylor Swift again."

Nolan tossed a pillow at his head. "Don't act like you weren't singing along with Shay this morning."

I smiled, grateful to see they'd moved past their dispute this afternoon. And despite my annoyance, I was relieved to see Brooks sitting with his brothers, hoping the contention between them had eased. But the relief vanished once

I turned to the sink, my stomach dropping at the sight of the dishes within. I let out a steadying breath and turned on the water, unable to make out what was being said behind me as I washed *their* dishes. To be fair, they'd never asked me to clean up their messes, but Declan hadn't either. It had been expected. I didn't know if that was the case here, but I knew it was better if they believed I served a purpose here. I didn't want them to kick me out. Just as I finished the last plate and switched off the water, they fell silent.

Brooks whispered something I couldn't hear to Nolan, and the latter groaned before he asked, "Hey, darlin', what's your next appointment for?"

"Um—" I faced him and leaned against the sink, stirring Cash where he lay at my feet. "It's the anatomy scan, remember?" I replied, almost positive I'd told him the other night.

"Will you get another one of those picture things where the baby looks like a blob?" Levi asked, grinning from ear to ear.

Nolan smirked. "You mean a tater tot."

I laughed, regretting when I'd shown them the ultrasound from my first appointment. "Yes, I'll get another ultrasound. And it'll resemble a baby more this time." I glanced at Brooks and my chest tightened. His eyes were questioning, lost. He hadn't seen the ultrasound, and I felt a twinge of guilt for leaving him out, but I quickly shoved it away. If he was interested, he would have asked.

And he hadn't.

Rather than filling him in, I shrugged. "I'm going to bed." I didn't know if Brooks had patched things up with his brothers, but he could ask them if his nosiness grew. "Good night."

I made my way to the stairs, barely touching the railing before Nolan teased, "Make sure you lock your window back up after you sneak in whoever dropped you off tonight."

I snorted. "Wren would terrorize you guys in your sleep," I said, not caring if I was admitting I'd fibbed before. I didn't want to play games, even if Brooks had moved on. Because no matter what, what I felt with him was real, and I wasn't going to lessen that by trying to hurt him. "I meant it when I said I didn't want to date anyone."

When I'd moved to Wallowpine, the last thing on my mind was dating. I'd come here guarded, determined to make a life for my child. But somehow Brooks had meddled his way through, then just as quickly ripped himself away.

And now I was left with a gaping hole of *what if.*

What if I'd told him sooner?

Would I have learned to trust and love again?

It didn't matter. We were over before we'd begun. But it hurt to see how quickly he'd moved on. How he'd detached himself from me, like he hadn't felt what I had. But I knew what I felt. Knew those feelings for him were real. They'd been growing before he'd even kissed me.

That didn't just go away.

No matter how much I wished it would.

Chapter Twenty-Nine

"Go ahead and lie down, the doctor will be in shortly."

"Thank you," I said to the nurse as she closed the door and dropped my bag atop the chair beside the exam table, this time leaving my clothes on. Typically, once the door clicked shut, it was go time. A race to undress and shove my panties in my bag so I could hide under a paper sheet before my doctor came in. Like she hadn't already seen me in all my naked glory. All modesty had gone out the window my first appointment, when the doctor pulled out this probe-looking thing and told me where she'd have to insert it in order to see the baby.

Yeah . . . we were real acquainted.

I searched the room, relaxing when I failed to find that intrusive device. I lay back, thrumming my fingers atop my stomach. I'd eagerly awaited this twenty-week appointment since I'd scheduled it. The last month had dragged by unbearably slow.

Other factors had contributed to that, but I wasn't focusing on anything but my baby and me right now. A baby that was *finally* starting to make its presence known. Even Nolan had commented on my bump, teasingly accusing me of sticking my stomach out.

I'd almost invited him to tag along and see for himself, but decided against it since Levi was already driving me. I felt guilty for relying on him, but he'd assured me he had errands to run in town. That didn't stop my insides from tangling together when I heard Brooks mutter under his breath that I was more than capable of driving Jake's truck.

In the midst of telling myself I'd start practicing again, there was a tap on the door. I sat up just as my doctor walked in. "Hi, Shay," Dr. Malitina said, flipping through my chart. "How are you feeling?"

"Good. You were right about feeling better during the second trimester." Despite a few uncomfortable instances—like when I'd blown grits on Brooks—my first trimester had been fairly mild. "My friend Layne thinks I'm going to have a boy. I guess her sister-in-law threw up all nine months, and she had a girl."

She just raised her brows. No doubt she heard all sorts of old wives' tales in her profession. "Guess we'll find out today—if you're wanting to?" she asked with a smile, turning on her computer.

I nodded, sputtering a short laugh. "Definitely. Maybe once I know the sex, Nolan will stop referring to the baby as Tater."

She hummed, scrolling through my digital file. "Is Nolan your partner?"

"No, not at all," I quickly answered, not surprised she hadn't asked if he was the father. During my first appointment, they'd had me fill out paperwork—one of the questions asking if the father was involved. Surprisingly, I hadn't been embarrassed to divulge that I'd be doing it alone, assuming they'd only asked so they could be sensitive to all situations. "He's just my friend—kind of like an annoying brother."

She went over my charts with me, asking questions and measuring my belly to ensure my growth was on track. Double-checking that I was avoiding stress and drinking plenty of water. "Oh, that reminds me—" she said, scooting on her stool across the room. She reached into a drawer and pulled out a handful of pamphlets. "You still have a while to go since you're not due until March, but it might be a good idea to look into some of these classes. They're not mandatory, but I know a lot of first-time parents appreciate them."

I grabbed the pamphlets and quickly flipped through, seeing one for a lactation class and one for a birthing class. My chest clenched, and against my will, grief and sorrow slithered their way in. I looked through the birthing class one, the front cover displaying several sorts of couples. I was okay doing this alone. I'd chosen this. But it didn't help that each time I came, I sat in the waiting room *alone*, where most women had supportive partners or family members with them.

"And just so you know," Dr. Malitina said, pulling me out of those thoughts, "those classes are for anyone. So whether you choose to go alone or bring a friend, you're welcome, okay? We want to make sure you feel as supported as we can." She smiled at me and tapped her pen on the pamphlets in my hand. "There's one in there about doulas too. You can never have enough support."

I nodded and dropped the papers in my bag to deal with at another time. "Thank you."

"Alright, alright," she said, switching off the lights. "I'm done with the boring stuff—time to see your baby." I rolled up my shirt and lay back, tapping my fingers along the side as she ran cold gel over my stomach. "I'll check the gender first, okay? Then we'll take measurements to make sure little Tater is where it should be."

I nodded and rasped a laugh, tears prickling at the edge of my eyes. My throat tightened, but I couldn't contain my smile, even as a different wave of emotions threatened to push me down. I was doing this—I was having a baby. But what if something was wrong? What if I'd inadvertently done something and the baby wasn't healthy? Was it my fault I was here alone? Maybe if I'd tried harder, done better, Declan would be here. Was I strong enough to do this?

How was it possible to feel so much at once?

But then, everything stopped. Every worry and thought vanished. And there was nothing else, nothing but the thumping heartbeat filling the room. I stared at the little baby on the screen, miraculously growing inside of me, trusting me to give it life.

And I knew nothing but love.

"Everything go okay?" Levi asked when I climbed into his Jeep, tossing his sketch pad into the back seat.

"Yeah." I wiped at my cheeks, my eyes exhausted and sore. I needed a nap. "Everything looks really great. All ten fingers and toes."

"So . . ." He drummed his fingers on the steering wheel, his brow raised. "Did you find out?"

"Kind of," I said with a light laugh. I pulled out an envelope, my fingers shaking with the urge to tear it open. "I asked her to write it down instead."

"Oh no," Levi groaned, dipping his head. "You're gonna make us wait, aren't you? Are you wanting one of those gender reveal parties?"

"No way." I scrunched my nose. "I mean, I'm sure they could be fun for someone else." Even if I had a family or a partner, I wouldn't want one. That sort of attention had me squirming beneath my skin. "I just decided to wait, save it for when I'm alone."

"Can I steal a peek? I promise I won't tell you."

"No." I laughed and tucked the envelope away, not wanting to risk losing my nerve for what I'd decided during the appointment. "Did you get everything done that you needed to? I'm okay if we stay longer."

"Nope. I'm all done." He pulled out of the parking lot and onto the road, starting the hour-and-a-half drive home from Hillshire. "Besides—" He paused as his phone rang, the music pausing and the speakers playing: *"Brooks calling."* "Again?" Levi muttered before he pressed a button, turning on the hands-free option. "Hello?"

There was static and rustling before Brooks asked, "Where are you at?"

Levi rolled his eyes. "We're barely leaving."

"That took a while . . ." I stared out the window, hoping the lapse in conversation meant the call had failed. "Everything okay?"

Levi shot me an apologetic glance, probably wishing Brooks had called me—not that he had my number. And even if he did, he wouldn't have called.

Brooks and I might be cordial, but we didn't speak. "Yup." Levi grinned, his wavy hair sharp at his chin. "Everything's great with me, thanks for asking. How are you, Brooks?"

"That's not what—" I smirked at Brooks's deep breath through the line. "Whatever. Come straight to the diner after you drop Shay off at home, okay? Anika's going to meet us there."

I stared out the window and avoided Levi's gaze, not wanting to see the pity there. It wasn't the first, and likely not the last, time the three of them had gone out with Anika. I didn't know if she and Brooks were dating—I'd only seen her at the house and then the shop that one time—but I wasn't about to ask. None of my business.

"You alright?" Levi asked once they'd hung up. "Want me to grab you something from the diner? Maybe you can come with us—"

"I'm okay, thanks." I cut him off, not because I didn't wish I had been invited along—of course I wanted to be included. But I had more pressing issues to deal with when I got home. "Thank you for driving me, Levi," I added, not wanting to take my nerves out on him.

"Anytime, Shay. I mean it."

I picked at a loose thread on my jeans, hearing the sincerity in his words and believing wholeheartedly Levi would be there for me. He'd proven it time and time again. "Hey . . . you mind if I ask you something?"

"Go for it."

I twisted in my seat, facing him. "I overheard a conversation between Nolan and Brooks . . . and Nolan said you knew I was pregnant." I paused, waiting until he nodded before I continued on, "So if you knew, why didn't you tell Brooks? You could've stopped him."

"Why would I want to stop him?" he asked, turning down the radio. "Shay, none of us care that you're pregnant—not even Brooks. I didn't think it mattered."

I stared at him and raised a challenging brow. Brooks very much cared. "I think most people might appreciate it if their brother warned them they were about to be strapped down with hormones and an extra mouth to feed."

He laughed, shaking his head. "Fine, I'll admit, I probably should've given Brooks a heads-up. Trust me, both he and Nolan have ranted to me about it. But the point is, I'd do it the same way again. It doesn't matter to me if you're having a kid or not. It doesn't change who you are." I nodded, silently appreciating the man that was Levi Graham. But he must've interpreted my silence wrongly, because he added, "Why don't you come with me to the diner? Maybe I can try to make Brooks explain—"

"No," I choked out, my cheeks burning at the thought of sitting there—with an audience, no less—as Brooks tried to explain why we couldn't be together. "It's really fine, I promise. It's just been on my mind and I thought I'd ask. Thank you for having my back."

His lips tilted up to the side in a smile. "You sure you don't want to come? We'd have fun."

"That's okay. Thank you." I reached over and squeezed his hand in reassurance. "I have plans tonight anyway."

I should've gone to the diner.

Enduring a meal with Brooks and his maybe, maybe-not girlfriend would've been better than this.

Cash whined beside me from where I sat on the front porch, somehow sensing my nerves. With shaking hands I rubbed his head as he nuzzled my belly, his large brown eyes holding mine. "I'm so scared."

He pressed closer, climbing on my lap, and I laughed, giving him a tight squeeze before I pulled out my phone. I hesitated on Levi's contact, considering calling him to come get me. Heck, I even considered grabbing the keys to Jake's truck. But instead, I shoved my needs aside and dialed a familiar number, one I couldn't forget no matter how much I'd tried.

My heart pounded with each ring, only to falter when the ringing halted. There was shifting on the other end, followed by a hesitant, "Hello?"

I swallowed. "Declan . . . it's me, Shay."

Chapter Thirty

My lungs burned. A slow, subtle burn. It wasn't enough. I pushed my legs harder, pumped my arms faster as I ran down the dirt road, chasing something I feared I'd never catch. I knew it was careless to be out here alone in the middle of the night, but I couldn't sit still.

I needed something to numb me.

I gently tugged Cash to a stop as I slowed. I was cleared for exercise, but I knew I shouldn't push myself too far. Cash leaned against my thighs, his presence like a gentle balm to my nerves. Feeling brave with a can of bear spray and my faithful companion, I plopped down in the meadow, the Grahams' porch light flickering in the distance.

Tonight had been a mistake, and it had cost me. I'd thrown away all the healing and growth I'd made, that moment of desperation leaving me raw. My phone buzzed in the side pocket of my leggings, but I made no move to reach for it. I knew who was texting me, and I didn't have to read his words to hear his voice in my head.

I set the envelope in the grass beside me and wiped my cheeks, afraid I'd ruin what was written inside with my tears. Calling Declan had been a long shot—a risk. I hadn't called him to take me back, or even for help with the baby. I called because of the guilt that had haunted me since my appointment.

I thought I'd robbed him.

But Declan didn't feel that way at all.

"Declan . . . it's me, Shay."

There was a long pause, so long I glanced at my phone to see if he'd hung up. But then, as crisp and as cool as air, he said, "What do you want?"

I should've hung up, but I was never smart when it came to Declan. "Nothing," I whispered. "I had an appointment today . . . Thought you might want to know."

It was quiet, but I knew he was there. He was calculating, planning the best tactic. "Why?"

I swallowed, my throat unbearably tight. I willed myself to be strong for my baby. If I wasn't strong, who would be? "You know how much it hurts me to not have a relationship with my mom. For my father to not know I exist. If you've changed your mind, I don't want to deny you the chance to be a part of this. I have the gender right here . . . We could find out together."

There was no pause. He laughed, the sound cruel and rough. "Did you finally realize how good you had it, butterfly? What, is life too hard? Did you find out no one wants damaged goods?"

I furrowed my brows. What was I doing? Why was I subjecting myself to this again? "I wasn't calling for me. That's not what this is. I was calling for our baby—"

"Your baby," he hissed violently, and I swore I felt the ghost of his touch on my neck, felt his punishing strength. "You made your choice, now live with the consequences. You threw everything away, and now you're alone . . ."

I pulled my knees to my chest, bundling myself up as tight as I could, forcing my mind to clear. I shuddered a breath, feeling like knives were wedged in my airway. I wasn't wrong in leaving—I was protecting *my family*. But now, my wounds were being carved open from the outside in, and it was agonizing.

"Shay—"

I screamed and scrambled to my feet, Cash barking. I backpedaled as I reached for the bear spray. "You—" I choked, grateful I hadn't sprayed as Cash stretched up on his hind legs, licking Brooks's neck. "You scared me."

"I scared you?" he asked, his voice shaking with nerves I didn't understand. And I thought I might've even seen the remnants of fear in his eyes before he pointed the light from his flashlight at the ground. "What are you doing out here? I came home and you were gone. I thought you left—"

"Don't pretend you'd care," I muttered under my breath, not caring how petty I sounded.

"I would care." The gentleness in his voice was enough to make me pause. Why wasn't he fighting back? "I cared when I went to your room tonight and found it empty."

"Why would you go to my room?" I asked before I could remind myself it shouldn't matter.

He swallowed hard. "I came home early from dinner. Levi had mentioned you seemed tired . . . and I wanted to check on you. Plus, I know Cash sleeps with you, so I figured I'd let him out to go to the bathroom. But you were both gone, and I guess my mind went to the worst-case scenario."

"Maybe you should take Cash with you the next time you go out with *your family*. Then you won't have to worry." I internally winced at the bite in my words. And because I thought there was sincere worry in his voice, I resisted the urge to remind him if he'd paid attention, he would've seen Jake's truck parked outside his house. And it wasn't like I had anywhere else to go. I shook my head and stared down at the spot where I was previously sitting, remembering why I came out here.

I had bigger things to focus on.

"What are you doing?" he asked as I crouched down and scanned the grass. "Shay?" Brooks shifted beside me, his flashlight shining on my searching hands.

"Do you see an envelope?" My voice was high, but my pride was not as I crawled on my knees, fervently searching. "It was right here."

"Why would there be an envelope out here?"

"Because it's mine!" I stood and snatched the flashlight from him, following the direction of the breeze. "Please, please, please," I begged as Cash walked beside me, his nose shoved to the ground. "Go find it, boy, go."

"He's not a bloodhound," Brooks teased from behind me. "Besides, there's at least a dozen more appealing scents to him. He'll probably lead you to a raccoon—"

I turned, not thinking as I shoved his chest. He didn't falter even an inch as I pushed him again. He gripped my arms, his eyes wide, when I made to leave—not to hurt, but to hold me there. "You and me—we're not doing that."

I froze in my writhing, my mouth open. I knew I hadn't hurt him, but what was I doing? Why was I taking my pain out on him? I suddenly felt no better than Declan. "I'm so sorry—"

"Shh." His hands traveled up to my jaw, urging me to meet his gaze. "I'm not mad, and you have nothing to be sorry for. But you and I do our best when we talk. So let's talk. Let me help you, okay?"

My lip wobbled. "I lost the most important piece of paper of my life."

He lowered one hand from my jaw and reached behind him, yanking something out of his back pocket. "You mean this?"

I gaped at him, snatching the envelope out of his treacherous hold. "You're a jerk." But it didn't carry half the anger I'd intended. I stared at the envelope, forgetting about what had just occurred with Brooks. "I called Declan tonight," I admitted, like Brooks was my friend and genuinely cared.

He stiffened, close enough his heat mingled with mine. "Why?"

I wiped my eyes with the back of my hand. "I was supposed to find out the gender today, but I had the doctor write it down for me instead. I don't know what I expected to happen, but I'm an absolute moron for thinking he'd care."

Ashamed, I stepped back, but Brooks halted me again, his hands wrapped about my elbows. "Shay—"

"Do you know what hurt the most?" I asked and let him pull me against his chest. I deserved a moment of weakness. "It wasn't how he insulted me, accused me of crawling back to him. It was how he spoke about Tater. He wants absolutely nothing to do with his own baby." At least my own father didn't know I existed. But Declan did. "How can he hate the best thing that's ever happened to me? I love this baby so much, Brooks. And he hates—"

"Shay." His voice was hot against my ear, his arms unbreakable around me. "He doesn't deserve to love you or *your* baby. Maybe I'm wrong in saying that, and he could change, but he doesn't deserve to have you in his world."

"I don't want to be with him," I said in a whisper. "Even if he changed his mind and stepped up to be a father, I will never be with him again. I just felt guilty, like I was being selfish and taking Tater away from more people to love them."

"Tater, huh?" He pulled back with a small smirk on his lips, his beard scruffier than the last time we'd been this close. "Don't tell me Nolan's name actually stuck."

I choked on a laugh, snot running down my nose. "No, I just don't like calling the baby *it*. It feels weird."

He smiled, his hands lingering on my lower back. "Tater is lucky to have you, Shay. That baby won't ever go a day not knowing how loved they are by you."

I sniffed, his words sending a wave of relief through my heart. "Yeah, well, Tater's only going to have me."

He shook his head, his eyes closed. "That's not true. You should hear my brothers, Shay—I caught both of them the other night looking up those playpen things so you could bring Tater to work." I laughed and rested my forehead against him, absorbing every word, every touch he was giving me. He swallowed deeply, and I shuddered as I felt his voice against my ear. "And you have me . . . Both you and Tater do."

"Brooks." My voice rattled, on the edge of breaking. His arms fell to his side as I stepped back, retreating from his hold and heat. I couldn't do this. I opened my mouth but stopped, deciding it was unnecessary to protest. He didn't need to know I didn't believe him. "Thank you."

But he seemed to hear my doubts and grabbed my hand. "Please," I cried—not because I didn't want to hold his hand, but because I *couldn't*. I couldn't risk being hurt again. I needed to be the best I could be by the time Tater came. "I can't do this."

"Do what?" he asked, oblivious to how my hand trembled within his. "Why are Nolan and Levi allowed to care about you, about Tater—but I'm not?"

"You hurt me," I said, not to further inflict pain, but so he knew, so he understood. "Maybe I'm being oversensitive. I don't know—"

"You're not." His hand was steady and sure. "I'll never regret anything more than what I did to you, Shay."

"It's okay," I murmured. The last thing I wanted was for Brooks to feel guilty. "I caught you off guard, and you were scared. There was no way you could've known what happened to me."

He still didn't know the entire story. He never would.

"You're right. I didn't know." His fingers edged my chin up, letting me see the sincerity in his words. "But I knew you'd been hurt—I knew it the moment I stepped foot in your cabin and you looked like you were about to come out of your skin from being alone with me. Regardless, it shouldn't have mattered. It wasn't my choice to make, and who am I to judge you? Even if Declan wasn't a prick, and had treated you how you deserved, it was still *your choice*." My choice. Declan had tried to take that away. He'd tried to force me into a corner, refusing to let us decide together if we wanted a family. Shoving his selfishness away, I focused back on Brooks's words. "But I let my anger and my past blind me, and in return, I hurt you. I was wrong, and I don't expect you to forgive me—but I'm sorry."

Tears brimmed in my eyes, and I was at a loss. The words *I'm sorry* were so foreign to me. Looking back at my entire life, I wasn't sure I'd ever heard such raw regret. Brooks could've twisted it around, tried to pin it on me—exactly like my mom and Declan would've done.

I licked my lips and told myself to be honest, to speak my mind. "I thought you wanted nothing to do with me. We haven't talked in weeks."

He blew out a heavy breath, likely remembering when he'd said those very words. "I've been trying to give you space. I don't blame you for this, but I didn't miss how you'd clam up each time I came around. I figured you only wanted to be around Nolan and Levi."

"I was trying to give *you* space." I shook my head, my voice no more than a weak rasp. "I know I'm not faultless in this. I really screwed up with how I told you."

"I don't *need* or *want* space from you," he said without hesitation, tucking his hands in his pockets. "Every time I've tried to push you away, I haven't meant it. But I'm sorry for saying it."

"I'm so afraid I'm going to mess up and you're going to kick me out." I needed to get my fears out, otherwise I was going to drown in them.

"Never. I meant it when I said I wouldn't run you out of your home."

I pursed my lips together, struggling to believe him. Why wouldn't he? How was he any different than the woman who gave me life? The man who promised to love me and even participated in creating a life with me?

"Shay." His lips curled into a frail smile. "I promise—my brothers would toss me out before I could even consider kicking you out."

I forced a laugh, and our breaths mixed, neither one of us having taken a step back. "I'm sorry if I've created tension between you three."

He raised a dark brow, chuckling under his breath. "We fought before you came into our lives. And we're gonna fight when you leave. You don't need to worry about that—we're fine."

I nodded and stepped back, feeling more at ease than when I came out here. If any good had come from my conversation with Declan, it was that I'd gotten the closure I needed. He wanted nothing to do with us. And *that* was just fine. And Brooks . . . I'd have to trust that he wouldn't toss me aside. But I hadn't missed his words, how he'd casually mentioned me leaving, reminding me this wasn't permanent.

"Okay." I wrapped my arms around myself. "I'm going inside. I'm tired, and my bosses get grumpy if I drag in the morning." I started back toward the cabin, smiling when Cash brushed up beside me. My faithful companion.

"Shay," Brooks called and I stopped, turning back to look at him. His voice was breathless from where he lingered behind me, his flashlight pointed at the ground. "I miss you. A lot. Probably more than I should." He ran a hand through his hair. "And I promise—someday, Declan will regret that he gave you and Tater up. You're both the best thing that could happen to anyone."

Fiery heat raced through me, and my heart danced. I hadn't anticipated that. I knew Brooks didn't easily speak his mind. On instinct, I wanted to delve deeper into his words, see how he might use them against me. Because now that I'd escaped Declan's grasp, I could see through the words he'd so finely crafted together, manipulating me. But the damage still lingered, and I questioned everything.

And I was tired of it.

I *wanted* to trust someone. I wanted to breathe easily and let down my walls. Believe my flaws wouldn't be used against me. I'd been waiting for this moment to come, to finally break free of those bonds once and for all. But I was learning it didn't work that way. Healing wasn't a swift motion, something that happened instantaneously.

It was painful. It took time, patience, and grace.

I wasn't instantly going to be better. I wouldn't climb this mountain in a day. But I could do it—someday, without even knowing it, I'd be through it. Or at least I would wear it differently. It wouldn't hurt, but remind me of where I started, how much I'd grown.

Someday I'd be there.

I'd have to trust I wouldn't be there alone.

My eyes brimmed with tears, pooling with the weight of today—the good and bad. "Well, I'm not sorry that he did. We're better off without him."

His throat bobbed, a bitter breeze stirring the grass at our feet. "Is it okay if I'm not sorry either?"

I laughed under my breath and smiled. "I miss you. A lot. Probably more than I should," I admitted, repeating his words back to him.

He seemed to waver on his feet, like he was holding himself back. "You think we should do something about that?"

I bit my lip, wishing he would close the distance and decide for himself. But I didn't voice that. Brooks had his own mountains, his own struggles to conquer. And I recognized what he was offering me, what him asking and keeping distance meant. He was giving me a choice, something he hadn't always done. Despite how much I wanted to, I couldn't risk running to him, not with much more than my heart on the line. We had so much between us—there was literally a baby between us. And it was Tater who kept me from going to Brooks and showing him just how badly I missed him. My choices no longer affected just me.

But maybe I could be brave enough to have a little bit of hope.

"You think you can stand to be my friend after all?" I asked, biting my smile as I backed away.

He grinned, like I hadn't technically friendzoned him, and shouted, "I'm going to be the best friend you've ever had, Shay."

Chapter Thirty-One

I needed salt.

Lots of salt.

Salt wards off spirits and demons, right? Surely it was capable of dismissing the Karens of the world, seeking retribution because their beloved Timmy didn't get pumpkin-shaped Reese's. *I get it—they're better than the originals—but you don't see me throwing myself on the ground, do you?*

And that wasn't just because I couldn't get back up.

But seriously, she could drive the hour and a half to the local Walmart—"the mall," as the townies called it.

"Are there any local priests who practice exorcisms?" I asked from the doorway of Nolan and Levi's office, keeping a close eye on the front door. "Maybe some purification."

Nolan's eyes gleamed off the computer screen. "Do I even wanna know, darlin'? Did you join a cult?"

I pinned him with a stare, waiting until he looked my way. "Halloween candy."

His eyes widened into blue orbs, and he stole a glance at Levi, who was already shaking his head. "Really, Nolan? Halloween is tomorrow—you told me weeks ago you ordered it."

"There's freaking candy out there," Nolan reasoned.

"You said you had it handled," Levi snapped, making me regret not thinking it through before I started this conversation. "I should've just done it. You've clearly proven you're incapable."

"Do you have any idea how much they mark up seasonal candy?" Nolan scoffed as Levi stood, his forearms strained as he stuffed his laptop and notebook in his bag. "Geez, if it's that big of a deal to you, I'll go out there and spray-paint them orange myself."

"It's not about the candy!" Levi grabbed the last of his things and stormed out. I averted my gaze. "We should've sold this place. Anyone could do a better job than we are."

Apparently needing the last word, Nolan shouted, "Forgive me for not instantly knowing how to run a business! We can't all be geniuses like you!"

I winced as the back door slammed shut, a roar of an engine not long behind. Nolan leaned back and ran his hands down his face before I said, "I'm so sorry. I shouldn't have said anything."

"Nah," he said, his gaze lost and empty on the floor. "This isn't your fault. It's mine."

I glanced to the front, double-checking no customers had come in. "Is there anything I can do to help?"

He rubbed at his sharp jaw. "There's nothing any of us can do. We just gotta get through it."

I swallowed, heart aching at the bleak pits beneath Nolan's eyes, the unknown weight on his shoulders. "Get through what?"

He gave me a smile, but it only made me sad. It was nothing like his full, contagious one. "It'll be a year in November since Dad passed." He let out a weak groan and raked his fingers through his hair. "I know it's hard on all of us—but I screwed up. I should've done better, tried to lessen what I could for Levi."

I frowned and put a hand to my chest. Sometimes I forgot Nolan wasn't all kicks and giggles. He felt pain too. "You're grieving. I don't think it's possible to lessen that for anyone, not truly."

"Maybe." His voice was hollow as he focused back on the spreadsheets on his computer screen. "Do you need anything else?"

I made to leave, pausing with a hand on the door. "Is there a reason you make special orders for customers? It seems like it could be . . . draining," I said, remembering the times customers had come in demanding things, complaining about out-of-stock items that had no business being in a game shop.

He groaned, shaking his head. "You want the truth?"

"Always."

"Let's just say I was drunk and trying to get laid," he said, his grin cocky—and every bit of the Nolan I adored. "There was this out-of-towner, real pretty girl with long legs. Anyway, I remembered my dad had his grocery permit, one he barely used. So in an attempt to impress her, I told her I'd order her anything her heart desired. But I was so plastered that I didn't realize until days later, when half the town was asking for special orders, that I'd told just about anyone in the bar."

My lips twitched, holding in a grin. "Did you get the girl?"

"No. Pretty sure I vomited on her." He frowned, shaking his head. "But now everyone pretty much expects it, and I'm afraid I'll piss them off and lose business if I tell them no."

I watched him, remembering what Brooks once confided in me about Nolan. How he'd drown himself in alcohol. I knew Nolan drank, but I'd never seen him out of control, and it was hard to imagine. Hard to picture my goofy, bright friend in a dark place.

"You should tell them no," I said, knowing how heavily the shop weighed on him. "It's your business. Run it how you want. Run it how you would have with your dad." I hoped I hadn't crossed a line. Nolan was my friend, and he never hesitated to call me out, to give me a little push. Maybe he needed that, too. "I'm proud of you—it's no easy task to come in and fill someone else's shoes. And if you need me to bare my teeth at the locals a little bit, I will. I'll blame my hormones."

His gaze never trailed from the computer, but his throat bobbed. "You've got your own things going on, Shay. You don't need any more burdens."

I almost let out a laugh—Nolan would never be a burden to me. And in that moment, I knew why he and his brothers never hesitated to help me. They cared about me. Just like I cared about each of them. I wasn't sure there was anything I wouldn't do for them. He and his brothers were always—always—giving to me.

I wasn't sure I'd ever given them anything in return.

"Okay," I whispered, hoping reverence was the key. "You listen here: you're no Betsy, but you're going to have to do. Alright?" I waited a moment, allowing Betsy Jr.—Jake's truck—the chance to protest before I started the ignition again, hoping the third time was the charm.

It was.

Grinning, I slid it into gear, the truck steady and true as I slowly shifted up, working it up to a steady pace. I'd only popped inside the cabin for an apple after work before I'd climbed into the truck, not wanting to lose daylight. I was enough of a hazard already. If I wanted to surprise Nolan and Levi, I'd have to make the trip alone.

I turned onto the paved road and started the drive to Hillshire. My stomach grumbled, and I'd just promised Tater I'd grab dinner soon when I passed a forest ranger's truck on the opposite side of the road, coming from the direction I was going. In my rearview mirror, I watched as the truck turned around.

The truck's lights flashed, and my heart did a somersault.

Especially when a certain forest ranger climbed out.

I cranked my window down, not sparing a moment. "I swear if you call me ma'am, I'm going to run you over."

Brooks, wearing blue jeans and a flannel, not his work uniform, grinned and slid his sunglasses atop his head. Before I could ask if he worked today, he said, "I was just on my way home—thought someone stole your truck."

I smiled and stared at my hands in my lap, grateful we were slowly easing back into our friendship after the night in the meadow. We hadn't interacted much, but at least we weren't walking on eggshells.

He leaned against the door, his arms resting on the roof. "Where ya headed?"

"Hillshire." I tapped my fingers against the wheel. "It's just a quick trip, but I won't be back until after dark. So Cash might end up in your bed tonight."

He smirked. "I doubt that." He glanced in the direction of the sun, its light barely resting on the treetops. "Are you meeting someone up there?"

"Nope. Just me and Tater."

He raised a brow, the side of his lips inching up. "You still haven't opened that envelope?"

I shook my head, not sure why I hadn't torn into the envelope containing the gender. Unable to bring myself to open it, I'd stuffed it safely in my desk back home. Nolan and Levi were eager to know and harassed me daily, but this was the first time Brooks had mentioned it.

A loose breeze stirred through the truck, and I pushed my hair behind my ears. "Did you not work today?"

"No." He looked down at the ground, lightly kicking at a rock. "I . . . I had a meeting."

"Oh" was all I said, realizing he wouldn't give me more than that. And that was fine—I hadn't told him where I was going. Besides, if he'd gone to visit Anika, I didn't want to know. I hadn't seen her in a while, so I assumed she didn't live in town.

"Alright." He drummed his fingers on the door, his hand lingering there before he stepped back. "I'll let you go. Hope it's okay if I have Nolan or Levi text you in a bit to see how you're doing."

I bit my lip and let him manage one step back from the truck before I blurted, "Or you could come with me?" He pressed lips together, and I couldn't stop myself from grinning at his attempt to hide his smile, his eyes bright and welcoming. In an attempt to break that smile free, I teased, "But I want to drive—and I'm sorry, but I'm not giving you a lap dance this time."

Chapter Thirty-Two

"You've gone insane," Brooks mumbled, his cheeks burning as he trailed me down the aisle, pushing our shopping cart. "Hormones have driven you wild and down a path I cannot follow."

I rolled my eyes and put a finger to my lips, scanning over the seasonal Halloween candy. I shrugged and grabbed an armful, silently promising that Karen and Timmy wouldn't get a single piece. "You can go wait in the truck if you'd prefer."

"Are you going to leave any for anyone else?"

I clicked my tongue. "Maybe."

He sighed but continued to push the cart behind me, letting me scan freely. "Are you going to tell me why we're buying fifty pounds of candy? If you're planning on this being for trick-or-treaters, we don't get any at the house. But if that's something you really want to do, maybe we could set something up at one of the trunk-or-treats."

I clutched two bags against my chest and stared at him, unable to find the words. Truth was, I didn't have a desire to hand out candy to trick-or-treaters, but the fact Brooks was willing to help me make it happen had me on the verge of tears. I didn't know how I'd ever thought the way Declan treated me was okay, but now that I knew I deserved better, I didn't want Brooks's kindness to go unappreciated.

Candy still in my arms, I wrapped Brooks in a hug. "That's okay, but thank you," I said, pulling back before he'd even had a chance to embrace me. "The candy's for the shop."

He raised a brow. "Why? Did all the kids raid the store already?"

"No. There was a mishap, and I'm trying to help, that's all."

"Everything going okay there?" Even if he didn't know what had occurred at the shop today, he knew the anniversary of his father's death was soon. He carried the same grief his brothers did.

It was why I chose not to say anything, to do what I could to lighten their load.

"I'm just trying to help where I can." I felt his gaze on me, silently pressing for more, but I wouldn't give in. It was a family matter, and I wouldn't implant myself in it.

Mercifully, he moved on, nudging my shoulder with his hand. "Are you going to grab some peanut butter while we're here?"

Yeah, because your girlfriend keeps eating it. Or wasting it, considering I'm always the one who has to throw away the untouched stale sandwiches.

Choosing not to voice my jealousy, I grabbed a jar of peanut butter and made my way toward the electronics. "Something wrong with your phone?" Brooks asked as I crouched down and searched through the prepaid phone stand.

"No," I murmured, grabbing the first phone I saw. I didn't care what it was, only that it was different from what I had now. "I just want a new one."

I set it in the cart, ignoring the prickling heat of his gaze on my neck. "Shay," Brooks said, his fingers snatching the cart, stopping me from leaving. "What's wrong?"

I bit my lip, embarrassment inching up my cheeks. I wanted to lie, but we were barely starting over. "When I called Declan, he must've saved my number. And now he's been texting me . . . awful things. And I want it to stop."

"Block him," he insisted, his nostrils flaring.

I blew out a dry laugh. Nothing with Declan was that easy. I'd stopped looking at the messages days ago, but I could guess what they said. If Declan would call me a whore to my face, I could only imagine what he'd say behind a screen. "I have blocked him, but I think he's using one of those texting apps or something. He keeps getting new numbers."

I forced a smile on my lips, hoping Brooks would drop it. But he saw through my mask and held out his hand. "Give me your phone."

I scowled. "No."

He tightened his jaw, hard enough to grind teeth. "Don't protect him. If that bastard wants to hurt you, then I should be allowed to hurt him, too."

"I'm not protecting him." I clutched my bag in case he tried to grab my phone. "I wasted too many years on him, and I'm not about to give him any more. He's nothing."

"He is nothing," Brooks clenched out, his voice rough. "But that doesn't mean I'm not gonna go to California and bash his teeth in."

Despite the situation, I smiled. "Oh, yeah? You don't even know what he looks like. Are you just gonna break every man's teeth that you see until you find him?"

"Sounds good to me," he muttered, sidestepping me.

I gaped at him as he walked away and pivoted down an aisle. I didn't have the slightest clue what just happened, but I couldn't stop the strange sense of warmth coursing through me. I sort of liked seeing Brooks riled up.

I grabbed the cart and followed after him, thankful we were the only ones in the aisle when I asked, "Is everything okay?" He nodded, but unless he was fervently searching for a new skin care product, I believed otherwise. "Are you mad at me?"

"Never," he said as he faced me, his frustration fading. "I'm sorry. I'm not mad at you. I just . . ."

I scooted the cart off to the side and walked up to where he stood, absent-mindedly scanning the shelves. "You just what?"

The last of the tension in his shoulders eased, and his voice was soft, but not weak. "I wasn't there to protect you before, but I am now. And I hate the idea of him hurting you—of anyone hurting you. He might be nothing . . . but you're everything, Shay."

My heart hammered, pounding harder with each passing breath. Brooks was making it really difficult not to have feelings for him. Not knowing what to say, I grabbed a bright pink face mask and tossed it in the cart. "I'm going to go look in the baby section," I said, willing my voice not to reveal how afraid I felt. "If you want to come, you're welcome to. And that's something Declan will never get to do."

Chapter Thirty-Three

Rainbows had thrown up . . . everywhere.

I scrunched my nose at a yellow onesie that screamed sunshine, with an attached tutu that resembled plucked feathers. I hadn't found a single thing I liked, though I could hardly focus with the six-foot-something grumpy man scouring the baby section.

I'd regretted inviting Brooks as soon as I said it. I wouldn't have second-guessed it if Nolan or Levi were with me. But Brooks was complicated. He wanted to be my friend, and I truly believed he'd try his hardest to make sure he didn't hurt me again.

I could shop baby stuff with him—as friends.

"Are all baby things so expensive?" he asked, frowning at the price tag on a stroller.

"I think so." I wished I'd gone home. All this was doing was reminding me how poor and unprepared I was. "I think diapers are what really cost the most."

"Are you thinking about doing cloth diapers?" he asked as he poked a breast nipple covering. He looked up, his cheeks burning when he realized I'd caught him, and mumbled, "I wanted to know what it felt like."

I might've teased him over it, had I not been so curious how he knew about cloth diapers. But before I could ask, he grinned and pulled out a little onesie that read: *I like big bucks and I cannot lie*, the words placed around a set of antlers. "You should get this."

I laughed. "Nolan would love that. I told him the other day how babies can hear music in the womb, so now he keeps playing 'Baby Got Back.'"

He chuckled and showed me another one—*I like big racks.*

I groaned, shaking my head. "You guys are going to make Tater into a hoodlum." I shifted closer, his arm pressed against mine as I pulled a navy onesie from the rack. "This one's cute."

"*Oh deer*," he teased, mocking the onesie. "How clever."

Groaning again in defeat, I hid my face in my hands. "Brooks, these are all horrible. Tater's going to be naked."

He laughed, and the sound filled my soul, even more so when he said, "If you want, we can go to Phoenix soon. Get you and Tater some things."

The thought was appealing. I did need to get serious about shopping for Tater—and considering I wore a hair tie looped around my jeans button, I needed maternity clothes too. But doing that with Brooks? I knew he was being nice, but he had no idea what he was doing to me. It was a miracle I hadn't fallen at his feet when he got all protective and told me I was *everything*.

But I couldn't be *his* everything.

I nibbled on my lip, avoiding his burning gaze as I sorted further through the clothes, needing a moment to clear the moisture from my eyes. But it worsened, blurring entirely after I found a tan shirt—so tiny and pure—that read: *Daddy's little hunting buddy.*

Okay—but seriously? What is with this town's fixation on hunting baby clothes?

"We should go," I murmured, just as his hand slipped into mine, holding me there. "It's late."

"Hey." His voice was low, smooth. "You can get that one. You know that, right?"

I furrowed my brows. "No, I can't—and it doesn't matter. It's dumb, and I don't even hunt. Plus, I'd never put Tater in something so cringey."

He laughed, the puff of air stirring the hairs around my face. "Agree. Tater will have far better taste." His hand squeezed and pulled me close, close enough there was nothing but him. "But you do have people who care about you and Tater and will do their best to fill that fatherly role. There's Levi, Nolan, even Jake." He paused, the edge of his tongue sliding over his lip. "And me. Especially me."

I stumbled away, the back of my thighs hitting the display table. Going shopping with him was a very bad idea—too many things were happening. "You can't say things like that to me, Brooks."

My insides might've whimpered when he came forward and placed both arms on either side of me, caging me in. "And why not?"

I willed my breaths to slow, my cheeks to cool. Willed my heart to reinforce its barrier and protect me. I was a woman on the verge of losing control. But there was nothing I could do when his lips skimmed my ear, my resolve melting as he rasped, "It wouldn't be the first time you've called me daddy."

Oh my—

"Brooks?"

I startled and squeaked, knocking off a stack of clothes. Brooks stepped back, his hands up as though we'd been caught. He turned as I did, settling on a girl with deep wine hair, her smile wide and beaming. "I thought that was you!"

He cleared his throat, dipping his head. "Hey, Bonnie."

Bonnie? As in his high school sweetheart—his ex?

"It's been what—ten years?" she asked, openly checking out—ogling, she was ogling—his frame, her beady eyes everywhere.

"Something like that," he murmured, kneeling with me to help gather the clothes I'd flung on the floor.

She smiled, her attention never once leaving him. "Hey, I meant to call you last year after what happened with your dad," she said, oblivious to how his back tightened and his knuckles strained white. "But I wanted to tell you how sorry I am for your loss. I thought about flying in for the funeral, but it's hard to get away with my husband working so often, plus I have the kids. I'm only here because—" She stopped short, her gaze drifting to me as I stood and set the rumpled clothes back on the shelf. "I'm sorry, I don't believe we've met. I'm Bonnie. I'm sure you've heard all sorts of stories about me." She winked at Brooks. "Though I can't imagine Brooks talking too much about the one he let get away."

Resisting the urge to reveal I'd never heard more than her name—*I am not a cave troll*—I smiled. "I'm Shay."

She gave me a half smile, lazy compared to the one she'd given Brooks. "Oh my gosh," she gasped, stepping back like I'd thrown hot oil on her. "You're pregnant."

I blinked. "Uh—yeah."

She smiled again and rushed forward, yanking Brooks into a hug. "This is so great." Her hands traveled down his arms to his hands, then fell limp at her sides when he stepped back. "I have to say, I'm a little surprised. You always said you never wanted kids. If I'm being honest, that absolutely played a role in my leaving."

He doesn't want kids?

I stepped closer to Brooks, my fingers brushing his in an act of silent comfort, wanting to shield him from this woman who might or might not have broken his heart. His fingers latched onto mine, holding me as I grappled with what Bonnie had revealed.

"Well, you're just glowing," Bonnie said, not seeming to care that the conversation was one-sided. "My lips swelled up just like yours when I was pregnant." She looked me up and down, somehow missing my clenched fist, how tightly I held Brooks's hand. "How many weeks are you?"

"Um . . ." I swallowed, not sure why heat was building on my neck. "I'm almost twenty-two weeks."

"Oh." Her eyes widened, surprise evident in her tone. "You're kind of small for being that far along, aren't you? Well, listen. I know it can be difficult to watch your body change." She glanced at our cart at the edge of the aisle, oblivious to me gaping at her. "That's not yours, is it? I know right now might seem like the perfect time to pig out, but it's important you give your baby and body the nutrients it needs. You know, when I was pregnant—"

"Shay's doing a perfect job." Brooks wrapped an arm around my waist and directed us away, likely sensing I was on the verge of going full-blown mama bear. "It was great seeing you, and as much as I'd love to stick around and catch up, I can't stop thinking about the lap dance Shay promised me, so we'll see ya around."

"Don't you listen to a single thing she said," he grumbled and grabbed our cart, keeping one arm looped around me, probably in case Bonnie was watching. But it was only for me when he pulled me tighter into his heat and pressed his lips to the top of my head. "I'll make you a sandwich when we get home to make up for it."

I beamed and didn't resist the urge to lean into him. "I kind of like you grumpy."

"I feel God in this milkshake tonight," I said, embracing the role of Pam Beesley. But instead of being intoxicated at Chili's, I was chugging a chocolate milkshake in Jake's truck as Brooks drove us home. "Wooo!"

"You know," Brooks drawled, watching me out of the corner of his eye. "When I offered you a taste, that wasn't an invitation to drink the entire thing."

I stuck out my lower lip. "But this is payment for Bonnie."

He laughed, shaking his head. "That's what you said the fries were for," he said, snatching a handful from the bag on my lap.

"I'm only trying to fatten Tater up," I teased, slurping another sip from his shake before I set it back down in the cup holder.

"Hey." He grew silent, rubbing his jaw. "About what she said . . . I hope you didn't listen to her. You're perfect."

"You mean when she thought she had the right to comment on my body?" I snorted. It wasn't the first time I'd heard remarks on my body—Declan had never failed to tell me how he wished I was *bustier*—but being pregnant seemed to grant strangers permission to comment on what I should or shouldn't be doing. "It's fine. You'd think after having kids herself—and being a woman—she'd know better than to comment on whether or not my lips were swollen."

"They're not," he said, eyeing me. "I like your lips."

I pointed a fry at him. "Ah, but you've only known me while I'm pregnant, so you don't know if they're their usual size."

He pinned me with a look, and my nerves quaked, his voice deep and raw. "I still *like* them."

I swallowed, fighting off the memory of when he'd tasted them, how he'd pulled—

"So you and Bonnie, huh?" I blurted, my voice squeaky. "Please tell me how you two didn't work out."

He groaned. "Do you really need an explanation?"

"Oh, absolutely."

"Fine, but I want those fries." I happily obliged him, not missing the way he smiled when I stole his shake again. "I dated Bonnie off and on throughout high school. As you can tell, she's a lot."

"I had no idea—"

"Anyway." He placed his ball cap on my head, apparently believing that was the way to silence me. Little did he know, I was never giving it back. "But she was fun, and at the time, that was what I wanted. So imagine my surprise when we're getting close to graduating and she mentions she not only wants me to follow her to her school back east, but she wants to get married and have babies. Specifically, my babies."

I laughed around the axe wedged in my heart, despite this being years ago. "Could you imagine little grumpy Brooks walking around? They'd be a menace to society—hey!" I whined when he snatched the milkshake and placed it between his thighs. He held my stare, likely daring me to wrestle him for it back. Deeming it not worth our safety, I sighed. "Fine. Go on."

He switched lanes, his attention back on the road. "Don't get me wrong, Bonnie's sweet. Or she was—but I was eighteen, and the thought of strapping myself down with anyone stressed me the hell out. So rather than being honest, I told her all these stories, like I never wanted to get married or have kids. And that I had zero intention of ever leaving Wallowpine—though I guess that one was true."

"Hmm." I brushed my hair behind my ear, glancing at him sideways. "Nolan made it sound like she broke your heart. He even said you've closed yourself off since her."

"What?" he choked, the disbelief in his voice evident. "That's ridiculously overstating it. I don't think I've given her a single thought since she moved away. When did he tell you that?"

I shrugged, toying with a loose string on my jeans. "That night he danced with me, after you—"

"After I told you no," he finished for me. His lips strained into a closed-mouth smile as he looked me over. "I regretted that the moment I did it."

I swallowed, the afterburn of his refusal still fresh, remembering how he'd said he didn't think it was a good idea. "Then why'd you do it?"

He rubbed the back of his neck. "I'm not always the most direct in going after things I want, and I didn't think it would do any good teasing myself with what I couldn't have." Before I might've contemplated his words, and understand what he couldn't have, he admitted, "And to be honest, your confidence kind of intimidated me."

I snorted. The entire thought was ridiculous. "I'm not confident—or at least, not *that* confident. I was terrified to ask you. I only did it because I was desperate for you to accept me."

"Shay . . ." He trailed off, shaking his head. It was quiet for a long moment, only the sound of the trunk clunking and me rustling atop the seat—remembering this freaking truck had no place for a car seat—until he said, "If you asked me now, I wouldn't say no."

"Yeah, well, I'd never ask you twice."

My words slipped out harsher than I'd intended, not meaning to cause a fissure in our fragile friendship. But they were true. I'd learned too often before what happened when I extended second chances—again and again.

People disappoint you.

"Wait—" I twisted in my seat to face him, seeing an attempt to salvage the night. "You do want kids?"

He shrugged. "If it works out, yeah. Why would I deny myself the chance to be a father?" A smile bloomed on his lips, and I should've anticipated it when he said, "Or a daddy?"

I groaned and hid my face in my hands, his laugh filling the cab. "You're never going to let that go, are you?"

"I like seeing you blush."

I looked up from my hands, his grin perfect and addictive in every way. "I'm sure there are other ways."

He lifted his brows and nodded, as though accepting the challenge. I smiled, but despite the joy fluttering through me, I couldn't help it when I said, "I'm sorry, by the way—for not correcting Bonnie that Tater isn't your baby."

His grin wavered, and his throat bobbed, but all he said was, "I didn't correct her either, Shay."

I fumbled with the ends of my hair, toying with my words. "Does Anika want kids?"

I glanced up when Brooks let out a startled laugh. "Why would I know if Anika wants kids?" I shrugged and twisted in my seat to look out the window, silently chastising myself for being nosy. I closed my eyes, ready to stay that way the rest of the drive when he asked, "Shay, why do you think I'd know that?"

I swallowed, hating that he'd make me say it. "Aren't you dating her?"

"No." He immediately handed me the milkshake, as though the chocolate deliciousness solidified his words. "Why would you even think that?"

I shrugged, praying he couldn't see the embarrassing moisture in my eyes. "I don't know . . . I saw you with her a few times . . . and you guys looked friendly. Plus, Levi and Nolan started joining you." I pointed my finger at him, having an aha moment. "And you made her breakfast that day—a peanut butter sandwich. And you've been making them ever since—"

"Shay." He nabbed my finger between us before I could lower it. "She's not my girlfriend, and I'm not seeing her in any sort of way. I hardly know her. Every time I had to meet with her was to discuss some business with the . . . shop. I never made her breakfast—she left that morning before it was even done."

He released my finger, only to wrap his hand with mine. "The only one I want to make sandwiches for is my very complicated best friend."

I hated the way my heart raced, despised how relieved and grateful I was to learn he hadn't moved on—at least, not yet. But it didn't change anything. There was such a thing as wanting to be with someone, all while knowing you couldn't—and that's all I was to Brooks. But it was okay. Having him in my life was better than not at all. "When you said you came up here for a meeting, I thought maybe you had come up here to see her," I said, revealing how insecure I was, the sort of power he held over me.

But this was different from the power Declan had wielded. The control he'd carefully woven within my very being, slowly binding *his butterfly's* wings together. I hadn't stayed with Declan out of love or desire. It was out of fear. But with Brooks . . . His power was because of how strongly I felt for him. I wanted him.

And I didn't believe Brooks would ever use it against me.

"I didn't go see her." His whisper was warm and soothing, much like his hand as he squeezed mine, pulling me back to the moment of only him and me. "About a year before my dad died, he convinced me to see a therapist. About my mom. I've gone since, but I slowed down for a while—I felt good. I thought I'd made some real progress . . . but lately I've been seeing him a bit more. Most of my appointments are over the phone, but I went to see him in person today."

"Oh," I murmured, at a loss for words. Not because he was going to therapy; I believed wholeheartedly it was a wonderful tool and thought often I might benefit from some sort of therapy myself. I was in awe that Brooks felt safe enough to admit it to me. "That's great. I'm really proud of you. Not everyone is even brave enough to try therapy. Or to admit they might need extra help."

He puffed out an empty laugh. "I wouldn't call it brave." He rolled his lips together, shaking his head. "It would be brave if I didn't need help and could figure out how to deal with my issues on my own."

"Then why are you doing it?" I asked, not loosening my hold on his hand, letting him see I was here with him. "Why not try it on your own?"

"Because," he started, his eyes fluttering fast, "what I was doing wasn't working—and I don't want to hurt anyone the way I've been burned."

I watched him as red crept up his neck, visible even in the night. Remembering when I'd said those very words to him. Told him he wanted to *hurt people exactly how he'd been burned.* If I could take it back, I would—it wasn't true. At Brooks's core, he was a genuinely good person. But he was human, and sometimes people mess up.

But he'd taken my words to heart. And he'd done something about them.

"I don't know whether to kick you or kiss you right now," I said, gripping his hand tight, needing him to understand. "I have been *hurt* by people I thought loved me, Brooks. And if they'd had an ounce of the selflessness and bravery you do, things might have played out differently in my relationships with them. So whether you did it for your brothers, or even me—heck, every person who comes into your home for the rest of your life—I think that is the bravest thing I've ever witnessed." I smiled to myself and turned his hand over in mine, his palm facing up. Gently, lovingly, I traced my finger along it. "Did you ever stop to think that maybe you aren't broken, but that instead you're being rebuilt?"

Brooks didn't respond, didn't even nod his head in acknowledgment. But I knew he heard me, felt how tightly he clutched my hand. He didn't offer an explanation as to why he was seeing a therapist—not fully, at least—and I didn't ask. It was his story to share, when and if he wanted to. I had a story too, one I'd slowly unraveled in my time here, and I couldn't help but think how freeing it would be to let it out.

And as I sat there, holding his hand, I couldn't help but wonder why the words I silently spoke to myself, when I'd tear myself down for not being enough, weren't nearly as gracious and forgiving as the ones I shared with others in their lowest points. Why I somehow believed my broken—or rather, rebuilding—soul was worth any less.

Chapter Thirty-Four

As a parent, it's your duty to thoroughly inspect your child's Halloween candy, right?

My mom never had, but one Halloween I'd gone out with a friend, and her parents had rifled through our candy. Searching for needles and wrappers laced in who knows what. If they found something, I didn't know, though my candy pile was suspiciously smaller than before.

It was why I was twelve—fine, fourteen—mini Snickers deep into a bag. I'd done it for the children. Not you, Timmy. *Kidding.*

"Shay?"

I scrambled and shuffled through the wrappers on the floor as I tried to stand. Why had I plopped down in the middle of the aisle in the first place? I swallowed the last of the nougat as Levi stumbled upon me. His eyes were wide, staring at the treacherous empty wrappers at my feet. "What did you do? Get bored and have a snack?"

"No," I mumbled, running my tongue over my teeth. "We were robbed."

"Robbed?" he scoffed with a laugh, walking down the aisle to me. "Who would steal—" He fell silent, as if the horrid orange-and-black shelves had stunned him with a spell. "Did you do this?"

"Eat half a bag of candy?" I hung my head in playful shame. "Yes, I did."

"No—you did this," he said, waving his hand at the candy. "How . . . why?"

I shrugged and knelt to clean up the mess I'd made. "It was important to you."

His throat bobbed as he grabbed the empty boxes from behind me. Brooks had dropped them off early this morning before we opened, in an effort to help me be discreet. "You didn't have to do this," Levi whispered, his voice strained.

"I wanted to." I didn't need to explain why. Levi knew all he'd done for me. "Want one?" I offered, holding out a Snickers that had somehow escaped my ravishing.

He grabbed it, staring at the aluminum packaging. "I made such a big deal out of nothing. It wasn't like my dad was even into Halloween. It was Brooks who always took me trick-or-treating as a kid anyway."

The thought sang to my insides, and I swooned at the idea of a teenage Brooks taking his brother out as he continued on, "I don't know if he stocked the shop every year with it anyway, I just remember the year before I left for school he had. And when I realized we hadn't ordered any, I kind of felt like I failed him." His fingers trembled as he held the sole candy piece, looking likely to toss it. "I should've paid more attention when he was alive, but I was so wrapped up in myself and wanting out of here. And now he's gone. He's gone and we're left alone to pick up the pieces."

"Levi." I was aware there was nothing I could say to lessen his grief or guilt. I hadn't known how much he was carrying, that he'd wanted out of this town. Levi was different from his brothers, perceptive and quiet, but I believed he experienced his emotions heavily, his wounds cutting deep. "You could never fail him. Never."

He looked up, his dark eyes pooling with disbelief. "But I have. If I hadn't started art school, I would've been here. I could've said goodbye to Dad. And now I'm taking these stupid classes I hate, and Nolan is stuck trying to figure out the shop on his own." He let out a guttural sound, wringing his fingers through his hair. "If I hadn't been so focused on myself—if we all weren't—we could remember how Dad did this."

My heart ached to save him from these thoughts he'd probably been stewing in since the moment his father passed. "Could I see your artwork?"

"What?"

I nodded with a smile, following the inkling leading me. "Your artwork. You never showed me that map you drew for me."

His jaw muscles worked, and he seemed to think it over before he stood. Without so much as a word, he walked away and returned with a notebook in tow just as I'd made it back to my feet. "I'm not as good as I used to be." He flipped through the pages, holding the sketch pad at an angle I could barely see, though I caught a glimpse of what looked to be a house. "Your map was the first thing I'd drawn since Dad died."

I rubbed beneath my eyes, regretting deeply that I hadn't cherished the gift he'd offered me, and was only now asking to see the map. How much else had I missed because I was distracted with my own sorrow? Promising to be better, I smiled and accepted his notebook, careful not to smudge the drawing.

"Levi." My voice was choked with awe. When he said he'd drawn a map, I'd expected it to have some trees and paths, maybe an arrow that said *go here*. But this was special, drawn in a way that was thoughtful and personal, ensuring I wouldn't get lost. He'd even drawn our cabins on the map, marking my way home. "This is amazing." He shrugged, hiding his burning cheeks.

Resisting the urge to flip through and admire more of his artwork, I closed and handed it over, assuming by the way he shifted on his feet he was antsy to have it back. "I don't know how your dad could ever be disappointed in you, Levi. You're the best of us." I dipped my head low with a tilt, trying to meet his eye. "I knew that the moment I met you. And I don't know your dad, but I promise he thought the same. He wouldn't want you to be anything but what you are."

His voice was low and rich, his gaze still hidden from me as he nudged his boot against the floor. "Dad would've loved you, Shay."

"Oh yeah?" I raised my brow. "What makes you say that?"

He lifted his head and gave me a small smile, letting me see just how young he was—yet wasn't. Life had aged him quicker. "Because Brooks is the most like him." He backed away, laying that on my heart. "Hey, if you feel like getting out of your room tonight, I heard Layne's throwing a Halloween party. Might be fun."

I laughed and grabbed the empty boxes from the aisle. "No way. Layne texted me about it too. And like I told her, I have plans."

"Really?" He smirked, though the light hadn't quite returned to his eyes. "What are you doing?"

"I have a date."

"What?" he choked out and crossed his arms across his chest, the black ink stark against his white shirt. "With who?"

"Cash." I smiled when he laughed. "He and I are going to snuggle up on the couch, eat popcorn, and watch *Halloween*."

He laughed quietly to himself, shaking his head as he walked to the front counter. "I hope you don't scare easily—Cash is a total chicken."

I scrunched my nose at him. There was nothing scary about the movie *Halloween*. As a kid, I'd made an effort to avoid scary movies since I was usually alone. But not this one. It was a family classic.

Grabbing the last of the boxes, I lugged them to the back, disposing of the evidence before Karen arrived. I'd called her with the shop phone not too long ago, so I imagined she'd arrive any moment—especially since I'd told her the candy was free. I wasn't about to get the Grahams in trouble for reselling something they shouldn't. I set them outside and grabbed the extra box Brooks had brought in this morning. I didn't recognize it, so Nolan must've asked him to pick something up for the shop.

I set it on the counter in the back, peeling up the tape as Nolan strolled up from behind me. "You're not supposed to open that." I raised my brow, not knowing how this was any different than other shipments I'd unloaded. Despite his warning, Nolan grinned, watching as I lifted the last of the tape off. "You're gonna get me in trouble, darlin'."

"What are you talking about—" I stopped when I saw what was in the box. This wasn't for the shop. Mouth drooling, I pulled out one of the single servings of peanut butter—the exact ones I'd been snacking on for weeks at work. "Why am I not allowed to see these? Wait—was I not supposed to be eating them? I'm sorry, I thought you and Levi had stocked them for me."

"Oh, those are for you. But they sure as hell aren't from me or Levi." He edged closer and pressed a chaste kiss to my temple. "Thank you for what you did, Shay. I can't tell you how much it means to me." He straightened and winked, walking away as he revealed, "Brooks has it in his head that you'll stop eating those, just like you did his sad little sandwiches, if you find out they're from him."

I opened my mouth, but the only thing that sprung out of me was a tear. I was ridiculous—absurdly ridiculous. It was only peanut butter, and I shouldn't be on the verge of becoming a blubbering mess. It was the hormones—it had to be. The other night, I'd cried while watching *The Lion King*. Who cries watching that? Fine, lots of people—but that was beside the point. I'd been given outrageously expensive gifts, an engagement ring that cost more than several months in rent. But this . . . this was the most priceless, considerate gift I'd been given. And I'd almost missed it.

Brooks . . . that man.

Chapter Thirty-Five

"That's weird." I rubbed Cash's head where he was nestled on my lap, both of us sprawled out on the sectional. "Where are the Sanderson sisters?"

I ate a piece of popcorn and then gave one to Cash, our cycle thus far. All three of my roommates were out for the night. Levi had decided to forgo the party after Nolan suggested they go camping. I couldn't help but wonder if the gesture was a way for Nolan to check up on his brother. They hadn't said if Brooks was joining them, but it was well after six and he wasn't home, so I figured he had.

I snuggled in, savoring having the house to myself. "Is this the extended version?" I voiced aloud, wondering why I'd yet to see Sarah Jessica Parker. And why was the camera focused on a little boy? What was with this creepy music?

"What is happening?" I cried as the music quickened, the screen showing only a shot of a stabbing knife. "Michael?" I gasped, realizing why Binx hadn't made an appearance when the camera focused on a bloody, emotionless child outside a house. "As in Michael Myers?"

"What are yo—"

I screamed, but rather than fleeing or fighting, I succumbed to death and hid under the blanket, leaving Cash to fend for himself. Beyond the blanket of faux protection, the movie stopped. Cash whined, his tail thumping, encouraging my intruder's deep laugh.

Beside me the cushion shifted, and hidden hands pried the blanket from my grip. I huffed a breath, and Brooks's eyes gleamed, his cheeks red from laughter. "Did you pee? You can be honest."

"No!" I tossed a handful of popcorn at him, and Cash hurriedly jumped down, gobbling the pieces. "I wasn't scared."

He raised a brow. "You sure?"

I narrowed my eyes and crossed my arms over my chest, the sleeves of my sweater hanging over my hands. "Yes."

He leaned back against the cushion beside me and draped his arms over the back, still dressed in his work uniform. "Who watches *Halloween* alone anyway?"

"Your disc is broken!" I frowned and pointed an accusatory finger at the TV. "That is absolutely not the same movie I watched growing up. Where the heck was Binx? Or Winnie Sanderson—"

"Wait." Brooks tipped his head back, his chest shaking as he laughed. "Do you mean *Hocus Pocus*? The Disney movie?"

My mouth hung open, realization settling in. How I ever mixed them up was beyond me, but I blamed it on pregnancy brain. Just last week I was mid-conversation with Elle, only to forget what I was saying—twice. Before I could muster a response, Brooks snagged a piece of popcorn and plopped it in his mouth. "Hmm. It needs Oreos."

I scrunched my nose. "Oreos?"

"Yeah, we'd eat it as kids. My dad would melt white chocolate, crumble up Oreos, and mix it in the popcorn." He leaned over and rubbed Cash, dipping his head toward the TV screen. "You going to finish your movie?"

I bit my lip, running my finger around the rim of the bowl. "I don't know . . . I've never really watched a scary movie. I tried once as a teenager, but I got all worked up. It wasn't something I liked to do alone."

Brooks hummed under his breath and leaned back, sinking deeper into the sofa. "Well, you're not alone now."

I side-eyed him, hearing the silent question in his words. I wanted to turn him down—I really didn't enjoy scaring myself—and I wasn't sure how I felt watching a movie with him. Alone. But then I thought of last night when we'd gone shopping and the peanut butter he'd secretly been buying for weeks, soothing my ridiculous craving. "If I made this Oreo popcorn, would you watch the movie with me?"

He rubbed a hand over his jaw, his lips twitching up a fraction. "Let me shower first?"

"I think I did something wrong," I whined to Brooks as he stepped out of his room, his hair slick from the shower. I frowned at the clumpy mess in the bowl, unsure why the chocolate hadn't melted into delightful bliss. I set the bowl down and wiped up the milk I'd spilled on the counter. I'd poured it into the white chocolate, hoping it would help, but it had stiffened it up more. "Does this seem right?"

He glanced in the bowl, his gray sweats low on his hips, clinging generously to that divine behind. "Looks perfect, Shay."

"Really?" I stirred it with a spoon this time, careful not to crush the popcorn more than I already had when I'd tried beating it together with the hand mixer. "Are you sure? It tasted kind of burned to me . . ."

"Can't pregnancy make your tastebuds sort of funky?" he asked, grabbing the bowl from my hands.

"Um—yeah." I fiddled with my hair, wondering how he knew that tidbit of information. "You really don't have to eat it."

"I want to." He wrapped an arm around my shoulder and pulled me in, pressing his lips to the top of my head. He lingered there, his chest rising beneath my cheek, breathing me in. "Thank you, sunshine."

I paused, not sure if I was more taken aback by the kiss or the fact he liked the popcorn. "Are you feeling okay?"

"Never better." He reached into a drawer, retrieving a spoon. "Are you having popcorn?"

I shook my head, deciding Tater must not be a fan, and grabbed a pickle from the fridge instead. "What an interesting way to eat popcorn," I noted, my eyes wide as Brooks plunged his utensil into the bowl and ate a spoonful like it was cereal.

Brooks might be a psychopath. Maybe I shouldn't watch this movie with him.

He shrugged, finding nothing wrong with eating burned, pulverized Oreo popcorn with a spoon—a spoon. Apparently he wasn't opposed to stealing as well, because without hesitation he claimed the corner of the sectional where I'd been. I glowered at him as he wrapped my blanket around his feet, probably still carrying my heat. Not in the mood to wrestle him for the spot, I'd moved for the recliner instead when Brooks said, "I thought you and I were watching this together."

I raised my brow and rubbed Cash's head as he leaned against my thigh, likely urging me to choose a spot so he could lie down. "We are. I'm just sitting over here."

With a shake of his head, he patted the cushion beneath him. "Come watch it with me, Shay."

I swallowed, suddenly finding my gray sweater and leggings rather frumpy. I hadn't even showered yet. Intent on ignoring his invitation, I lowered, butt grazing the recliner as Brooks said, "Don't make it into something it's not. I need you closer so I can push you down in case Michael breaks into our house."

"Ha ha, very funny." I rolled my eyes, ignoring the way my stomach dropped. I should be relieved snuggling me wasn't a big deal for him. Sure, we had a moment—or I thought we had—on the way home from Hillshire, even held hands. But that was nothing. Friends held hands. Just like how friends watched scary movies together.

I was too petrified to let this be anything more than friendship.

I offered him a wobbly smile and sidled up to him, my thigh pressed to his so I wouldn't hang off the couch. Waiting until Cash settled in beside me, I held my arms up until he put his head on my lap, running my fingers through his brown marble coat.

I glanced up to see why the movie hadn't started, to find Brooks watching me. "What?" I asked. Oh my gosh—had I misunderstood him?

Before I could scramble away, Brooks shrugged and pressed play on the remote. "I've never seen Cash take to anyone like he has you."

I bit my smile as I rubbed his ear, wondering if Cash had known I was pregnant long before his owners did. I settled deeper in the cushions and focused on the movie, not the way Brooks's muscles shifted each time he grabbed a bite. My nerves seemed to ease, relaxing when he sat up and placed the half-empty bowl on the coffee table. But apparently, I was as sensitive as a bomb, positive he could hear my treacherous heart rate spiking when he tossed his arm over the back of the sectional, resting behind my head.

But forty-five minutes in, I'd forgotten about anything but this cringey yet fantastic movie on display. "We can turn it off if you want—I'd hate for you to be scared," I teased, even though the movie was more amusing than terrifying.

"I'm not the one who keeps hiding behind my hands every time Michael pops up." His fingers playfully tugged on the ends of my hair, grazing the side of my neck.

"He's creepy. He doesn't even speak! Pretty sure you'd pee yourself if you woke up with me in the corner of your room just breathing."

His breath was enticingly warm, welcoming against my ear. "Are you afraid, Shay?" I swallowed and shook my head, staring at the movie, struggling to focus with the heat of his gaze. My sweater grew unbearably hot when he quietly admitted, "I'm scared too."

I looked at him then, knowing that not to be true. He'd laughed several times, even called the film cheesy. But behind his full lashes, his eyes were intent and vulnerable, and I wondered if he meant something else. "You are?"

I shivered as his thumb edged beneath the collar of my sweater, skimming my collarbone. *I'm going to pass out.* "Terrified."

I bit my lip, mouth parched as I looked from his eyes to his slowly rising chest, seeing how I might fit. Cash grumbled in protest when I shifted to my side and drew closer to Brooks. For a moment—a terrifying, paralyzing moment—I was filled with regret. But it vanished just as quickly when he slung his arm around my back and pulled me in close.

I settled in against his chest as he adjusted the blanket over us, draping me in comfort and safety. My bump was lightly pressed to his hip, my hand on his hard stomach as I remembered how I'd once touched him skin to skin. But then something bewildering and breathtaking occurred, something within me. I smiled, in a near daze at the tiniest, yet mightiest movement within my belly. It was the most I'd felt Tater move; I still hadn't experienced its kicks on the outside.

And in that moment, with Michael Myers murderously chasing Laurie, peace washed over me. A creeping, wandering thought reminded me it wouldn't last, but I chose not to give it air and savored this for what it was now.

"Did you like it?" Brooks asked as the credits ran, his hand touching not me, but Cash where he lay pressed against my back.

"I did." There was something about older movies that today's films couldn't touch. "It was a little corny, but I liked it."

He laughed under his breath, the puff of air caressing the top of my head. "Want to watch *Friday the 13th*?"

I sat up and twisted to look at him. "Doesn't that take place in the woods?" He nodded, a smile growing on his lips as though he knew where my thoughts went. "Nope." I kicked off the blanket, struggling to get it off my feet. "There's no way in heck—"

He laughed and his hands locked around my waist, stopping my retreat. "No," I cried with a choked laugh as he rolled onto his side, pulling me down beside him. "Brooks!" His chest rumbled against my back, and I screamed as his fingers tickled my side, each stroke leading us into mutual laughter as my legs flailed, completely at his mercy. "If I pee on you," I gasped, "it's your fault."

His hands halted in fear but stayed on my frame, his breathless laugh entwining with mine. One hand slid out from beneath me and rested somewhere above our heads, but his other stayed on my hip, holding me there. I swallowed, nerves on the edge of combusting as he urged me closer against him, spooning me.

"Thank you for tonight," I said in a low rasp, afraid if I moved, I'd startle him and this moment away.

His hand clutched my hip, thumb sliding over my hip bone. I closed my eyes and lay my hand on my bump, focusing on how well his body flushed with mine. "Shay," he breathed, and I shuddered, the heat of his words on my neck. A wild fever raced through me as his lips skimmed my throat, his beard teasingly scraping my skin, his fingers holding me with need.

I opened my mouth, perhaps to say his name, to suggest I go to bed—or that *we* go to bed—but words failed me. I held my breath and blocked out everything but the pressure beneath my hand. *No freaking way*. I smiled, a laugh bubbling out of me at the movement, feeling like something was tapping my palm. "Brooks," I squealed, running my fingers over my bump, searching. "I felt Tater move."

Caught up in chasing Tater's movements, I almost missed the way Brooks's body tightened behind mine. His hand departed my hip, and his heat left too, as if he'd pressed himself back against the sofa as much as he could. His voice was quiet, almost distant. "That's great, Shay."

"Yeah." My throat throbbed, my heart pounding in my ears. I rubbed my fingers over my palms and counted to five before I stood, deeming that enough time to not let on how hurt I was. He didn't protest, not even when I walked away and paused at the edge of the staircase. "I'm going to bed—it was a long day. Thanks for staying up so I wouldn't be scared."

I didn't wait for a response, moving as soon as I heard Cash's nails on the wood floor, following me up the stairs. Each step worsened the alarming belief that perhaps Brooks cared for me, but not for Tater. I tried to calm my nerves, reminding myself how he'd assured me he would be there for both of us—but his actions were saying otherwise. And that wasn't enough.

Chapter Thirty-Six

I checked behind the still-wet curtain of the upstairs shower again, ensuring no one was hiding and waiting to murder me before I left the bathroom. My damp hair dripped down my back as I walked down the hall to my bedroom and rubbed a towel through it. I froze, realizing it wasn't just Cash on my bed.

"Brooks?" I asked in disbelief, like I hadn't been with him twenty minutes ago, nor cried over him in the shower. "Did you need something?"

"I'm sorry." His voice was hushed, but his gaze was unfaltering, as though he needed me to see—feel—how genuine he was. "I'm sorry for how I reacted downstairs."

"You didn't do anything," I whispered and pulled at the hem of my fresh sweater, making sure every bit of me was covered.

"That's the point," he said, shifting to his feet. "I did *nothing*, Shay. Absolutely nothing for a moment that deserved to be celebrated."

I bit my lip, hiding how it wobbled. "You're not obligated to do anything you don't want to do. I shouldn't have said anything about it."

"Shay," he groaned, rubbing his jaw. "You have no idea what I want."

You're right, I don't.

But I didn't say that, didn't voice how confused I was. I didn't have the chance to before he said, "Every single day, I've regretted how I reacted when you told me you were pregnant. I hate what I said to you—"

"Brooks," I started, only to stop when he said, "Please—please let me get this out."

He didn't hesitate, didn't wait for me to agree, the words flowing out of him. "If I could take it back, I would. I would do anything to never see the hurt I saw on your face that night. And while I know it's my fault, and I deserve it—I hate that you can't trust me. That I have to beg my brothers to tell me how you and Tater are doing, because you trusted me once with your baby and I blew it." He let out a deep breath, not giving me even a moment to absorb his words. "I've been waiting, grasping on to every little detail you share with me, in hopes of gaining your trust again. But then tonight, you gave me a chance and I panicked. I was a jerk, and I'm sorry."

I leaned against the doorframe as Brooks sat on the edge of the bed, watching me—waiting. I didn't know what to say, to do. Lately, his words weren't the problem. He'd built me up countlessly, promised me he was here for us. But words weren't enough.

I let the towel fall from my hands and onto the floor before I sat at the head of the bed, leaving the entire length between us. "You've never asked to hear about my pregnancy. Or at least, you never really asked me."

He twisted on the bed to face me, his hair mussed as though he'd wrung his fingers through it. "For a while, I felt undeserving to ask about it, you know? I mean, you gave up your entire life to protect your baby. And after what I did . . . I thought you might believe you needed to protect Tater from me too."

"Brooks," I whispered, shaking my head. "That's not true—not at all. You're my friend."

He smiled meekly to himself, his gaze focused on the jean quilt beneath us. "Then why doesn't our friendship feel like what you share with my brothers? You don't come to me like you do them."

I shrugged. "Our friendship is different."

"Why?" he pressed. "Why does our friendship have to be different?"

"Because I haven't kissed your brothers," I said with a laugh, tossing a pillow at him. "And I can't say I've daydreamed about tearing off their clothes like I have you."

He feigned a smirk, but his freshly trimmed beard was incapable of hiding his flushed cheeks. "I won't deny that brings my jealousy down a notch."

I rolled my eyes, but my voice was careful. "You have nothing to be jealous of. And I'm sorry you thought I was trying to protect Tater from you. If you'd just asked, I would've told you anything."

"I'm sorry for not asking." He bent over and grabbed a pillow that had fallen on the floor, settling it between us. His hand lingered there, pausing. "Shay, I've gotta be honest. I'm at a loss on what to do." I licked the seam of my lips and pulled my knees as tight as I could to my chest. Where was this going? "I'm not trying to pressure you, okay? If you need time, that's okay with me, sunshine. I'll wait. But I'm not sure what you want. I keep hoping you'll lead, at least let me know what sort of relationship you and I are going to have."

I swallowed, my chest rising fast, my heart pounding in my ears. "Why do I have to lead?"

That seemed to take him back. He blinked slowly. "Well, I kind of thought you might need that. I know—" He pursed his lips together, seeming to gather his thoughts. "I know I don't know every detail about your . . . previous relationship. But I got the sense you were sort of dragged around. And I want to make sure I don't do that with you."

I stared at Brooks as a balmy, reassuring feeling washed over me. An emotion I was barely beginning to know. All my life, I'd thought I knew this emotion well—thought I'd felt it for my mom, for Declan. But this . . . I'd never felt this. It was pure, raw and refining.

It was terrifying.

Not in the way that made me want to run in the other direction and hide in the shadows. This was the exhilarating, stomach-twisting sort of fear you felt before you dove into the unknown. The kind where your scream was intertwined with a laugh, because in the back of your mind, you knew you'd be okay. You were confident you'd land on your feet.

And in my case, I knew Brooks would catch me.

"I can't tell you how much that means to me," I admitted, forcing myself not to retreat from his gaze—to be bold, brave. "And there are times where I really want to . . . but then moments or emotions from before pop up in my mind, and it can be really difficult for me to put myself out there." I rubbed the side of my arm, heat prickling up my neck. "But I don't mind if you lead, because I don't think it would feel like I was being led at all." I smiled at him, lifting one shoulder in a shrug. "I sort of think it would just feel like you were holding my hand, like we were a team. And I would like that. A lot."

Before I might've regretted it and panicked, Brooks rolled to his knees atop my bed and pulled me toward him, wrapping me in a hug. I closed my eyes and breathed him in. "A team," he murmured, his hold every bit as sturdy and reassuring as his words. "I would like that."

I didn't know how long we knelt there, holding one another. But neither of us attempted to shift the hug to something more, to express ourselves in a way that words couldn't. And something told me this embrace, and even our words to one another, weren't necessarily romantic. Yes, I felt something deeply for Brooks, but this moment was the building of a foundation, a promise to be there for one another.

Brooks pulled back with tired eyes, and I yawned, as though our confessions had drained us. I didn't want him to leave, but I scooted back to the top of the mattress and said, "I should probably get some sleep."

He cleared his throat and moved to stand, but rather than saying good night, he lingered by the door. "It's Sunday tomorrow . . . Are you going to be around?"

"I think so. But I thought maybe I should check with your brothers and see if they need me to do anything around the shop while they're away."

"Don't worry about it," Brooks said, stopping me before I could reach for my phone on the nightstand. "The shop's closed—and I doubt they have service anyway."

"Okay," I agreed absentmindedly, grabbing my pillows from the top of the bed and rearranging them in the middle. "I guess you're kind of my boss too."

"What are you doing?"

I turned my head to look at him, not understanding why his eyes were wide, his brows pinched together. "I'm going to sleep?"

His lips twitched, fighting off a grin. "Why are you building a wall of pillows?"

I waved my hand at the small round bump that was now my stomach. "I'm usually a back sleeper, but I'm not supposed to lie flat on my back for too long now. I feel like I can never get comfy, but throwing my leg over these seems to help."

I frowned when he didn't laugh, not understanding why his lips downturned. "Are you hurting?"

I shrugged, my heart turning molten at his concern. "Not really. I mean—my legs cramp up and my back aches after a long day, but that's normal."

His gaze drifted to my bump. It wasn't completely visible beneath my sweater, but it was obvious I was pregnant. I fought the urge to turn off the lights or nestle beneath the blankets and hide. Brooks had admitted he wanted to be a part of this as much as his brothers—maybe even more so. But even knowing that, I couldn't say my mouth didn't hang open when he offered, "I could give you a massage."

I sputtered a laugh, my heart racing at even the thought of his hands roaming over me. "Oh, no. No, it's fine—I'm fine. I haven't shaved my legs in a few days."

It was his turn to laugh, apparently not mortified like I was. I wished the sky would fall and obliterate me and my hairy legs, especially when Brooks snagged the bottle of lotion off my desk. "If you think I'm scared of a little hair," he said as he rolled the cuffs of my pajama bottoms up, oblivious to how I gaped at him, "then you must've forgotten about when you vomited on me. Twice."

I groaned, smothering my face in my hands. "That was humiliating."

He chuckled, and I did my best not to fidget and yank my leg back as he squeezed a dollop of lotion on his hands. This was Brooks's way of leading. Before I might've wondered what the heck I was getting myself into, his thumb began kneading my calf and I gasped. "Okay." My voice was breathless—I hadn't expected his hands to feel that good. "You can rub my legs. And maybe my feet. But that's it."

He smiled at me and fell into silence, letting his hands speak for him. I bit my lip as he roamed my legs, edging barely past my knee, my sweats rolled up to mid-thigh. Tears welled at the corner of my eyes, not solely because of the pain and tension within my muscles—but because of his attentiveness.

His kindness.

I settled deeper into the mattress, my eyes heavy. His calloused hands were careful, but not cautious, as though he knew my body as well as his own. I wondered if he knew what he was doing, if he was aware how deeply I trusted him.

"Anywhere else?" he asked as he unfolded my sweats and covered my legs, now gleaming with lotion.

I shook my head, gratitude filling my soul. "No, but thank you. Thank you for this."

He shrugged like it was no big deal, oblivious to the pain he'd relieved, much more than any sort of physical kind. He glanced down at my bump, and I opened my mouth, the invitation on my lips. I wanted him to touch me, to touch Tater. But for a fleeting second, it felt like I was transported to a different room, with a different man.

One whose hands weren't careful and considerate. Whose eyes weren't full of kindness, but disdain and bitterness. Whose words were sharp and degrading, eager to tear me down.

I hadn't heard from Declan again after I'd successfully disconnected my old phone. He couldn't reach me anymore, couldn't hurt me—yet somehow he was still doing it, with hundreds of miles between us.

It was time I stopped letting him.

"Would you want to spend the night with me?" I asked instead, choosing a different route of bravery.

He sat at the edge of the bed beside me, cocking his head. "Are you scared?"

"Yes . . . but not because of the movie." I hoped he'd understand and wouldn't need me to reveal how terrified I was of my feelings, how strongly he consumed me. I was scared of the future, of what could go wrong between us.

"I'm afraid, too." His fingers skimmed my cheek, brushing my hair behind my ear. "And sometimes fear takes time to work through, so I think we should go slow. No timelines, no pressure—it'll just be us. We'll go slow together." His fingers tangled deeper in my damp hair, his palm cradling my jaw. "Does that sound okay with you?"

I nodded, leaning into his touch as a silent *thank-you*. My heart was light, at ease as he stood and walked to the opposite side of the bed and pulled back the covers. I grabbed the pillows in the middle to make more room, tossing them onto the floor as he said, "You might want to keep that wall up. I've been holding myself back since the day I met you, and if you knew how close my restraint came to breaking downstairs, you might not let me in bed with you."

I laughed and tossed the final pillow at him, hitting him square in the chest. "You're so full of it."

He clutched it to his chest as he teased, "You think I'm lying?"

"No." I fiddled with the strings of my sweats. I didn't think Brooks would lie about finding me attractive just for the sake of appeasing me. When I'd first come to Wallowpine, my confidence had been shattered, but it had never been over what I looked like—but *who I was*. I was learning to see myself with different eyes, but I wasn't oblivious. "But I'm pregnant, and I wouldn't fault anyone for not finding me particularly sexy."

He stuck his tongue against the inside of his cheek, his eyes dark and heavy in a way that had me wanting to retreat. He lifted the blanket and set the pillow between us. His gaze held mine as he rubbed Cash where he lay at the foot of the bed. Only when he flicked off the lamp did I lose sight of him, but I felt every bit of his heat as he lay down, the mattress shifting.

There was no way in heck I could sleep with him next to me.

I lay on my side, the pillow cradled between my legs like my life depended on it. On the verge of counting sheep—or sprinting out the door—I froze when Brooks breathed, "First time I saw you, you drove me out of my mind. You were a tad infuriating, and you smiled a lot. I thought if I gave you a bit of hell, maybe scared you off, that you'd stop—but you gave it right back to me." His fingertips dusted the top of my head, playing with the loose strands. "If Jake wasn't waiting for you, and I hadn't gotten that radio call, I would've tossed you in my truck and taken you home."

I smirked. "I'm not sure your house is a great place to hide a body."

I couldn't see his smile, but I felt every bit of it in the puff of air teasing my nose. I gasped, slowing my breaths as Brooks's legs grazed mine, aware how near he was. "I thought you were beautiful. But I was so blind." His fingers stroked my cheek, soothing the swelling panic within me. "I didn't know how selfless and considerate you are. You've got a bit of fire in you, and when I see it . . . I want you to burn me alive until I'm a part of you. You're the cutest thing, who scrunches her nose and cries over trees." He chuckled, skating his knuckles down the side of my arm, leaving a trail of desire. "You guard your heart, but you've never let it stop you from being kind. And when I came home tonight, and saw you cuddled up with Cash with your hand on your belly, I've never thought you were more beautiful."

His hand cradled the back of my neck, holding me still as he leaned closer, his forehead against mine. "I ate that popcorn tonight until I was sick because it was taking everything in me not to pull you onto my lap and make you forget about ever being alone. If I hadn't made a fool of myself, I might've offered to join you in the shower. And we wouldn't have left until you fully believed how consumed I am by you." My breaths were short, sparks fluttering beneath my skin, and I ached for Brooks. I wanted to shred this pillow and entwine my legs with his. I needed to close the teasing inch between us and taste his words. My lips parted, my lashes fluttering shut as the mattress shifted, ready for him to kiss me.

I opened my eyes, confused as his heat left me and the comforter pulled tight. I stretched my hand out and patted around, finding him more than an arm's length away. "If you think you're allowed to roll over and fall asleep after getting me all hot and bothered, you're mistaken. Get back over here."

His laugh was a low rumble, completely unapologetic. "Good night, Shay." I gaped at him, on the verge of curling up behind him, consequences be damned. Somehow sensing my next move, he murmured, "I want you, Shay . . . but I need to move slow. And if for some reason, this ends with us only being friends, I need you to know that even then, *you own me*. Both you and Tater do."

Chapter Thirty-Seven

"I'm going to break you into a million pieces." I jumped back with a yelp as the bacon within the wicked cast-iron skillet popped, daring me to try. "Just you wait—tomorrow morning, you'll be gone."

Letting the threat sink in, I grabbed the plastic tongs and fished out the cooked bacon. "Oh, come on," I muttered as the plastic began to melt, drizzling onto the crisp slices. Silently cursing, I tossed the worthless tongs in the sink. Ensuring the pan was free of plastic, I cracked and plopped a few eggs into the grease pit.

Cash grumbled beside the stove, likely agreeing that I had no place in the kitchen. But when I'd awoken this morning to an empty bed, and the only proof that I hadn't slept alone was a note, I'd known what I wanted to do.

When my relationship with Declan was fresh, I was excited to cook for him. I'd wanted him to know I thought of him often, wanted him to taste my appreciation. But soon, that excitement was replaced with stomach-twisting anxiety. I was afraid of messing up, of not being enough for him. The last time I'd done anything out of pure love, and not obligation, was for Tater—when I'd left Declan.

But this morning, after I read Brooks's note telling me he'd gone to work on Jake's cabin, I wanted him to know how much he meant to me. And there was nothing scary about that.

Unless I accidentally poisoned Brooks—that might be scary.

Cash jumped to his feet, paws scattering across the wood floor as the front door opened. Heart racing, I fumbled with the spatula and stirred the eggs. I frowned at them, the mixture more brown than yellow. I should've done something else. Like invited a stripper over. Even better, the stripper could've made him breakfast. Wait—no. I didn't want a stripper making him breakfast.

Maybe I should strip for him . . .

No. Bad. We're taking things slow.

Bracing myself, I slapped on a smile and turned. And then, as though I'd been hit with a gust of wind, I stepped back into the stove.

His chest was bare, his jeans low on his hips with the buckle of his belt undone, like he'd planned to strip out of them immediately. I realized why when I noticed the wood shavings on his thighs, the brown stains splattered over him. "Morning." His voice was low and meek. I gulped and forced myself to meet his curious stare and not ogle the flushed, gleaming ridges of his stomach. "What are you doing?"

With all the restraint in the world, I managed not to tackle him. "I made you breakfast," I murmured, twisting to face the stove. I scraped the eggs onto a plate, clearing my throat as I opened a cabinet and fetched a loaf of bread. "I can keep it warm for you if you want to shower first. Or if you want something else, that's fine. Cash has been eyeing it the whole time."

"Are you suggesting I smell or something?"

I bit my smile. "Maybe."

A barstool skidded across the floor, and my smile grew as he said, "Well, I guess I'll eat now then."

I slathered peanut butter and butter—extra butter, always extra butter—on a slice of bread and plated the rest of his meal. My grin was nothing but smug as I slid the plate across the counter to him. It looked dang good. And by the way his eyes gleamed, he must've thought so too. "It looks delicious, thank you."

"Thank you for working on the cabin." I tapped my fingers on the kitchen island, hesitating. "And thank you for last night."

Before he could reply—or worse, voice that he regretted sharing a bed and telling me just how strongly I possessed him—I moved to the opposite side of the kitchen to make my own breakfast. I was slicing strawberries when Brooks cleared his throat. "So I started staining the kitchen cabinets down at your cabin . . . but I got to thinking. Is there a color or stain you'd prefer?"

I shrugged and took a bite of my sandwich, waiting until my mouth was clear before I said, "I don't know—it's Jake's cabin. So whatever he wants."

"Yes," Brooks pressed. "But is there a color you want?"

I furrowed my brows. I'd never once thought I'd have a say in how the renovations went; I was just a renter. "I don't know. I like the color green."

"Green?"

"Yeah," I mumbled, wishing I'd picked a different color. *Like taupe—taupe is fine, taupe is whatever.* "Not just any green. Definitely not the color of snot or vomit. Sort of like the color of the . . ." I pursed my lips, searching for the best explanation. "You know that time of day when the sun is setting, but you can still see? Where it seems like there's a glaze? That's my favorite—when the trees are that deep, almost moody green."

Brooks made a humming sound in his throat and straightened where he sat. "Can't say I've ever stopped to notice what color the trees are at dusk. I'm usually too busy catching the last bits of the sunset."

"Sunsets are pretty," I said with a shrug. "Please don't paint the cabinets green. It might be my favorite color, but I'm not sure it would be a good fit."

He gave me a small, amused smile. "Alright."

"How is the cabin going, anyway?"

He shoveled in his last bite of eggs, and a part of me screamed inside: *Look at that! He likes my food!* "Good—it's slow. I'm decently handy, but there's a few things I haven't done before, so I'm having to learn." Somehow sensing my next thought, he added, "I'm doing my best to make sure you're in before Tater gets here."

I strained a smile. *Don't panic.* There was plenty of time before Tater came—eighteen weeks. *And now I'm sick.* No longer hungry, I packaged up the remaining fruit and wrapped my sandwich up for later. With Brooks still eating,

I moved to the living room and picked up. Blankets folded and pillows back in place, I grabbed the leftover Oreo popcorn bowl. I set it on the counter and switched on the sink faucet, planning on cleaning the rest of the dishes first.

I set the first plate in the steaming water just as Brooks switched the faucet off, placing both hands on my waist. I squeaked as my feet left the floor before I was twisted and plopped down on the counter, facing him.

He stepped between my legs, his eye level at mine. As though possessed, or fearing the intensity I read in his overwhelming gaze, I blurted, "Hi."

He grinned, the heat of his breath skimming my cheeks. "Hi, sunshine." I sucked on my bottom lip, hiding how much I loved it when he called me that. "Thank you for breakfast—I can't tell you how much it meant to me. But you don't have to do anything for me. You don't need to pay me back, or owe me some sort of favor. I would've been happy to come home and find you still wrapped up in bed right where I left you." Before I might've protested that I did it because I wanted to, his hand came up and cradled my jaw. "This isn't conditional."

"That's not—" I closed my mouth. Was Brooks wrong? I hadn't done anything I didn't want to this morning, but had my fears still played a role in it? Fears where I was scared Brooks—or anyone, really—would leave me if I didn't give them a reason to stay, to keep me around? "I'm sorry." I didn't know what else to say.

"Please don't apologize." He urged my gaze up to his, his thumb beneath my chin. "If you want to do it, then by all means do it. Clean the whole damn house, dust the rafters. Whatever you want. But don't do it because you think you have to earn your keep. And I'm sorry if I hurt you—I wasn't trying to. I've wanted to say something for weeks, especially when I came home and all my laundry was folded. And while I appreciate it, you're not here to take care of me. Or my brothers. You're here because you want to be—and because I want you here. That's all."

I leaned into his touch, letting myself relax into him. "So if there's a stack of dishes and a pile of laundry, it doesn't mean you're leaving it for me?" I asked, my tone teasing and light.

He smiled, but I didn't miss the twinge of heaviness in his eyes. "Never. It just means we're bums. But if you get sick of it, feel free to kick us into gear."

I raised a brow. "And if I leave my laundry hanging off the staircase?"

He grinned wickedly, the heat of it igniting my own. "What sort of laundry?"

I leaned back on my hands, resisting the urge to wrap my legs around his waist. "Oh, you know . . . a few muumuus, and at least thirty pairs of granny panties."

He chuckled and lowered his hands to the counter, caging me in. "I don't know what the hell a muumuu is—but I'd love to see you in one. And as for those granny panties . . . I'm not so sure that's what I saw in your suitcase before."

I choked on a laugh and flicked his chest. He caught my finger before I might do it again, watching me with a playful smirk. And I watched him right back, wondering how I'd ever lived without this. How I'd ever live without him again.

I wanted to kiss him. To learn what he tasted like in the morning, to feel his calloused hands discover my body. But I didn't close the distance, didn't dare taste more than his air. We were moving slow. Brooks said *he needed* to move slow. There was an insecure, hidden piece of me that wanted to be hurt over his admission. But that would be unfair, and I didn't blame him. I didn't know his reservations, what exactly had him wanting to pump the brakes. Though I imagined it had to do with taking on a baby, and all the baggage I carried.

But it was okay. I would never want him, or anyone, to commit before they were ready. I wasn't sure if I was ready, if I could ever commit myself to anyone again. What lay between was new and complicated. And our choices affected much more than just each other. But the fact that he was willing to try, and even understood why we couldn't rush this, made me care for him that much more.

"I have something for you," I said as he stepped back and leaned against the far counter. I reached into my back pocket and pulled out the other tidbit I'd decided this morning. My hand was steady as I held out an envelope. "There's an ultrasound inside of Tater. You can keep it if you want. They gave me a few copies—Nolan and Levi have their own," I added, suddenly second-guessing myself. Was this too much? Before I could chicken out, I tossed it at him, smacking him in the chest. "The gender's inside too—I thought it might be fun if you found out first."

"Oh." The word was almost nonexistent, nothing more than a puff of air. "Shay . . ." He ran his fingers through his hair. "I don't know—I think that should be something you learn first."

I shrugged and did my best not to let disappointment wiggle into my heart. I'd made this choice knowing he might decline, and I needed to be okay with it. Just as I owed him nothing, he owed me nothing. "If you're comfortable with it, I'm giving you the option to know first. And then, maybe another time, when it's just you and me and it feels right, you can tell me."

He stared down at the envelope in his hands, his fingers carefully grasping it. "Are you sure? I mean—" He looked up, a slow smile creeping on his lips. "I want the ultrasound—I do. I tried stealing Nolan's from his truck, and he threw a fit. But I just want to make sure this is something you really want." I nodded, and his smile grew. "Okay, wow. Yes."

"Hurry and open it before I change my mind," I teased, growing impatient. My fingers fidgeted at my sides as he faced the sink, and I could hear the sound of paper unfolding and folding. Just as I was about to jump down and rip the envelope out of his unsuspecting hands, he finally turned. "Well?" My heart fluttered at the sight of Brooks's smile, the fullest and brightest I'd ever seen. "Tell me."

He laughed and tucked the envelope into his back pocket, the ultrasound still in his hand. "Not yet, sunshine."

"Please," I whined, not opposed to snatching the envelope out of his *Wrangler butts drive me nuts* jeans. "I changed my mind. I want to know now."

"Not yet." He stepped forward, catching my hips before I hopped down. He leaned in, his lips toying with my ear. "Soon. I promise."

He pulled back, and I watched his gaze, saw how he glanced at my lips. I swallowed, my throat bare, my skin hot. Slipping into temptation, I lifted my finger and traced it along his rigid stomach.

He shuddered beneath my touch, resting his head in the crook of my neck. "Hey, Shay?" he murmured, his lips leaving a ghost of a touch.

"Yeah?" I rasped, frozen where I sat, resisting the urge to wrap my arms around his back.

He smiled against my skin, and I trembled before he said, "Do you think Tater sort of looks like—"

"If you say an alien, I will find Michael Myers and set him loose on you," I warned, flicking his side.

He stepped back, grinning as he stared at the ultrasound in his hand. "Cutest alien I ever did see."

"You and your brothers are a bunch of overgrown children." He smirked but said nothing more and focused solely on the ultrasound before him, watching it with all the wonder and attention in the world. But my words were enough to remember why we were alone in the house. "How are you doing . . . with your father?"

He glanced up with glazed eyes, taken aback by my question. But rather than brushing it off, he jumped up on the counter across from me. Still looking at the ultrasound, he said, "I'm okay. Some days are better than others."

"And today?"

"Today is good." He set the photo beside his thigh, a lingering smile on his lips. "Thank you for this—and for breakfast, and last night. I almost went with Nolan and Levi. I'm worried about them. But I'm trying to give them space."

"You're a good brother," I quietly reassured him, even if he did sometimes come on too strong, hovering over his brothers. But when I tried to view it through his eyes, understand how it might feel to be the oldest of a family who'd lost their dad, I could see why. I couldn't help but wonder if Brooks had carried the burden of being the oldest far longer than a year. "I don't know or see everything, but I think they're okay. I worry about them . . . about you. It makes me sad when Nolan is hard on himself. He stresses about the shop—and I think it's heavy on Levi too. It's like they both think if the shop fails, then they failed your dad."

He sucked in a deep breath, and I second-guessed myself. Maybe I should've minded my own business. But then he said, "It wasn't supposed to be this way. My dad was supposed to be here. He chose to stay, you know? It doesn't seem all that fair that he could leave us in a matter of minutes. We never had the chance to give him a real goodbye."

I bit my lip, toying with what I should do. Trusting my instincts, I hopped down and leaned against the counter beside him. "What was his name?" I asked, always treading carefully when it came to their family, never wanting to push too far.

"Wayne." His voice was steady, not shaking like his hand in mine as I traced gentle strokes over his palm. "When he had his first heart attack, the doctors reassured us it was just a fluke thing. He was fairly young and in decent health. Plus, Dad never liked a fuss, so we all kept going on with life as normal. Levi went back to art school, and Nolan was slowly taking over the shop, learning from Dad." He fell silent, his eyes distant, like he was pulled back into those last moments with his dad, what he might've done differently. "He had another one in the middle of the night a few weeks later. And that was that. So now we're just trying to figure out how to make something of this mess."

I hadn't experienced loss before, at least not from death. But I wished I could take Brooks and his brothers and lock them in this house. Protect them from the inevitable agony and discomfort that was a part of life. If I could, I would carry their grief and breathe air into their lungs, anything to ease their burden.

But I couldn't.

It was impossible to avoid. There was no amount of light, no amount of love that could absolutely overpower the darkness. It lingered, the pain a constant reminder. But I liked to believe, had to believe that there was something to be found in the shadows, in our darkest moments. Perhaps an extra morsel of strength. That maybe, when we were consumed by darkness, exhausted and lost—only then did we learn who we were.

But I would be their friend. Sit with them in the bleak, lonely shadows of grief.

"We should do something," I started, abandoning my former idea of suggesting we stay inside and watch movies all day. I was a homebody to my core, but there was nothing quite like getting out in the sun. "We could go for a hike, maybe a drive. Fishing?"

Brooks pushed off the counter, his brow raised. "You want to go fishing?"

"Yeah." I shrugged, my hands tucked in my pockets as I backed away, putting plenty of distance between us. "You wouldn't need to shower. You'd fit right in with the fish."

His eyes flared, a grin playing at his lips. "If you think that cute lil' bump of yours will keep me from tossing you in the lake, you're wrong, sunshine."

I made a small humming noise, pretending the thought didn't have my heart racing. I stopped, my heel hitting the edge of the staircase. "So you'll teach me, then? How to fish?"

I bit my lip and stayed where I was as he approached, watching me as though he knew the effect he had on me. But if he did, if he was aware how he held me in the palm of his hand, he didn't let on. "I'll teach you. But only if you promise to let me come home and make you dinner with whatever you catch."

"And if I catch nothing?"

"I'll make you dinner anyway."

Chapter Thirty-Eight

Two weeks had passed since Halloween. We were in the midst of fall, edging in on winter. I had little experience with snow, and based on the blistering heat I experienced driving through Arizona this summer, I assumed I never would. But here in Wallowpine, the temperatures were dropping and change was in full effect. It wasn't immediate. The aspen trees didn't wake up one morning and decide to shed their leaves, leaving their ivory branches bare. It took time, patience, as it gradually settled in. As did all the best changes.

With Brooks, there wasn't a monumental change either. One fishing trip, a quick dunk in the lake, and a delicious meal didn't change our world. But those little shifts . . . wow. Those meant everything. We hadn't shared another night in bed, but there was the sincere, steadying way his fingers brushed mine in passing, reminding me he was here. Sometimes I'd wake up to a peanut butter sandwich—with a sticky note attached to the plate, so I wouldn't wrongly assume he'd left it for someone else. On the mornings I'd wake up early to run, I'd start his truck so it was nice and toasty by the time he left for work. No longer did I do the dishes or laundry unless I wanted to. Nor did I scurry up the stairs to hide when he'd get home, instead staying firmly planted with Nolan and Levi on the couch, unwinding from the day.

Which is exactly where I planned to plop down as soon as I finished the drive home from my doctor's appointment. I took Nolan's truck instead of Jake's, but I drove myself. All three brothers had offered to drive me, but it was time I took my training wheels off. And I didn't want to put unnecessary pressure on them with the anniversary of their father's death.

I hopped out onto the driveway, stretching my legs from the drive. Today had been only a simple checkup, ensuring the baby's heartbeat and growth were steady and my vitals were healthy, but I'd be grateful when the appointments were over with.

"Hi, handsome," I crooned to Cash as he greeted me at the door. He jumped up and lathered me with kisses, somehow always careful with my belly. "Good boy." I glanced around, searching for a sign of my roommates. All four vehicles were out front, but the house was empty, save for their father's guitar set out on the kitchen table. I'd expected Brooks to hide it when I officially moved in weeks ago, but until today it hadn't left its spot beside the fireplace.

Actions spoke louder than words.

Brooks trusted me.

I smiled to myself and followed Cash to the glass door, assuming his wagging tail meant his owners were in the backyard. I slid it open, watching from the threshold as the three brothers rifled through a shed.

Before I might've said a word, Nolan turned with a wide grin. "Hey darlin'," he said, setting down what looked to be a folded-up canopy at his feet. "How's our baby mama?"

I rolled my eyes but embraced him back as he pulled me into his hold. "Good. The appointment was quick, nothing new to report."

"You hear that, Brooks?" Nolan hollered into the shed, his arm slung around my shoulder. "She said they're both good—so you don't need to ask me later."

He jumped, hissing, when I pinched the skin beneath his ribs and gave him a pointed look. I knew Brooks had pushed his brothers to ask about my pregnancy when he felt he'd lost that right. But the closer we became, and his confidence grew, the more Brooks asked and not his brothers, and I wasn't about to give him a hard time for it. He was showing me he cared. I gave Nolan a innocent smile as I said, "Thanks for letting me drive your truck."

"Anytime." He pushed his golden hair out of his eyes, leaving a smudge of dirt on his forehead. "When's your next one?"

"In about a month." I scrunched my nose, my stomach already turning at the thought. "I'll drive Jake's next time. I have to do this glucose test, and it's longer."

"Is that the appointment where you drink that really sugary juice?" Brooks asked as he stepped out of the shed and lowered a bale of firewood to the ground.

"I think so," I said, fighting off a smile at the sight of him. To hell with suits and ties. I'd cut off my big toe and toss it in a stew—okay, too many scary movies for me—if that meant I could see Brooks wear Wranglers and flannels every day.

He shoved his sleeves up his arms, looking at me. "You have to fast too, right?"

I raised my brows, shocked with how much he knew about pregnancy. Before I could agree, Nolan patted him on the shoulder and smirked. "Guess I'll go help Levi since you're too busy showing off."

"Are you guys going camping?" I asked, assuming so since Levi and Nolan were both lugging camping supplies through the gate that led to the front.

"Yeah." Brooks teetered on the edge of the porch step, his hands in his pockets. "Nolan wanted to get raging drunk before spreading Dad's ashes—so we compromised and decided to go camping instead."

"Oh." I hadn't realized their father had been cremated, or that they had his ashes. "I'm glad you guys are going out together to honor your father."

He pressed his lips together and looked up at the sky. "You coming with us?"

"Oh—uh," I started, fumbling for a response. "That's okay. This is something you should do with your brothers. Plus, someone needs to open up the shop in the morning."

"We're closed," Levi said, surprising me when he slipped out the back door. "We weren't open the day Dad died, so there's no sense in being open. Come with us, Shay."

"Don't worry—we'll still pay you," Nolan added, leaning against the porch railing.

"No. You're not paying me if I'm not working." I reached for Cash, avoiding their gazes. "I'm going to stay here. Someone needs to stay with Cash anyway."

"Nope," Nolan pressed, shaking his head. "Cash is coming with us, darlin'. And I'd really rather not deal with a pissed off dog all night, so would you please come?"

"This is something you should do with your family." I wrung my hands together behind my back. "Not the random girl you're letting crash in your house. I promise I'm fine here. I don't mind being alone."

"I'm going to pretend you didn't say that." Nolan bent and grabbed the bale of firewood. "Go upstairs and pack a bag—we're leaving in thirty."

"Come with us." Levi squeezed my shoulder in reassurance before he followed after Nolan, leaving only Brooks and me on the porch.

Brooks waited until they were out of earshot before he said, "Ignore them—you don't have to do anything you don't want to do, alright?" Before I could thank him, he hooked a finger through my belt loop and tugged me to the edge of the porch. "But I want you to come. We all agreed on it before you got here. So if that's what's stopping you, don't let it."

I stared at his hand as he wound it through mine, unable to deny it did something to me when he admitted he wanted me around. "It's going to be cold." It was mid-November, still warm enough during the day to wear short sleeves, but at night the temperature dropped. And it wasn't a personal goal of mine to become a human icicle.

His laugh was light, and I looked up to find him grinning. "We packed you a tent, extra blankets, and an air mattress. Maybe even a pillow or two."

My eyes burned and I swallowed, keeping that emotion at bay. "You promise you don't mind?"

"Not at all." He tightened his hold on my hand. "Tomorrow wouldn't be right without our whole family there. And that includes you and Tater, Shay."

Chapter Thirty-Nine

Family.

I carried that word with me the rest of the evening. Stored it deep in my heart as I mulled it over. Is that what this was? Had I somehow meddled my way into this family of brothers and found an unexpected place with them?

It was true I'd come here in search of a home.

But I hadn't known I'd find a family, too.

I pulled my beanie down over my ears and scooted closer to the fire while we ate our tinfoil dinners. I'd thought Brooks was kidding—or was high—when he handed me a shovel and told me to start digging. I'd never cooked anything in the ground, and I was wary about dirt or worms sneaking through the foil. But even if they had, it was the best worms I'd ever had.

"You did a great job with the tent." Brooks pulled his chair up beside mine, the four of us gathered around the fire. He leaned over, rubbing Cash where he lay at my feet. "I'm proud of you."

"Thank you." I smiled, pretending it hadn't taken me three tries. But I'd done it on my own, leaving them to set up the rest of camp. "You guys are going to freeze out here," I said, shivering despite the Carhartt Brooks had loaned me. There was no way the three of them would last the entire night out here with nothing to break the cold. Light flurries of snow had fallen earlier this week, not enough to stick, but it was only a matter of time before it was a dreamy winter wonderland.

I was in the middle of imagining my first Christmas in Wallowpine when he leaned in close, his voice deep and low. "If you're so worried, maybe I'll sneak in with you. Keep you warm."

Heat crept through me, having absolutely nothing to do with the fire. I brought a finger to my lips, and Brooks tracked the movement, his eyes matching the desire in mine. Every day, no matter how innocent our touches were, how little or much time we spent together, it was growing harder not to make Brooks's body a part of my own. Before I might've accepted, Nolan doused the fire brewing in me. "Well, I hope you're gonna invite me along, Brooks. Levi and I will be sad if we have to snuggle out here without you."

Brooks laughed, stretching out in his chair. "I'm not snuggling either of you while you both reek of beer."

"I've only had one," Levi chimed in, kicking his legs back.

"One too many," Brooks chided back and crossed his arms over his chest. He and I were the only ones not drinking—me, for obvious reasons, and Brooks didn't drink at all. "You shouldn't be drinking anyway."

Levi scoffed. "I'll be twenty-one in six months." He pointed a finger at Nolan. "If I don't start now, he'll have drunk the world dry by then."

I laughed under my breath and wrapped my jacket tighter around me, tucking Tater in. They'd done this the whole evening, harassing and joking with one another. I watched in awe, unable to stop myself from wondering how differently my childhood might've played out if I'd had a sibling.

Nolan lifted his beer to his lips. It was the most I'd ever seen him drink. I didn't know much about his history, but I assumed by the cautious way Brooks had watched him all night, he was keeping a close eye on him. "You ever wonder what she did with it?" I froze, and silence pressed in. Even the crackling flames seemed to still, giving me no clue as to who Nolan was speaking of. "I mean, ten grand is a lot of money. But not enough to make her pop into town to see her boys."

I glanced at Brooks, but his thoughts seemed to be lost in the fire. Levi's attention was diverted to the bleak sky. Was Nolan talking about their mom? There was something heartbreaking about the image, about this moment. They were silent. They had no answer to why their mom didn't come home. Didn't choose them.

I folded up the last of my tinfoil dinner and pushed through my nerves. "I don't know your mother—"

"We don't either," Levi muttered, bringing his beer to his lips.

I shuddered a reinforcing breath, refusing to lose my nerve just yet. "But sometimes guilt keeps us from those we love most. I'm not excusing her leaving—not at all. But maybe she never came back because she couldn't forgive herself. Maybe she felt undeserving to exist in your world."

Nolan eyed me through the flames, his voice the driest I'd ever heard it. "You know, Shay, from the day Mom left, not one of us heard from her again. At least, not until she called the shop years later. Someone from town must've told her about Dad dying, and she wanted to check in. I'd thought a lot about what I'd say if I ever saw her, how I'd tell her to screw off—but she caught me at a weak point." He grinned, and I didn't smile back. There was nothing contagious about it. "I won't bore you with the details, but she started calling regularly enough that the one time I didn't hear from her, I was worried. For once, I called her—and she told me she was in trouble. She needed money." His gaze was heavy and demanding. No matter how much I silently wished it, I couldn't bring myself to look away, couldn't ask him to stop sharing this tale, already knowing how it played out. "I wanted to help, so she gave me an address for a check. But I thought I should deliver it by hand, see if she was okay. I hadn't come clean to my brothers about us talking until then, but they must've thought it would spark something in her too, because they didn't hesitate to pile in the truck with me and make the drive to California." I glanced at Brooks, seeing the unveiled rage pooling in his eyes. "I can't speak for them, but I was almost excited to go. I imagine that's why these two stayed in the truck and I walked up alone to deliver money to the woman who left us. The whole time I'm looking around this fancy neighborhood, I'm thinking: this is what she gave us up for.

"I suspected something was up, but I knocked anyway—I guess because I'm a stupid bastard. I imagine that's exactly what she thought when she opened the door and didn't know who I was. She just stared, waiting for me to say something. It wasn't until Brooks and Levi climbed out of the car that she connected the pieces. And you know what she said, Shay? Before she took that generous check and closed the door in our faces?" I ached to my core, and tears welled in my eyes. "She said: 'I'll tell you what I told your father—I want no part in your family.' So no, Shay, I don't believe she thinks she's undeserving. If anything, to her, we're the undeserving ones."

A harsh breeze whizzed through and the fire stirred, thickening the tension. I didn't know how to respond, how to put into words what I was feeling as I pieced it together. Brooks had told me of his mother, how she'd left when he was a child—but he hadn't told me this. Hadn't shared how she'd blatantly walked away from them even as adults, leaving them to grieve over the death of their father alone. She'd had the audacity to accept money, but not her own sons. Was this what Nolan and Brooks had spoken of that night in the kitchen, when Brooks said they'd been fooled before? Why he offered me cash all those months ago, and seemed shocked when I'd denied his money? No wonder he'd hated me. I was from *California*—the state his mother had run off to, never looking back. He'd believed I was here to take and leave, to drain their hearts and pockets, exactly like their mother.

I ran a trembling hand down my face. I was feeling too much.

I stood, jolting Cash awake at my feet. Based on the way Brooks jumped and his brothers' wide eyes, I'd shocked them too. "Give me that," I hissed, yanking the beer right out of Levi's hand and then Nolan's, ignoring their protests. Before I could truly process what I was doing, determine if my fury was worth setting the mountain on fire, I tossed the near-empty cans into the campfire.

But the flames only rose a lick. Brooks sat back down with half a smile on his face, and I deemed that as permission to continue. "I have no problem if you want to get drunk and mourn your dad." I snatched two half-empty beers beside Nolan's boots and tossed them in the flames. "But I'm not going to sit here and let you mourn a woman who doesn't deserve to hold that sort of power over you."

Nolan stared up at me, both he and Levi resembling scolded children, their hands folded neatly on their laps. "If you want, we can sit here and cry about how the ones who were supposed to love us didn't. We can whine all night about how much they suck. How much I believe your mom sucks for deserting you. I promise you—I am on your side in this. I hate her for hurting the people I love most, and for making you doubt yourselves. So if that's really what you want, I will be on this mountain of misfits with you and tell you you're not alone. But in the end, it doesn't change the fact that we're all human, and sometimes we do shitty things that hurt others. So if that's what you need, I—" I covered my mouth as my voice broke, anger and grief pulsing through me.

I cleared my throat, needing to say these words as much as I needed to hear them. "I will do it. But the truth is, I don't want to be a misfit, a stray, or anything like that. I'm tired of being angry and wondering what I could've done differently—when deep down, all four of us know we did nothing wrong. I don't care about who left us. I care about you and your daddy, who stuck around and loved you because you were enough without even trying. And that is why we came out here—to celebrate the phenomenal man who managed to raise even more amazing sons. That is who I want to know about."

Hot tears fell down my cheeks, streamed down my jaw. I didn't wipe them, unable to do anything but stand there and wait. Had I crossed a line? I hadn't meant to get so worked up, but Nolan stirred something in me. My anger wasn't at them, but that they'd allowed their mother, a woman who didn't know them, to define their worth. But I knew them.

And I knew how much they were worth.

And maybe . . . maybe some of that anger was directed at myself too. For too long, I'd carried the burns inflicted upon me, acting as if someone's carelessness and selfishness determined my worth. It was time I stopped that.

I was worth more than that, too.

"Well shit, Shay." Nolan cracked a laugh and rubbed at his eyes, smearing the tears. "Way to suck the fun out of the night."

I laughed as they did, each breath one of relief, confirmation I was where I belonged. A sturdy, firm hand found mine and tugged me back until I was swept off the ground. Brooks pulled me onto his lap, adjusting himself in his chair. My legs were draped over the side of his, and his hand cupped my face, looking at me with all the kindness and wonder in the world. His thumb skimmed my bottom lip, his other hand resting on my thigh. "Nolan and I didn't learn how to swim until we were around ten and twelve."

"I was nine," Nolan said from across the fire, leaning back in his seat. "I hadn't turned ten yet—don't try to make me as much of a loser as you."

Brooks laughed, and with a wide smile, he flipped his brother the bird. I rested my cheek against his chest, and Nolan and Levi both edged their chairs closer to the fire, to their elder brother. "But I guess Dad was tired of us not knowing how, so he dragged all of us to the lake. Only he said we were going fishing." His chest shook, a laugh bubbling within. "He had us paddle out to the middle of the lake, and then he basically shoved us out. He said: 'You're either gonna learn how to live or drown today, boys.'"

"Remember when you convinced Levi to hand you a paddle, and Dad chucked it across the lake?" Nolan laughed, tipping his head to the sky, so different from the man of moments ago.

"Your dad didn't make you?" I asked Levi, craning my head to see him.

"I was only four!" Levi smirked beneath his jacket hood. "And don't be fooled into thinking they were victims, Shay. Both of them dragged me out there the next year. They were real assholes. Held out a rope, but they made me work for it and chase it the whole time."

"He could've drowned," I gasped at Brooks, my eyes wide. "He was practically a baby!"

Brooks laughed, and Nolan called out, "Oh, he was a big baby, alright. He cried about it to Dad afterward. Got us grounded for two weeks."

"That's because you stole Dad's truck to take us out there and you know it," Levi shouted, but there was nothing angry in his tone. "We're forgetting the only reason Dad did that in the first place, and that's because Brooks was too chicken to learn on his own."

"You were kind of old." I pinched his chest, only to yelp, nearly coming out of my skin, when he returned one on my butt.

His lips were heavy with a smirk before they found my ear. "Says the girl who barely learned how to fish and drive a standard."

I scrunched my nose at him, my heart warm with bliss as I thought of Brooks taking me out fishing. He'd been different than when he'd first tried to teach me how to drive stick shift. Quieter and patient, letting me go at my own pace. Pep-talked me through my squeamish stomach as I tried to bait the hook, even more so when I gutted the fish. He'd told me it was because he had to be, something about not scaring away the fish—but I knew differently. There was a change in Brooks. Somewhere down the line, he'd learned me. Realized I couldn't be pushed in the way his father had taught him and Nolan to swim.

I skimmed my nose along his, his lips so tauntingly close. "Thank you for teaching me."

Brooks looked inclined to reply, but he pulled back as Levi said, "Dad played the guitar—bad. He was absolutely horrible, and we all begged him to stop. But he insisted that he loved it, and that not being good wasn't enough of a reason to stop."

Nolan's eyes were glazed, distant. "Dad worked harder than anyone I've ever met. During slow seasons, I remember him sneaking out to strip copper or chop wood while we all slept so he could bring in extra cash."

Tears slipped down my aching cheeks, sore from smiling and laughing as I listened to them share moments of their father, both hilarious and heartbreaking. I absorbed every moment, cherishing that they'd trust me with this—with him. Never before had I felt so robbed for not having met someone. I would never know what his laugh sounded like, if he preferred Pepsi or Coke. But as I sat here with his sons, in the arms of his eldest, I thought I might already know him.

My back throbbed, my bones chilled to their core, but my heart was filled to the brim. We'd sat by the fire for hours, the three of them sharing stories to honor their father. Only after I fell asleep did they stop. I woke to Brooks carrying me to my tent, and despite his initial offer to sneak inside, I didn't ask him to join me. I knew he not only needed but wanted to be with his brothers tonight. So I meekly kissed his cheek and sent him on his way. I fell back asleep with a smile on my face, Cash nuzzled against my side, as I listened to their whispers and laughter outside.

At the brink of dawn, we were awake, packing up camp. Rather than loading up to leave, Levi started through the woods, carrying his father's guitar. Nolan followed after him, holding an urn. An urn I'd mistaken as a vase, not realizing it held the ashes of Wayne Graham.

"Are you okay to walk?" Brooks asked, lingering behind. "We're going to the meadow to spread Dad's ashes." Before I could agree, he added, "I can drive the truck around too. There's a road that connects beneath—"

I stopped him with a shake of my head. "Just hold my hand."

His throat bobbed, and he wrapped his hand with mine, gripping like I might slip away, my other hand holding Cash's leash. The crunching of needles and leaves spoke as we slowly trailed Levi and Nolan through the forest until the trees thinned and opened into the meadow. Fog seeped through the raw morning air, a layer on the rosy sunrise. With summer gone, the colors had faded with it. The evergreen pines held true, but the aspens were bare, crisp golden leaves scattered on the forest floor.

I looked to Brooks when Levi and Nolan did, silently asking their oldest brother to take the lead. Dark pits lay beneath his eyes, and his shoulders were tight. I couldn't imagine the exhaustion he carried, feeling like he had to lead the family. If he resented it, he didn't voice it. He squeezed my hand once more before he grabbed the urn from Nolan, and Levi set the guitar on the straw-like grass. "Um—" His laugh was scratchy, full of nerves as he ran a shaking hand through his mussed hair, his face blotchy and red. "I don't know how to do this."

I stuffed my hands into my pockets and leaned back on my heels, resisting the urge to hold him, letting him work through it. "If I'm being honest, I don't know how to do any of this, Dad. I thought I was grown and didn't need your help—but now you're gone, and I have no idea what I'm doing." He grew silent and the forest followed suit, watching in reverence. "I don't know how to fill the void you left, how to be half the man you were. And I'm sorry. But thank you—thank you for choosing us every day. For setting the example of the type of father I hope to be, and I promise, I'll do my best to follow the path you set."

He clamped his mouth shut and with shaking hands reached into the urn. "Love you," he whispered, and the wind lifted his father's ashes off his palm, setting him free.

Nolan swallowed, his face taut when he took the urn, nothing like the carefree man I'd grown to know and adore. "I love you." His voice broke, tears falling hard and fast. "But I'm mad at you. I'm so mad you left us. And I'm sorry I didn't grow up sooner, and you'll only remember me as a jackass, and not the man you wanted me to be. I'm sorry for being selfish and not realizing earlier our time with you was limited. I'm sorry for drinking too much, and not going to church. And I'm sorry for not ordering that damn Halloween candy." He stammered out a choked laugh, the rest of us following suit. "I miss you. I miss you every day." He opened his mouth, only to close it. His words must've failed him, because he only reached into the urn and spread his father's ashes before handing it to Levi.

I bit my lip and held back tears at the sight of each of them red-faced and fighting to hold it together. Brooks wrapped his arm around Nolan's shoulder as Levi said, "I don't know what else to say—but I think you already know. I think you hated leaving us as much as we hated you leaving. But if anything good has come from this, it's that it's forced us to lean on each other." He stared at the guitar near his feet in a daze, his hand quivering around the urn. "I'm sorry that it had to take you dying for us to realize how good we have it. Brooks and Nolan will probably give me hell for it later, but I like to believe, despite how lost we all feel right now, that you're still here, existing within each of us." He opened the lid and pulled out a handful and let it go. "Missing you is an honor, Dad."

I lowered Cash's leash to the ground, trusting him to stay with them, and stepped back, wanting to give them their space as they finished their goodbye. But then Levi held the urn out to me. "Shay."

I didn't dishonor this privilege, accepting the urn immediately. I clutched it to my chest and searched for what to say about a man I didn't know, yet did. I slipped off the lid and held the ash in my fist. "I love your sons." I opened my hand and the breeze stirred, carrying the ashes away. "I know everything that they are is because of you."

I replaced the lid and handed the urn to Brooks, his green eyes vulnerable and pooling with tears. He set it down and tugged me into his side, one arm holding tight as Levi and Nolan joined, creating a messy group hug. We cried, them for their father and me for them—and perhaps what I'd missed out on. Eventually the tears slowed and the sun rose past the tree line, but we stayed, holding one another.

So this was love.

Chapter Forty

Grief was strange.

Watching those you love mourn was stranger.

But I was thankful they'd trusted me to see them at their lowest.

We didn't remain in the meadow long, leaving shortly after they scattered the remaining ashes. Every bit of their father was free, the flowing wind spreading him throughout his home. The ride back was silent, vacant of tears or laughter. But the windows were down, and the breeze and shifting of the trees somehow filled the void. We went straight inside when we got home, leaving the camping supplies for tomorrow. I longed to be with Brooks, with all of them, but I went upstairs instead, offering them clarity and air.

I climbed into bed at the first sign of night, leaving the window cracked open. It was growing colder, but there was something soothing about listening to the obscurity of the forest at night. With Cash beside my feet, I closed my eyes just as there was a knock on the door.

"Shay?"

I stirred out of bed and cracked open the door. Brooks stared at me with heavy and solemn eyes, the bags prominent beneath them. I held out my hand, and it felt like I was offering him much more when he wrapped his hand with mine. I led us back to the bed, grasping his chilled fingers as I pulled him down with me.

Pulling the blankets over us, I faced him on my side, watching. Waiting for nothing. I'd lie here all night with him if he asked. But needing him to know, I whispered, "I'm proud of you."

"Thank you for being there today."

"Always." I felt the surety of that proclamation in my bones. "No matter what, Brooks, I promise to always be here for you. For all of you."

"I was wrong for ever thinking you'd hurt my brothers." His hand found mine between the space of our bodies. "Sometimes I worry that I'm the only one in their corner, the only one looking out for them. But you've made me not feel so alone."

I smiled, and a single tear ran down my temple. We'd come so far from who we used to be. I loved his brothers, loved him. I didn't understand how anyone couldn't. As I thought of their mom, and why Brooks was so wary to trust, I thought of the night when I'd overheard him and Nolan. Not wanting anything between us, I said, "That night I slept on the couch, I was awake when you came home and talked to Nolan. I don't care about what you said—we're not those people anymore—but I wanted you to know." I gripped his hand. "And I'm so sorry about what your mom did to you and your brothers, and if you ever need to talk about her—"

"Wait," he said, his voice low as he stopped me and backtracked to what I revealed—that I'd listened in on a private conversation. "You heard everything I said to Nolan?"

I swallowed, my throat tight as I thought of what I'd overheard. How he was hurt I'd kept my pregnancy from him when he was vulnerable with me. His anger at Declan. His confession that he'd messed up, and his fear I was using them. How they'd been fooled before. But he said something else, too.

I can't be with her.

Before I could reply, Brooks said, "You said something last night, and it's stuck with me." He shifted beside me, and half a beat later, the lamp was switched on. He lay on his side beside me, his eyes as exhausted as before—but there was something else there. A determination I hadn't seen before. "I've carried my mom abandoning us for a long time. It's impacted me and the choices I've made. And sometimes, I worry I'm going to end up like her. That someday, I'm going to have this beautiful family . . . and leave." He glanced at our joined hands, and I hoped he saw what I felt. He would never do anything like that. His heart was too big. One hand clutched mine, and his other skimmed my cheek. "So when I told Nolan I couldn't be with you, I *was* afraid of hurting you and Tater in the way my mom hurt me. It was why I kept pushing you away when we first met. Even then, I didn't believe I'd be good for you. But therapy and you, especially you, have helped me see how much more I could be. I don't want to be defined by the person who left me."

My lip trembled, and I was at a loss for what to do. I thought I'd regret admitting to Brooks I'd eavesdropped on him, and I certainly hadn't expected him to react how he had. I thought he'd be angry, or at least hold it against me. But Brooks wasn't Declan. And he wasn't his mother either.

I didn't know what we were becoming, if this was us taking another step forward. I knew I couldn't give him all of me, at least not yet. But I could give something. Fear laced through me, but I didn't let it take root as I sat up against the headboard. I unraveled our hands and, without any hesitation, set his palm on my stomach. He didn't look at me, but at his hand, my gray sweatshirt keeping us from being skin to skin. Maybe I should've been uncomfortable, but I wasn't embarrassed to share the greatest thing that had ever happened to me.

Nolan and Levi had said the thought of feeling the baby move grossed them out, apparently reminding them of a scene from *Aliens*. So I expected Brooks to touch me for maybe a moment, long enough to not hurt my feelings. I probably should've asked him first, but I wanted him to understand I didn't think he was capable of hurting anyone how his mom had. But then he said, his voice shy, "I want to see you."

I blinked.

He wants to see . . . me?

Beyond Dr. Malitina, no one had seen my stomach bare. The last time Declan had seen me naked, neither of us knew I was pregnant. I nodded anyway, wanting to share this with him. But because I hadn't found a way to sever Declan's abuse completely, I whispered, "I have stretch marks. They're small, but I have them. And there's this brown line that runs down from my belly button. It's normal, but I thought you'd want to know, in case it weirds you out."

I hadn't realized how afraid I was, how exposed I felt, until Brooks brushed his thumb over my cheek and caught a single tear. His voice was thoughtful, gentle, as he said, "You're safe with me, Shay."

I closed my eyes, blocking out the memories of Declan commenting on my body. No longer did I live with a man who controlled me. Who belittled me for not having the biggest breasts or a tight ass. Never again would I lay on the freezing bathroom floor and silently plead with God to save me from the man who I thought loved me.

Never again would I be made less than.

Never again would I accept anything but what I deserved.

I bit my lip and rolled my shirt up. Not even the brisk air seeping through the open window could cool the burning within me. At first, only his fingertips grazed my stomach, a featherlight touch. But the longer he traveled, the more prominent his touch was. Soon, the entirety of his hand was against me, spanning my stomach. "Do you feel Tater moving?" he asked, his voice light with wonder.

"No," I whispered. Tater's movements had increased; not a day passed where I didn't feel a kick or some sort of wiggle. But right now, beyond the rise and fall of my breaths, there was nothing. This moment was just between us. "Must be hiding."

I watched with amusement as he nudged and prodded at my stomach. Tater was perfectly safe inside me, but I hadn't expected such confidence from a man who knew next to nothing about pregnancy or babies. I scoffed a laugh, smiling as he gently poked me beneath my belly button. "Are you trying to irritate Tater?"

The corner of his lips tipped up. "Maybe."

"You know," I started, teasingly pinching the arm propped up beneath his head. "Bonnie would lose her mind if she saw you right now."

He laughed under his breath, the only acknowledgment he gave me, apparently too focused on the task at hand. He ran his palm over the curve of my belly, searching for movement. Wanting to be brave and touch him too, I smoothed my fingers through his hair. "I wouldn't mind if you told me the gender now. Then we can stop calling it Tater."

"But I like Tater." He pressed two curious fingers down. "I'll tell you soon, sunshine."

"Okay." I liked having this between us. It was intimate, special, to share something that was only ours. "Thank you for letting me experience this."

He glanced up then, a crease between his brows. "Experience what?"

Heat crept through me, and I teared up. I wished the lights were off so he couldn't see how close I was to breaking. "As much as I don't regret my decision, there are times where it's incredibly lonely." I thought of the times I'd sat at the doctor's office alone and watched women with their partners, knowing it would never be that way for me. The harsh reality that my only support when I delivered would likely be the hospital staff. I knew I could do it, but I ached regardless. "You've made me not feel so alone, too."

The crease between his brows eased, recognition settling in those lovely green eyes. He unfurled my sweatshirt back into place and tugged on my hand until I lay back down beside him. One arm slid under me, the other above as he pulled me into his hold. I burrowed myself against his chest, gripping his shirt. His chin was atop my head, his breaths stirring my hair. "You can give me your pain, Shay."

How? How did I show him my scars, my tattered spirit, without him seeing me as weak and broken? I loved how tender and kind he was to me, but I didn't want him to treat me like I was fragile. And I didn't know how to put such ugliness into words. "Sometimes . . . putting it into words feels too heavy. You know?"

His fingers slid through my hair, his chest rising beneath my head. "I know." Despite the ache in my chest, I smiled, grateful Brooks didn't push for more. His lips brushed the top of my head, hovering there. "You're not alone anymore. You have a family here."

I believed him.

I didn't know what sort of family that might be. What role Brooks would play in my life, in Tater's. And when he flicked off the lamp and lovingly caressed my stomach, I thought he might want to be something more than an uncle of sorts to my baby.

I wanted that for him, too.

But I didn't know how to hand him my heart.

Brooks was good, and he was still young. I didn't want him to commit to more than he could handle. I'd grown tremendously in my time here, but I'd gone so long being treated like a burden, reminded how unlovable I was.

What would I do if Brooks saw me and walked away?

My mother didn't love me—or, at least, not in the way I wanted to love my children—and Declan hadn't shown an ounce of interest in his own child. So how could I trust Brooks, or anyone, to take on a baby who wasn't theirs?

The thought made my soul throb, but it might be better to stay alone. I couldn't be hurt, and Tater would never feel the pain I had. We would be alone, yes. But we'd be safe.

But what if Brooks, and the life we could have together, would be worth the risk?

Chapter Forty-One

"I never should've let you talk me into this," I whined, frowning at the pink strands in my hair. "I look like a flamingo."

"Stop that." Layne pointed a finger at me, her fingers stained from coloring my hair last night. "It's barely a few pieces. Besides, after you have that baby, you're going to lose all your hair." She nodded, as though it was set in stone. "Yup. It happened to my sister-in-law."

"That's fine." I leaned over the diner counter and pulled on her braid, where green was woven through—a failed attempt at trying to color it blue. "At least my hair isn't green."

She hummed under her breath, no doubt biting back her response as she checked out a customer. Despite spending the night at Layne's, I'd come to the diner for lunch. She would be leaving for college in a few weeks, and I wanted to spend as much time with her as I could.

She made her way back to me, dipping her finger in the whipped cream atop my mug. "I think you messed up on purpose. Probably as punishment for making you leave Brooks to warm your bed all alone."

"I told you I'd never colored hair before," I reasoned with a laugh, heat sneaking up my neck. I hadn't expected Brooks to sleep with me again, assuming he'd only come for comfort after spreading his father's ashes. But the next night, he was there. Again and again. Sleeping with him was now familiar—he preferred to sleep on his stomach with his arm tossed over me, keeping me close. Despite the intimacy that came with sharing a bed, we'd done nothing more, not even kiss. My fears and reservations still existed, creeping through the back of my mind.

But wow, I really wanted to kiss him.

"Gross," Layne muttered, like she had a front-row seat to my thoughts. "Oh, don't come any closer, Lila," she warned as my former boss exited the kitchen. "Not unless you want to hear Shay talk about how good Brooks looks naked."

"Layne!" I screeched.

"Oh, leave the poor girl alone—and stop pretending you haven't thought about it too." Lila tugged on Layne's hair, eyeing the green. "Stop talking and do your job, you Grinch."

"Let me know about Thursday," Layne called over her shoulder, stepping into the kitchen.

"You want more whipped cream?" Lila asked, glancing at my hot cocoa. She smiled when I nodded and filled the cup until it was nearly a mountain. "Are you going to Layne's for Thanksgiving?"

"Probably not. It's her last Thanksgiving at home before she leaves, so I'll let her spend it with her family." I shrugged. "But I'm fine hanging around home—I never liked turkey much anyway."

"That's probably because you've never had it fried," she said, wiping the counter down. "I'm sure you and those Graham boys can figure something out. I imagine they'll be home too, since Wren's still in the hospital."

"Maybe," I whispered, my throat tight and achy. Two nights ago, I'd been in bed with Brooks when she'd called him and delivered the news she wouldn't be home for the holiday. She assured us she was fine—she was feeling a little worn down, and they were keeping her as a precaution. But the treatment was working, and she was due for her next set of scans soon. I was hesitant to believe her, but by the way she scolded me for not saying hello and keeping her updated on the baby, maybe she was fine. Since then, I'd made a promise to call her nightly.

"Hey, Shay. I've been meaning to say something," Lila said, her arms braced on the counter. "I'm really sorry about the timing of letting you go. Had I known you were pregnant, I would've tried to make it work."

I reached out and set my hand over hers. "Please don't apologize for that. You had no idea, and even if you had, you need to do what's best for your family."

She smirked, shaking her head. "You should've heard Layne tear into me—I was expecting her to light this place on fire."

I laughed and took a sip from my mug, not doubting it one bit. But never once had I felt bitter toward Lila and Seth for letting me go. "Really, it's fine. I like where I'm at now."

The door opened and I followed her gaze, my heart fluttering at the sight of Brooks. He smiled and pushed his sunglasses up his head, pinning every bit of his gaze on me. I would've walked to him in a trance had Lila not said, "I'll let you go—but why don't you stop by sometime next week? I have a bunch of baby items you can have."

"Really?" I cleared my throat, my voice all high and funny sounding. "You don't have to do that."

She lifted one shoulder in a half shrug. "You'd be doing me a favor. Some of it's used, but it's in good condition." She sighed and jabbed her thumb to the kitchen. "Last summer we had our grandson for a bit, and Seth went overboard on buying things for him. He's back home with his mom now, so it's just collecting dust."

"That would be amazing," I said in a rush, despite not knowing if I was having a boy. I'd saved up money and planned to buy baby items soon, but I wasn't about to be picky, and I seriously doubted a newborn baby would care about what they wore. "Thank you. I can pay—"

She put up a hand. "Please."

Lip wobbling, I stood and ran behind the counter, pulling her into a hug before she could squirm away. "Thank you."

She laughed under her breath, her arms stiff beside her. "You'll let us know if there's anything else you need? You have help here, Shay."

I pulled back and stole a glance at Brooks. He leaned against the doorframe, his eyes gleaming. "Well . . . there is one thing you could help me with." I looped her arm through mine and half dragged her into the kitchen just in case Brooks was being nosy.

Five minutes later, with what could either be a wonderful or a disastrous plan, I strolled out of the kitchen. Brooks held out his hand, and I accepted it immediately. "Everything okay?" he asked, leading me to where I'd parked Jake's truck across the street. I was slowly getting braver with driving it.

"Yup," I said, with a little extra pep in my step. "What are you doing here? I thought you'd be at work until tonight."

"I swung by the shop on my way through town—thought I'd stop by and see you on your lunch break. Levi said you were here."

"Ah." I spun on my heel and faced him, leaning against the door to the truck. "You missed me."

"Maybe." His voice was a low growl, skidding through my nerves. "Or maybe I wanted to let you know I hardly slept last night with all the whining Cash was doing."

I brought my hands to my chest. "Oh, my poor baby."

"You've spoiled him into a baby." He braced one arm by the side of my head. "He wasn't like this until you came around."

"Is that right?" I looked up at him through my lashes. "Well, maybe I oughta get lost then."

"Nope." He placed his other hand on my side, the edge of his palm on my stomach. "I'm sorry, but I can't bear to hear him cry for the rest of my life. So I think you're stuck here." I made a humming noise and smiled at him, cherishing the way he was looking at me, touching me. It reminded me of the way I'd seen Jake watch Wren, like I was his entire world. "I like your hair." The corner of his mouth lifted as he ran a pink strand through his fingers. "Pink just might be my new favorite color."

"It's a good color," I offered, struggling to keep my face straight. "Especially when you're wearing a face mask. The pink really made your eyes pop, don't you think?"

His eyes flared, likely regretting that I'd talked him into joining my spa night the other evening—as if he didn't love the scalp massage I gave him. He smirked like he was planning something, but all he asked was, "Can I take you on a drive?"

I lifted my brows. "Don't you need to get back to work?"

"I took the rest of the day off. I'll go in earlier tomorrow to make up for it." He shrugged, the corner of his mouth tilting up. "I missed you."

I rolled my bottom lip between my teeth, hiding how hearing those words from him affected me. They had little to no effect on the "no nonsense and absolutely no hot men" part of my brain. Alas, the "let's go make out with Brooks in the woods" side won out. "Okay, I'll go—but if Levi and Nolan fire me for ditchin' and kick me out of the house, you'll only have yourself to blame for sleeping alone with a heartbroken Cash."

The corner of his eyes crinkled. "I already let them know you'd be out the rest of the day. C'mon, we'll take my truck." He pushed off the door to Jake's truck and grabbed my hand, not giving me a chance to change my mind.

"Oh. I talked to Wren last night, and I was thinking about going up to Phoenix to visit her. Plus, I've saved up some money, so I thought I'd get Tater some things." I bit my lip, my stomach squirming with nerves and maybe a little bit of baby too. "Would you want to come with me?"

Without hesitation, his hand squeezing mine, he said, "Only if you let me get Tater something too."

"Deal." He opened the passenger door for me, and I stopped with one foot up, remembering what I'd meant to ask him before I got sidetracked. "And while you're in such a generous mood, I have a huge favor I need from you. But you can't ask me what it is."

He raised a brow, a smirk teasing his lips. "And what do I get in return?"

I scrunched my nose at him. "Nothing. Some grumpy man told me to stop feeling like I owe everyone something."

Chapter Forty-Two

Was this my end? This was my end. *What else could it mean when the man whom I may or may not love takes me on a forty-minute drive into the forest?* We were so deep, I'd lost sight of the sky until he parked at the edge of a cliff, offering us the perfect view. The lush and full valley, the tops of the pines, the sun's rays shimmering on the lake. The mountain range was endless. It felt like a hidden secret, a space where I could see everything, yet nothing could see me.

Ah, the perfect spot to be murdered.

I feigned a smile at Brooks when he hopped back in the truck, the tip of his nose and ears as bright as a cherry from when he'd gotten out to pee. He must've smelled my fear or seen the nerves in my smile, because he reached over with a chilly hand, his fingers skimming mine. "Say the word and we'll go home. I just thought it might be nice for us to get away for a bit."

"Thank you," I said and meant it. Not only because I fully believed Brooks would drive us home without question, but that he truly seemed to like having me around. *He wants to get away with me.* "Where are we?"

He stared at his hands on his lap. "I used to come up here with my dad. And I know you're probably wishing I'd stop talking about him—"

"Never," I said in a rush, not wanting him to spiral down that thought a moment longer. "I will never think that. I love when you share him with me."

He tilted his head and watched me, his eyes beaming like he might believe me. "I wanted to bring you here the other night after we'd spread my dad's ashes. But I wasn't sure how keen you'd feel about me dragging you out of bed in the middle of the night. Something you said—about words being heavy—it reminded me of this place." He shifted in his seat to face me, his large legs twisted beneath the dash. "I think I know that feeling you're talking about. My dad must've too. I don't know if he could sense it, or if he knew me that well, but when I was struggling, he'd load me up and we'd come out here for a bit. Sometimes we'd talk, and other times we'd sit here, maybe play a card game. It didn't really matter what we did, because no matter what, every time we left, I felt better." He huffed a small laugh. "He said there was nothing a dose of pine couldn't fix."

Before I might've replied, voiced how much I loved that, Brooks reached over and opened the center console separating us. He pulled out a notebook and set it on my lap. "It's nothing much," he murmured before he twisted away in his seat and looked out the window. I stared at what I realized was a journal, the cover simple and green—almost matching the color of trees at dusk. "I don't know anything about writing, or if you have much of an interest in doing it anymore. But I thought it might be nice for you to have when your thoughts are loud, or words seem too heavy to say aloud. And if you need something more than that—someone to talk to, or even bring you up here for a nice dose of pine—I can do that too."

With teary eyes, I looked up at him, my voice lost in awe. *I think I'm in love with you*, I admitted in the safety of my thoughts, not yet brave enough to confirm it aloud. But as I watched him, and him me, words weren't necessary. Somewhere in his evergreen eyes, I thought he said it back. *I think I'm in love with you, too.*

"Thank you," I rasped, my voice wet, no more than a frail whisper. "I might love this more than those peanut butter cups you buy me."

He let out an abrupt laugh, red creeping up past the edge of his collar. "Was it Levi or Nolan who snitched on me?" I shook my head, stifling my own laugh. "Those weasels had me pay them fifty bucks each to keep it secret."

"I like knowing you were thinking about me," I murmured with a shrug.

"I'm always thinking about you."

I smiled, the feeling radiating to my core. The fear I wore was loosening, and I could see the path set before us, the fork in the road. One where we'd need to decide which path we took. Together or separate. I knew we had time—we didn't need to make that decision right now.

But I could take another step. Trust that Brooks would stay with me.

"Declan wanted kids." I wasn't sharing this because I felt pressured; I knew Brooks would never push me to share when I wasn't ready. All he'd done was give me a space of safety, where it was peaceful and hidden. Somewhere I might find strength. "I was sort of indifferent to it. I'd always taken care of myself, so I wasn't really interested in the idea. But Declan wanted a big family, and I loved the home he envisioned for us. It was so different from anything I'd had. He talked about moving us to a smaller town, maybe the suburbs. One of those picture-perfect homes with the white fence."

I'd imagined it too. I would stay home with the kids. We'd do crafts, bake special treats for their daddy. I'd write while the kiddos napped, maybe plant in the garden. I'd nourish a home full of laughter and love.

A home that was safe.

But I quickly learned that the home he'd drawn up for me was nothing more than a picture. A two-dimensional dream. It didn't show what dwelled behind those doors, the flaws on the inside. And had it, that white picket fence would've been cracked and rotten, overgrown with weeds.

"We hadn't been happy for a while, but when I found out I was pregnant, I thought maybe this was what we'd needed all along. Maybe if *he* was happy, *I* would be happy." I could still feel the way my hands shook, the eager smile I wore as I handed him a white box, one I'd wrapped earlier that day. Stuffed inside was my positive test, along with a white onesie: *Surprise, you're a daddy!* I could barely contain myself, I was so giddy—until Declan told me to stop hopping around and sit down.

I was on the edge of my seat, my glee overflowing as he opened the box. He had no clue our world was about to turn upside down—for the better. But then he opened it, and time froze. And rather than my world turning upside down, it was torn completely apart.

"He didn't take it well." I clutched the journal in my lap, not letting myself get lost in those memories. They didn't deserve my attention. "He called me a whore, accused me of cheating on him. But he knew I hadn't. So then he gave me an ultimatum: either I end the pregnancy, or I get out and leave with nothing. I didn't know if he was bluffing or not, but I refused—and that surprised him. Declan had a temper, but I'd never seen him this angry. Like I'd just intentionally ruined his entire life. He'd never been physical before, but I thought for sure he was going to hit me. But all he did was throw the box at me and storm out of the house."

Brooks stretched his arm out across the back of the seat, and I closed my eyes at the gentle, soothing pressure of his fingers on my neck. "Is that when you left?"

"No," I admitted, shame, such shame and regret filling me. "I stayed. I didn't think he'd actually follow through on his threat. He just needed some time to calm down." Despite my fear, the agony I was unbinding, I willed my voice to be strong. I'd already survived the worst of it. *I can breathe.* "It was after midnight when he came home. I hadn't heard him at first . . . I was crying, and I think with that, plus the hormones, I'd made myself sick. Declan must've slipped in sometime during that, because all of a sudden he was at my side. He reeked of alcohol, and I threw up again, but then his hands were in my hair, pulling it out of my face." My fingers trembled over my lips. I'd been so relieved, so happy that he'd come *home.*

"I told him I was sorry . . . and he slapped me." My voice was hollow, as empty and worthless as I'd felt after that. When I'd experienced the smart of his hand against my cheek, felt the burn in my scalp as he fisted my hair. "I just kind of sat there. I was so shocked. And then he yanked my head and threw me back against the tile."

His grip on my hair had been painful, wrenching my head so I was forced to meet his rageful gaze. I was gasping for air, from both the shock of being thrown back and his hand at my throat. I remembered thinking, in the midst of that panic, how strange it was that he looked like *my Declan*. I'd thought he'd be different, something off about him. But he was every bit of the man I'd fallen in love with, whom I'd given myself to over and over again. I'd been just blind before.

And then I wasn't.

"It was all so fast . . . one moment he was on me, and I was choking, and the next he was off. I think it kind of scared him, like maybe he hadn't meant to go that far. Whatever it was, he helped me to my feet and into the shower. I left the next morning."

I didn't know how long I stayed in the shower, afraid Declan would join me. Sex had always been his way of *apologizing*. But the thought of his body in mine—in the body where I carried his child—made me physically recoil. But what would he do if I denied him? Would he hit me again?

Thankfully, I never had to find out.

Declan had never been a huge drinker, and he must've been drunk enough he passed out somewhere in the bedroom. But even when the water grew cold, I couldn't find the will to move. I was numb. I'd always excused his behavior, justified his sharp tongue because he'd never gotten physical. But when he hit me, I realized it didn't matter. He'd made me feel worthless before he'd ever laid a hand on me.

Fear, anger, and adrenaline pumped through me. And there was a piece of me that knew if I was there when Declan woke up, I'd forgive him. He'd convince me to stay—again. After years of manipulation, there was no way I could unravel his control in one night.

But he wasn't awake, and my thoughts were my own.

When the rising sun peeked through the bathroom window, I rose with more resolve than I'd had in years. Wrapped in a towel and shivering, I called my mom. But she turned me away. No one was coming for me. I didn't have a family to rescue me.

But I did have a family, I realized. One I needed to rescue.

There was a tiny bead of life inside me. Counting on me. I'd never felt protected, never really tried to protect myself—but I'd protect this baby. Make the family I'd never had. I'd build our white picket fence.

I walked down the street in only a robe and called Elle. She came immediately, and after losing her mind that I hadn't called her before then, she saved me. She was on maternity leave with her third baby, so she didn't have to worry about run-ins with Declan at the firm. Not that he sought me out anyway. Those first few days, I was afraid he'd come to Elle's. He knew I didn't have many options to run to. But he never showed.

Because he didn't care.

I stayed with her for a few weeks. Got myself back on my feet. I helped Elle with her kids, and she helped me. She stood by me, and it was because of her I didn't drown. It was there that I experienced the true, unconditional love that only comes from a mother.

And I wanted to be that, too.

Once I'd saved enough money—Elle insisted on paying me as a nanny—I bought Betsy, and I moved. I left everything behind in hope there was more awaiting me.

I blew out a refreshing, relieving breath. Those moments had weighed on me for too long. I didn't want to carry them any longer. Declan didn't deserve my energy. But in spite of my acceptance, I was eerily aware of how silent Brooks was.

I rolled my lips together and picked at the edge of my sleeve. "I'm sorry for dumping that on you. I know you're probably thinking I should've left him before it ever got to that point. I've thought about it too. I know there's plenty of things I could've done to prevent it—"

"No." Brooks's voice was hard and low, and I could see the anger in his eyes. But I didn't flinch when he flipped up the center console and pulled me onto the middle seat. Nor was I afraid when his hand cupped the back of my neck. I was silent, still, as his fingers glided through my hair, and I wondered if he was piecing it together. If he knew why I'd cut it, if he suspected it had been a way for me to remove the grief and pain I'd experienced before him. "He had no right." His eyes softened, shifting to nothing but love and concern. One hand moved to my jaw, and the other cradled my stomach, as though comforting both Tater and me. "I don't care if he was drunk—he had no right to lay a hand on you. Even if you'd run him over, or set his house on fire, he still would've had no right. He's responsible for his own choices. He chose to get drunk and come home when he shouldn't have. He chose to suffocate you, drain you for years. We both know the only reason you stayed for so long is because he made you think you were weak and needed him. He saw what a light you are, and he takes what he thinks he's entitled to. And no matter what, even after I'm dead, I will wholeheartedly believe there was nothing you could've done to stop him."

I knew he was right. Elle had said the same. But while I believed there was nothing I could've done, guilt lingered within me. All the things I'd missed, what I wished I'd done differently. But maybe with time, someday I'd stop blaming myself.

"Sunshine," Brooks said, the tension in his shoulders easing. He twisted further in his seat to better face me and wrapped me in his hold. "I'm sorry if I reacted poorly. I don't like feeling helpless, and I know nothing I can say or do can fix it. I don't know what to do—"

"Just don't see me differently." I closed my eyes as his lips brushed my neck. "I didn't tell you for pity, Brooks. I thought you deserved to know . . . so you know what you're maybe getting yourself into."

"Pity you?" Brooks eased back, his brows pressed together. "I don't pity you. I'm in awe of you. But I felt that way before now." His fingers slid over my temple, brushing my hair behind my ear. "I didn't need the full story to know he'd hurt you. You'd hinted at it already, and I suspected enough. But I've never thought less of you because of it. You're the bravest person I know, Shay. I'm proud of you."

I choked on a laugh, the sound mixed with a sob. "I'm the furthest thing from *brave*."

He pressed his lips together, and when I looked away, he brought two fingers to my chin, not letting me run from his gaze. "How are you not brave? How is not surviving what you did—"

"Because that's all I did. All I did was survive." My voice was hoarse, rough. Blood pounded in my ears as my thoughts ran rampant. I was drowning. The pressure in my chest was swelling, increasing each moment. I waited for Brooks to speak, to pull me out of this—but his mouth stayed closed. But when I stared at his hands, unwavering in mine, I realized he wasn't silent.

He was here. He wouldn't leave me to drown.

"Declan used to call me his butterfly." Bitterness coated my tongue. Funny how such an innocent, harmless word could be ruined. "When I met him, he made some comment about how he'd clip my wings so I'd never leave him. And sometimes I think he did. I feel like he took everything worthwhile about me and broke it. But there are moments where I feel okay and I'm happy." I ran my fingers up Brooks's forearms. "This town, your brothers, Wren . . . and you have made me incredibly happy. Sometimes so much that I think I'm healed. But then the pain swells, and I remember what I've lost. I feel like a butterfly with no wings, barely surviving."

My breaths were easy and slow, and I wiped at a tear on my cheek, something that felt like peace stirring in me. It felt good. I thought I'd be full of regret, but there was something relieving about being vulnerable. It was exhausting—but in the best sort of way. Like by allowing myself to feel, to process these emotions, I was giving myself a chance to breathe.

"You remember how you told me your favorite color? The pines at dusk? And I told you I'd never noticed because I was busy looking at the sun?" If the journal in my lap wasn't enough proof of how well he listened, then that alone was. "You see the world differently than me, Shay. You see beauty in the shadows, and I find it in the sun. I see it in you." I shuddered, my heart frantically pounding, as though undecided if it was about to overflow with love, or shatter into pieces. "You're *my* sun, Shay. But I don't want to possess you, keep you for myself. I'm on my knees in awe of you, at your mercy. I will never overpower you. I want to watch you rise and experience your warmth and light—because, Shay, whether you believe me or not, you are a *light*." His hands cradled my jaw, gentle but firm—not to hurt, but for me to feel his surety, his strength. "It's okay to not feel okay. Even the sun needs rest."

I rested my forehead against his and wrapped myself in his reassurance. His faith in me. Months ago, I would've searched his words. Looked for how he might hurt me, use my weakness against me later. But this wasn't that. This was Brooks building me up, offering me strength, as I'd done for him. This was friendship and loyalty. And dared I say it . . . *This is love.*

I thought of when we'd hiked to the controlled burn zone and I learned how new life could grow from ashes. That was what I wanted. I'd shared my lowest moments, and now I wanted us to nourish something good and whole. So that one day, when my grief flared up, it would be overwhelmed with life, with him.

I brushed my lips over his in a featherlight kiss. Once. Twice. His lips were smooth and slow, savoring this moment. But on the third kiss, when I wrapped my arms around his neck, his restraint dissolved. His hands slid up my jaw, fingers tangling in my hair, and there was no stopping now.

How we'd gone so long without touching was beyond me. He kissed desperately, like a man who hadn't drunk water in days and his thirst had driven him to the edge of madness. I let him drink from me willingly, let him drive me to that place of insanity, too. His hands roamed me, his fingers walking a line of blissful roughness, and if not for the building heat consuming me, I might've sobbed with relief that while Brooks respected and cherished me, he didn't see me as delicate or broken.

Returning the thought, I bit down on his lower lip. He groaned in my mouth and kissed me with a delicious force I'd never experienced. One hand cupped the back of my head as he hooked the other under my butt and lifted me up, pulling me onto his lap.

My leg kicked the steering wheel, and I opened my eyes when something skidded along the window. I twisted backward to try and turn off the windshield wiper. "Sorry," I muttered, as the blades flapped faster and water shot out, raining down on the front window. I leaned back, accidentally honking the horn, and the heat of his laugh tickled my neck. It beeped again, and I was on the verge of losing it when I hit the hazard button, still struggling to turn off the cursed wipers.

"I got it." His voice was smug as he leaned against me and switched off the wipers and hazards.

I glanced down at our position, seeing how tight a fit it was, my back resting against the steering wheel, my bump pressed against his flat stomach. Cheeks flushed and the heat of the moment gone, I said, "I'm beginning to think making out in trucks doesn't work for us."

He smirked, his hair mussed from where I'd dragged my hands through it, and with a shrug, he said, "I was having a good time. But if you're thinking it could be better, I'm willing to kiss you everywhere. You know, just to be sure."

I smiled at him, and he smiled back, and the warmth that washed over me was more powerful than even his all-consuming kiss. I couldn't help but think how nice it would be for him to smile at me for the rest of my life.

Chapter Forty-Three

Screw fried turkey.

And curse the buttery fingers of a six-month pregnant woman who believed it was a *fantastic* idea to prepare a Thanksgiving feast. Fine—I hadn't prepared it. I'd paid Lila and Seth to do it, but I set the table. And tripped on thin air, watching in horror as the crisp turkey splattered into a mess on the floor.

I gagged, something about the slimy coating making me sick as I picked up the last of the turkey and tossed it in the trash. Back aching like I was eighty-seven and not twenty-four, I knelt and wiped the floor clean. I groaned as the oven beeped and hustled to my feet. I'd forgotten about my banana bread in my haste to ensure Cash didn't eat any turkey.

I pulled it out, sighing in satisfaction at the crisp, perfect bread, and set it on a rack to cool at the table. Lila and Seth had been kind enough to cook the whole meal, but I wanted to contribute. I'd thought about trying a recipe from a cookbook, but Brooks loved my banana bread, so I'd stuck with the original one I'd made up. It seemed like a good way to thank him for occupying his brothers this morning and afternoon, without even asking for an explanation.

I beamed down at the table like a true modern housewife—minus the wife. With the turkey in smithereens, it left only mashed potatoes, gravy, corn, stuffing, green beans, and rolls—but I doubted they'd mind. I opened the fridge to heat up some leftover hamburgers Brooks had made earlier this week, but stopped as I heard the running of an engine outside. My time was up.

I ran my fingers through my hair, the loose curls falling just above my shoulders. I smiled as I caught a glimpse of pink strands, happy I'd done it after all. I was afraid I had no business having pink hair as a mom, but to hell with it. I'd be a good mom with or without pink hair. I smoothed my hands down my white babydoll shirt and made sure my belly wasn't peeking out. I'd officially *popped*, as Layne called it—I looked like I'd sliced a basketball in half and glued it to my skin.

I bounced on my toes, squealing with excitement as the front door opened. A rush of familiar voices drifted in, singing to my soul as they mixed with Cash's whines for attention. I smiled and held my arms out when all three Graham brothers filled the entryway. "Surprise! Happy Thanksgiving!"

Nolan and Levi muttered something to one another, their faces wary. But I hardly paid them any attention, too enthralled in Brooks, feeling the heat of him even across the room. Other than our make-out sesh, we hadn't acted on our desire again. After that afternoon together, we'd come home and sprawled out on the couch, where I'd watched *Friday the 13th* in exchange for a foot massage. But as Brooks looked me over and chills formed beneath his gaze, I knew it wouldn't be long until we crossed that line again.

I blinked, blaming hormones and an unsatisfied, heightened libido for distracting me enough I'd missed what Nolan had said. "Sorry." I cleared my throat. "What did you say?"

Nolan's cheeks reddened as he strangled down a laugh, not looking at me, but Brooks. "You have to tell her. I'm not—" He paused and covered his mouth with his hand, composing himself when he faced me. "I'm sorry, darlin'. You know I love you. But—"

"Nolan." Levi jabbed his elbow into his ribs. "Don't be an asshole."

Eyes burning, I fought my mind from slipping to the worst. "Tell me what?"

Nolan dipped his head toward Levi and lowered his voice, but not enough that I missed it. "You want to get sick again? I'm telling you, I will actually die—"

"Stop," Brooks murmured and grinned at me, his hand gripping the back of Nolan's neck. "I can't believe you did this, sunshine—"

"Save it." I narrowed my eyes, not trusting one bit of the trio of fidgeting brothers before me. "What's going on? Did I do something wrong?"

"No!" Brooks and Levi said at the same time Nolan shouted, "Yes!"

Nolan slipped out of their hold, weaving and dodging them when they reached for him. "No! Shay's my friend, and dammit, she deserves the truth."

My stomach knotted and tears welled in my eyes. Even though I knew it couldn't be true, I feared my days in this house were numbered. "What's the truth?"

Nolan paused at how my voice broke. But then he shook his head, his jaw set with determination. "Screw it." He stepped forward and took my hands in his. "Darlin', I'm sorry. I'm so sorry—but I can't eat this."

"What?" I choked out.

He gave me a tight smile, his tanned fingers squeezing mine. "You know I think you're amazing, darlin'. You're so brave and smart, not to mention sexier than hell. But you can't cook."

I blinked. "I can't . . . cook?"

Levi face-palmed his forehead, and Brooks gripped his hands into fists, looking liable to Hulk smash at any given moment. Oblivious, Nolan continued on in a soothing voice, "No. I'm sorry. But you're awful. Terrible. And as much as I love and appreciate you going out of your way to cook us this meal—I can't eat it. Levi was sicker than a dog the last time he ate your bread."

An abrupt sob bubbled out of my chest, the sound crossed with a laugh. "But—" I pointed a shaking finger at the table. "I didn't cook this, you asshole."

A deep howl of laughter burst past Levi's lips, and Brooks leaned against the wall, hiding his face in the crook of his arm. Nolan blinked, his blond hair falling across his forehead as he cocked his head. "What do you mean you didn't cook it?"

"I paid Lila and Seth . . ." I narrowed my eyes, realizing something. I tilted my head in a way that was purely predatory and had all three men stepping back, likely believing the six-month pregnant lady living in their house was about to be their end. "What do you mean my bread made Levi sick?"

"Uh—" Nolan glanced back with wide eyes at his brothers for help. In an exchange of silent words that only siblings could share, all three surged for the table as I did.

"Give it to me now," I hissed at Brooks, who'd snatched the bread and held it above his head. "Give me my bread."

His chest shook with laughter, tears sliding down his cheeks. "No, it's mine. I love it and want it all."

"See, there you go with that nonsense again." Nolan pulled out a chair and leaned back, watching the chaos he'd created. "You're the one who kept having her bake you loaves because you're so damn in love with her—and Levi and I had to suffer the brunt of it. I mean, you get the girl. What do we get?"

"You get bread!" Brooks said, holding the bread impossibly out of my reach, ignoring how I relentlessly twisted his nipples. "That's what you get!"

"Give it to me," I whined, Levi and Nolan bickering behind us, the former calling the latter a giant dingbat. "Brooks, if you don't give that to me right now, I will never let you use my cotton candy face mask again."

"Cotton candy face mask?" Nolan asked, both him and Levi wearing wide, devious grins. "I gotta say, of all the things I figured you two were doing upstairs, I didn't imagine it was Shay slathering girly shit all over your face—"

"Shut it," Brooks hissed, his palm pressed to my forehead, playfully holding me back. "When you guys look like hell at fifty and have beer guts, I'll be glowing and freaking delicious."

I rolled my eyes, and before I thought better of it, I cried, "Ow!" I stopped fighting Brooks and clutched my side. "Oh my gosh—"

All laughter and taunting ceased as the three of them came to my aid. Brooks knelt with wide eyes, one hand still holding the bread. "Sunshine, talk to me. What's going on?"

I stomped on his boot and snatched the loaf out of his hand with more stealth than I believed I possessed. Cash was fast on my heels as I darted to the living room, barking in encouragement. Before anyone could get their hands on me, and having lost my mind, I bit a chunk out of the loaf.

"Shay!" Brooks rubbed his jaw, his voice exasperated. "That wasn't funny. Don't scare us like that."

I might've felt guilty for what I'd done had I not been on the verge of vomiting. Without thinking, I gagged and spat out the bread, wiping at my tongue. "What the heck is this?" I held the loaf out like baby Simba—that is, if Simba had been rotted from the inside out. "This tastes like actual garbage."

Nolan and Levi were bent over, shaking with silent laughter. Brooks watched me, his lips twitching with a grin as he fought to hold it together. I pointed an accusing finger at him. "You lied to me."

He lifted his hands in defense. "I did no such thing."

I clutched the bread, nails digging in. "Was the popcorn I made bad too?"

Brooks shook his head, but Nolan groaned. "Yes! I'm sorry, I know it was a day old when I tried it, but c'mon—how do you mess up popcorn? You disintegrated it!"

I flipped Nolan off, keeping my gaze hot on Brooks. My voice was lethally calm. "And the eggs?"

"Delicious." Brooks stepped back as I inched closer, making my way back to the kitchen table.

I rolled my eyes, but inside I was on fire. Not with anger or embarrassment. But love—so much love. But that didn't stop me from tearing off a piece of bread and tossing it at him. It bounced off his head and he blinked, staring at where it had landed on the floor. "Did you just throw bread at me?"

"Maybe I did." I raised my brow and threw another chunk at his chest. "Maybe I didn't."

"Alright." Nolan cleared his throat and sat at the table, making himself a plate. "While you two act like lovesick children—and since we've now deemed this food safe—I'm gonna dig in."

I glared at him, and I must've blacked out in a feverish rage, because next thing I knew, potatoes were sliding down Nolan's jaw, the remnants of said freshly tossed potatoes coating my fingers.

"Oh, darlin'. Now you're in for it," he warned and flung a roll, nailing me in the forehead.

I ran to the kitchen as Nolan stood on the table, clutching the potato bowl like his life depended on it and firing globs across the room. Brooks reached for me and I screamed, smashing the remaining banana bread against his chest. He scooped me up in his arms, ignoring my pleas as he hauled me back to the table. Levi, being the noble man he was, defended my honor and pelted Brooks with gobs of stuffing. I squirmed with laughter, on the verge of peeing when Nolan slipped and fell off the table, the gravy pot falling with him. After that, I lost track of who was on whose side. Who smeared potatoes across my cheeks, who shoved green beans up Levi's nose, and who Cash tackled first.

Next thing I knew, we were all on the floor, the kitchen as covered in food as we were. Levi flung corn out of his hair, his shirt drenched with gravy, as he walked in from putting Cash out back, not wanting him to eat something he shouldn't. "Next time, Nolan, keep your mouth shut and eat the bread."

I laughed with them, my smile genuine and full. But as I did, my chest ached and my vision blurred. I hadn't realized I was crying until they fell silent, all three warily watching me. "Sunshine." Brooks was on his hands and knees, crawling over to me. "We're so sorry—"

"I can't cook. And if I can't cook, how am I going to feed this baby?" I whispered, my voice breaking before it rose. "And it's not like I can drive Tater anywhere to get food, because I traded my car away, and Jake's truck can't fit a car seat, and the baby will just roll around inside. Oh my gosh—I need to get a car seat. Or do I not need one if I don't have a car?" I rambled, running my fingers through my filthy and knotted hair. I froze, frowning at the strands of pink. "I have pink hair—"

"I love your hair," Nolan piped in. His grin was cocky, like he believed he was about to fix everything. "And don't you worry. I bet little Tater will love your boobie milk."

"And I'm gonna be stuck living with you," I cried, pointing my finger at him, his eyes wide and horrified. "And then the baby won't want to hang out with me because you guys are way cooler and cook better—"

"Shay." Brooks crouched down in front of me, his fingers pushing my hair out of my face. "It's alright."

"It's not *alright*," I snapped, my chest shaking, spiraling more and more with each breath. "I don't know what I'm doing. I don't know how to be a mom. I can barely drive myself to my own appointments. How am I supposed to have a baby?"

"We're going to figure it out."

"How?" I rubbed my eyes, wincing after smearing who knew what into them. "I can't live upstairs forever. I can't keep mooching off you guys—"

"Don't let yourself think like that," he whispered and peeled my hands off my face with gentle fingers. "We benefit from having you in our lives more than you'll ever understand."

"I don't even have a bed for Tater." My voice was raw and scratchy, guilt seeping out with each breath. "I've been so focused on me, on fixing me. And now I have absolutely nothing to give this baby."

"Shhh," Brooks soothed. His voice was slow, cautious, sensing my mind was elsewhere. "I'm going to pick you up, okay?"

He slipped his arms under me, one in the crook of my knee, the other around my back, and lifted me up against his chest. "I'm sorry for ruining Thanksgiving," I murmured, realizing the kitchen was empty and Levi and Nolan had stepped out.

"You didn't ruin anything, sunshine." He pressed a warm, thoughtful kiss to my forehead, and I wished his confidence could somehow seep into my mind.

Rather than carrying me up the stairs, he turned down the hall and pushed open his bedroom door, leading me to the bathroom inside. He shifted me in his hold, setting me on the counter. "Let's get you cleaned up, okay?" he offered, waiting until I nodded before he turned on the shower. His hands were wet and dripping on my thighs. "Did you want to get in with your clothes—"

He stopped short when I lifted my arms and peeled off my shirt. Any other time, I might've been embarrassed for Brooks to see me this way. My bra was a size too small, and bright, angry stretch marks traveled over my breasts, matching the ones on my stomach. But I didn't care.

And I sensed he didn't either when he hooked his hands on my waist and lowered me to the floor. I stared at his slowly rising chest and kicked off my leggings, not thinking anything of it when I unsnapped my bra. My mind was numb and so blind with panic that I didn't hesitate to slip off my underwear—entirely bare in front of him.

His throat bobbed, but he only offered me his hand, his fingers trembling. He checked the water before he pushed back the curtain and helped me into the tub. My mind was elsewhere, but my heart wasn't. I gripped his fingers, stopping him when he made to leave and give me privacy. I didn't speak, but my face must've said enough, because he nodded and shucked off his clothes before he stepped into the shower with me.

"Let me hold you." He held his arms out as though we'd seen one another naked countless times. But because we hadn't, I made a point not to trail lower than his chest, aware his eyes hadn't once left mine. He folded me against him, and I leaned on him, the feeling so natural and right, and accepted the strength he was offering me. "Let it out," he breathed, running his hand through my hair and down my back. "I promise you can rest—I've got you, sunshine. You can trust me. I won't let either of you go."

I did trust him.

So I cried. Not silent, fleeting tears. But ugly, soul-writhing sobs. Raw, all-consuming fear had at last surfaced and threatened to destroy me. Paralyzing thoughts whispering I would fail, sneering that I was selfish and this baby was better off without me. With each ragged breath, I only uncovered more anguish and heartbreak. I'd been on the verge of drowning for months, kicking and thrashing to keep my head above the surface. And now, with my soul weary and the fight in me nearly gone, I was sure I would drown.

But I didn't.

Because Brooks held me through it all.

Chapter Forty-Four

I ran a hand through Cash's coat, stroking his back where he lay beside me. He hadn't left my side since Brooks and I stepped out of the shower. I didn't know how long he held me, how long he stood silent as he washed my hair. A service that brought forth further tears. All I knew was when I was on the cusp of shivering and had fallen quiet, my throat raw, he lifted me out. He wrapped me in a towel and carried me inside his room. With his back to me, I slipped on my bra and underwear, then accepted the faded flannel he handed me from his closet. He smirked at how it engulfed me, and with careful, purposeful fingers, he buttoned it up. After he tucked me in bed, he reached into his closet for some clothes, and with the towel still wrapped around his waist, told me he'd be back.

There'd been a long-festering wound inside me, and I'd done my best to ignore it. Foolishly believing that if I didn't acknowledge it, its power would cease. But all I'd done was run and hide.

I'm having a baby.

Alone.

I'd known this. I'd accepted this reality the day I left Declan. But until now, I hadn't let myself delve down the entirety of what that was. I might've made improvements, grown in some way, but it felt selfish now. I'd wasted time on me, and now with my allotted time nearly spent, I had nothing figured out. I was going to bring an innocent baby into a world I was struggling to build.

I needed to make arrangements with Declan. I didn't believe he wanted to be involved whatsoever. But were there legal obligations I needed to take? Would the baby share my last name or his? Did Declan, or at least his family, deserve a chance to be in this baby's life? Had I been wrong to leave California? Could a judge force me to move back?

There was so much to do, to face. And I just wanted to hide from it all.

Cash stirred at the slight tap on the door as Nolan said, "Darlin'?" The door creaked open, and there stood the Grahams. Did they regret the disaster they'd invited into their house? "Is it alright if we come in?"

I nodded, and with how tight Cash had wedged himself up to me, I stayed on my side. Nolan huffed a smile and sat beside my pillow, with Levi at the foot of the bed. Brooks leaned against the doorframe, his face at ease, but there was something there I couldn't read.

I sucked in a breath and readied myself for what was to come.

"I'm sorry," I started. "I know this is way more than you bargained for, and I promise I'll be out of your hair—"

"When are you going to stop doubting how much we love you?" Nolan murmured, running a finger over a pink strand in my hair. "I should be the one apologizing. You did a really sweet thing for us, and I was a smart-ass. I'm sorry."

"You were just afraid you'd catch food poisoning like Levi did," I teased, hoping it would ease the pressure growing in my chest.

"Nah. He's just got a weak stomach." His blue eyes gleamed, and he smiled mildly, sincerely. "I'm sorry, Shay. I shouldn't have even teased you about that—"

"I'm not mad at you." I grasped his hand, needing him to understand. Nolan didn't know how Declan had belittled me. Nolan would never do it maliciously, never as a way to remind me I was replaceable. Though, I'd be lying if I said it didn't sting a little to know I actually sucked at cooking and could no longer chalk it up to Declan being miserable to please. "You didn't hurt my feelings. I love when you mess around with me, so please don't stop." I loved when Nolan and Levi—even Brooks—would make teasing jabs at me. It made me feel like I was one of them. "It just sort of reminded me I have no idea what I'm doing."

"That's not true." Levi sat at the foot of the bed, his elbows resting on his thighs. "Clearly we don't know everything about your life before us—we only know what led you here. But you don't give yourself enough credit. You gave up everything and started over on your own. And you're doing it, Shay. Regardless if you believe you're failing or not, you're still doing it." He squeezed my foot through the blanket. "And don't forget one of your biggest successes—you moved to the middle of nowhere and managed to tame the biggest ass of us all." He smirked and jabbed his thumb at Brooks. "None of us know what we're doing, you know that. You've watched Nolan and I stumble around at the shop. And I know you think you have to do this alone, but you don't. We want to help you—"

"No." I sat up, stirring Cash awake. "You guys are good people, some of the very best. So it makes sense why you want to help me, why you've always wanted to help me. But this is different—I'm having a baby. And I refuse to come in and blow up your world."

"Shay." Brooks's voice was warm and soothing, sneaking into my heart even from where he stood in the doorway. "You changed everything about our lives, my life, the moment you became our neighbor."

"It's true. I mean, how could we not love you? You looked so damn cute pedaling your Barbie bike around town. I just knew you had to be ours," Nolan chimed in, nudging my shoulder with his palm. "I don't know how you pictured our lives before you, but it's not as pretty as you're thinking. You remember how annoying Brooks was when we first met you, with his controlling, protective bullshit? Well, imagine that twenty-four seven—except on 'roids."

I choked on a snotty laugh, wiping at my nose. "He was just looking out for you."

"Ah, that's just because he's got you under his spell, exactly where he wants ya." Nolan winked at Brooks, earning an eye roll in return. "But the point is—we were lost before you, Shay. You don't know how much light you've brought into a home that, I can promise you, was very gray before you showed up carrying that forsaken banana bread."

I shook my head, giving him a frail smile. "It's a wonder that you're single when you talk like that."

"Perfect as I may appear, we both know I've got my own issues. We all do." He moved to his feet and soothed a loose strand of hair behind my ear. "But we're all working on it, and like Levi said, you don't have to do it alone. Now—" he started, clearing his throat. "I need you to do me a solid and just sit here and truly think this over. We don't want to hear your excuses yet."

I furrowed my brows, my eyes wary and tired. "Okay . . . ?"

With a crooked smile, Nolan nodded at Levi, who reached under his sweatshirt and pulled out the sketch pad he'd apparently stuffed inside. "There's something in there for you."

I bit my lip and leaned over Cash to grab the notebook, the same one he'd shown me on Halloween. My confusion only grew after I flipped one page and looked up, not understanding why each of them was grinning. "What is this?"

"It's your home." Brooks's voice broke as his smile did. He cleared his throat, composing himself. "It's yours if you want it."

The burning in my heart was fierce as I looked between them and the sketch—a blueprint of a home. But not just any home. "Is this Jake's cabin?"

"Not anymore." Brooks's voice was low, like he feared it would fail him. "We bought it from him."

"You bought it," Nolan corrected, his eyes kind, full of admiration as he bumped his shoulder with Brooks. "If it was for any other girl, I would've thought you were crazy for wanting to buy her a home so soon after finding out she was pregnant."

"You bought the cabin?" I asked, my words coated with disbelief as I unraveled what they'd done. "You bought the cabin . . . for me? But—" Heart racing, I ran my fingers through my hair. "Jake told me it was infested with termites."

Each of them quietly laughed. Levi shook his head and scooted further up on the bed until he sat beside me. "We just asked him to say that. We figured it was a smart move since you almost bit my head off for trying to give you a bike light."

"I thought for sure we'd have to tell you when it looked like you might smash Anika's head with a pan," Nolan teased, waggling his brows. "Wouldn't look good if we let you hurt our realtor."

"I . . ." I wrung my fingers together, struggling to form words. Anika was a realtor? Jake had sold his cabin to Brooks? "But it's all broken inside. I can't afford to fix it up, and *you*—" I pointed a shaking finger at Brooks. "You dummy. I'll never be able to pay you back."

"Don't panic about the money." Brooks ran a hand over his beard, scraping at his jaw. "Dad left it for me, and I couldn't think of any better way to use it. Wren and Jake needed it more than I did. And don't think it's just been on me. I've been putting the rent you pay to stay here toward it."

I scoffed, and Tater kicked my side in encouragement. The amount they'd charged me was a joke, ridiculously low. "Why?" I asked, not understanding in the slightest. It was one thing to care about someone, but this . . . "Why would you do this?"

"You know why." His voice was steady, the challenge in his tone evident. "You know exactly why."

Clearing his throat, Nolan tipped his head to the door. Levi moved to his feet as he said, "We've already started fixing the cabin, but there's a couple sketches in there for you to choose from. And no matter what you decide, the cabin is yours, Shay."

Levi and Nolan left, taking Cash with them. I fidgeted on the bed, wanting to run after them. I didn't know if I was brave enough to face this. Was I ready? Before I could flee, Nolan poked his head in one last time. "I like the second sketch the best, darlin'. Takes the most work—but it's my favorite."

Chapter Forty-Five

The door shut, and I blinked. Blindly, I stared at the sketch pad as the mattress dipped, Brooks now sitting beside me. With shaking fingers, I turned to the second page, careful not to smudge the drawing. It was similar to the design of Jake's cabin when I'd lived in it—but now was larger, an addition sketched in. I raised a hand to my chest and smiled at the small block marked off as *Tater's room*. And beside it lay another square indicating a bedroom, this one reading *Shay's room—and Brooks's if she doesn't make him sleep on the couch.*

I closed the pad, protecting the greatest piece of art I'd ever seen. "Why?" I rolled off the bed, needing distance. My back hit the wall. I felt entirely bare and exposed in nothing but Brooks's flannel. "Why do you want this? You're young, handsome, and so dang good. Why would you give up the chance to start a family of your own?"

I winced, regretting the words as I said them, seeing the way his hands trembled between his legs. *He's as terrified as I am.* But if I'd hurt him, he didn't voice it and instead straightened himself where he sat on the bed. "I want a family with *you*, Shay. That's what I want."

My heart burned—oh, did it burn. Not in pain, but something stronger, refining. "If it was just you and me . . . you know I'd choose you. But—" I waved a hand at my stomach, not daring a step away from the wall. "I'm having a baby, Brooks. A tiny human with an even tinier heart. And if you and I don't work—"

I swallowed, the thought gutting me. This was the only thing holding me back. "I can't risk hurting my baby."

"I know that." His voice was firm, but kind, patient. As patient as he'd been with me, I realized, when he said, "Don't you think I know that? Why do you think we've gone slow? Why I haven't pushed to be with you, even though I've never wanted anything more?" He stood and stepped forward, grasping my fingers between his. "Sunshine, I wouldn't do this if I wasn't sure." He squeezed my hands and dipped his head, waiting for me to meet his gaze, see the truth lying there. "I'm in this for the long haul. I'm not going to leave you or Tater."

"It doesn't make sense." I stared at our joined hands, too much of a coward to face him. "It doesn't make sense why you'd take on the task of raising a baby who isn't even yours, or why you'd take me on."

He wrapped an arm around my lower back, the other hand cradling my jaw. His eyes were bright and earnest, full of dreams and hope. "I'm not taking on anything," he assured me, his thumb stroking my cheek. "You're not a task, Shay. Not you, and especially not this baby. You're both a gift, and I promise, I will cherish you. But I need you to let me—I need you to trust me."

"I do trust you." That truth was as sure as the air in my lungs, the blood in my heart. "I know you care about me, Brooks."

"Then what's stopping you?"

I brought my hands up to his chest, his heart rampant beneath my palm. "Because you deserve the absolute best. And as much as I want to have a family with you . . . it feels selfish to drag you into this. The entire situation is messy, and it's only going to get messier when the baby's born—"

"If you're worried about Declan, it doesn't bother me. I'm here whether or not you decide you want him to have a role in Tater's life." He bent lower and rested his forehead on mine. "I want messy. I want sleepless nights and diapers. I want to see you at your best and worst, and I promise you—I'll hold you during both. I want to do more than share a bed with you. I want to lie down every night and wake up every morning with the surety that you're mine." His fingers tangled themselves in my hair, his eyes brimming with intensity and need. "I want you to make me those awful eggs," he said with a soft laugh, his air mixing with mine. "Though I won't know, because I'll believe they're the best thing I've ever had. Because that's what you do, Shay—you somehow manage to take the bleak, painful parts of life and turn them into something amazing. And I want to share that with you."

He pulled me against his chest, cocooning me in his safe and sturdy hold. "I know I didn't make this baby with you. And I don't love Tater as much as you do—at least, not yet." He leaned his head back and held my gaze, his throat bobbing. "But I love you. And I know without a doubt if you and Tater give me the privilege of being in your life, I will treat your baby like it's my own." He managed a frail smile, putting himself on the line. "Let me prove it to you. Let me love you how you deserve—and in return, you can love me back. That's all I want."

He folded me back into his hold and rested his head atop mine, his voice a low murmur. "I know you're afraid. And you're right to be. I'm terrified, too. But nothing scares me more than not sharing a life with you. I can't stand the thought of not watching you become a mother, not learning if Tater will crinkle its nose like you do."

I closed my eyes and gripped his shirt, holding on. I'd known all along what this could be. What he and I could share together. But I'd been too afraid to claim it, fearing I'd get my heart broken. I'd left my home, given up my life so I could offer my baby a world I'd never had.

But now . . . now I wondered if I was letting my fears get in the way of me giving Tater the best life I could offer.

"I have to figure some things out," I said into the safety of his chest. "I know I've done a lot of good for myself in my time here, but I should've been doing more. I need to talk to Elle, maybe get a lawyer here. I'm pretty certain Declan doesn't want any sort of rights, but I need to make sure Tater stays with me. I need to do things right." I blew out a breath, praying I wouldn't regret this. I was trusting Brooks, *trusting me.* "So if you're in this . . . we'll need to decide some things, together. It's not like the movies, where just anyone can sign the birth certificate and be called daddy without taking the proper steps first."

Brooks stiffened and I did my best not to freak out. I didn't know if he would be interested in legally adopting Tater, if Declan would relinquish his rights. I didn't believe I was ready to take that step with Brooks. I might never be. But these were choices we'd have to discuss, see what sort of life we'd have together. I couldn't continue to run from this.

I leaned into him as he relaxed, his hands roaming my back. "I want to have those conversations with you."

I nodded, accepting what he was giving me, refusing to let myself spiral on what could go wrong. I was grateful Brooks was willing to communicate with me—he'd always been up for difficult conversations. Declan would've bulldozed over me.

"I can't cook." I stepped back, Brooks's arms falling to his sides. He raised a brow, like he hadn't endured several of my meals and had no idea. "So if you're expecting to come home after a long day of work to a hot meal, I'm afraid you've picked the wrong woman."

His lips twitched at the corners. "As long as it's you in our home, I'm happy." He lifted one shoulder in a shrug as he added, "Besides, I like to cook. I'm pretty sure you'd live off my peanut butter sandwiches for the rest of your life if you could, so I think we're set there."

I pressed my lips together, hiding what his words did to my heart. He winked at me, likely aware of how many points he'd just scored—but I knew the truth and value in his words. Brooks didn't make promises for the sake of telling me what I wanted to hear. He made them because he meant them. "Okay." My back tapped the door as I stepped away, straining to keep a healthy distance from him. "I heard you before, how you care about me—"

"I said I love you." He stepped toward me, not backing down from the path before him. "I care about you, yes—but I want to make sure it's clear that I love you."

"Right." Heat crawled over every inch of my skin. I glanced at my hand and picked at a nail, struggling to look him in the eye. "I think you know that sometimes I get wrapped up in my head, and I know it might be annoying, and it's ridiculously insecure, but I might need you to remind me . . . that you love me."

"I can do that." His voice was steady and clear. He stepped forward, the last of the distance between us dissolved. "I've stopped myself from saying it at least sixty times before now, so I doubt I'll have any problem letting you know." His hand found my hip, curving around my side. "I know what you're doing. You're trying to scare me, hoping some silly reason will make me think we won't work." His nose skimmed mine, his words hot on my cheek. "But the truth is, we both know we work, Shay. We've been doing this for weeks—the only difference is now we're putting a name to it. This has been real since the moment I pulled you over."

I glanced down at where my bump separated us, a frail inch of empty air keeping him from being against me. Before, when I looked down, I'd see what stood between us, the near-impossible mountains we'd have to climb. But now . . . now all I saw was what could exist between us.

A family.

"So, what, am I your girlfriend now?"

Brooks laughed, the corners of his eyes crinkling with amusement. "I'd say you're a bit more than that. I'm not sure there's a word to describe what you are to me."

His fingers skimmed mine, and I twined them together, raising my brow. "What if I wake you up at three a.m. and ask you ridiculous questions, like if you'd still love me if I was a worm?"

Brooks rolled his eyes, but I knew he wouldn't mind. He'd answer every one of my questions. "What kind of worm are we talking about here?"

I laughed and leaned up on my toes, wrapping my arms around his neck. "You shouldn't have bought Jake's cabin." I put a finger to his lips, seeing how his eyes widened. "I know you were trying to give me a home. But you already have. You're my home."

Beneath my finger, his lips stretched into a smile, so radiant I believed I'd never be afraid again. "You're my home, too."

"I love you." I leaned against his neck, whispering those words into his skin. "I love you and I promise to never leave you—"

His lips found mine, hard and desperate, as though I'd pushed his patience to the very end. I met him with equal force—I'd waited just as long. "I love you," he said in between teasing kisses. "I'm yours, sunshine. I'm both of yours."

He wanted me. And not solely me, but Tater too—a child who wasn't his. But as he rubbed my back, his large hands occasionally stroking my stomach, I knew it didn't matter. Not as I thought of Wren and Jake, the Grahams, even Elle and Layne.

Blood didn't bind a family. Love did.

Brooks was my family.

I peeked up from beneath my lashes at him, and there was such love there, such adoration, that I didn't think twice when I set my hands on his waist and guided him back to his bed. His throat bobbed, and he held my gaze with every step, only breaking it to glance at the door.

Without a word, he left my side and locked it. "Your brothers." I blinked, the fog of desire parting, the need to give myself to Brooks right this moment easing. "I should go talk to them, thank them for their part in the cabin."

"They're fine. We've lived together our whole lives—if they don't know when to make themselves scarce, that's their own fault." Heat licked my spine as Brooks made his way back to me, his steps full of purpose, like he had no intention of ever leaving this room. "You can thank them later."

His hands found my waist, lowering me onto the bed. I settled myself on my side just as he lay beside me. I leaned for him as he did me, our lips meeting in between. Our kiss wasn't hard or desperate, nor was it tender and cautious. It was confident and freeing. We'd both waited for this long enough, since before we'd even known one another.

We kissed and kissed, until his lips were swollen and the skin beside mine was raw from his beard scraping me. I watched him as we lay, sharing the same pillow. He smiled, his fingers skating through my hair, and made no move to deepen this moment, as though content to watch me for the rest of the night.

But I set my palm against his shoulder and nudged him onto his back, wanting more. Maybe it was greedy of me, but I wanted everything with Brooks. He shimmied himself up to sit against the headboard as I straddled him.

I slipped my fingers beneath his shirt, feeling the smooth, firm ridges below. "Do you still want me as bad as you did on Halloween?"

"More." His voice was husky, his lips on my ear. "That first night in Jake's truck, when you sat on my lap, I could barely sleep because I kept thinking about what it would be like to have you moan my name." I bit my lip, doing just that as he left a trail of fleeting kisses down my neck. "I've dreamed of making love to you, feeling your skin against mine. But mostly, I've just dreamed of having you, and your trust." He kissed the hollow of my throat. "And I'll do anything to keep you—so there's no rush. We've got time."

My hands stilled beneath his shirt, I lingered on his lap, seeing nothing but truth in his eyes. There was desire and heat, but there was also concern, not wanting to push me too far. Make me give something I wasn't ready to give. He was letting me lead, I realized—sort of like he'd done this whole time. He might've nudged me along, kept us on track, but he'd never led me. Somehow, he'd eased me into it, so effortlessly I hadn't noticed until long after it happened that I was in love with him.

I lifted the hem of his shirt, and he obliged me easily, raising his arms. I pulled it off, tossing it somewhere behind us. "I've dreamed about those things too, Brooks." I skimmed my hands over his frame, feeling his strength. "I've wanted to share a life with you for a long while—I've never wanted anything more. And I don't want to wait."

He rubbed a hand over his jaw, failing to hide his grin. But rather than accepting what I was offering, he admitted, "I didn't plan this—I don't have any condoms."

I raised my brow and glanced down at the bump between us, almost pressed against his tight stomach. "I'm no doctor, and maybe you have mighty sperm, but I think the odds of me getting knocked up again are pretty slim."

He laughed, shaking his head. "I love talking to you."

"I love it too," I whispered, unexpected moisture building in my eyes. I loved talking to Brooks. I'd never shared so much with anyone before. I hadn't known how healing words could be, for both of us, until now.

His thumb caught my tear and lingered there on my cheek. "I'm clean. I haven't been with anyone in years. And I've always used protection."

I'd only been with Declan before, and we'd always used protection—Tater was just a force that couldn't be stopped. "I'm clean too. They ran a bunch of tests at the beginning of my pregnancy. And there's never going to be anyone else for me but you."

He wrapped his hands around my waist. "I've never had sex with a pregnant woman."

I laughed, tilting my head back. "I'm happy to be your first and *last*. If it helps your nerves, I've never had sex pregnant," I revealed, the last time being when I'd *gotten* pregnant.

His fingers gripped my shirt—his shirt—knuckles white, as though his restraint was going out. But somehow, he had enough left to look me in the eye and say, "I'm never going to hurt you."

I blinked, the words taking me aback. I knew it was inevitable, that someday, even if unintentionally, Brooks would hurt me. But I heard his promise for what it was: a declaration that he would never raise a hand to me. Never plan and plot his words, never scheme to bind my soul. My voice was a low rasp. "Never."

"And I'm not going to hurt your baby."

It wasn't a question, but I answered it anyway. "You won't."

I didn't know if he meant during sex—I was cleared, and Dr. Malitina had said it was healthy during pregnancy—or in general, but I believed him without a doubt.

With nothing else left to say, Brooks wrapped his hand around the back of my neck and brought my lips to his. The kiss was slow and earnest, savoring what lay between us. His fingers traveled the course of my back, not stopping until they made their way around to my front. "This is still my favorite look." His fingers were precise as they unbuttoned my borrowed flannel. I swallowed, my skin flushed as he peeled it away, the cool air failing to ease my nerves. "Beautiful," he murmured, his voice wet with awe. "You're absolutely beautiful."

I felt beautiful. Felt nothing but lovely as he devotedly caressed my body, like the angry stretch marks were worthy of such attention. I gasped, my nerves awakening, as he pressed his lips to the swell of my breast and unsnapped my bra. I let it slide down my arms and to the side, baring me entirely for Brooks. Despite the hunger in his eyes, looking like he might eat me alive, I laughed.

Brooks blinked, seemingly coming out of a daze. "I'm sorry." I covered my mouth, stifling my laugh. I glanced between his wary smile and his heaving chest, his muscles straining. "I'm sorry—you're perfect. I think I'm just nervous, and it doesn't help that you look like freaking Superman and I'm just plopped down on you like Pooh Bear."

"Pooh Bear?" The corners of his eyes crinkled with his grin. "Who's to say Superman doesn't have the hots for Pooh Bear?"

I snorted, shaking my head. "Oh my gosh—maybe that's what I'll write. Fanfic about Superman and Pooh Bear."

Brooks groaned and flopped back down on the mattress, rolling me onto my side beside him. "Well, do you think you could do it after?" he teased, brushing my hair behind my ear. "If you're willing to wait, I bet we could come up with some great inspiration."

"I can wait," I said with a laugh and kissed him long and hard, swirling my tongue with his, only to pull back a fraction of an inch. "I just wish I wasn't stuffed full of a peanut butter gremlin for our first time."

He smirked and ran his hand over my stomach. "I happen to love you stuffed full with a peanut butter gremlin."

Having had enough with words, Brooks pulled my mouth back to his, consuming any and all worries, until I was unable to think of anything else as he familiarized himself with my body. His hands and mouth were starved, claiming, only stopping to allow me to do the same to him. Letting me feel every inch of his skin, learn his body as well as I knew his heart, his soul. I moaned his name, and he breathed mine as we touched one another, ensuring there was not a single wound left unhealed.

"You found me." My hands shook as I cupped his jaw, our slick legs entwined. Our skin was flushed, breaths heavy as we watched one another in awe. I didn't know it could be like this. This was love. It wasn't perfect. It was messy and flawed, and we'd have to work for it for the rest of our lives. But with Brooks, I didn't mind. He was worth it. We were worth it. "Don't ever let me go."

"Never," he said, and I kissed him, sealing the promise, trusting him as we worked our way together. And when he and I were one, I knew nothing and no one outside of this moment. No longer did I remember the pain, the fear of being abandoned. I only felt him.

I was home.

Chapter Forty-Six

"What do you mean you're going to bust down the walls?" I frowned as a wintry breeze swept through the open doorway of Jake's cabin—or I supposed, my and Brooks's cabin. Snow painted the forest floor and treetops, pops of evergreen sneaking through. Though anywhere that wasn't alabaster white, was brown sludge, the sight remained pure and beautiful. Alas, I couldn't wait until it was warm enough to spend evenings in the meadow again. Sighing, I closed the door, admiring the new hardwood floors beneath my feet, replaced by Brooks himself. "You just barely fixed this place up."

He'd fixed it up, all right—it was beautiful. The floor was sturdy, the color a deep red oak. He'd stained the cabinets the same color and rehung them on the wall. The mattress was new—big enough for two, I'd noticed—and the wood stove was clean, with freshly chopped firewood beside it. It was December, and with several inches of snowfall already on the ground, I imagined we'd use it plenty.

"Well," Brooks started, interrupting my daydream of us curling up together beside the fire, "if we're building an addition, I'd need to take down at least one so I can extend the frame."

I raised my brow, still struggling to process that this cabin was ours. "Shouldn't you have done that before?"

He barked out a laugh, the sound inviting a smile to my lips. "When I bought it, I wasn't so sure you'd let me join you. So I just wanted to get it livable for you and Tater. Didn't think you'd like me very much if the floor caved in on you."

I rolled my lips together and walked over to where he sat on a stepladder. "Thank you for the cabin."

He widened his legs and pulled me in close. "Thank you for letting me tag along."

I snorted. Brooks was doing much more than tagging along. I shifted in his hold and sat on his thigh, glancing around the cabin. I loved it, even more so because every time I was in it, I'd think of his love. How he'd given me a home, both in him and this cabin. "I'm just sorry you have to do more work." I ran my fingers through the hair on his neck. "Are you sure it's okay to bring Tater home to your dad's house? Maybe it would be best if I stayed here. What if the baby cries a lot? Or I cry a lot? And then you and your brothers can't sleep because everyone is crying—"

"Hey." He pressed his thumb between my brows, easing the worry lines there. "We've been over this, sunshine. We'll have the entire upstairs to ourselves—and I'm sure Tater will cry. But as long as it's not as loud as those creepy screaming plants from that Harry Potter movie you made me watch last night, I think we're set." I huffed and rested my head against his shoulder, smiling as he skated his fingers over my stomach. Since we'd made it official, he could barely keep his hands to himself. And while I loved the moments of heated passion and desire, I cherished this more. *He loves us.* "It's only temporary. I'm going to give it my best shot, and if I need to bring in contractors, I will. But who knows, maybe we'll have the addition done before Tater is born in March. But we have a plan, okay? My brothers won't mind. Levi will be happy to get extra time with us before he goes—"

"Oh, don't get me started on that," I cried, slinging my arms around his neck. It turned out, the cabin wasn't the only surprise. The day after Thanksgiving, Levi had admitted he was considering enrolling back into graphic design school, the same one he'd dropped out of in Boston. Nothing was set in stone, and while

I was happy for him, I selfishly didn't want him to leave. "We could just skip the addition. I don't mind the space being small."

He sighed, his shoulders falling with the motion. Rather than protesting, telling me there'd barely be enough space for a crib, and that Tater would only continue to grow, he said, "It's your choice. If that's what you want, we'll do it."

I kissed his temple and eased myself onto my feet, pulling him up with me. "Technically it's your cabin," I teased, poking his side. "Shouldn't it be your decision?"

"Our cabin," he corrected, even though it was his name on the deed, as well as his money going to it. Though I imagined the few scraps of cash I'd paid in rent had at least bought the stain for the cabinets. Maybe a paintbrush too. "I know it works for some couples, but I'm not really for all that this is *mine*, and this is *yours*. So I hope you're okay with me considering it all *ours* from now on."

I raised my brow, a playful grin on my lips. "Oh—so is your truck mine?"

He leaned back against the wall, his arms crossed over his chest. "Considering it belongs to the Forest Service, I can't really say it's mine. But if you want to ask them for it, go ahead."

I hummed. "Is Cash mine, too?"

"He's sure as hell not mine anymore."

"Is this mine too?" I asked, walking my fingers up the buttons of his flannel.

He smirked, his gaze hot on my lips. "You wear them more than I do, don't you?"

I shuddered as his fingers slipped beneath the hem of my jacket, toying with my skin. "Most couples wait to share everything until after they're married."

His fingers edged their way up, and no longer did I feel the bite of the air as he said, "Yes, but I have every intention of marrying you. So why wait?"

My pounding heart filled my ears. Heat spread over me, having nothing to do with his touch. It didn't matter if we'd already made promises, shared a bed, and were now making plans to live together and raise Tater together. Hearing he wanted to *marry me* set my heart to a completely different pace. How I'd ever believed I loved Declan was beyond me. Never once had I felt a fraction of what I did with Brooks—not even when things were good. But maybe that had something to do with me, now that I'd grown and accepted myself. I knew what I wanted, what I deserved.

I pressed my lips to his, intent on making this cabin a little bit more ours. But just as I'd wrapped my hand around his belt buckle, his tongue stroking mine, my phone vibrated. Brooks twisted us and backed me up against the wall, oblivious to my vibrating butt cheek. I reached into my back pocket, enjoying the way he nibbled and kissed at my throat too much to ask him to stop, and glanced at my phone. "It's Wren," I gasped, my eyes fluttering shut as he nipped at my ear. "I should probably answer—"

"She's fine." His fingers were in my hair, scraping delightfully against my scalp. "I'm sure she just wants to make sure we're still coming up in a few days—and like you told her last night, we'll drive to the city as soon as we finish up at your doctor's appointment."

I looked at the phone vibrating in my hand, unable to convince myself to answer it as Brooks unzipped my jacket. "You know," I huffed, letting him push it off my shoulders and down my arms. "If I didn't know better, I'd believe it was you who was twenty-eight weeks pregnant and plagued with insatiable hormones that made you want to tear my clothes off constantly."

He grinned against my lips, likely wishing I'd stop talking. "Maybe I am. Haven't you ever heard of a sympathy pregnancy?"

I laughed, the phone now silent in my hand. "If that's the case, then I better see those abs of yours disappear, and you put on at least thirty pounds."

"I thought Pooh Bear loved Superman," he teased, pulling at my bottom lip.

"Very much." I kissed him hard, believing it would always be like this. He was my partner, my best friend. "Oh my gosh," I groaned as my phone vibrated again, wishing I'd chucked it across the room. Despite his persistence before, Brooks pulled back and let me read the screen. "Oh." I blinked, realizing it wasn't Wren after all. "It's a text from Elle. She sent me the information to that lawyer in Phoenix."

As though an icy bucket of water had been dumped on us, we straightened our clothes. Brooks cleared his throat and stepped back, giving me space. "You alright?"

I bit my lip, fidgeting with the zipper on my jacket. "Yes—I don't know." A few days ago, I'd asked Elle if she could connect me with any family lawyers in Arizona. I would rather have used her, but her license restricted her from representing clients outside of California. "I wish I didn't have to deal with this at all."

"You're doing the right thing," he assured me, somehow comforting me without a single touch. "At least now you'll have an idea of what you should do if Declan decides he wants to be involved."

I would never have admitted it aloud—that was a lie, I'd said it several times—but I didn't want Declan involved. Not because of what he'd done to me, though it did weigh on my mind, but because he'd made it clear *he didn't want our baby*. But I also wanted to do the right thing, so I could at least look my child in the eye someday and be honest that I'd tried. My mom had never given my biological father a chance to be in my life, and I'd hate myself if I did the same. Selfishly, though, I hoped Declan walked away. But then it broke my heart to imagine him giving up what could be the best thing to ever happen to him.

This was messy, and too much. No matter what I did, I felt like I would doubt it was the right thing.

"Shay," Brooks said, likely sensing my thoughts. With two fingers beneath my chin, he raised my gaze to his. His eyes were sincere and bright, a reminder that good still existed. "No matter what, Tater will be loved. You've always loved this baby—I've never been more sure of anything than that."

"Thank you." I leaned into his touch, kissing the palm of his hand. "I'm so grateful we have you."

"Always."

I believed him. No matter what happened, even if we didn't work out, I'd have him to rely on. It was why I pushed past the nerves fluttering through me, ignored the thoughts telling me to run, and said, "I'm only asking because Elle will probably ask me later, so no pressure—and you don't have to answer right away. And you can say no now, and change your mind in a few years—"

He silenced me with a gentle kiss, slowly unwinding the unease snaring me. "If Declan signed away his rights, I'd adopt Tater, yes." His eyes flickered, moisture building within. "But there's not a timeline to that. So even if he walks away, I can wait—for as long as you need. This is your choice."

"Thank you." I could never correctly convey how much that meant to me. I was grateful he understood why I couldn't immediately go down that route. I was willing to give Brooks my heart, but no matter how much I trusted him, I was cautious with Tater. But maybe . . . maybe someday this baby would *choose* Brooks. And that might be even more special. "I think it would be smart not to rush into anything. But if I could choose anyone, it would be you."

He nodded, the corner of his lip tilted up. "We're a family regardless of what any paper says. And even if Declan's involved, the same applies. I'll be a father to your baby in the ways that matter."

"Our baby," I rasped, failing to muster the teasing manner I'd been going for. "I thought you said you didn't want to be a *yours* and *mine* couple."

"Fine," he grumbled—or at least tried to, the tear falling down his cheek betraying him. "*Our* baby."

Chapter Forty-Seven

I could count on one hand the moments when I'd experienced true bliss. A joy so pure, so blinding, I seemed to have stepped past reality for a moment and into something brighter. A moment that was strong enough to escort me through darkness.

The most recent was my first doctor's appointment after learning I was pregnant. I'd been so nervous, so unsure. I was on the verge of running out and never looking back. But somehow, I found the courage to stay. I told myself to make it through the appointment and go from there. One scary step at a time. I hadn't known how many that would be, but after I saw Tater on the sonogram, and heard its mighty heartbeat—I knew I'd take all the steps in the world.

And as I lay in bed with Brooks, firing baby names back and forth, I knew this would join the list.

"Chewie."

Brooks groaned and rolled over, hiding his smile in his pillow. "We are not naming our baby after a Star Wars character."

"Hmm." I peeked at him over the laptop I'd borrowed from Levi earlier, wanting to search through baby names. It was Sunday night, and Nolan and Levi were both out, but we'd spent the better half of the day in Brooks's room. The addition was set to start in a few weeks, and we'd stay here in the meantime—there was no need to move twice. "What about Han?"

"Shay."

"Solo?"

He laughed and shifted to face me, his head propped up on his arm. "Are you telling me someone actually compiled a list and put those names on it?"

"Maybe." I was sure they were on some lists, just not ones I'd come across. I'd looked through a few before I'd gotten sidetracked. Aware of the way Brooks was closely eyeing me, I saved the link for a crib and closed the tab. "It's kind of hard to look for names when you haven't told me the gender yet."

He grinned, his eyes gleaming. "You'll find out soon enough."

I set the laptop on the nightstand beside me and shifted up onto my knees, wearing one of Brooks's flannels—my favorite pajamas. "And there's nothing I can do to convince you otherwise?"

He lay back with a smirk, his bare chest an open invitation. "You can try."

"Oh, really?" I leaned forward, close enough to feel his heat but nothing more. "I see how it is."

He closed his eyes, anticipating my kiss as I pressed closer. Wickedly, I weaved to the left and licked his cheek instead. I smiled at his shocked laugh and rolled off the bed. "What are you doing?" he asked, wiping at his cheek as I patrolled his bedroom.

I searched the top of his dresser, finding nothing of value—no sign of the envelope I'd given him. When I'd initially given him the gender, I was fine waiting, but now time was ticking, and I had an urge to plan. *Am I nesting?* Elle had teased that I was after I told her about my weird compulsion at one a.m. to organize the kitchen cabinets. Let's just say the Graham brothers didn't appreciate being woken up by banging pans and early morning Taylor Swift jams.

I rounded the bed, intent on searching the nightstand on his side. My eyes must've been on the prize, as Brooks jumped to his feet, blocking me. "It's not in there."

I furrowed my brows and reached around him, his hand catching mine. "What's in there, then?"

"Nothing."

I eyed him and then the drawer, curiosity getting the best of me. But something must've washed over my face, because Brooks sighed. "I'm not hiding anything. I just . . . I'm afraid you'll think I'm crazy."

I bit my smile, weaving my finger through his abs. "If you have a voodoo doll of me, Brooks, it's okay. I used to sleep with yours every night."

He rolled his eyes but sat on the edge of the bed, giving me access to the drawer. I pulled on the handle, not sure what I'd find—maybe some trashy magazines or a bottle of lube. But I hadn't expected this. I swallowed, my throat aching as I pulled out the book: *What to Expect When You're Expecting.*

"Shay," he whispered, misinterpreting my stunned silence. "Please don't take that the wrong way. I promise I had no expectations of you and me ever happening . . . I just wanted to know how to be there for you."

I shook my head and clutched the book to my chest. I didn't know why seeing this book made it real for me. Made me see how deeply devoted Brooks was. I didn't know how long he'd had this, but based on the wear and tear on the pages, and the random tidbits he knew about pregnancy, I sensed he'd had it for a while. I set the book back in the drawer and closed it. "You love me."

He sputtered a laugh, relief washing over his face that I wasn't angry—as though I could be at a man who only wanted to support me. "I do, Shay."

I slipped my fingers into his hair as he pulled me between his legs. His fingers lingered at the hem of my shirt, his gaze holding mine, waiting until I nodded. He plucked open the buttons, stopping when only my stomach was exposed. I closed my eyes, bracing my arms on his shoulders as he set his palms above my hips, searching.

I was twenty-eight weeks, and the baby's movements had grown more prominent. Sort of like something knocking on me from the inside. It was wild and weird and amazing—and something Brooks had yet to experience. With his attention captured, I revealed, "I think I'm going to get another job."

He hummed under his breath, distracted enough with his earnest search for kicks that he nearly missed what I said. He looked up, his brows furrowed. "Did something happen at the shop?"

"No," I assured him. "I mean a second job. Layne told me her sister-in-law works for this online company. They teach English to children in other countries. So I could still work at the shop, and teach at night."

I was dreading the thought of losing sleep; I was exhausted already. But the job was a good deal. They didn't require a teaching degree, just experience with kids, and I could set my own hours. This baby wasn't going to pay for itself—unless there was a magical wad of cash stuffed inside me, too.

"Shay." Brooks leaned back on his arms, watching me from the bed. "If you're worried about money, you don't need to. I'm not loaded, but I make decent money. I'll help you—"

"I know you will," I said with a smile, shaking my head. I knew Brooks would help me, that he likely had every intention of doing so. But after Declan, I'd promised myself I'd never be entirely reliant on someone again. I didn't see it as a weakness like I had before, but I'd feel better having a little cushion beneath my feet. "But I'd also like to be able to help myself a little bit." The extra money could also help set me up while I was on maternity leave. Not wanting Brooks to think I didn't trust him, I teased, "Don't worry, there'll be plenty of times for you to be my sugar daddy."

He smirked, and I captured it with my lips, wrapping my arms around his neck. His tongue stroked mine, and I paused, feeling a nudge beneath my ribs. Not breaking the kiss, I brought his hand up to the spot and gently pressed his palm down.

He froze, and I smiled, leaving a parting kiss on his lips as I leaned away, not wanting to miss this. He stared at his hand, his brows furrowed in concentration, as though he couldn't discern if the squirming beneath it was real.

There was a tap below my ribs, just as Brooks's eyes widened. "There's a baby in there."

I tipped my head back in a laugh. "There is."

He leaned in, and I shuddered as he kissed the spot above my belly button. Unexpected tears welled in my eyes as he left a trail of kisses, whispering sweet nothings into my skin. Promises to always be there. That he and I would make this work. He believed our family was a family as much as anyone else's. And we were his home.

I pressed deeper against Brooks's chest, running my fingers over his smooth skin. My eyes were closed as the bed groaned, and I smiled lazily as I felt Cash lie at my feet. I'd stayed up later than I planned, losing myself in Brooks, and I was exhausted. I stirred as his phone rang. He ignored it and rolled us onto our sides, his arm strapped over me. He groaned as it rang again, the screen lighting up the room. "It's probably Nolan." He pressed his lips to my forehead. "If I don't answer, he'll keep calling."

Eyes still closed, I rolled to my other side, a pillow wedged between my legs. I was nearly gone when Brooks sat beside me, his fingers skimming my side. "Sunshine, that was Jake."

I smiled in my pillow and stretched. "Did you tell him to remind Wren to be patient, and we'll be there tomorrow night?" I waited, but when Brooks said nothing, I sat up. "Is everything okay?"

"Wren's not doing so well." He gave me a tight-lipped smile. "Um—they're stopping treatment and she's coming home tomorrow."

"Stopping treatment?" I asked, unease swirling through me. "I—I don't understand."

His eyes gleamed. "It's spread. It's in her lymph nodes, her lungs—" His voice broke, and I rolled onto my knees, wrapping my arms around his neck. His breaths were heavy, his chest shuddering as he held the emotion in. "They're bringing some supplies back to make her as comfortable as possible. Jake asked if I could come up tonight and help."

He pulled away, and I sat back on the bed, watching as he slipped on a pair of jeans. "Can I come?" I asked, knowing there was nothing I could do. But I wanted to be there for him, for Wren. I didn't know much about cancer, but I could only assume if she was stopping treatment, it wasn't good.

"I was counting on it," he said, buckling his belt. "She was expecting us tomorrow anyway, so it works."

I slipped his shirt back on—all my things were still upstairs, and I didn't want to be entirely naked in case Nolan or Levi came home. "Shoot—" I ran my fingers through my hair, remembering why we'd chosen tomorrow to see Wren in the first place. "I have my appointment for the glucose test in the morning."

"Okay," he said, already grabbing his phone. "I'll see if Nolan and Levi can drive up to help instead."

"No." I put my hand over his, stopping him. "Go help them. I've gone alone before, I'll be just fine."

He shook his head. "I promised I'd go with you to the rest of your appointments. I want to be there."

"And you will—after tomorrow." I put a finger to his lips, stopping his attempt to protest. Wren was in Phoenix, hours away from Wallowpine and Hillshire. There was no way we could make both work. "It's just the glucose test tomorrow. You're not missing anything."

He looked downright conflicted, his throat bobbing. "I wanted to be there for you."

"You are." I leaned up on my toes and kissed his cheek. "But Wren needs you more right now. I'll be home when you get here."

He watched me, and I could see his hesitation. Not wanting to leave me, but needing to be there for Wren and Jake, the rest of his family. But like the man he was, the man I fell in love with, he swept his thumb over my lip. "I love the sound of coming home to you."

Chapter Forty-Eight

Sugar rushes are a load of garbage.

At least, they are when you're a twenty-four-year-old pregnant woman.

I'd chugged a hundred grams of sugar crammed into a three-and-a-half-ounce bottle, and I was *not* bouncing off the walls. It was taking everything in me to not hurl all over them. Pure will was the only thing that stopped me, not wanting to do the inevitable three-hour test if I failed.

I'd never been so happy to have blood drawn after the hour was up. I was drooling for the PB sandwich I'd packed in Jake's truck. I was mid-bite, my mouth full, as my phone rang, Brooks's number popping up.

"Hey, sunshine," he said. "Are you all done?"

"Yup." I wrapped up the rest of my sandwich, leaving the rest for when I got home. "You know, when I gave you my number, you swore you'd only call if the planet was being invaded." I smiled, just knowing he was doing it alongside me.

"Well, I'm sorry I broke my word. How are you feeling?"

"Like I never want sugar again," I whined, smiling wider when he laughed. How was it possible I missed him already? "I should probably get on the road."

"Do you feel okay to drive? I can send Nolan or Levi up to get you."

I rolled my eyes, secretly loving his protectiveness. "I ate and I'm good to go. Plus, I'm sure they're busy at the shop." Not wanting to give him a moment to insist, I asked, "Have you guys left yet?"

He sighed heavily, likely knowing I couldn't be swayed. "Just about. They're finishing up some paperwork, and then I'll follow them home."

"How is Wren?"

There was a long pause, nothing but an empty line, worsening the swelling panic in my heart. "She's alright. I'll tell you more when I get home—and once they get settled, I'll take you over to see her. Wren kept asking about you and the *babe*."

"Okay," I rasped, my throat lined with regret. I should've done better at keeping her in the loop, checked in more.

Likely sensing I was on the verge of tears but needed my mind clear to drive, Brooks said, "You drive safe, okay? And call me when you get home—and then I want you to soak in a bubble bath."

"A bubble bath?" I wiped my nose, not knowing the last time I'd taken a bath. But my aching back and the thought of having the house to myself had me considering otherwise. "That sounds amazing."

"Good." His voice was low, making my heart race even with miles between us. "It'll make me drive faster, too."

"Freak," I teased and hung up, grateful for his attempt to lighten the mood. I switched off the radio, needing silence. I was decent at driving a standard now and had gotten here with no problem—but I wasn't taking risks, especially with the inches of snow on the ground.

Only a few minutes into my drive, my phone buzzed. Normally I'd ignore it while driving, but when I glanced over and saw it was Elle, I answered it anyway. "Helloooooo," she called, not giving me a chance to talk. "I'm absolutely honored you chose to take your tongue out of that mountain man's mouth and answer me."

I laughed, rolling my eyes as I clicked the phone to speaker and set it on the center console. "How are you? The kids?"

"Let's just say I'm really happy to be at work right now. Theo pooped in the middle of his nap and smeared it all over the wall. Pretty sure my nanny is going to quit."

I scrunched my nose, grateful her kids had never done that to me. "That's disgusting."

I imagined her maniacally laughing as she said, "This is your future, Shay. Enjoy your freedom while you can." Before I could reply, she continued, "But in reality, it's better now that I'm back at the firm part-time. I'm slowly settling back in. It's felt really good to have something to myself again."

"I'm so happy for you." I knew the guilt Elle carried for not only wanting but needing to be out of the house. Our situations were different, but I could sympathize with her—it was why I had been so miserable with Declan. I'd had nothing that was *me*. "I think it's awesome that you show those three babies of yours you can be a good mom and still be your own person." There was a long pause, and I peeked at my phone, making sure the call hadn't failed. "Are . . . are you crying?"

"No," she said, her voice wobbling. She was totally crying. "My hormones are still out of whack from having a baby, okay—and dang it, Shay. I totally called you to talk smack, not cry. So thanks for being a total buzzkill."

I laughed hard and crossed my legs, afraid I'd pee myself. I missed her so dang much. "What were you going to tell me?"

There was a bout of sniffling, followed by the blowing of a nose, before she said, "So we had the firm's Christmas party on Saturday. And Declan was there—he brought mommy dearest as his date, by the way." I swallowed, not sure I wanted to hear about him at all. "But I was a little tipsy—don't judge me, I pumped and dumped before I fed the baby—but just seeing his face pissed me off. My legs practically moved on their own . . ."

"What did you do?" I groaned.

"I was possessed," she reasoned. "But . . . I might've told him I'd smash his marble balls with a hammer and called him a baby deserter, along with a few other choice words." I laughed, not sure if I should be encouraging her. "Hold on, I'm not done. I'm pretty sure his mom didn't know you were pregnant.

You should've seen her face, she looked like she was about to gouge his eyes out. And the best part—you know our law firm manager, Janet?" she asked, and I failed to picture her in my mind. I'd only gone to a few events with Declan, and if I wasn't following him, I was glued to Elle. "Well, she heard the whole thing. And rumor is, this morning she asked him about you, and he told her you weren't pregnant." I gasped, stunned into silence. I didn't know if I was angry, sad, or downright pitied him. But most of all, I was relieved. So relieved to be away from him. Hopefully for good. When I didn't reply, Elle said, "I'm sorry, I wasn't thinking. I thought it would be funny, but now I can see it was totally insensitive to tell you—"

"Marble balls, huh?" I teased, knowing Elle would never go out of her way to hurt me. I was too busy picturing running Declan over—twice—to be angry. "They probably shriveled up inside of him and died."

She barked a laugh. "I'll be sure to ask him at our staff meeting later."

"So," I started, needing a change of conversation, "I called that family lawyer you recommended. Brooks and I are going to meet with her next week."

"Mountain man's going?" she asked, and I could've sworn I heard swooning in her voice. "I love Howard, but I'd be lying if I said my ovaries didn't squeal when you told me he fixed up that cabin for you." She sighed, and I did with her. *I have a home. Not a house. A home.* "I'm proud of you. I know it seemed pretty bleak there for a while, but you kept pushing, and you've made something worthwhile. I haven't heard you this happy . . . ever. I mean, can you imagine what your life will be like in a few years?"

A few months ago, I wouldn't have let myself. I was living day to day. But now . . . now I wasn't so afraid to dream. Tater would be with me—though with a real name—and Brooks would be, too. We'd be in our cabin, and he'd make us dinner as I sat with Nolan and Levi. Maybe by then, they'd have started families of their own. Maybe I'd have a degree, or at least have stopped resisting the itch to write again. Maybe I'd run a marathon and convince both Layne and Elle to join me. I'd visit Wren and Jake often, let her finally make me Sunday breakfast. And who knows, maybe I'd be pregnant with Brooks's baby.

I didn't know where I'd be, but I knew I'd be happy.

"I should probably go," Elle said, pulling me out of my daydreaming. "I have that staff meeting soon, and I have some paperwork for a case to catch up on. But let me know how it goes with that lawyer—"

I cursed when the phone slid off the console onto the passenger seat. "Hold on!" I shouted, unable to piece together what Elle was saying. I checked my mirror twice, making sure the road was clear and no one was around me. Taking my eyes off the road—for just a second—I reached across the seat and grabbed my phone with ease. But by the time I glanced up, the truck was off the road.

Chapter Forty-Nine

Time was strange.

Twenty-four hours before, I'd been in bed with Brooks, brainstorming names for our baby. Our baby. Blood or not, Brooks was this baby's father. A father who swore to love us, to protect us.

But he didn't know he'd have to protect our baby from me.

I'd never forget the ringing in my ears, the blurring of broken glass as I slipped in and out. But even as I struggled to keep consciousness, I'd had one steady thought. *My baby.*

Even now, as I lay alone in a hospital bed, I thought only of Tater, even as the nurse checked the stitched-up wound atop my head. "You're sure the baby's okay?" I rasped, running a bandaged hand over my stomach.

"Yes." She smiled, gently squeezing my hand, careful of the IV. "We can do another ultrasound to ease your mind, but I promise, we were thorough with our last two." She lifted my gown and adjusted the heart rate monitor on my stomach, a thudding heartbeat filling the room. "See? Your little Tater, as you call it, is steady and strong. You're showing no signs of preterm labor. We're only keeping you for observation as a precaution." She straightened the hospital gown draped over me, making sure I was covered—even though she'd seen every bit of my goods when she helped me change—and reached for my cheek, wiping my tears. "The best thing you can do right now is stay calm and be grateful for the miracle you both made it out nearly unscathed. I'll be right back with a soda—it'll calm your nerves."

"Thank you," I whispered before she left the room and closed the door, trapping me alone with myself. My eyes strained, but I refused to close them, knowing I'd hear the thunderous sound of steel hitting the ground. The haunting of blood dripping down my face from jarring my head on the steering wheel, the truck tipped over on its side. How eerily quiet the world had fallen as I'd touched my stomach, searching for any sort of movement.

But there were miracles.

It was a miracle—the absolute stupidest miracle—when I'd somehow managed to hold on to my phone in the midst of it all. All I'd heard was Elle's panicked cries on the other side of the line before I'd hung up and called 911. It was a miracle that a car hadn't been too far behind, a set of college-aged girls who were kind enough to stop and wait with me. The biggest miracle was Tater was safe, and beyond being bruised, I wasn't seriously injured, despite having driven off the side of the road and tipping into a ditch.

Miracles that shouldn't have had to take place.

How could I have been so reckless? So careless?

"You can't do anything right, can you?"

"You're worthless. Good for spreading your legs, and that's it."

"Be grateful I haven't walked away like everyone else, butterfly."

I shook my head, shuddering a shaky breath, and focused on the tiny television on the wall. I needed to stay calm. Half-heartedly, I watched Monica Geller yell the number seven, distracting me enough I didn't roll over when there was a tap on the door.

I glanced over my shoulder as it creaked open, expecting it to be the nurse. I froze, lip wobbling as I settled on Brooks. He closed the door and leaned into it. He looked as bad as I felt, with red eyes and messy hair. He fervently scanned me, his gaze lingering on the stitches along my hairline, likely ensuring I was in one piece. But when he didn't come for me, I couldn't slow the pounding of my heart. "I'm sorry," I rasped, feeling like a rock was wedged in my throat. "I'm so sorry, Brooks—"

He closed the distance in three strides before he knelt beside the bed. "Breathe." His hands were careful as he grabbed mine. "You have nothing to be sorry for."

Hot tears sprawled down my cheeks. "I almost killed our baby—"

"Don't," he said softly but firmly. Not because he was angry, I realized, but because he was struggling to keep it together. He'd been on the road less than an hour when I called him. But rather than telling him I was in the bubble bath, I'd told him I was on my way to the hospital. I'd assured him I was fine, but I couldn't imagine how agonizing the four hours it took him to get to me were. "Don't do that to yourself, Shay. It was an accident. It could've happened to anyone."

I shook my head, refusing to hear his words. *I'm angry at me.* "It's my fault. I was the one who reached for my stupid phone. I can't believe I did that. I'm so sorry."

"You have nothing to be sorry for. I don't care if you made a mistake—it's done and over, and we'll deal with it," he said, brushing his thumb over my lip.

"You're not listening—"

"It was a mistake," he pressed, his voice thick with emotion. "Accidents happen, sunshine. And I'm sorry, but as perfect as I think you are, it won't be your last."

My lip wobbled as I struggled to accept Brooks's words, to see it through his eyes. "I might've broken Jake's truck."

He cracked a laugh, a tear spilling out of the corner of his eye. He kissed my lips, catching my sob before it broke free. "It's okay. I don't care about that, and neither does he, I promise. All I care about is my girls. And as long as you're both safe, I'm happy."

I nodded and clung to that truth. *We're safe.* I was angry at myself, at how quickly I could've lost everything. But I could be angry and grateful. We were safe. Brooks's girls— "Wait . . ." I blinked at him, my voice a frail whisper. "Your girls?"

"My girls," he murmured, in a near daze as he put a hand on my stomach, careful of the monitors strapped to me. His fingers froze, and he looked up, realization hitting him. "Oh, Shay. I'm so sorry. That's not how I wanted to tell you. I had this whole thing—"

I shook my head, not caring a lick about what he'd planned. If I hadn't been so concerned about Tater while they'd done the ultrasounds a few hours ago, I would've asked them to tell me. I was done waiting. Tears dripped down my cheeks again, not of guilt, but joy. "She's a girl? We're having a girl?"

He smiled and choked on a noise, caught between a laugh and a cry. "We're having a girl, sunshine."

"Shay," Brooks whispered, his cheek resting atop my head. The room was dark, and it was the middle of the night. He'd left my side only at the nurses' wishes, needing to check my vitals. I'd been afraid they'd ask him to leave, but the nurse only winked after bringing him a soda, too. He was on his side, while I lay on my back, the bed having me in a slightly angled position.

"Hmm?" I breathed him in, engraving the smell of pine and him in my mind.

After hearing nothing but beeping machines, I closed my eyes, assuming he'd fallen asleep, only to open them when he said, "I want to marry you." I blinked real hard, believing I was dreaming. "I know we haven't known each other long, and we don't have to do it right away . . . but I feel like I've loved you forever."

I ran my fingers over my lips. My grin was wide, blooming from deep in my core. Inside, I was saying: *HOLYMOLYWHATISHAPPENING?* But on the outside, I was as cool as a cucumber. "Okay."

He laughed, his chest shaking against my shoulder. "Okay? That's all?"

"That's all." I craned my head and kissed his jaw, content to stay here for the rest of my life. Well—not here, in a hospital bed—but with him, yes.

I felt his smile against my head, heard it in his voice. "Do you want your ring?"

"Of course." I stretched out my arm, wiggling my fingers. "Pop it on."

"Are the doctors sure your head is okay? Because you're being way more mellow than I expected. I was expecting you to put up a fight, make me beg."

"Mmm." I hummed under my breath. "I do like the idea of you begging."

I laughed, squirming as he nibbled at my ear. His voice was a low growl. "Marry me."

"Okay," I repeated, warmth spreading through me. I twisted onto my side, wincing at the stiffness beginning to settle in. "I'm calm because I'm happy—plus a little sleepy. But trust me, I'm absolutely undressing you in my head right now."

He sank deeper against the bed, holding me close, and kissed my forehead. "Get some sleep, sunshine."

"Wait." I waved my left hand in the air. "My ring, please." He groaned but must've known I wouldn't let it go and reached into his pocket. Plastic crinkled, and I smiled wide. I laughed, fully awake as I smacked his chest. "Brooks Graham—if that's a Ring Pop in your pocket, I'm going to marry you twice."

He leaned against me, burying his head in the crook of my neck. His smile was hot on my skin. "I grabbed it when I fueled my truck up this morning in Phoenix. It was dumb, I'm sorry. Forget I asked. Let me get you a real ring, and I'll ask you when you're not half asleep—"

"Put it on," I rasped, feeling nothing but surety. Doubt didn't exist with Brooks. I'd marry him right now if I could. "Please."

He must've heard the sincerity in my voice, as soon the wrapper crinkled and tore open. I couldn't see him, but I felt every bit of his love when he solemnly grabbed my left hand and slid the ring on. "I love you."

"I love you." My voice was full of awe as I ran my finger over the massive candy ring. I didn't know what color it was, but it was better than any diamond. And the man who gave it to me—who thought of me always, and saw me in the sun—was better than any other man. I knew we were moving fast, but I trusted myself more than I ever had before. With Declan, it had felt like I had to cut myself down to fit into his world. But Brooks and I . . . we were creating our own world. Together. *This is right.* "Thank you for turning one of the worst days of my life into the very best."

"I wish I could take all your worst days and turn them into the best."

I closed my eyes and leaned into his hold, into him. "You already have."

Chapter Fifty

I stayed at the hospital for another day, though I'd begged the doctors to let me leave. I wanted to see Wren and longed for my own bed, but I'd stopped complaining after they promised me it was for the best, wanting to ensure all was well with me and my daughter.

My daughter.

I still wasn't over it.

"Are you going to be okay if I run out and bring the truck around front?" Brooks asked. He hadn't left my side once in my time here. Since he'd come immediately after my hysterical call, most of Wren's items had still been in his truck, and Levi and Nolan had driven up yesterday to grab her things. Both slipped into my room and delivered a gentle scolding, along with a careful kiss on the forehead goodbye.

"I'm good. I have paperwork anyway." I held up the massive stack I'd been given, praying my insurance would cover it. I hadn't begun to let myself think about the expense to cover Jake's truck. "Your girls will be waiting for you to hover over us when you return."

"Say it again," he whispered, something gleaming in his eyes.

"Your girls," I whispered back, feeling the truth in my heart.

He grinned and shook his head like he didn't quite believe it. "I love that."

"Me too." And just to take it a step further, I waved my hand in the air, where I wore a bright pink Ring Pop. "Almost as much as I love my ring."

Brooks's eyes flared. He probably regretted giving it to me, especially when I told the nurses how much I loved my *fiancé*. He paused with a hand on the door, his lips straining to hide his smile. "If you eat that thing right now, I promise I'll get you a real one as soon as we get home."

I held it out, admiring it like I'd never seen anything so lovely. I hadn't. "I'm not eating it."

With a shake of his head, he walked out the door. I smiled and worked through the pile of paperwork, stopping only when my phone vibrated. The dumb thing had survived. I pulled it out of my pocket, assuming it was my OB's office returning my call to schedule the appointment that the hospital advised I get, only to see it was Elle. I'd texted her briefly after the accident to let her know I was fine, but otherwise we hadn't spoken. I wasn't angry—it wasn't her fault—but I'd been heavily distracted, and now I was antsy to get home. I'd call and make up for it later.

"Are you back already?" I asked when the door creaked open, keeping my eyes on the forms, signing signature after signature. "I'm surprised you didn't try to drive your truck inside."

When he said nothing, I looked up. It wasn't Brooks.

I swallowed, putting a hand to my stomach. "What are you doing here, Declan?"

Chapter Fifty-One

He was exactly how I remembered him. Same stoic, hard face. More pretty than handsome. The same pressure from his brown eyes. The only difference was how I felt beneath them. Every nerve in me was telling me to run, but I stayed—I was done running. Declan was quiet, assessing, leaving me without a clue as to what he was weaving in his mind. How had he even found me?

I glanced at the door behind his tall, athletic frame, wishing Brooks would open it and prove Declan wasn't real. "What are you doing here?" I repeated, knowing he wasn't a figment of my imagination.

He swallowed, and his gaze dropped to my belly. I shifted, blocking his view with my bag. "I was at the firm when it happened—Elle told me you'd been in an accident. Once she told me where you were, I came as soon as I could."

I blinked. His answer wasn't the one I wanted. "What are you doing here, Declan?"

He furrowed his brows, apparently not understanding why I was confused by his presence, like he hadn't told me and his unborn daughter to get lost. "Are you kidding me, Shay? I came all this way, to the middle of nowhere, and you have the nerve to hound me for why I'm here?" He stepped back, smearing his hand through his freshly styled hair. "Obviously I care about you. I wanted to make sure you were okay, butterfly." He glanced down, my bump still hidden from his view. "That you both were."

My hands shook as I clutched my bag tighter, not realizing how much resentment and anger I still carried for him. Before I could utter a word—or maybe chuck my bag at him—the door opened, hitting Declan in the back.

"Shoot—I'm sorry," Brooks said, easing the door open when Declan stepped out of the way, letting him into the room. Brooks eyed him for a moment before he turned his attention back to me, oblivious to who stood in the room. "Are my girls ready?"

I stared at the ground, wishing I could wither into nothing when Declan said, "Girl? We're having a girl?"

"I'm having one," I rasped, barely able to hear my words over the pounding in my chest. *I can't breathe. He can't be here.* "Brooks, this is Declan."

"I gathered that." Ignoring him, Brooks leaned down and met my gaze, searching for words I might not be brave enough to say aloud. Only after I nodded did he turn and face Declan. "We're on our way home. We have some family we need to get to. But I'm sure we could arrange something—"

"No. I'll talk to Shay now," Declan cut in, staring not at Brooks, but at his hand holding mine. I winced, realizing how he might see it as Brooks staking his claim, even though it was me who'd slipped my fingers into his, wanting his comfort. His gaze slowly trailed Brooks and sized him up. While they stood at similar heights, Brooks's frame was sturdier, solid. He seemed to hesitate, likely wondering if Brooks would deck him—not knowing how tender his hands were—and instead looked to me. "She's my baby too. I have rights, butterfly."

I bit my tongue, resisting the urge to scream. He had no rights—he hadn't wanted her. Up until now, he'd refused to acknowledge her existence. But I knew I needed to protect her, and that wasn't always done by fighting tooth and nail. I could protect her by listening, by advocating for her well-being. I looked up at Brooks, wanting to tell Declan that anything he had to say to me, he could say in front of him. Brooks was a part of her too. But I knew I couldn't, seeing how that might set him off.

I was certain I'd never loved Brooks more when his hand cupped the back of my neck, soothing the pain that once lived there, and whispered, "You're the sun."

I blinked through tears and smiled, cherishing his gentle reminder of my strength. I held on to his words, steeling my spine with them when he left. Despite who I was with, I was filled with gratitude and love when the door didn't fully shut, assuming Brooks had propped it open. I moved to the window, leaving the bed between Declan and me.

Declan didn't wait long, shaking his head with the laugh I used to love. I hadn't realized until now how lacking it was. "Really, Shay? Really?" He pointed a finger at the door. "First, you not only left me but disappeared entirely. And now you have the audacity to whore around with another man while carrying *my* baby?"

I raised my brows. I wasn't surprised by his bluntness—I just was no longer attracted to assholes. "I didn't leave you—you kicked me out. You told me to get rid of the baby or get out of your life."

"That's still leaving!"

I blinked and let out a low laugh. "You're pathetic."

"You're right, Shay. I am pathetic." The harshness in his tone eased, his hands falling to his sides. "I shouldn't have tried to force you to choose. I know it was wrong. But I didn't think you'd actually leave."

"You hit me."

His face faltered, and I didn't know if I'd stunned him for calling him out on it, or if he hadn't remembered. He confirmed it was the former when he said, "I was drunk."

I crossed my arms over my chest. "I have been around plenty of drunk men, and not one of them has wrapped their hand around my neck."

"Really?" he scoffed, his voice dry. "I mess up one time, and you're going to punish me? After all I've done for you? After all the promises we made to each other?"

I fidgeted where I stood, resisting the urge to glance at the door. I didn't want Declan to see me as weak. "You didn't seem to care about any of our promises when you found out you knocked me up."

"Because I was scared." He ran a shaky hand down his face. "I'm at the peak of my career. I thought I was going to lose everything—

"Well, you did," I muttered.

He looked me over, his eyes solemn, and sat on the edge of the bed. "And I have regretted it every day—you have no idea what I've gone through these past months. I tried finding you, but then you changed your number. And Elle wouldn't tell me where you'd run off to. I tried your mom, and she didn't answer."

I swallowed, willing his words not to affect me. Declan was intentional with his words; he'd wanted them to hurt. "I moved fourteen hours away—we both know you could've found me if you wanted to. And I called you, Declan. I gave you a chance, and you didn't want it."

"I know, butterfly," he said, the nickname grating against my nerves. "I was mad and I'm sorry. But I'm not mad anymore—and I want you to come home."

I scowled at him. "I am home," I said with all the certainty in the world. I would've felt that way even if Brooks and I weren't together. *Wallowpine is my home.* "I got lost, Declan. Just like you wanted me to. And I'm sorry—but for the first time, I've been found. And I'm not leaving."

"Really?" He stared at me, something sparking in his eyes. "After everything we've been through—all I've done for you—you're going to throw that away? For what? Some Podunk loser who will probably knock you up, one kid after another? And then he'll be too busy to take care of them cause he's screwing half the trailer park."

I rolled my eyes, wanting to pound in his ridiculous, closed-minded head. But before I could tell him just how blind he was, he begged, "Butterfly, please. Don't do this. I want to be a family. Don't we owe it to our daughter to try? Wouldn't she want that?"

I knew what I wanted to say. I believed wholeheartedly blood didn't make a family. And Brooks and me—the Grahams, Wren and Jake, the whole town—could be that for her. But Declan . . . He was her biological father. And he was here.

I swallowed my pride and found the will to say, "You and I don't have to be together for you to be her father, Declan."

He raised his brows, stunned. But rather than seeing how that situation might play out, how he could still have a role in his daughter's life, he moved to stand beside me at the window. His voice shifted into tenderness, as deceptively warm as the sun beating against my skin. *I hate it.* "I miss you, Shay. And I'm sorry for not realizing how good you were for me until you were gone. But—" He grew quiet and put a hand on my back. I froze, but I didn't shrug him off, reminding myself who I was doing this for. "You're being careless here. You're not thinking straight. And it's clear you haven't been yourself. There's pink in your hair like a child, and you're wearing a piece of candy on a finger that used to be mine." I ground my teeth and stepped away from his touch, turning to face him. "I'm sorry," he claimed, his hands up. "I won't lie and say it doesn't hurt. Because it does hurt—what you've done to me, how quickly you've moved on. You've hurt me. But I care about you, and I want you to ask yourself: do you really think you can be happy here? Think about how hard it's going to be. I know you think that man out there is going to help you, but you're wrong, butterfly. He has no reason to stay. He doesn't know you like I do—"

"You're wrong," I rasped, hating how weak I sounded, how weak I felt.

"I'm not." He leaned back against the window, looking so much like the man who'd loved me and who'd hurt me, I couldn't discern which was which. They were the same man. "I know with your . . . childhood, it makes sense that you would easily latch on to someone. You're trying to make sure our daughter has the father you never did. But, butterfly, you know how easily people leave. And that man will leave you."

"You left me," I pointed out, my fingers trembling. He was wrong. I hadn't been in search of a father for my daughter. *Brooks found us.* "You were never with me."

"I'm here now, aren't I? And I'm never going to leave you again. You or our daughter." He smiled at me, and my stomach twisted. "I know you're angry at me, but you need to think clearly. I'm sure right now you're thinking you can do this. And maybe you have been. Elle mentioned you have some sort of job. That's great—I'm so proud of you—but what are you going to do when our daughter's born? Surely you can't keep working. And I imagine you totaled your vehicle." He let out a low laugh. "Look where you are—you're in a hospital. And had you never left me, this never would have happened." He stepped forward, either not seeing or not caring how my hands shook, and propped a finger beneath my chin, raising my gaze to his. "Come home, butterfly. I need you. And whether you like it or not, you need me, too."

One tear slid down my cheek, the most I would allow. Not for myself, not even for my daughter. But for who I used to be. The girl who would've believed every word of the garbage he was spewing out, who couldn't see through his carefully set traps, who was blind to the tale he weaved.

I allowed one tear to mourn her.

And then I moved on.

"I am not your butterfly. And I don't need you," I said softly, but not weakly. "Maybe I *thought* I did before—but I don't now. I don't need anyone, at least not how you had me believing I needed you." It was true. While I craved Brooks, wanted him and his brothers in my life, it wasn't out of dependency. They'd always ensured I knew how capable I was. I lowered his finger from my chin and looked him dead in the eye. "I'm not sure what you expected to find when you came here, but I'm not the same woman who left you. So I suggest you stop talking before I make sure you never share the same air as *my* daughter."

He stared at me, wearing something that looked like surprise. But then it was gone, his face composed and cool. He straightened and adjusted the collar of his shirt, oblivious to how I eyed his tie, imagining how I'd strangle him with it. "I know you want this baby—you've made that clear. You want to make the family you never had." He brought his hands to his chest. "And I want to give that to you. It's why I came. So maybe you should take some time to think. Sure, you might be able to raise this baby alone, but that's only if you get the chance." He must've seen my confusion, sensed my resolve fracturing, because he pounced. "Oh, butterfly," he tsked, shaking his head. "I'm positive you'd be a beautiful mother, but I'm not sure a judge would see it that way. You're a college dropout. You work in a run-down, dinky tack shop. You live with your bosses and warm the bed of at least one. You have no real family or support to fall back on. I don't know your finances, but I can't imagine you have much. Especially with these unexpected medical bills. Now, maybe a judge will look past that. I know what I'd do—and that would be to put the child's best interests at heart. Are you sure that's you? Are you really willing to lose her because I made you a little mad?" He lifted his hands slowly, and when I didn't react, he set them on my shoulders. Only then did I understand his words, feeling the entirety of them upon me. "I don't want to take that from you—I want to give you your family. But if you walk away from this, from me, I have rights. I'm not afraid to seek sole custody if that's what I have to do."

I faltered at that, not knowing if I wanted to claw his eyes out or cry. Maybe both. Never once had I imagined he'd want sole custody—I'd hardly thought he'd go for partial. He'd literally lied to his boss and told her I wasn't pregnant.

But he wanted to take her from me entirely.

And for what? Because I'd moved on? He'd hurt me, manipulated me, for years, and yet I'd never tried to take her from him, at least not entirely. I'd always wanted it to be his choice—and he hadn't wanted her.

"Are you saying that if I don't come home with you, you would try and take her from me?" My voice was breathless, not quite believing it myself.

"I'm saying I want to be a family." He blew out a tired breath and shook his head, like it pained him to do this. But he did it anyway. "You know I don't lose, butterfly."

I stared at him. That's all this was to him—a game. An attempt to mark his territory, claim himself the biggest and mightiest man. But it terrified me that within this game, this ploy to have me submit, there might be some truth. I was a college dropout with hardly a dime to my name. I didn't have a house of my own. The only reason I had a roof over my head was because the Grahams had given it to me. And not only did I not have a vehicle, I'd potentially totaled one after being illegally on my phone. And unfortunately, I didn't have a glowing family behind me, at least not the sort Declan came from. Would that be enough for a judge to rule me as an unfit mother? Was Declan's threat serious, or was it all empty talk?

In the back of my mind, I knew it was nonsense. I could feel it in my bones. I was a good mother. I was more than my shortcomings and I'd grown. But as sure as that, I could feel my world unraveling, could see my dreams slipping out of my reach. I'd once thought I had nothing—but now I could see.

I was about to lose *everything*.

I'd called Declan on his bluff once before, when he told me to end the pregnancy or get out. I'd made the wrong choice and stayed—and I'd suffered at his hand because of it. I wasn't willing to see if he was bluffing now, wasn't willing to let my daughter suffer the brunt of it.

Because I knew Declan didn't lose—or at least, he didn't like to.

And in a world where Declan wins, she loses.

I looked up at him, and despite my hesitations, the fears firing through my mind, I managed an ounce of bravado. "Go ahead and try to take her from me, Declan." I narrowed my gaze and smiled, feeling none of it in my heart. "I didn't want this. I never wanted to take her away from you—I just wanted away from you. But fine, we'll go to court. But I'm not the only one who has something to lose here. If you think I won't smear your name and let it be known how you manipulated and abused me for years, then you're wrong."

"Abused you?" He reared back, his eyes wide as though I'd hit him. Like I was the one who'd wrenched his neck back and tossed him against the tile floor. Like it was me who'd gripped his throat and held his gaze, watching as I taunted his lungs with air. "You're pathetic," he spat, such disdain in his voice that I flinched. "Stop acting like you're some victim—"

"It's time for you to leave."

I didn't have to face the door, knowing exactly who the hard, gruff tone belonged to. I knew whose heat was pressed against my back, who offered me strength without even a word.

Declan shifted where he stood, turning to face Brooks. "I'd get out while you can," he sneered, his gaze following the movement of Brooks's hand as he wrapped it with mine. "She's a leech. She'll take everything from you."

My hand fell limp in Brooks's, and I wanted to curl up and hide. But Brooks held on, his voice effortlessly smooth. "I hope she does." He tipped his head to the door. "Now I'd take your own advice and get out while *you* can."

"Is that a threat?" Declan clenched his hand into a fist, assessing Brooks once more. But because he wasn't an idiot—or not a total one—he unraveled his fingers. "Enjoy my scraps. She's always been an easy lay, but at least you got a taste before that baby wrecks her—"

Brooks lunged forward, his hand leaving mine as he shoved Declan against the window. His forearm was wedged against his throat, and he leaned in, muttering something in Declan's ear I couldn't hear. Before I could beg Brooks to stop, he pushed off the window and joined my side again. Declan slumped against it, his eyes as stunned as I was as he spat, "You'll regret that, you son of—"

"Oh, cut the act, Declan." A new voice slipped in, a fresh breath of air. "Don't make a bigger fool of yourself than you already have."

If not for Brooks gripping my hand, I would've believed I was hallucinating as I stared at Elle. Her dark hair was shorter than I'd seen it, cut in an edgy pixie. Her skin was tan, full of California sun. She wore daunting red heels and a pencil skirt, not looking at all like the exhausted woman I'd last seen. But the fire in her heart was the same. "It was a mistake to let you come. You can find your own way home. And I suggest you run, because I'm going to make sure Janet hears every word of this visit."

Declan's eyes darkened at the mention of their firm manager, but he shook it off, waving a dismissive hand. "You're full of shit, Elle."

"Yeah, and you only spew it." She smiled and held out her hand, waving what appeared to be a phone. "Care to listen?"

Before I could process what she said, Declan turned to me, his jaw clenched, looking likely to shatter teeth. "See you in court."

I waited until he walked out the door before I slipped my hand free of Brooks's. I ran my fingers through my hair, gripping it by the roots as I sucked in deep breaths. I couldn't afford to panic—I needed to think.

I dropped my hands, wiping my palms on my pants. "Are you leaving with him, Elle?"

She lingered in the doorway, her gaze on the hall, likely trailing Declan and making sure he left. "No. I've got the keys to the rental car too, so that sucker's on his own."

I nodded, unable to return the smile she gave me, no matter how relieved I was to see her. "Do you have time to hang around for a bit?"

She furrowed her brows and glanced at Brooks, whom I'd done my best not to acknowledge, ignoring how his fingers brushed mine. "Yeah." She pulled her purse higher on her shoulder. "I'm here as long as you need—I'm just going to walk around for a bit, stretch my legs."

I nodded and kept my gaze on her until the door closed. My lip trembled, and a tear streamed down my cheek as Brooks put his hand on my neck, soothing the tension there. His voice was warm, reassuring. "You did good. I'm proud of you."

I brushed off his words as I did his hand and twisted to face him, my arms wrapped around me like the coward I was. "I need to go home."

"I know—I'm gonna take you home. Wren and them are waiting for you at the house." His hand reached for my elbow, missing when I stepped back. "Shay—"

"I need to go home," I pressed, willing my heart to accept what my mind had decided. "To California."

"Don't do this, Shay." His plea threatened to shatter the frail resolve I'd barely built. Enough that I allowed his heat to mix with mine, his hands cradling my jaw. "I know you're afraid. I heard what he said. But you're not going to lose her—"

"How do you know?" My voice was harsh, rough. "You heard him—he wasn't lying! Everything he said was true, and there's a real possibility a judge could decide to take her from me."

"That's not going to happen," he promised, the confidence in his voice unable to ease the fire building in me. "*Nothing* he said was true. You have built a beautiful life, Shay—"

"No." I stepped back, shrugging out of his hold. "You made me a beautiful life, Brooks. You did. I knew better than to let you in, to let you take care of me." I scrubbed my face with my hand. "I'm such an idiot. I've wasted so much time. I should've been preparing, doing everything I could—but I was so caught up falling in love with you, and now I'm going to lose her."

"You've done everything for her," he pressed, a hint of wild desperation in his tone. "Who do you think you rode that bike for so you could get to work? When you felt broken and worthless, what made you get out of bed in the morning? You're exhausted, and you didn't even complain about getting a second job. You've had your heart broken, but you were willing to risk it all and trust someone again. Who do you think that's for? I sure as hell know it wasn't for you or me—you did it for *her*." His eyes flickered, hard with anger and what looked to be sorrow. "You've made plans, Shay. We'll call your lawyer tonight. We can try and see her sooner—"

"Yeah?" I snapped, fear hot on my tongue. "And how do you think it'll look when I tell her my *fiancé* attacked the father of my child? What if they think you're violent—"

"I'm not violent," he cut in, the hurt evident on his face that I'd even suggest such a thing. "Do you have any idea how painful it was listening to him tear you down? I don't think you do—part of me thinks you're numb to it because that's how he treated you daily. And if you think I'll stand by and let anyone hurt the best thing that's ever happened to me, then you're wrong."

He didn't give me a chance to reply, to combat with another excuse, and grabbed my hands. "I know you're scared and doubting yourself, Shay. So lean on me, trust me when I tell you you're not going to lose her. We'll do everything we can to make sure of that." He weaved our fingers together, clutching as though he knew he was about to lose me. "Go get in our truck. I'm taking you home." I stayed where I was. I had no intention of leaving with him, but I couldn't form words to say it. It was taking every bit of my strength to not fall apart. Red seeped up his neck, his voice thick with emotion. "You're coming home with me, Shay."

"Wallowpine was never my home," I said, the words foreign and wrong. "It was only meant to be temporary. I needed to get away and clear my head. You helped me do that. Now it's time for me to leave."

Brooks rubbed at his jaw and scoffed like he didn't believe a word I was saying. *I don't believe it either.* "You can try to lessen it all you want, but nothing about us is temporary. We're as real as it gets, Shay. Please just get in our truck."

I shook my head. It was wrong of me to have let it go on this long. "I got distracted in my time here. And I think you and I . . . we found each other when we were trying to come out of a dark place. We were lonely and lost—and we might've confused our feelings, made it into something more than it was."

Brooks watched me, seeming to consider his words. His shoulders were low, his hands tucked in his pockets. The fight in him seemed almost gone. He wasn't going to beg, not after his mom—when he'd begged her to stay and she'd left. But I realized how wrong I was when he said, "I know you're scared, and that he put doubt in your head. But I made you a promise, and I'm not walking away from you. You're my family, and I'm going to fight for you—I'll help you fight for her."

My lip trembled, and my eyes burned, but I refused to let the emotion fall. I believed him. I knew firsthand how fiercely Brooks would come to his family's aid. How quickly he'd help me. But I couldn't have him fighting my battles.

I couldn't trust my daughter with anyone but myself.

So I said the words I knew would hurt him. What would make the love in his eyes disappear, make him stop seeing me as the sun. Maybe then, he'd finally see me for what I was—the broken butterfly with no wings. "You always said this was my choice . . . and I don't want to be a part of your family."

If my words affected him, he didn't let it show, didn't bleed from the knife I wedged in his heart. I thought he might argue some more, attempt to change my mind. Instead, he grabbed my bag from where it sat on the hospital bed and handed it to me. I accepted it and waited, foolishly waited for him to meet my gaze. Except when he did, I wished he hadn't—if only so I hadn't seen the coldness, the distrust there. He hadn't looked at me that way in so long. But somehow, he managed to ask, "Do you need a ride to the airport?"

A tear slipped down my cheek. "No."

"Did you leave anything behind at the house that you need?"

Everything. His brothers. Cash. Wren . . . oh, Wren. I was leaving her. I was leaving everyone I loved.

My breathing hitched, my blinks quick. I hadn't expected this, for our ties to be severed less than twenty-four hours after I said I'd marry him. But it was better this way, to get out before we hurt each other worse. "No," I rasped. "There's nothing there for me."

Brooks flinched, like my words had physically harmed him. But rather than hurting me back, all he said was, "I hope someday you meet someone who you're brave enough to stop being lost for."

Chapter Fifty-Two

I straightened myself at the soft tap on the door and blotted the lingering tears on my cheeks. "Hi," I croaked as Elle entered the room, closing the door behind her. "Um—can I stay with you for a while?"

She gave me a sad smile, one that didn't reach her eyes. "Of course. I kind of sensed it was heading that way. And then Brooks said something about it in the hall."

"Was he okay?" I asked, only to regret it when she gave me another look—I already knew he wasn't. "Right. Don't answer that. It doesn't matter anyway." I blew out a breath, strengthening my resolve. "All that matters is making sure I don't lose custody of Tater."

Elle snorted, shaking her head. "Like that would ever happen."

I raised my brow, blaming the bite in my words on the last hour. "Would you care to share some of your confidence with me? Because I could very well lose her." She hummed under her breath and flipped through the stack of paperwork I'd left on the bed. Why was she so calm? "Elle, he literally told me he was going to fight for sole custody—"

She looked up when my voice broke, and her eyes widened, as though she didn't understand why I was on the brink of hysterics at the thought of losing my child. "I'm sorry, Shay. I suck at this." She pulled her purse off her arm and rustled through it, then yanked out what looked to be a dirty cloth and extended it to me. She must've seen how I curled my lip in disgust, as she then explained, "It's the baby's burp rag. It's fine."

Oh, right—I love wiping my tears with baby vomit.

Not caring, I dabbed at my eyes, allowing her to steer me to the bed. She smiled, a little too wide for comfort, waiting until I finished blowing snot into her vomit rag. "Okay, let's rewind." She gripped my shoulders, turning me to face her. "You're not going to lose her. Declan's as entitled as they come, and that's saying a lot because I've worked around my fair share of men like him. I know it's hard, and it's easier to not look at what's right in front of us. And I know you—you've always tried to give him the benefit of the doubt. To see him for more than what he is. But everything Declan just did—*that's who he is*. He's a coward. He doesn't want Tater. He never asked about you, never even told his mom you were expecting. It wasn't until I had one moment of stupidity and thought you were seriously hurt that he popped back up." Moisture built in her eyes, like it pained her to say those words, but she knew it was what I needed to hear. "And you know why? Because he expected to come in here and save you. He thought you'd be weak and broken, nothing like the strong woman who left him, the one who faced him today. He came in with the intention of pissing all over you and marking you his, but you didn't let him. And that's why he walked away with little to no fight—because in the end, Declan doesn't fight hard. You want to know why he always wins? He picks the easiest cases, the quickest fights. But fighting you for Tater wouldn't be easy—you'd go in kicking and screaming, probably stop just short of killing him for your little girl." There was something fierce in her tone, and I knew it was because she understood the unwavering sort of love I felt for my daughter. I'd seen firsthand how unconditional, how powerful her own love for her children was. "He doesn't care about you or Tater. He cares about himself. And you said it best—his reputation would be ruined. Who wants to be represented by a man who abused and kicked out his pregnant fiancée?" With a little bit of a wicked gleam in her eye, she reached into her purse and waggled her phone in my face. "And if necessary, I'll help you take him down."

I frowned at the phone, not understanding when Declan's voice began playing over the speaker, mixed with pieces of mine. "Wait—" I clutched her arm, nails on the verge of breaking skin. That wasn't a phone. It was her damn recorder. "Did you record our conversation?"

She shrugged and tucked the recorder away. "I told you—I always do."

I bit my lip, not feeling the least bit comforted. She was absolutely insane. "You can't use that in court—"

"I don't need to." She grinned, her sharp brow raised. "But I can show Janet. It'll be pretty hard for him to talk his way out of this, especially when he lied to her face about you being pregnant. She won't stand for that sort of behavior. Trust me. He's already lost you—he won't risk losing anything else. Especially his reputation."

I ran a hand down my face, not sure how to process what she'd done. It felt too easy. Worse, it meant I'd let Declan manipulate me, work my nerves up into a frenzy for nothing. "What now?" I rasped, something leaden dropping in my heart. "I can't sit around and hold my breath, waiting for him to potentially take her from me. I need a plan—I need to know what he wants now. What if he pops up in ten years and decides he wants her? That would shake our entire life, everything I could've built for her—"

"Shay." Elle craned her head to look at me, her smile full of sympathy. "We take it a step at a time. I think it's really admirable that you're trying to make sure your daughter comes into a world more stable than the one you grew up in. But that's sometimes easier said than done. Especially when there are multiple hands trying to build that world. So this is what you're going to do: you're going to call your lawyer. I can't tell you exactly what she'll advise, but she'll probably tell you nothing can be done until your baby is born. But until Declan establishes paternity, he has no rights to her. She'll assure you that it takes a hell of a lot for a mom to lose her kids. She'll help you form some sort of plan." She put her hand on my knee, giving me a reassuring squeeze. "And then she'll tell you to love your little girl and be the best mom there ever was. That way, if Declan decides he wants a role in her life, it won't really matter. Because you stayed—and no one can say otherwise."

Her words had barely settled, hardly eased into my mind before she stood, cracking her neck. "My nanny quit—I need to get home. But am I driving you home to Wallowpine, or are you coming with me to California?"

Even with the reassurance Elle had given me, my breaths were raspy, my body still wild with fear. I glanced down at the ring on my finger, a reminder of what I'd done, what I'd given up in a matter of a few panicked moments. I'd barely given Brooks the chance to talk, listened to what he had to say. Yet I'd given Declan that chance. I'd let him tear me apart—it was only because of Brooks that he'd stopped at all. He'd protected me, cherished me.

And I'd thanked him by telling him I didn't want to be a part of his family.

It shouldn't have mattered, but I asked it anyway. "Did . . . did Brooks say anything outside to you?"

She gave me a tight-lipped smile, and just when I didn't think she'd reply, she said, "We didn't say much—I wanted to make sure I got it all on tape. He looked like he was about to come out of his skin the entire time, but I've never seen a man smile wider than when you told Declan off. My husband's not even that proud at our kids' T-ball games."

Brooks was proud of me—he'd told me so himself. He always told me how proud he was, and it had never been for the sake of saying it. It was the truth. He'd built me up, made me strong. Helped me find my footing and get my confidence back. He gave and gave, and I took in return.

And then I left him.

Left when I promised I wouldn't.

I cleared my throat, washing away what my heart longed to say. "Take me with you to California."

There was no going home. Not when I'd burned it.

Chapter Fifty-Three

I was sixteen when I realized I was capable of more than I believed.

It was one of those moments of pure bliss—the ones I could count on one hand.

I was in the midst of a race. The sun was blistering. My tongue felt like cotton, my lungs burned, and my legs were near numb.

But something kept me going. Whether it was competitiveness or some unknown force, I didn't know. But I kept pushing, somehow finding the will, even when my mind screamed I was done. And then I saw the finish line. It was far off in the distance, and I should've felt discouraged, out of breath. But I'd somehow uncovered another well of energy. One I'd never experienced. I'd never pushed myself that far past the point of comfort. And soon, it stopped feeling like running at all.

I was flying.

That's how I could best describe it. The experience of when your body takes off and breaks free of your mind's bonds, unleashing your full potential. When your legs no longer feel like your own, and you give in. You trust your body, your instincts. You trust your heart to carry you the rest of the way and remember you possessed the strength to do this all along.

So when I left the hospital, made the drive to Phoenix, and boarded a plane, I told myself that feeling was coming. I'd done the right thing, and this pain wouldn't be forever. I wouldn't always ache, be this hollow.

I was going to build a home, a life for my daughter and me.

She was the extra strength I never knew I had.

Chapter Fifty-Four

California sucked.

Wiping poop off chubby, toddler-sized fingers sucked.

Being thirty-four weeks pregnant sucked.

But thankfully, this wasn't permanent.

"Are you sure you have to leave?" Elle asked, nursing her wine like her life depended on it. "Can't you stay at least until after she's born?"

"I was supposed to leave last week," I reminded her, watching from her back porch as her two toddlers ran through the backyard, squealing and howling at the moon. I glanced at the baby monitor on the table between us, surprised they hadn't woken their sister. "Besides, we know once she's born, you'll only try harder to get me to stay."

"It's my kids, isn't it? They're driving you crazy, and now you're doubting if you actually like kids," she whined, plopping her head back against the chair. "I promise it's different when they're your own. But really—I appreciate you coming out here to help me with the kids. It means a lot."

Elle's kids were great, but I'd definitely questioned my sanity the last month and a half. I'd stopped having fun somewhere around Christmas, after her three-year-old wiped his booger on me and licked it off my arm. Couldn't say I blamed her last nanny for quitting.

I stretched out my legs and rested my hands on my belly—my own personal shelf. Don't have a table? No problem—I've got a belly. "I didn't come here out of the goodness of my heart. More like I was desperate and hungry."

She grinned from behind her glass, wiggling her brows. "Some could say I took advantage of a vulnerable, helpless woman. It could probably hold up in court."

I laughed—a real one. "I've loved being here, Elle. So thank you."

I hadn't anticipated staying long in California. I wanted to clear my head, maybe go to the beach. But it was just the place I was born—not home. I did go to the beach, only to realize I hated sand when I couldn't easily bend over to clean my toes. The waves were too loud, different from the breeze shifting through the mountain meadow. The streets were too busy, the air too muggy. It was all wrong.

I missed Arizona.

So I'd go back. Not to Wallowpine, but to Hillshire. I loved living in the mountains, craved that slow pace. It was larger than Wallowpine, but it made sense to live close to Dr. Malitina and the hospital. At least I wouldn't have to worry about delivering on the side of the road. I'd planned to go after Christmas, but Elle had convinced me to wait, finish the holidays with her family. Make sure I really wanted Arizona as a home, and not just a hiding spot.

I wanted it.

I had two jobs waiting for me. I'd already started one, teaching English online to children in other countries. The late nights had aged me at least twenty years, but most of my students were great—except the one who'd nicknamed me Humpty Dumpty. Little shit. But my savings had grown, and I'd probably quit when I started my job in Hillshire. It was a receptionist position at a local optometrist office. They must've been as desperate as I was, as they hadn't even batted an eye when I told them I'd likely only work a few weeks before I went on maternity leave. It wasn't my dream job, but it would work while I figured out what I wanted to do.

"Does mountain man know you're coming home?"

My gut twisted, but I blamed it on my daughter. She was running out of room, and any day I expected my stomach to explode. "No. And unless we have a run-in at Walmart, I'll never see him."

I hadn't heard a word from Brooks or his brothers. I'd checked my phone constantly those first few weeks, hoping at least one of them would reach out. On Christmas, I'd peeked out the window more than once, foolishly hoping they'd surprise me with a visit. I missed them badly, and the holidays seemed to make it worse. I was grateful to be with Elle's family, but it wasn't *my family.*

I'd broken my family.

But not enough that it stopped one person from Wallowpine from reaching out.

As though summoned, my phone thrummed inside my jacket pocket. It was seven, and she was calling right on the dot for our nightly visit. We hadn't once broken our routine, not even when I'd moved. She'd called that first night I left, and I thought it was to scream at me. But she acted as though nothing had happened—she told me she hated the snow, and that Phoenix might have its perks after all. Aware of the routine, Elle raised her glass in parting. "Good night," I said, squeezing her hand. "See you in the morning."

I waited to answer until I was alone inside the casita, away from any children's ears. I never knew what Wren might say, and I loved it. "Hey, Wren."

"It's about time. I thought maybe you rolled down a hill again and were too busy trying to get back up to answer your phone."

I groaned. It was a good thing I was leaving. Elle's kids were going to be the death of me. Last week, on a day they were being particularly rowdy, I'd taken them on a walk. The weather was overcast and mild, perfect for stir-crazy demons. At least it was, until the two oldest took off, and I chased after them—thus falling down a hill.

I was fine. But I was seriously questioning if I liked kids.

I plopped down on the bed, setting the papers I'd left scattered on it this morning onto the nightstand. "I think you might need an extra dosage of those gummies, Wren. You're sounding all cranky."

She rasped a laugh, and my heart ached, missing the loud, full one she once bellowed. "How much longer until you pop that baby out? I'm tired of your moods."

I laughed, running a hand over my stomach. "Six weeks." *Forever. I have forever left.*

"Hm—doubt I'll be around then. Do me a solid and push Tater out now."

I swallowed, my throat tightening. Wren had stopped treatments weeks ago. The cancer was too aggressive, moving at a faster rate than the treatment could touch. Rather than trying another route, Wren had called it quits. She hated the hospital, and the city even more. Maybe I shouldn't be surprised, heartbroken—after all, she'd told me on more than one occasion she was dying—but the thought of Wren . . . It was too heavy. I glanced at my journal on the nightstand, fingers itching with the need to jot down the words I couldn't say aloud. When I'd left Wallowpine, I'd only had my bag with me. I'd known it was in there, but it was still quite the knife to the gut to find the journal Brooks gave me. I'd stuffed it away, intent on forgetting about it—but then, on a night when the grief was too heavy, I grabbed it.

And I wrote.

Nothing significant or life changing. I was rusty and awkward, but I wrote words I'd never speak aloud. Mostly because I'd lost the one person I felt safe enough to share those thoughts with. But somehow, it felt like I was still sharing them with him.

I cleared my throat, swallowing the emotion there. "You're just gonna have to suck it up and wait. I need you when I'm delivering."

I leaned back against the headboard and closed my eyes, pretending I was in a world where that wasn't Wren hacking in the distance. She coughed again, the sound deep and throaty. "Trust me, sugar. You don't want me there. I'm liable to hit that doofus baby daddy of yours with my cane."

I laughed, imagining the sight vividly. I could only hope she'd let me take a swing, too. Though Declan wouldn't be at the hospital while I delivered. I was still clueless about his intentions—he'd ignored both my calls. I thought of when I told my mom I wanted to live with my biological father, the fear that seemed to cross her face at the idea of losing me. I understood that fear now. The thought of losing my daughter made me sick.

But I wasn't my mother. I wouldn't live in fear.

As soon as she was born, my lawyer was set to request a paternity test. I could do it now, but I'd decided to wait, let emotions settle. Regardless, Declan would have to acknowledge her, decide if he wanted rights or if he'd sign them away. But I wasn't going to live for him—he'd stolen too much from me already.

I shouldn't be surprised I hadn't heard from him. Maybe he was busy. After all, a little birdie had told me he was looking for another firm to join, after being dismissed from his former one for questionable behavior. Not that I had any idea about that.

"Well, I want you there." I kicked off my sandals and frowned at my swollen toes, not knowing the last time I'd fit in a real shoe. "I'll need you to tell me if I poop or not when I'm pushing—"

"Are you coming home, Shay?"

I scrubbed at my face with my palm, dreading where this was going. "I leave in the morning. It'll give me a few days to get settled before I start that job in Hillshire."

"Don't be a tease. I want to know if you're coming home."

"No, Wren," I sighed. "I'll come visit you, but I'm not moving back."

"I can't believe you just gave up," she mumbled, so faintly I strained to hear her over the beeping machine in the background.

"I haven't given up," I rasped, feeling like a ton of bricks had dropped on my chest.

"How have you not?"

"What about you?" I asked before I could stop myself, finally voicing what I'd held in these past few weeks. "You stopped treatment. You quit fighting—"

"I am fighting," Wren said, an edge of fire in her tone. "I have been fighting for months and I'm *exhausted*." Tears welled in my eyes, my throat constricting, even more when I heard the emotion in her voice. "I'm seventy-six, Shay. I'm old, and my body is done. I've given months to this disease, sacrificed time when

I'd rather have been with my family. And I'm not giving it any more. My life isn't over yet, and I want to be home."

"But you kept telling me you were fine—"

"I might've fibbed a little and said I felt good, but I didn't know it was spreading. Even if I had, I wouldn't have told you or anyone," she said, her voice surprisingly steady. "People treat you differently when you're sick. They pity you. They hold their tongue and walk on eggshells. And if my days were numbered, I just wanted them to be real. I didn't want this disease to take anything else from me."

"I'm sorry," I said, remembering when Wren had confessed she hated people hovering over her. Shame and regret filled me. I knew it was different, that our journeys weren't the same—but I thought of how I didn't want to be defined by what had happened to me. I wasn't my abuse, and Wren wasn't her cancer. "I'm so sorry. I just don't want to lose you—"

"Never," she breathed, her tone even fiercer than before. "I told you, not a day goes by where I don't think about my kids. And you're a part of that, Shay. That sort of love doesn't bow to time or distance. I'm with you always."

I rolled onto my side, tears dripping onto the pillow beneath my head. I could remember my life before Wren, but I couldn't fathom a world she wasn't a part of. It was quiet for a long moment, and I thought she might've fallen asleep, but still I said, "I hurt Brooks. Bad."

"So?" she asked, as though I hadn't intentionally gutted the man I loved. "Who's to say he can't forgive you? You've forgiven him before."

I shook my head. It wasn't that easy. Maybe if I'd hurt him differently. Brooks had trusted me. Opened himself up to the sort of intimacy not all were brave enough to share. He'd removed his armor, his mask, fully vulnerable and raw. I'd seen his fears, his flaws, his burns. I held his heart. But then I'd taken the pain and insecurities he'd shared with me and made them into a weapon. *I don't want to be a part of your family.* I'd broken my promise and left him. If the roles were reversed, if Brooks had chosen to hurt me in the way Declan had, reopening those old wounds, I didn't know if I could forgive him.

"He hasn't tried calling me," I tried, dismissing her. "He could've reached out."

"Have you?"

No. I was a coward and couldn't bear it if he rejected me. Somehow sensing I wouldn't respond, Wren said, "This might be a surprise—but I have a few regrets in my life. That's what death does to you. It forces you to sit and wait, watching as you torture yourself with what you would've done differently." I sat up, wary at the sound of her choppy, labored breathing. "It's a living hell. Because a lot of good, wonderful moments are being tainted with pain. And I think you're doing the same thing. I don't know what happened, because neither of you will talk about it. But you're allowing your pain, your fears, to ruin what were likely some of the best moments of your life—both of you are. But you're not dying, Shay. You don't have to sit in it and wait. You can change it. You can claim the life you want. It's yours for the taking."

I knew she was right. I believed it with every fiber of my being. But I also knew not everything was forgivable. Some steps couldn't be wiped away. Not all burns healed. I couldn't claim the life I wanted if I'd broken it.

"I should get ready for bed. It's a big day tomorrow," I murmured, scooting off the mattress. "I'll call you tomorrow night?"

"Of course," she whispered, all the previous fight in her voice gone. "I want to hear all about the big day."

Chapter Fifty-Five

You know what I hate about airplanes?

Peanuts.

But my daughter must have had the nose of a bloodhound, because all I craved on the short flight from California to Phoenix was a peanut butter sandwich. Emphasis on the butter. I'd cut myself off cold turkey since I'd left, and I was feeling every bit of withdrawal.

"This is better." I gagged down a hot ham sandwich, one I'd bought from the deli inside the airport after I'd landed. "We don't need peanut butter."

We did, we really did. But if anything, at least I had my sweet Betsy.

Being the stubborn woman she was, Wren had somehow convinced one of her kids to drive my car up to the airport a few days ago, ensuring I'd have the transportation I needed. In the end, Jake's truck hadn't been totaled, so I didn't feel all that bad taking Betsy back. Plus, the checks I sent weekly to cover the repair costs lessened the guilt. But I was afraid with Wren's kids temporarily staying with her, it meant she was worse than I thought and I'd need to face Wallowpine sooner than I'd like. I couldn't stand the thought of not seeing her one last time.

I fished the extra key she'd mailed a week ago out of my purse, never thinking I'd be on the verge of tears at the sight of my dear Betsy. I sucked in a deep breath of fresh air—it was the city, so not that fresh—and climbed in after tossing my suitcase in the back. I rubbed my cramping thighs. I'd have hell to pay once I completed this drive. I turned on my phone and texted Elle to let her know I'd landed and I'd see her in a few weeks. Having learned my lesson the last time, I went to power off my phone, only to notice a missed call.

Wren.

Not willing to face her wrath, I called her back, assuming she wanted to know if I made it. But when the ringing stopped, it wasn't her voice that said, "Hello?"

"Um—" I glanced at the screen, making sure I'd called the right person. "Is Wren there?"

There was a pause and what sounded like distant chatter before she said, "Is this Shay Graham?"

I winced but didn't correct her. It was no doubt an attempt from Wren to get me to reconsider coming home. "Yes?"

"This is Jules, Wren's daughter. I know we never officially met, but I helped you rent the cabin."

"Oh yeah—" I bit the inside of my cheek. Why had she called me? "I don't live there anymore, if that's why you're asking. Your parents sold it . . ."

"I know." Her breaths were rapid and shaky. "Um—there's really no other way to say this, and I'm sorry it's not in person, but my mama passed away last night."

"What?" I rasped. My voice sounded all wrong, distant. But . . . but I'd just talked to her last night. "She's gone?"

"Yeah," she said, her words edged with a sob. "She never woke up."

My vision blurred, a cry lodged in my throat. I shoved it down, knowing what Jules must be feeling was a hundred times worse. She'd lost her mom. "I'm so sorry, Jules. I can't imagine what you and your family are going through."

"It's okay." It wasn't, but I didn't counter her. What good would it do? "She's not hurting anymore. She's free."

"Yeah." I wiped at my cheeks, clenching my jaw. "How's Jake?"

"He's alright. Been sleeping most of the day."

I nodded, not knowing what to say. I waited, expecting her to wrap up our call, surprised when she asked, "Mama told us last night you were coming home today. Are you okay to drive? Do you need someone to come get you?"

"Um—" I closed my eyes, tears seeping past my lashes. She was in the midst of great loss and grief, and she wanted to help me? But of course she did. Her mom was Wren. "I'm okay."

"Alright. But we'll see you at the service tonight, right?"

"Tonight?" I asked, certain I'd heard her wrong. I'd never been to a funeral, but could it really be thrown together that quickly?

"I know," she said. "Mama started declining pretty quickly this past week, so everyone came home. We decided it was best to honor her while everyone was in town." Through the line, a door slammed shut and an engine started. "It's at the chapel at six. Listen, I've gotta go and get things ready. I know you've got a drive, so no pressure making it. I'm sure my dad would love to see you though."

"Okay." The word was a puff of air, empty. "Goodbye."

The line fell silent and I stared at my phone, letting it rest on my palm. What was I supposed to do? How did I grieve, process what just happened? I'd talked with her last night. I'd laughed and argued with her, felt her love—and now she was gone. Worst of all, I hadn't known she'd declined so rapidly. I knew she wouldn't get better, but I hadn't anticipated it to be so soon. Had she known?

She'd had to. She'd asked me to come home, but I'd thought that was for Brooks, not for herself. *And I didn't.* I'd been too much of a coward, consumed by my own fears, to say goodbye to the woman who was a pivotal force in my life.

I'd never see her again.

A sob slipped past my lips, and I cried, sucking down gasps of air. I didn't know how to do this. There was too much in me, and I couldn't breathe. I couldn't breathe, it was too heavy—

I reached for my bag and dumped its contents on the seat. Fingers shaking, I found a pen and grabbed my journal, needing the words out. I stumbled through the pages, not realizing I'd opened it backward. Tears pooling, I flipped it over, stopping when I noticed the last page wasn't blank. I wiped at my eyes, smearing mascara on my fingers, and blinked rapidly to clear the tears, not sure if I could trust what I was seeing.

Shay,

I hope if you're reading this, it means you found the courage to write again and used every bit of space in this journal. But on the high likelihood you opened it up immediately to the last page as soon as I handed it to you, I love you. And now I'm praying you didn't read this page first, because I really don't want the first time I tell you I love you to not be with my lips. But wow, I love you.

Maybe you're reading this with me beside you in bed, maybe you're laughing and calling me cheesy. (I really hope that's what we're doing.) But on the chance you're not with me, and you're somewhere across the world, I want you to know I still love you. I think I might've loved you the first moment I saw you, and that might've been why I was the grumpiest man on the planet, because holy hell—I was in love and that was terrifying.

I'm proud of you. So proud. And no matter what, if our paths stay the same or break apart, I know I'll always love you. And every time the sun rises and sets, I'll think of you. I'll be grateful that I was able to experience your warmth up close, and that I can still witness your light even from afar.

I told you once I thought Dad brought you into our lives. Maybe you brushed it off, but I meant it. Maybe this is wishful thinking, and maybe it's because he never left when he was alive, but I have a hard time believing that sort of love and devotion just disappears because he died. Regardless if it was fate or not, I'm grateful you're in my life. And if you aren't in it, I'm really hoping Dad can pull some strings and bring you back to me. Or maybe he'll kick my ass, and tell me to go find you. So, I guess the point I'm trying to get across is, whether you're at home waiting for me or across the country—I'm coming for you.

Brooks.

NOLAN, IF YOU'RE READING THIS—GET OUT OF SHAY'S STUFF.

I stared at the page, reading it again and again. I didn't know when Brooks had written this. Where we'd been at the time. Did he remember it? If so, would he regret it now? I didn't know, but all I could think of was the massive weight pushing in on me and how badly I needed to relieve it. What was Brooks feeling? His brothers? They'd lost their aunt, a woman who'd stepped in when their mother left. Were they hurting? Were they safe?

I wiped my eyes and blew out a shuddering breath. I couldn't drive until I calmed down. I'd never been confident in what happened after death, if there was a resting spot for our spirits. Brooks believed his father brought us together, that his love and devotion didn't go away just because he died. And as I glanced through the window and peeked up at the sky, I thought there might be something more too.

I was going home. And I couldn't help but wonder if Wren and Wayne had planned it themselves.

Chapter Fifty-Six

Holy balls, it was freezing.

When I'd landed in Phoenix, it was a balmy eighty. Similar enough to California's weather that I felt comfortable in leggings, sandals, and a thin sweater. But hell must've frozen over and sent a blast to Wallowpine.

I trudged my way through the inches of snow and up to the church. It was after six, but I hoped to catch a bit of the service. If I wasn't so afraid of Wren striking me with lightning, I wouldn't have come at all. I wanted to honor her differently, but once I drove into town and saw the snow, I knew there was no way I could safely drive Betsy off-road.

I paused at the chapel doors, my toes bright red from the snow. What was I doing here? I looked like hell—I had no business stepping into a church. I wasn't even wearing black. Deciding I'd wait in the car and find Jake after the funeral, I turned.

Carefully, I inched down the steps—if I fell, there was no way I'd get back up—freezing when I caught sight of a red Jeep pulling in. *Oh, please don't be them.* What was I thinking coming here?

They didn't want to see me, didn't want my comfort.

They didn't need me like I needed them.

I hastened my steps, waddling as fast as I could to Betsy. Fingers numb, heart racing, I pulled open the door and stuffed myself inside. I inhaled a deep breath and blew it out, breathing myself through my tightening stomach. It wasn't a real contraction, I knew that by the lack of pain, but man, Braxton Hicks were a real Karen.

Ready to go, I opened my eyes—then screamed, shocked to find a set of blue eyes peering down at me through the window. I patted my legs and made sure I hadn't leaked pee, holding on to my dignity. Confirming I was dry, I rolled down the window.

"Darlin'."

The word hit me like a force of air. It took all I had to not climb out and wra myself around Nolan. His hair was combed, neater than I'd ever seen it, and h wore a white button-up and black slacks. "Hi," I whispered, not missing th tight strain of his lips. "I heard about Wren. I—I hope it's okay I came."

He didn't voice it, but I knew it was when he arched a brow, his dimpl popping through with his smile. "You don't own a dress?"

I choked on a laugh and shook my head. "I wasn't aware I'd be attending funeral when I boarded my plane this morning."

He smirked before he glanced up over the hood of my car, and when followed his gaze, there was Levi. "Come on," Nolan said to me, the do creaking as he pulled it open.

I started to protest, but there was something about the weight in his eyes, th redness within them, that had me pausing. I hadn't come here for me, I'd con here for *them*. Pushing my insecurities aside, I climbed out of the car. Had I n been dried out, I would've cried when Nolan slipped his hand into mine.

I let him lead me around the car to where Levi was. He was dressed similar to his brother, wearing a black suit jacket that made him look older than he w He must've seen the way I shivered, as he shucked it off and extended it to m

Having no interest in being a human popsicle, I accepted and shrugged suit jacket on. "I'm sorry about Wren. I know you guys loved her."

"We did," Levi agreed, tucking his hands in his pockets. "But you loved her, too." The corner of his lips tipped up in a half-hearted smile. "She'd be happy you came home. We're happy you're here."

I nodded, swarmed with more emotions than I'd anticipated. Especially when I scanned the parking lot, searching for who was missing. Knowing exactly who I was looking for, Nolan softly said, "He's not here."

My heart ached, and I must've shown it, or maybe they needed someone to lean on as much as I did them, but Levi grabbed my hand too, his fingers cold in mine. But then, when they steered me away from the chapel, I wondered if it was so I couldn't run away. "I thought we were going to the funeral?"

"I hate funerals," Nolan stated matter-of-factly.

I raised my brow—I was pretty sure no one *loved* funerals. I was about to tell him that when Levi said, "Wren won't mind. She knew how much we hated Dad's funeral. She wouldn't expect us to go to hers."

"Pretty sure I heard her tell Jules the only reason she was letting them host one for her was because she wouldn't be there to suffer through it," Nolan quipped back, dropping my hand as he opened the passenger door to the Jeep.

Despite the circumstances, I snorted. *That* sounded exactly like something Wren would say. "Wait," I said as Levi released my hand and Nolan motioned for me to climb in the passenger seat. "If you weren't planning on going, why are you here?"

Nolan gave me a smile, the sight more sad than anything. "We knew you were coming today. And when we heard you weren't in Hillshire, we came here."

"We didn't want you to be alone," Levi said, his voice a soothing chord.

I shuddered a breath, feeling like it was the first one I'd taken in weeks. Waves of grief, gratitude, and relief washed over me. I didn't care how they knew I hadn't gone to Hillshire, and I didn't know how I could possibly deserve them. But I was so thankful for them.

They didn't want me to be alone.

I climbed into the Jeep without another thought. It didn't matter where we were going. Anywhere with them was home. But still, I asked anyway, "Where are we going?"

Nolan squeezed my shoulder from the back seat as Levi shifted the Jeep into gear and said, "A dose of pine sounds good to me."

Chapter Fifty-Seven

Maybe I'd been too quick to assume Nolan and Levi had forgiven me.

I assumed we were going to where Brooks once took me, where his dad would take him and his brothers when they needed to be away from the world. It was where I'd wanted to go to honor Wren before, only to have my plans thwarted by the snow. Levi's Jeep was a champ and maneuvered the slick mountain roads without a problem.

It was when he pulled to the side of the road and flicked off his lights that I realized there might be a problem. I tapped my fingers on the side of the door, telling myself nothing was wrong. If they wanted to yell—or maybe murder me—they would've pulled the trigger already. Sitting in the complete dark in silence, except for the radio faintly playing, was completely normal.

Unable to take it anymore, I said to Levi, "Did you end up applying for that art school?"

He nodded, his voice low. "Yeah. I'm not sure if I got in, though. I haven't heard anything back."

"You will." There wasn't a trace of doubt in my mind. Levi was talented, even more so for being brave enough to face it again. I glanced in the back seat at Nolan as his phone flickered, lighting up the cab. I rubbed my temples, my eyes heavy from the stress of the day. I didn't want this to end, but I was afraid I'd fall asleep if I didn't call it quits now. "I should probably go," I started, stretching out my legs. "I was supposed to meet my landlord in Hillshire hours ago. I don't want her to think I ditched her."

"So you moved back, huh?" Nolan asked, texting on his phone. "California wasn't working for ya?"

It never worked for me.

But I didn't voice that. They knew me, so they knew it didn't work for me. "I left to clear my head. I only stayed longer because my friend needed help with her kids," I said, sensing Nolan wanted an explanation. "I was afraid. I thought Declan was going to take my daughter from me. I panicked."

"And is he?" Levi ground out, his voice uncharacteristically hard. "Is he going to try and take Tater from you?"

"I don't think so . . . I reached out, but he's been silent. Maybe it's dumb, but I like to think if he really wants a place in her life, he won't risk losing her altogether." I shook my head, shame filling my heart. "I overreacted, and I'm sorry."

Nolan surprised me when he said, "I'm not sure I'd call it overreacting. I mean—I would've liked to say goodbye, and it would've been better if you were around to help us move your stuff out, but we always understood, darlin'."

I internally winced, not expecting my heart to throb at the realization they'd moved my things out. *They've moved on*. I needed to do the same. "I'm sorry for not saying goodbye. And even more so that I left you behind to deal with my mess."

"It's alright," Levi murmured. "I'm sure you can find some way to make it up to us."

I nodded, hoping I didn't come across too eager. I was thrilled at the possibility of being in their lives at all. I glanced at Levi as he thrummed his fingers on the dash, making no move to leave at all. "Um . . ." I hesitated, not wanting to be a pest, but I was thirty-four weeks pregnant and couldn't hold my pee in much longer. "I really should go—"

"Remember that time you ripped me a new one when I kept complaining about my mom leaving?" Nolan cut me off, his voice eerily calm as he set his phone down. I opened my mouth to protest, never once thinking he'd been *complaining*, but he shook his head, beating me to it. "Well, I thought about doing that to you after Brooks got home and I realized you weren't coming. I wanted to holler at you for allowing that *man* to get in your head and make you believe you were small. That the life you built was any sort of less than. And maybe someday I will give you a little grief over it—but right now, I'm happy you're home. And I really hope you stay. Not in Hillshire, but *home*."

I burned. Everything in me *burned*. He couldn't know how much I needed to hear that, to know I hadn't completely lost everything. And while I could sense his hurt, his frustration toward me, I was so grateful for it. All my life, I'd been a shadow. No one cared where I went, so long as I stayed out of the light. I'd thought I was nothing, but I could see that I was *something* to Nolan, to Levi.

"It's not that simple," I murmured, not knowing what better explanation to give.

"Why?" Levi pressed, not letting me have an out when I shook my head. "Tell us why. Help us understand."

My voice was a low rasp, choked with grief. "Did he tell you what I said?" I looked at both of them with tearful eyes, waiting until they nodded in confirmation. "Then you know why I can't come home after what I did. How is me leaving any different than your mom leaving you guys?"

Nolan reared back, his eyes pained in a way I'd never seen. So much, I couldn't bring myself to look away, not even when a pair of headlights appeared on the road. "We're not your kids, Shay . . . And yeah, our mom left us. But you know what hurt us the most?" he asked, his eyes pooling. "She never came home. She didn't come back for us. But you did." He grabbed my hand and grasped so hard, I thought he would never let go. "There's nothing to forgive, Shay."

I crumbled, hot tears sprawling down my cheeks. "Shit," Nolan cursed and inched his way up into the front as far as he could. "I'm sorry, darlin'—I wasn't trying to make you cry. I just wanted you to know there's nothing you could do to make us stop loving you."

I opened my mouth to tell him I loved them too, but a sob broke out instead. It was as though a dam had been broken, and I was releasing the tears of every overly emotional pregnant woman in the world. "Please stop crying," Nolan soothed, like he expected that to work. His hands cupped my jaw, his words edged with a nervous laugh. "Darlin', if you don't pull it together in two seconds, you're gonna get my ass kicked."

I looked up then, about to tell him to shut up and get comfortable with tears, when I realized there was a truck pulled up beside the Jeep. Not just any truck—a forest ranger's.

My forest ranger?

No. Not mine anymore.

I glanced at Nolan, and then Levi, both giving me nervous smiles, probably not having a single clue what to do with me. I didn't believe it was real, that it was really him, until Brooks climbed out of his truck.

I didn't know if he could see me through the tint of the window, but I felt every bit of his gaze on me. He wasn't wearing a suit like his brothers, but a flannel and jeans. His beard was longer, his hair scruffy—but he looked every bit like the man I loved.

Sensing I didn't know quite what was going on and needed an extra push, Nolan said, "He went to Hillshire, Shay. And I imagine the speeding ticket he got for hauling ass back here, combined with the cold, has made him pretty damn grumpy. So I'm gonna need you to do us a solid and bat your eyelashes at him."

I snorted, both at the idea of Brooks getting a speeding ticket and that Nolan believed batting my eyelashes would have any effect on his older brother. But I didn't voice that. I was too dumbstruck. Brooks had gone to Hillshire . . . for me?

I looked at him, and then at his brothers, thinking of the woman who'd brought us together again and remembering what Wren had shared with me last night.

You can change it. You can claim the life you want. It's yours for the taking.

Tater kicked my ribs, apparently believing I needed the extra nudge. So, telling myself to face my fears, to let them work with me, I reached for the handle. A gust of frosty air swept in as I opened the door. "Are you guys not coming?" I asked when neither made a move to leave.

Levi shook his head and started his Jeep. "We'll see you at the house." His throat bobbed as he watched me, eyes full of emotion I hadn't seen him often wear. "In case you forgot," he said with a small, reassuring smile, "I've always wanted to be your friend, and that doesn't change, whether or not you and my brother are together, alright? So don't run from us. We'll find you every time."

Fearing I'd cry again, and not wanting Nolan to get his ass kicked, I stepped out of the Jeep, feeling stronger yet more vulnerable than I ever had. I wasn't a risk-taker. I'd done what I needed to survive, whatever would make the least ripple effect. But I was going to take one now. I'd put my heart, my soul, everything on the line, because I knew if I didn't, I'd lose even more.

Brooks was worth the pain.

I only had to hope he thought I was, too.

I rounded the hood of the Jeep and faced the man who held my entire heart in his hand. Before, I'd hoped he wouldn't realize how much power he held over me. But now, I wanted him to know. "Is it too late to get in our truck?"

Chapter Fifty-Eight

The world was big.

It was also kind of small.

At least, that's how it felt when I climbed in the truck, and Brooks drove the remaining distance to the spot in the woods he'd gone with his dad. Where he'd once taken me, giving me a break from the world, a chance to free myself of words I'd carried for too long. Neither the silence nor the darkness of night had broken by the time we made it. Our view was obscured, the stars not offering the faintest hint of the cliff within our reach. And as I sat there, without the slightest clue if Brooks could forgive me, I thought of what was below. How I could hop out of the truck and, with one misstep, plummet to my end. But I didn't focus on that. I focused on the surety of Brooks beside me, on the sticky candy ring I clutched within my purse, proof that he once loved me.

There was a big, unknown world out there.

There was one here, too. One between him and me.

Trying to figure out how I might heal it, I asked, "How are you doing about Wren—"

"I'm fine." His gaze stayed ahead of him, never once straying my way. He'd rather look at nothing than face me. But somehow, he must've seen the way my mouth fell, heard the stammer of my heart, because he whispered, "I'm sorry."

He looked at me then, and I could only see the shadows and lines of his face, but I felt the unsteadiness in his eyes. "I don't know how to put what I'm feeling into words yet . . . but thank you for coming here with me."

I nodded, fearing his lack of words was because he didn't want to share them with *me*. But as I thought of where we were, what the purpose of this spot was, I quietly reassured myself. His thoughts were heavy right now, and I was as much a refuge for him as this spot was.

"And you?" he asked, his gaze straight ahead again.

"Today's been . . . a lot." I fidgeted with a loose button on Levi's suit jacket. "I don't think I've quite absorbed it." There was a cocktail of emotions swimming through me, and I didn't know how to process it. But I wasn't running from it like I'd done before, when I'd hidden, stuffing away the grief, fear, and guilt consuming me all those months ago. Now I acknowledged it, finding comfort in finally understanding I couldn't conquer it all in one day.

Day by day, step by step, piece by piece, I'd sort my way through it.

I'd have to do the same with Brooks.

I thought he might realize that too when he asked, "What are you doing here, Shay?"

I stared at my palms on my lap, thinking of the first time he'd asked me that, at the cabin soon after I'd come to Wallowpine. We'd been in a much different place at the time, though I supposed it resembled where we were now, too. Dancing around one another, never turning our backs, afraid of getting hurt. Before, I'd brushed the question off—I hadn't known the answer. But now I did. "I wanted to come home."

He plucked his hat off his head, smoothing his fingers through his hair. "Thought you said this wasn't your home."

"I said a lot of things I didn't mean." I bit my lip and waited, resisting the urge to wander off and hide. No more running, no more being lost. If Brooks wanted to face this head-on, then so would I. "I can't tell you how sorry I am. How much I've regretted how I reacted, what I said." I swallowed, panic rising the longer he stayed silent. "I was scared, and I took it out on you. I shouldn't have done what I did—even as I was saying it, I knew it wasn't true. Yes, I was lonely and lost, but that played no role in me falling in love with you. I fell in love with you because you're a good man. You're fiercely loyal and you love large. But most of all, you never made me feel like I needed to change. And I never thanked you for that. For finding a way to see past how broken I was—"

"Broken?" Brooks asked, my heart burning at the softness in his tone. "I never saw you as broken. Every part of you was always just Shay to me. And I don't think you'd be whole without every bit, even the parts of you that hurt. It's made you who you are. So I don't see how that's broken at all." He leaned against the steering wheel, his gaze still onward. "I'm sorry, too. I never should've reacted how I did with Declan."

"You were just protecting me." It hadn't taken me long to see that. It had been a shock to see Brooks react physically, even if he hadn't taken it far. And while I didn't want him protecting me that way, I understood why he did it. If our roles had been reversed, and I was forced to listen to anyone tear him down, I would've stopped at nothing to defend him.

He faced me, the moonlight hitting the sorrow in his half smile just right. "I could've protected you differently. I should've protected you both. Not put you and your daughter at risk of being separated."

I shook my head. I didn't want Brooks to feel guilty in the slightest way. "It wasn't your fault—Declan knew what he was doing. He would've threatened to take her whether or not you were there. He's always known how to hurt me." I pursed my lips, gathering the words I knew I needed to say. "I can't blame him for everything. Yes, he scared me—and I was terrified to lose Tater. But I didn't have to push you away, too. I mean, you were afraid, but you didn't hurt me. And I'm sorry. I know I can't undo it, but you should know, I'll forever be grateful for you and what you did for us. You gave me a home, Brooks. I'll carry it with me forever."

Brooks watched me, and I did my best not to squirm beneath his searching gaze. "Why did you come back?"

I furrowed my brows, my voice less sure than before. "I . . . I wanted to come home."

He rolled his lips together, and I thought the light might be deceiving me when I saw a hint of a smile there. "So you're here because you want to be? Not because you have nowhere else to go?"

I shrugged. My options were limited, but that wasn't why I was here. This wasn't a last resort, a desperate attempt to find a home. If that were the case, I could've gone anywhere. *This is home.* "I'm here for me." I glanced warily at Brooks, not understanding the reason behind his deep breath. Afraid he'd tell me to get lost, I said, "I'll be in Hillshire, though. So if you're worried about me bugging you, I doubt you'll even see me—"

"I've never wanted to live anywhere but Wallowpine. It's always been my home," he said in a rush, like he couldn't hold the words in any longer. "But then you left, and I realized it wasn't home without you." I stared at him with wide eyes, hanging on to every word. "I can't tell you how many times I wrestled with the thought of bringing you back. I barely made it through Christmas morning before I got in the truck. I made it halfway to California before I turned around."

He'd come for me? Even after what I'd done, how I'd hurt him—he still thought of me as his home? "Why did you turn around?" I asked, making myself focus on that, not wanting my hopes to get out of control.

"I know you've been cornered a few times in your life, and I wasn't about to do that to you," he said as he folded up the center console separating us, though it felt like more. He was lifting his walls. "I wanted you to *want* to be here—that's all I've ever wished for. When you first came here, you were running, searching for something. And as badly as I wanted you home, I didn't want you to do it for me. I wanted you to do it for *you*." He reached for me then, and I didn't realize I was shaking until he grabbed my hand. "When we got the news about Wren, all I could think about was you. I knew you were coming today, but it wasn't until then that I decided to go to Hillshire. It wasn't to bring you home—it was just to be with you. I knew it would hurt like hell if you asked me to walk away, but I didn't care. I thought if you needed someone half as bad as I needed you, it would be worth it."

"I didn't need someone . . . I needed *you*," I admitted, my voice low so it wouldn't break. "I was drowning, I couldn't breathe—and then I opened the journal you gave me. I found your letter, and somehow you were there with me even when you weren't."

"You wrote again," he said, his voice filled with all the admiration in the world.

A single tear ran down my cheek. "You made me believe I could." It was silent for a long while as we watched one another, as though trying to find the next step. "Is this real?"

He reached for my seat belt and released the buckle, carefully pulling me onto the middle seat. His voice was smooth, confident, filling me with hope. "We're real."

My lip wobbled, and though I saw no hesitation or doubt in his eyes, I couldn't help that it appeared in my own. "I don't understand. It doesn't make sense that you could possibly still want this after I broke our family."

"You didn't break our family." His voice was soft, but there was a sort of intensity there, like he believed it with his entire being. "Yes, I was hurt, sunshine. But when we started this, I knew we'd go at our own pace. It would be unfair of me to expect nothing but smooth sailing. I knew we'd hit standstills—even take steps back. But I knew we'd do it all together."

"I'm so sorry," I repeated, believing he somehow didn't understand what I'd done. This was too easy. *I don't deserve easy.* "I was so afraid, and I know I can't take back the pain I made you feel. But I promise you, I didn't leave because I didn't want you. I left because I chose her. I had to choose *her*."

Before I might've continued to reason with him, he silenced my words with his lips. His palm rested at the back of my neck. His hold was unfaltering, as though he sensed I might try to run. I didn't deserve him—but wow, I wanted him.

I melted into the kiss, savoring his gentle firmness, letting me share what I wasn't brave enough to say aloud. He pulled back, and I followed him, afraid I'd never get the chance again, only to stop when he said, "I chose her too, Shay." His hands lingered on my hips, and he stared at my stomach, hidden beneath

Levi's jacket. I thought he might touch me there, but he looked up, holding my gaze. "I chose her. I'll choose her every time, and I know you will, too. But to do that, we also need to choose each other. No more fear, no more walking away—this is it. I'm yours, and you're mine." His throat bobbed, his voice a shaky rasp. "And she is ours."

I closed my eyes, feeling nothing but the warmth of his lips on my cheeks, catching my tears, removing the pain. "I don't know what the future is going to look like, what Declan will do. He may never acknowledge her. He might not sign away his rights—"

"I don't care." His fingers were tangled in my hair, his forehead against mine. "I don't care about him. The only good thing he's ever done is make Tater with you, and even that required minimal effort on his part. If he chooses to and is worthy to be in her life, then fine. But I'm not going to allow him to control one more moment of our life. I never cared about a piece of paper. That's not what binds me to her, or you."

I leaned into him, borrowing his strength. This was real. I hadn't lost the only family I ever wanted. "I was prepared to beg," I said, a shaky laugh following the words. "I thought it would take months before you could begin to forgive me." He leaned back, his smile holding a twinge of sadness. He looped his hands under my butt, and before I could protest, he lifted me onto his lap. My cheeks warmed, a laugh bubbling past my lips as I fidgeted, my back pressed firmly against the steering wheel. The fit was even tighter than before. My stomach had grown so much, you couldn't even wedge a peanut butter sandwich between us. "I told you making out in trucks doesn't work for us."

He grinned, and it was a surprise I didn't faint at the mere sight of it. "And I'm set to convince you otherwise." But rather than making good on his word, he skimmed his thumb over my bottom lip. "There's nothing to forgive—there never was. I only stayed away because I thought that's what you wanted. But you read my letter, and I promise—I would've come for you eventually. I would've found my sun." I leaned into his palm as he cupped my cheek, his skin feeling so right against mine. "It scares me how much I love you, how much you own me. But you're worth the fight, Shay. And I promise, I'll spend the rest of our lives making sure you know it." He dropped his lips to my neck, and I arched bac giving him better access. "You've got one minute to change your mind, becau after that, I'm not letting you go."

I shuddered as his lips brushed my collar bone, at the hint of possessivene in his tone. "Don't let go," I whispered, not needing the extra minute to decid Brooks was it for me.

"Tell me what you want," he murmured, the words feverish on my skin. "L me give you the world."

You can change it. You can claim the life you want. It's yours for the taking.

"I want to live in Wallowpine, with you," I said quietly, but not meekl claiming the life I wanted. "I want to finish the cabin—"

"It's done." He must've felt my intake of breath, tasted the tears on my lip because he added, "You were always coming home, Shay. It was just a matter when. I'm not saying the cabin's perfect. You still might have to bang the show wall for hot water, but it's waiting for you. Everything's there . . . even that cri you thought I didn't notice you looking at."

I closed my eyes, my heart overcome with what he'd done. How could I ha walked away, thinking he wasn't worth the risk of being hurt? Never again. H was worth everything. "I want to work at the shop—but I also want time write. And I might take an online class or two, because I really don't know wh I want to do. I kind of want to stay at home, at least for a while. I want to g on hikes and sleep under the stars. I want you to dance with me, because yo promised you would. I want you at my doctor's appointments, and I need yo to hold my hand during labor and promise me I won't die, because I'm real scared Tater's going to rip me in two. I want you to be deliriously in love wi our daughter and tell me she's the most beautiful girl in the world, even if s looks like an alien. Make love to me, and laugh with me always. Give me yo highs and lows, and let me cheer you on. I want you to make dinner for m and I want you to teach me how to cook. And I promise I'll give you all the la dances in the world—"

His eyes crinkled as he laughed against my lips, the sound filling my sou "Anything else?"

"Everything." I cupped his jaw, his beard thicker than the last time I'd touched him. "But I'd be okay if you just gave me you."

"You have me." His eyes were clear and bright, so full I thought that if I peered close enough, I'd see our future in them. "And what about what I want?"

I raised a brow, feeling nothing but joy in my heart. "And what is that?"

"You and Tater will do. Maybe Cash, too. And I imagine my brothers will hang around for a bit." He hummed under his breath as his hand found mine, running his thumb over my finger. "I wouldn't be opposed to you being my wife, and making that damn banana bread just for me."

My voice was gentle, wet with emotion. "Yeah?"

"Yeah."

I tipped my head toward the passenger seat, my bag open and waiting. "My ring's in my bag. You can pop it on right now."

He eyed me, failing to conceal his grin before his lips found mine. "I might just make you wait, then."

"Liar." I trapped his response, not letting him leave my kiss. I wound my fingers in his hair, faintly aware of the heat of his arm leaving me. I pulled back as the door opened, an invasion of bitter air sweeping through. "What are you doing?" I gasped as he swung his legs around the seat, his hold relentless on my butt. I wrapped my arms around his neck and my legs around his waist as much as I could manage, refusing to fall as he climbed out of the truck. "Is this the part where you murder me, bury me in the snow, and leave my body for the wolves?"

He chuckled against my ear, my insides heating as he lowered me to my feet, sliding every bit of my body against his. "I need to see you."

I looked up at him then, hearing the need in his voice. With the truck door open, and the cab lights on, I could finally see Brooks. His beard was longer, his hair grown over his ears, like he hadn't cut it since I'd last seen him. There were tired, heavy lines beside his eyes, but all I could truly see was the deep love and devotion in them as he looked not at me, but at my stomach. I didn't care about the cold or anything at all as I shrugged off Levi's jacket, wanting him to see every bit of me.

His chest heaved, his eyes wide, and something that looked like grief washed over him. "You've grown." His throat bobbed, and there was such emotion there, I thought my knees might give out. "I knew you would . . . but wow. You're beautiful, Shay."

I offered him my hand, understanding what he'd missed out on. His boots nudged my sandals, reminding me they were two seconds short of falling off, but I didn't care as I rolled my shirt up to my breasts, revealing my round belly. The skin was stretched taut, round enough I had to bend to see my toes, and if he looked below my belly button, he'd find a web of stretch marks. When he didn't reach for me, I teased, "If you don't say hello to her, she's probably going to kick my ribs."

He smiled, and I gasped, shivering, as his palms landed flat on my skin. A gust of wind blew, swirling up a patch of snow, but he made no move to stop. We both missed this. One hand traveled up my side and cradled my jaw. He kissed me, long and slow, as his free hand roamed my stomach, earnestly searching.

"There you are," he murmured when she pushed up, and I fought the urge to grimace. I was so ready to stop being a baby's house. "I missed you," he said to her, his voice full of awe and fascination. "I missed you both. But you're home now."

I closed my eyes, absorbing this moment of pure bliss. As the man I loved, the man I would marry, cherished and adored a daughter who wasn't his—at least, not yet. There was a time when I wished Brooks and I had made this baby together, but no longer did I dream of that. This was how it was meant to be. Everything, the highs and lows, the pain and sorrow—it had all led to this.

I was lost, and had been for some time—but in the end, that was the only way I could be found.

"What is your mama gonna name you?" Brooks asked as he stroked my stomach before rolling my shirt down. He lifted me by the hips, helping me back into the comfort and warmth of the truck, letting me see every bit of love in those green eyes. "Is Chewie still a contender?"

I laughed as Brooks did, grateful it was something we could do together. And if we could do that, if we could still find happiness and moments to celebrate in the midst of our pain, I knew our life would be *everything*. I brought his hand to my stomach, holding it there with mine. "I was thinking of naming her Wren."

For the one who called me home.

Epilogue

Brooks—The Following Christmas

The rich aroma of smoke wafted through the cabin, and I set the last log on the arrangement I'd built in the wood stove. I shut the door, wincing as it groaned. Holding my breath, I peeked over my shoulder towards the darkened hallway and listened. As excited as I was to start Christmas morning, I wasn't eager to face the wrath of my wife or daughter if I woke them up.

Deeming it was safe, I crept over to the Christmas tree shining brightly in the corner, smiling to myself as I thought of the night before. You would've thought by the way Shay had squealed and bounced on her toes the presents were for her, and not Wren. I stared at the towering pile of gifts, the full stockings on the wall, and wondered if we might've gone overboard. Wren—Winnie, as I liked to call her—was only nine months old, and though I knew she was the smartest baby in the world, I didn't know how much she'd understand.

But after seeing the way my wife smiled, I didn't care. I'd do anything for her happiness.

Anything for both my girls.

I hadn't known how it would work—becoming a father. I'd put on a brave face for Shay, but the closer her due date got, the more terrified I was. I no longer feared I'd inherit my mom's inability to love—I was intimidated to be a father. Shay had told me she considered herself a mother the moment she saw those two lines, but that hadn't stopped the immense terror she'd felt for months. I believed her, but from my perspective, I'd seen nothing but gracefulness. There'd never been a doubt in my mind that she'd stop at nothing to be the best mother.

But I didn't know how to do that. How to naturally step into this role. What if I failed?

Not for the first time, nor the last, I longed for Dad. It didn't matter that I'd watched him be a father; I had no idea how to be one. Assuming my brothers didn't either, I'd sought Jake out instead.

But when I told him my fears of failure, he'd given me a sad grin—one he'd worn often after losing his wife, Wren—and told me I'd do exactly that. Fail. I'd stumble and fall my way through fatherhood, through life in general, but all that mattered was if I got up and tried again. Gave every bit of my heart to my family.

It hadn't comforted me much, but on that early March morning when Shay lay on a hospital bed, bearing more physical pain than I could fathom and I watched her give birth, it no longer mattered. I was afraid, but as I peered into my daughter's pale blue eyes—her mother's eyes—I'd known loving her would be easier than breathing.

My phone vibrated, and I pulled it out of my pocket, seeing it was a text from Nolan. Levi had a last-minute final at his art school in Boston, so he'd taken a red-eye flight home to Arizona. Nolan had driven to Phoenix to pick him up, so I assumed it was a text letting me know they were on their way back.

Boy, was I wrong.

I groaned, the sound edged with a laugh as I stared at the picture of my brothers in Nolan's truck—and the bright pink Power Wheels car piled in the back seat. The message read: **I wanted to get Tater a motorcycle, but Levi convinced me this was better. Can't wait to see Shay's face**.

I knew exactly what face Shay would make, no doubt seeing red. *I can't wait either.* After telling them I'd see them in a few hours, I tucked my phone away, ready to join my wife back in bed.

I stopped mid-step, smirking at the shadowed figure in the hall and whispered, "Looks like I'm not the only one who can't sleep." She crept down the hall, Cash hot on her heels. I'd thought Cash might've taken to Shay because she was pregnant, but it turned out he was just obsessed with my wife.

"I'm too excited." She plopped down on the couch, wearing nothing but a pair of tube socks and one of my flannels. "Can we just wake her up?"

I laughed quietly and joined her on the sofa, pulling her against me. "I'm not sure how much she'd like us waking her up at two in the morning."

She scrunched her nose at me, and it was an effort not to unwrap her from those clothes. I didn't blame my dog for his obsession. I bore the same one. It didn't matter if we'd been married for six months or sixty years—I knew I'd always feel the same. *I love her.*

"Please," Shay asked, her lips in an adorable pout. "She wakes us up all the time. It's only fair."

I chuckled under my breath. "If you want to go head-to-head with a teething baby, go get her." Despite the way her foot bounced with excitement, she made no move to get off the couch. As much as we loved Wren, neither of us wanted to wake a sleeping baby.

Instead, she sighed and climbed onto my lap, facing me. "I guess you'll have to keep me company."

I settled deeper into the couch as her fingers danced over me, bringing my nerves into a frenzy. Despite the desire, the absolute want consuming me, I said, "If we lie down now, we can still catch a few hours of sleep."

She shook her head, setting her palms on my shoulders and kneading at my muscles. I resisted the urge to ask her to stop, to let me take care of her instead. No longer did Shay do anything she didn't want to, and if she wanted this, I'd let her have it. But as I noticed the faint circles beneath her eyes, I promised to return the favor.

She'd never complain, but I knew she was tired. She was enrolled in online classes, and that was hard enough to juggle on its own, let alone as a mom and wife. And she was still helping Nolan occasionally down at the shop. I'd asked her more than once if she should slow down, possibly stop working at the shop, but she'd assured me this was the best kind of exhaustion. The gratifying feeling you felt after a day of hard work.

It didn't ease my worry, but I trusted her, and I knew she trusted herself. I'd be lying if I said I wasn't filled with love and pride when I watched her confidently make decisions, knowing she hadn't always been that way. Someone had once tried to snuff out the fire in her.

I cradled the back of her neck with my hand and pulled her lips to mine, kissing her hard. I didn't know how long the honeymoon stage lasted, but I didn't think I'd ever stop wanting her. I hitched her up against me, and she threw her head back in a gasp when I nipped at her collarbone.

I shifted and laid her down atop the couch, then knelt beside her and peeled off her socks, leaving a trail of heated kisses and goosebumps down her calves. I reached for the buttons of her top, and despite her heaving chest, she snatched my hand, stopping me. I raised my brow, knowing she loved to make me wait. Little did she know I'd wait forever for her. "You're playing a dangerous game, sunshine," I murmured, leaning forward until my lips skimmed hers.

"I have something I want to give you."

I leaned back and eyed her, running my finger along a pink strand in her brown hair. I'd never forget the first time she did it, not knowing I could be so damn affected by a color. But it had little to do with her hair, and everything to do with watching Shay grow into herself.

I was so grateful to be a part of it.

I kissed the hollow of her throat and whispered into her skin. "I want you. I can wait for my Christmas present a little longer."

She shook her head, apparently holding strong. "I want to do it before your brothers and Jake come over."

I sighed but let her sit up, still kneeling on the ground beside her. After hearing she wanted to do this alone, and seeing her fingers fidgeting on her lap, I glanced at her stomach. "Are you pregnant?"

She shook her head with a meek smile. We weren't in a rush to have another baby, but we weren't necessarily preventing one either. If it happened, it happened—and if it didn't, that was okay. I'd be happy either way.

"Sunshine." I wrapped my hands with hers and squeezed, not understanding her nerves. No matter how much she trusted me, knew I wouldn't hurt her, it made sense for her to be wary after what happened when she'd told Declan she was pregnant. But if she wasn't pregnant . . . "Talk to me."

She gave me a shaky smile. "I've run this through my head so many times. I keep looking for the best way to go about this, the best words to use. I want to do this right." I sat up, wedging myself between her legs. There were tears lining her blue eyes, but they didn't look to be of sorrow. It was why I said nothing and waited, letting her set the pace. Thankfully, I didn't have to wait long when she reached into the top pocket of the flannel she wore and plucked out a folded piece of paper. "I think this says more than I ever could," she whispered, holding it out to me.

I grabbed it and smiled, assuming I'd find Shay's words inside. After I'd written her the letter in her journal, and she'd fallen in love with writing again, she'd gotten in the habit of leaving me notes. I'd find them everywhere, in the shower, my truck—one was even hidden in my sandwich. But I only had to read the title in bold font to realize this wasn't a letter from Shay.

PETITION FOR ADOPTION

I rubbed my jaw and stared at the form, confronted with an overwhelming wave of emotions. After Wren was born, Shay's lawyer had pursued Declan for proof of paternity. It hadn't matter if Shay was still healing from giving birth—she was prepared to fight. I was, too. But when the lawyer called, she'd informed us not only was Declan the biological father, but he was relinquishing his rights. I couldn't deny my heart had broken for Shay, for Wren. We were relieved, overjoyed with the surety she'd never leave our home, but there was a cost. Shay loved Wren something fierce, and it gutted her that Declan hadn't tried to be in his daughter's life. Not for herself, but for what Wren might feel later in life because of it. But there was comfort in him giving up his rights, his conscious decision not to make Wren's life harder as an attempt to further hurt Shay. I hated the man, hated what he'd put my wife through. But he'd walked away, and I was grateful for that.

"Shay—" I stopped myself, deciding against the words on the tip of my tongue, and instead reminded myself what I already knew. I hadn't pushed Shay for this, hadn't even broached the subject. This was entirely her own decision. So instead, I whispered, "Thank you for trusting me with her, with you." I peered down at the paper, not seeing any of the words as my vision blurred. I'd meant it when I said a piece of paper didn't determine a family, but wow . . . I hadn't let myself acknowledge how badly I wanted it until now. "You're both my entire world, and I can't tell you how much this means to me. But I'll spend the rest of my life, and even after, cherishing this gift you've given me."

If I wasn't already on my knees, I would've fallen to them at the sight of pure love and trust in her eyes. Not trusting myself to speak, I kissed her, showing her my gratitude in a different way. I'd once doubted my ability to love, if I could care for Shay in the way she deserved. But loving Shay . . . it was as natural as the sun rising and setting.

I'd barely plucked open the last button of her top, felt the soft heat of her skin, when a cry filled the cabin. It wasn't until we'd pulled apart, our breaths heavy, that I realized we'd found ourselves on the floor. We waited, listening, and after Wren cried again, confirming she was awake, Shay straightened herself.

"I've got her," she murmured and kissed my forehead before rolling to her feet. "Go back to sleep, I'll wake you in a few hours."

I watched her walk away before I slipped back on my shirt, having no intention of sleeping. I padded down the hall, but rather than slipping into the door on the right, I paused at the one directly across from it.

Warmth washed over me, an overwhelming sensation as I watched my wife cradle our daughter in her arms and hum a soothing tune. It was a feeling I'd only experienced a handful of times, one of them when we'd spread Dad's ashes. And just as I'd felt him there, I felt him here, too.

Her back was to me, but she must've sensed me at the door as she th whispered, "Your girls are waiting for you."

I smiled and walked to them, like I'd been doing it for years. And I had been was just blind before. But now I could see, and I'd follow them anywhere. Th were my lifeline, my guide, my home.

My girls.

Thank you!

If you enjoyed The Burns We Carry, please consider leaving a review. It helps so much with reaching other readers.

And if you can't get enough of the Graham Brothers, hang tight—Nolan and Levi's stories are coming!

Acknowledgments

When I first started writing, I had zero plans to ever write a contemporary. There's something so intimidating to me when it comes to writing within the real world. But on a day when I was feeling particularly exhausted and in need of a break, I sat down to write a story about a woman moving to the middle of the mountains for a fresh start. Because, let's be honest, it's way easier to write that scenario than pack up your family and moving across the country! I thought I'd have some fun, escape a little bit, and move on. However, the characters quickly took over, stole my heart, and the story became something I never anticipated. Sometimes the best things truly are unexpected.

First, I must thank the women who shared their stories with me. Shay's story is her own, but it's your strength, resilience, and tenderness that shaped her. You opened my eyes and taught me bravery comes in many forms. You helped make her real for me, and I'll forever hold Shay, and each of you, dear to my heart.

To my beta readers: Thank you for your feedback and helping me see what I couldn't. It's no easy task to brave a rough draft, and I'm so grateful for your help! To my street and ARC team: I feel so fortunate to have you in my corner. Your excitement and support has truly fueled me and I can't thank you enough. To the readers who picked up this book: It's absolutely terrifying, yet exhilarating to take an idea from your head and put it onto paper for others to read. I never would've dreamed this would be my reality, and it's because of you that it is! Thank you, thank you, thank you.

To my editor, Kara Aisenbrey: I truly believe I scored in the editor department! I'm so grateful to work with someone who is as talented as they are genuine. Thank you for always giving your best effort and helping me put into words what I sometimes struggle to say. I promise to someday get my ellipses right lol! You're a gem, and you have the cutest editing assistant! To Jessie at Book Blurb Magic: What you do is truly magic! Thank you for taking my messy notes and forming them into a beautiful blurb. To Kody Taylor: Thank you for the amazing cover. You captured the story beautifully and I'm so grateful to work with you.

To Teresa and Ashley: For keeping me sane with endless Henry Cavill memes. I'm so grateful to have stumbled into the same Discord server as you two. I'd be so lost without you. To Kallie: I never thought I'd form such a genuine relationship online, but here we are. You're a real one. Thanks for being at least ninety percent of my book sales. You're the ultimate hype girl, the queen of buddy reads, and an even better friend. And to Mady: I'm convinced you are the epitome of sunshine and if I could pocket you up, I would. Thanks for being such a bright point in my life. Let's cut our hair and move to Florida.

To the Bookstagram community: I haven't always been the biggest fan of social media, but the best perk is you. It's really something to connect with people who live across the world, and have the chance to share your passions with them. I am so grateful for each of you, and knowing I'm not alone in my obsession with fictional men. And a special thank you to: Alix, Alyssa, Amanda, Amber, Ashley L, Bailey, Brittny, Chloe, India, Julia, Jacqlin, Jessica, Katie, Laura, Lindsey, Mary, Megan, Moe, Molly, M & J, Nicole, Rain, Sarah, Taylor, Tori, Tessa, Vanessa, and the Booksta weekend crew (and many more). Thank you for your constant support and friendship! You build me up more than you'll ever know!

To my Good Family: So grateful to be a part of this family. I'm typing this before we go on our family trip, so we'll see if we all come back in one piece lol!

Thank you for your endless support, and for your love. And to Cori and Kiley: You're the best sisters I could ask for.

To my clients: I think I've done a fairly decent job at keeping this side of my life hidden from you, but if you're here—Hi! So sorry for hiding this from you! I adore all of you, and I'm so grateful for you. I promise to never write your stories into a book.

To the girls at the salon, Alicia, Sasha, and Stacey (I'll always consider you a part of the salon, Stacey): Thank you for your endless support, laughs, and your friendship. You three have taught me much more than just hair.

To my clone: You're the best friend I could ever ask for, and the inspiration behind every friendship I'll ever write. Thank you for loving my girls, and for at least tolerating Brody. Our phone calls are still my favorite, and so are our movie nights, even when you pick the movie every time. Sorry for not reading any of the books you recommend to me, but thanks for always reading mine. Remember when we read so many books in a month, we killed our brains? If you can't tell, I'm rambling a bit so your paragraph will be longer than Brody's. Oh, and thanks for "helping" me with my website. Love you and your little family so much. (P.S. You should probably add another star to your side of the mountain.)

To my daughters: You're my everything and my why. You changed my world and taught me a whole new sort of happiness. I love you both more than I could ever say. And to Butter: You're still the best kind of crazy.

To Brody: Thank you for never believing any dream is too large, nor small. I couldn't ask for a better husband, and there's no way I could write one either. The girls and I are so lucky to have you. Thanks for embracing my weirdness, for always seeing me, and for not losing your mind when I ask you to fix the blanket at two a.m. I love you forever.

To those who broke the cycle: Keep going, keep healing, and continue learning. Unless you've lived it, no one quite understands how lonely breaking the cycle can be. But I see you.

Lastly, I must thank my Heavenly Father. I have no doubt it was your hand that guided me to writing. Thank you for staying with me on the hard and easy days.

About The Author

Marae Good was born and raised in Arizona, where she currently lives with her husband, two daughters, and their sassy Yorkshire Terrier, Butter. After an episode of crippling depression forced Marae to reevaluate her priorities, she found herself returning to an old habit: reading. Mesmerized by the worlds she could escape to, Marae started creating her own. When she's not writing, Marae loves to dance with her littles, run and hike in the mountains, or stay up far too late bingeing TV shows (most likely *Vampire Diaries* or *Gilmore Girls*).

Follow Marae's bookish adventures on Instagram: @maraegood.writes

Made in the USA
Las Vegas, NV
09 June 2024